G-Strings and Sympathy

G-Strings and Sympathy

Strip Club Regulars and Male Desire

KATHERINE FRANK

Duke University Press ∗ Durham & London 2002

© 2002 Duke University Press

All rights reserved

Printed in the United States of

America on acid-free paper ∞

Designed by Amy Ruth Buchanan

Typeset in Dante by Keystone

Typesetting, Inc.

Library of Congress Cataloging-in-

Publication Data appear on the last

printed page of this book.

In memory of

my grandfather,

John Murawski

Contents

ACKNOWLEDGMENTS, ix

PREFACE Skin Brings Men, xiii

Part One

CHAPTER 1 Observing the Observers: Methods and Themes, 1

CHAPTER 2 Laurelton and Its Strip Clubs: The Historical, Physical, and Social Terrain, 39

Part Two

INTERLUDE *Strawberries* (fiction), 79

CHAPTER 3 Just Trying to Relax: Masculinity, Touristic Practice, and the Idiosyncrasies of Power, 85

CHAPTER 4 The Pursuit of the Fantasy Penis: Bodies, Desires, and Ambiguities, 121

Part Three

INTERLUDE *Fakes* (fiction), 159

CHAPTER 5 "I'm Not Like the Other Guys": Claims to Authentic Experience, 173

CHAPTER 6 Hustlers, Pros, and the Girl Next Door: Social Class, Race, and the Consumption of the Authentic Female Body, 203

Part Four

INTERLUDE *The Management of Hunger* (fiction), 231

CHAPTER 7 The Crowded Bedroom: Marriage, Monogamy, and Fantasy, 241

CHAPTER 8 Disciplining Erotic Practice, 273

APPENDIX, 281

NOTES, 285

BIBLIOGRAPHY, 311

INDEX, 327

Acknowledgments

Writing this book has been an exhilarating and often wonderful process from the very beginning, and it is a pleasure to thank those who helped to make this so and who nurtured my thinking along the way. This book would not have been possible, of course, without the interviewees and the other customers who shared their stories with me, and I am thankful for their openness and for their willingness to take the time to speak with me. I also learned a lot—professionally, intellectually, and personally—from the spirited and brave sex workers I've met and worked with over the years that I have been engaged in this project. I look forward to a time when sex workers of all kinds do not bear the brunt of others' fears about sexuality and when only those individuals who *want* to work in the industry do so.

I have always felt extremely thankful that I ended up at the Department of Cultural Anthropology at Duke University for my graduate training. The education, guidance, and support that I received during my years in graduate school, and afterward, have been remarkable. Anne Allison has been an amazing teacher, advisor, advocate, and friend over the years and I am grateful to have had the opportunity to work with her. She has provided me with a model for careful and exciting scholarship, in addition to offering me guidance and encouragement at each step of my own journey. Each of the other members of my committee also contributed to this project in unique and significant ways, and their mentorship and support from start to finish have been invaluable to me. Jean Hamilton responded enthusiastically to my original ideas for such a project. Claudia Strauss was always ready to help me map out my ideas and clarify my arguments. Charles Piot was excellent at pointing out the underlying assumptions and blind spots in my writing. Wendy Luttrell guided my work with careful and patient questions, always encouraging me to interrogate my experiences and supporting my tendency to learn through emotional reactions to the material.

Many people have offered helpful comments and suggestions on particular chapters of this book or on my research in its various phases: Michael Kimmel, Deborah Durham, Gary Brooks, Judith Lynne Hanna, Jo Weldon, Keith McNeal, Merri Lisa Johnson, Lynn Hempel, Amy D'Unger, Brent Shea, John Anderson, and others. In particular, Naomi Quinn offered me encouragement and careful readings of my work and is always willing to talk when I come knocking on her door. I would like to thank my editor at Duke University Press, Ken Wissoker, the conscientious and helpful reviewers of my manuscript, and the others at Duke Press who helped me with this project.

My research was made possible by a fellowship from the Sexuality Research Fellowship Program of the Social Science Research Council, with funds provided by the Ford Foundation. The Sexuality Research Fellowship Program supported me not only financially but also by enabling me to develop a network of talented, dedicated, and encouraging researchers, some at the beginning of their career and some established, in a variety of academic disciplines. My interactions with the other fellows have greatly enriched my thinking and the writing of this manuscript, and I would particularly like to thank Celine Parrenas Schmizu, Diane Tober, David Valentine, and Russell Shuttleworth for their comments and our ongoing conversations. I would also like to extend a special thank you to Diane di Mauro for her support and encouragement over the years. The completion of the manuscript was funded by a Richard Carley Hunt Postdoctoral Fellowship from the Wenner-Gren Foundation for Anthropological Research. This support allowed me the luxury of focusing solely on revising the manuscript for several summers, and was much appreciated.

It would be impossible to list all of those individuals who have influenced my thinking more generally on the issues I take up in this book, but there are some that bear mentioning here. My colleagues and students at the College of the Atlantic, along with the staff, were supportive and encouraging, and their commitment to the world and to a better future, as well as their shared passion for learning, continue to inspire me. Those late-night conversations with Ben Peacock and John Vincent, though they seem so long ago, shaped me irrevocably. My friendship with and love for Shelly Manaster also line these pages—she was the brilliant, creative, wonderfully rebellious, and inspiring friend for whom I had searched for years and lost far too soon. I cannot help but think of her when I write or dance.

My family and friends have also contributed in myriad ways and I am grateful for their faith in me. Buddy Frank was supportive during my fieldwork, listening to me at any time of the day or night that I needed to test new ideas, offering insightful comments and questions, and complementing my work with his own. David and Victoria Rauch, Ed Dorrington, and Scott Battaglini all played important supporting roles during those nomadic summer months while I was revising the manuscript, including providing me with housing, understanding, and excellent company. My mother, Lyn Baldauf, read and commented on the entire manuscript, always asking me to keep my writing accessible. As she was the earliest feminist influence in my life, I often felt as though I was writing to her. My utmost gratitude goes to my parents for supporting me in all of my endeavors, no matter how far away they take me, and for always keeping me a place at home.

Skin Brings Men

Hi, sexy, you starting tonight? Got your permit from the police station? Good. Kind of like a mug shot, huh? Let me see those fingertips—yeah, you can start work even before the ink dries. Well, I'm your DJ. I do all the training of new girls here—I've been around a lot longer than any of these managers and I know what makes us money in this business. What's your name gonna be? Okay. We haven't had a Kate in a while. Well, here's how it works here at Tina's Revue, Kate, here's the spiel I give all the new dancers here. I know you're coming to us from Diamond Dolls, but I always like to start everyone off on the same foot. Have a seat on my stool there, or you're gonna be standing in those high-heeled shoes just a little longer than is comfortable for you. Don't worry, I'll have you out on the floor while the money's still here.

Your shift is eight hours. That's a long time. You've got to pace yourself, darling. Change your outfits, take a break when you need to. Have some dinner—it's okay to eat. But don't drink too much—they're gonna give you a breathalyzer when you get off work, and if you're drunk, you're not driving.

I take 10 percent of your money, sweetheart: 10 percent. I'm just like you, okay? I make a living from gratuities. Before you leave here each night, you're gonna tip me 10 percent, tip your floormen a couple of bucks each, tip your bartenders if you've been drinking, tip your housemom who's taking care of things backstage. You can't forget your housemom. She's gonna do your scheduling, get you some mascara if you forget your own, give you tampons if you suddenly need them. We all get tipped out. That's how it is. You got to realize that we're all leeches in this business. I'm sorry, but we're leeching off y'all.

You can write down the music you like on this little card but I can't guarantee you that I'll be able to play it. I've got lots of people that I'm working for—management, dancers, customers. The girls right now all want to dance to Nine Inch Nails, they all want techno. Well, these customers don't want techno—they don't know it. They're from another generation. They don't get piercings, they don't get tattoos, they don't buy techno. I'll do my best to make you happy but that's all I can do. I've only got about twenty girls a night—that's a quarter of the girls that they've got at Diamond Dolls—but I still can't make everyone happy.

Now here's some tips on how to work. First, you've got to do your stage sets. It's very important that you come to stage for me when I call you. On every third song, the last song of the set for the girls who are up, I'll say "up next will be Carrie and Jessie." And then I've got a minute and a half, two minutes before the third song is over with and I need you up there. After the song, I'll call you again. You've got to be ready. So if you're one of those girls who needs to pee before you get on stage, then go pee when I say it the first time. Don't wait until there's a minute and a half left when you know it takes you three minutes to pee. Because it's a show, sweetheart. There's no excuse for you to miss your stage and I need you to be up there within twenty seconds of me firing your first song. If you're doing a table dance, you put on your dress a few seconds early. Wear practical clothes, okay? That cocktail dress looks fine. You don't need buttons and zippers that waste everyone's time.

In this business you got good girls, you got bad girls, you got girls in between. You've got drug users in this business. You've got alcoholics, okay? Just like anywhere. You've also got lawyers and schoolteachers. You've got girls like you that are gonna be professors or doctors in a year. You've got girls that are gonna be nurses. You've got girls that are going to college and gonna be something. You've got girls who are bitter, who hate dancing. You've got little girls like Serenity, young girls that are sweethearts. Supporting her mother, basically trying to just have a good time right now and, you know, no hassles, no real bills, okay. I can handle just making a hundred and fifty dollars a day. Hell, I really don't have to work. I'm hanging out in air conditioning in a bathing suit. You know?

As for the job, if you've ever wanted to be a flirt and a tease, then this is your chance. If you already are a flirt and a tease, then shift it into high gear, sweetheart. Let's make some money, okay? If you're not a flirt and a tease and you think you've always wanted to be an actress, then *act* like a flirt and a tease. Okay? So the thing is, you're a party girl. It may not sound like a good thing, but you can make a whole lot of money out of it. So if you can think "happy happy joy joy, let's party and have some fun," and if you can handle taking your clothes off in front of guys and knowing that you're in a good clean place and nobody's gonna touch you or do anything rude, you're set. You're golden. Nobody's allowed to touch you. Even if there's instances where you might want to let him do something, it's against the law and WE don't let you do anything except maybe give him a peck on the cheek to say thanks, and that's with all your clothes on.

You've got to have a good attitude. You can't be moaning and groaning and saying "I need money" because then customers will think you're popping 'em. You've gotta know that these guys come here to have fun and if you can make it fun for them then they don't mind leaving broke.

Okay, here's the rules and then the ropes. Always take tips in your garter—never your mouth, never your knees, your tits, or anything else. No bending over, no kneeling down. Your feet can touch the stage and that's it, you got it? Don't ever take off your shoes. I don't care how much your dogs hurt. The Health Department'll shut us down in the blink of an eye.

Look, eye contact is important. Smile when you're on stage! You've got to try to talk to these guys, look them in the eye. If you've got a guy who's sitting there, sort of walk up to the end of the stage, look at him, smile . . . Use your facial expressions. Tease the guy, okay? And then he's gonna give you some money. Go up and say "Hi, how you doing?" What's so hard about that? That's what this is all about. Some guys'll give you ones on stage, some will give you fives or better. But if a girl is smart, she'll treat the dollar guy the same way she treats the five-dollar guy when she's on stage. Okay? You give no one special treatment when you're on stage. When you get off stage, that's when you can go over to that big tipper, you know, now you can give special treatment.

Say it's a slow night, and no one's tipping. Remember this: Skin brings men. So, say you don't feel like you've got enough money to take any clothes off the first song. Girl, I can live with that. But baby, if you're smart, when you're on the second song you'll pop your top or drop your drawers, whichever you're most comfortable with. I suggest popping your top even if you don't have large breasts, okay? Just to get the clothing off . . . Because by the time I fire that third song, you still have your top and bottoms on, they're gonna go, well, she's not gonna get naked during this set. Why do I want to tip that bitch? And it's over for you. You may as well just hang out. You may as well just walk the hell off the stage. I mean, I'm not gonna let you leave the stage—the show must go on, so to speak. So even if you don't feel like you've got enough money by the middle of your second song, take something off anyway. Skin brings men. And there's a good chance by the third song, somewhere along that line, they will give you enough money so that you will get naked. I mean sometimes, you've got to go for broke.

Now look, when you get off the stage, you go to the floor, to go talk to these guys . . . You're trying to sell table dances, okay? Ten dollars a pop when they ask you for one. Private table dances—that's where you make your real money. They pay you directly, but if they run out of money they can waddle up to the bar and get funny money on their credit cards. Don't forget about that—you turn it in at the end of the night when you pay your taxes and it's the same as cash. So when you get off the stage, put on your clothes and go talk to these guys and say thank you for the tips, even the dollars. Use your voice, learn how to talk sexy. Lean over, maybe kiss them right by their ear, and use a low voice, say, "Well, I really appreciate that tip. If you'd like a table dance, all you have to do is ask." Okay? You set it up so that if he wants a table dance, all he's gotta do is ask. And you're asking without asking him, because in Laurelton it's illegal for you to ask directly for a table dance. It's considered solicitation.

As you're walking through the room, okay, you've gotta watch these guys. Watch his body language. You can tell if he's watching you and if he's interested in you. Look, like I said, eye contact's important. A guy smiles, he's a potential tipper, okay? If you want, you can sit down and talk to a guy. Remember, there's nothing more interesting in this world for men than to talk about ourselves. Okay? Ask him his name! Remember his name when he tells it to you! Ask these guys: What do you do for a living? What are your hobbies? You know, do you race trucks? Do you like speedboats? Do you ski? You know, what do you like to do? So you start trying to get personal on him. Now these guys are gonna ask you a lot of questions about yourself, and you be real careful. Just ask them right back.

Couple more things, darling, are you comfortable on that stool? Okay. We're almost done. Now you can hang out with a guy two or three songs if you want to, but if after two or three songs he hasn't asked for a table dance, you now say, "Hey, I've got to make a living, I'm going to go see if I can find a table dance with someone, you know, but do you mind if I come back in a minute?" If he likes you, he'll ask you for a dance so that you'll stay.

Part of table dancing is planning ahead. You've gotta be looking around the room. Guys are gonna sneak a peek at your table dance so if you're watching, that's gonna be a clue to you . . . they're a potential table dance, too. And if you can, while you're turning around, you've got your backside to your customer at your table dance and you're arching your back for this guy and maybe you're winking at that other guy across the room! He says, oh wow . . . And you finish with your table dance and hang out with Guy #1 another minute or two and then, you say, "I'm gonna go see if that guy wants a table dance over there" and that guy's gonna buy a table dance from you too. They know you're out there making money, they see that other guys want you. And they'll start competing with each other.

If he's a big spender, we've got the VIP room. The way VIP rooms work, it's twenty dollars to the house right off the bat. Not like Diamond Dolls, it's a lot more money to do the VIP thing there. I think they charge up to five hundred an hour to go in those rooms, don't they? I thought so. Well, a lot of these girls think they're gonna make big bucks just by going in there. Let me tell you something. A new guy, not the regulars, but the new guy gets in the VIP room and thinks he's gonna get a blow job or that he's going in there to get laid. Or at least to touch, feel, whatever. And you've gotta make it clear to him that that's not the case. And if they try to do something in there, then doggone it, baby, I want you to step out of the room and let one of us know. That's not gonna make any of us money. But you can charge double for your dances and you can get a lot of money from him up front if you play it clean.

You need to get regulars, you probably know that. That's what keeps you going here. I mean, you got a girl like Carmen, over there on stage, okay, and she's not that beautiful but she's got six customers that she has trained. Okay? And she gets three of those guys every other week coming in. Regular as clockwork. She schedules them. And the three days she works, okay, she makes a quick two hundred from each of those guys every day she works. She knows how to do this work. You get Ashley—she's got this same fellow, day after day, poking around in here looking for her. Okay? And that's what you've got to do.

My job is to get them tapping their foot and forgetting time, okay? Your job is to help me make them forget time. So what we've got to do here is we've both got to make this guy forget. Forget everything. The man's changed but in his mind's eye, he can go back in time. I'm looking out at the audience all day or all night. My job is to look out in the audience and get an average age in my brain. Okay? Like, look at this guy over here, right now, he's fifty-five years old at least, okay? Look at this guy over there, we've got a twenty-two-year-old over there at Sheena's stage. We've got four forty-year-olds over here, not talking to any girls yet, and a couple thirty-five-year-olds over here near the pool table. Now I'm just guessing, so I can be off by three years here and there, but you know, I think my average age in this room is about forty-five or younger. Okay? You know what I should be doing, as a good disc jockey? I should say, okay, my average age is forty-five or younger, that means when these guys were seventeen to twenty, that was twenty-five years ago. Okay? So I should be playing music from when these guys were young and sowing their wild oats and drinking booze and smoking pot and getting wild. And all of a sudden while you're dancing on stage and they're having that extra beer or a shot that we talked them into doing, you become that girl that they remember back in the seventies, okay? And suddenly instead of these guys coming in here for lunch or happy hour and leaving in forty-five minutes to an hour they stay here for an hour and a half, almost two hours, and then they got to leave because they're fucking broke.

When I got a hot crowd going, I know some things to say to get them laughing, okay? "Don't get your shorts so hot, it's like your crotch pot cooking. Say hello to the chef." Or "If you're a Republican, it's called trickle down economics. If you're a Democrat, it's called having a damn good time! If you're an Independent, then for crying out loud, act independently wealthy!" You know? Little shit like that. "Guys, you'd slap your momma's cousin's uncle a week past Thursday just to get

close to that lady! And all you've got to do is just walk up to that stage!"
You know? And you'll have men laughing and they're chuckling and
they're having a good time and that's what it's all about. Let's get drunk!
Shots, yeah! And you know, when they get drinking I can do toasts.
Look, "Here's to women in high-heeled shoes; they'll smoke your dope,
they'll drink your booze. They lost their cherries a long time ago, but
they'll say with a grin that that's no sin. They've still got the box their
cherries came in!"

I say to the customers, "You are the king of your dreams. You're the
king here at Tina's, gentlemen, now find the queen of your dreams."
Okay? And that's just it. It doesn't have to be a really beautiful girl.
Some guys, a beautiful woman intimidates them. They don't want to
go to Diamond Dolls. They don't want model types. But a chubby little
plain girl that's still willing to take her clothes off, that's . . . that's the
queen of their dreams. I say, "Every man has his vision of the perfect
lady and we've got them all here. Tall, small, short or fat, blondes, red
heads, and brunettes. Who's your perfect lady?" You know?

Look sweetheart, I've told you you're a party girl. You've gotta realize this and what comes along with it. You're gonna have guys say "Oh
baby, I'd like to eat that pussy." You're gonna have guys say "I'd like to
fuck you." You're gonna have guys tell you what you're doing for a
living, you're nothing but a whore. Look, honey, these guys don't know
what they're talking about. Some of them, it's just their hormones
running crazy on them, or the liquor, or whatever. Okay? It's gotta be
water on a duck's back. You've gotta be secure enough about yourself to
know that what they're saying is just bullshit. It's a job, it's a business.
We sell the *idea* of sex. We do not sell the act of sex. We sell a sexual
fantasy without actually copulating. We've caught guys in here jacking
off sometimes and we throw 'em out! And then, there's guys that are
straight out looking for sex, you know? Asking all the girls. And those
guys you've just got to blow off, kick 'em out, send 'em elsewhere.
There's plenty of other places to go.

Like I said, most customers, they're looking for a fantasy girl and
they're looking for someone to fall in love with, but not be in love with,
how's that? They're looking for someone to lust after.

Looking for that fantasy girl.

Yeah, sweetheart. This business can eat you alive or you can eat it alive. And if you eat it alive you're gonna make money and you're gonna use your head and you're gonna do all right. But if you let this business get to you, it's gonna buck you out.

All right, Katie, girl. Are you ready to start working? You ready to dance?[1]

*

When I began stripping in 1996, as both a means of earning extra cash for graduate school and as part of a feminist theory project investigating female objectification and body image, I had no idea how fascinating the world of adult entertainment would become to me. Quickly, however, my questions began multiplying: What did it take to be successful in this business? What was I actually selling to the customers, as I was providing no direct sexual release and no actual bodily contact? Who were these men who were so willing to open their wallets to the dancers night after night, paying us double or triple or quadruple the amount of money that we would make at our day jobs, to receive only a seemingly intangible, ephemeral service in return? What were the customers hoping to see, to discover, to buy in our young bodies, our attentions, and our complex financial, sexual, and emotional transactions in these dark, smoky rooms? This book, after dancing for over six years in more than six strip clubs, is my attempt to begin answering these questions and others that arose over the course of my research on the industry and my experiences as a dancer.

This ethnography specifically explores the personal and cultural fantasies underlying visits to strip clubs for certain groups of regular heterosexual male customers in the United States and, to a different degree and in a different manner, those of the women who dance in them. My primary argument is that the customers' understandings of their visits to strip clubs are deeply intertwined with cultural discourses about masculinity, sexuality, and consumption, but also that their visits become meaningful in relation to their everyday lives and relationships and their own personal and emotional experiences of gender and sexuality. Despite popular beliefs to the contrary, strippers[2] are generally not selling sex to their customers—although they are indeed selling sexualized and gendered services. Rather than fulfilling a biological need for sexual release or a masculine need for domination, strip clubs provide a kind of intermediate space (not work and not home, although related to both) in which men can experience their bodies and identities in particular pleasurable ways. The sources and forms of this pleasure, as well as how the meanings of visits to strip clubs are intertwined with material inequalities and constraints, focus my investigation. Further, strip clubs, as part of the sex industry more broadly defined, are not necessarily antithetical to marriage, as some social theorists and community members would like to think, but neither are they unrelated to it. In fact, visits to the clubs are related to particular ways of *practicing* marriage (and heterosexual relationships more generally) that make this a desirable venue for some men.

Commercial sexual services and activities have long been a part of the entertainment and leisure industries in the United States. Given the continuing emphasis on leisure, entertainment, and pleasure in the American[3] economy, it is not surprising that the sex industry has grown and diversified even more rapidly throughout the second half of the twentieth century. In 1996 Americans spent "more than $8 billion on hard-core videos, peep shows, live sex acts, adult cable programming, sexual devices, computer porn, and sex magazines" (Schlosser 1997: 44).[4] In terms of strip clubs primarily catering to heterosexual men, the changes have also been dramatic. According to market researchers, the number of major strip clubs nearly doubled between 1987 and 1992, and an estimate for late 1998 puts the number of clubs at around three thousand (Hanna 1998b), with annual revenues ranging from $500,000 to more than $5 million (Schlosser 1997). In major cities, convention business and high-end gentlemen's clubs have become symbiotic. Strip clubs and exotic dancers have become a consistent presence in popular culture in recent years, both glamorized and stigmatized. Books about stripping written for popular audiences abound, such as *Strip City* by Lily Burana, *Ivy League Stripper* by Heidi Mattson, and *The King of Clubs* by Jay Bildstein, and movies set around women in the industry—*Show Girls, Striptease,* and *Exotica*—have been shown in mainstream theaters. On television, HBO recently ran a series called *The G-String Divas,* chronicling the lives of several exotic dancers, and another of their popular productions, *The Sopranos,* features a strip club as a hangout for several of the gangster characters. The number of scantily clad, suggestively dancing women in a recent string of R&B and hip-hop music videos has reporters wondering about "stripper mystique" (Jones 2001). Strippers are also recurrent guests on daytime television talk shows, often being subjected to repeated appeals to get out of the business and clean up their lives. Media attention to the *customers* of strip clubs, however, is far less pervasive.

A strip club represents a different, perhaps even self-consciously aberrant social space for the customers, especially when it is contrasted with other spheres such as home and work. Compared with prostitution, however, strip clubs certainly fall on the more acceptable side of sexual behavior due to their legality. Part of the allure of strip clubs for their patrons lies in part in their very representation as somewhere out of the ordinary, somewhere proscribed—yet a *safe* space of play and fantasy where the pressures, expectations, and responsibilities of work and home can be left behind. Strip clubs thus provide a type of service that is distinct from other sectors of the sex industry. If a man is looking for quick sex, for example, there are usually many other arenas in which this desire can be met and he would be very unlikely to get it by going to a strip club. Similarly, if he wants a more private sexual experience he might visit a massage parlor, call a phone sex line, or rent a pornographic movie, depending on the level of interaction he desires. Moreover, he might have different desires on different occasions and thus avail himself of multiple services.

One important aspect of the contemporary strip clubs that I studied, then, is the fact that sexual release on the premises is generally not part of the experience. Although there are certainly exceptions, strip clubs in the United States generally privilege *looking* over touching or enacting sexual scenarios.[5] In many cities regulations prohibit any contact between the dancers and the customers. In such cases management is usually motivated to enforce these prohibitions inside the clubs, and if not, the dancers often do so. There are adult entertainment clubs in the United States that offer lap dancing (or "friction" dancing), a practice that involves varying amounts of contact between the dancer and the patron and can lead to sexual release for the customer, who may even wear a condom underneath his clothes. However, I consider this a different kind of entertainment because of this overt possibility of sexual release and did not select for my ethnographic sites clubs that offer this service. Table dancing, on the other hand, was one of the services offered at the clubs I investigated. Table dances were offered to the customers at their seats, either on a raised platform or table or while standing on the ground between the man's knees. These "private" dances involve a more individualized interaction between the dancers and their customers, but although a dancer could disrobe completely and place her hands on the customers' shoulders, other forms of bodily contact were prohibited and she was required to keep at least one foot of distance between herself and the customer. Customers were not allowed to touch either the dancers or their own genitals. I was interested specifically in the customers who returned again and again to such a venue where contact and sexual release were prohibited, for whom voyeurism and conversation were the eroticized practices. The significance of this distinction is one to which I return throughout the text.

Despite the fact that some American customers do avail themselves of other services that involve sexual contact (illegally or legally inside strip clubs or lap dancing clubs, with prostitutes, or in other venues such as massage parlors), there is a significant population of heterosexual American males who are willing to spend their money on such a public, *voyeuristic* (although interactive) *fantasy.* Certainly, the desire to simply look without touching cannot be considered only American, as similar formats can be found in other countries as well. The particularity of the American male customer who explicitly does not want direct sexual release, however, is something that must be explored in more depth.

Another important aspect of contemporary American strip clubs is the public nature of the encounters involved. Semiotician Terry Prewitt terms modern exotic dance "porno-active performance" and distinguishes it from pornography in several ways: viewers are visible to both other customers and to the dancers, may become participants in the action in various ways, and may engage in a dialogue with the performers (1989: 140). As the dancers circulate among the customers to sell table dances, the individualized interactions that take place become an extremely important part of the experience. Although table dances are private in the sense that the dancer's gaze and attentions are focused on the man who has commissioned her for the dance, they are still public in that the man and his reactions remain visible to all. Dancers may also sit with customers between their sets and their table dances, and thus conversation becomes a (public) service in and of itself. The significance of the different kinds of visibility and intimacy involved in these transactions is also discussed throughout the text.

Strip clubs do not cater only to heterosexual males, of course. Numerous clubs around the country feature male exotic dancers and cater to a female clientele, a homosexual male clientele, or both. Lesbian, bisexual, and heterosexual women may also visit clubs featuring female dancers. These populations and practices are significant and cannot be ignored when contemplating the changes that have occurred in the realm of adult entertainment in recent years. In this project, however, my focus remains on men who repeatedly visit strip clubs featuring female dancers, as this particular gendered pattern remains the most prominent in scale and scope and allows me to draw on my own experiences working as an exotic dancer.

Not all American men, of course, enjoy visiting strip clubs. Some may dislike them entirely, preferring another form of adult entertainment or preferring their own fantasy life to the options presented in the marketplace. Some visit only occasionally, such as for a bachelor party or other special event, or only during a particular period of their life. Some enjoy going to the clubs but do not because their wife or partner does not approve. Some men visit only with business associates; others visit only alone. Still others are "regulars," men who frequent a club or a number of clubs daily, weekly, or monthly and find these visits particularly satisfying for a variety of reasons. The focus in this text is on those male customers who visit the clubs *often enough to consider this a significant personal practice.* For these customers, visits to strip clubs are part of a meaningful and desirable repertoire of sexual and / or leisure practices, and are a form of consumption that is integrated with their other activities, pursuits, and relationships. These are not men who just happen to wander in off the street wondering what a strip club looks like inside or who accompany their friends or business acquaintances on a special excursion to the neighborhood "tittie bar." Men who do not find their desires represented here are urged to consider the *meaning* of visits to strip clubs in their own lives; this book may not be about them. However, though my focus is primarily limited to this particular group of customers, the themes taken up in this text—masculinity, sexuality, power, pleasure, erotics, authenticity, and commodification—are relevant to much broader debates about subjectivity, intimate relationships, and modern consumer practice.

This ethnography is also concerned with the differences among clubs in terms of "classiness." With the fairly recent advent of gentlemen's clubs, many of which trace their genealogy to the famous Rick's

Cabaret in Houston or Scores in New York City (Bildstein 1996), has come a highly stratified arrangement of strip clubs in terms of luxury, status, and other distinguishing features. Whereas strip clubs were once primarily located in red-light areas of towns and cities associated with crime and prostitution, the upscale clubs are now often quite visible and work to develop reputations for safety, comfort, and classiness. Drawing on cultural markers of status such as the provision of luxury liquors, fine dining, valet parking, and private conference rooms, upscale clubs advertise themselves as places for businessmen to entertain clients or for middle-class professionals to visit after work. Inflated drink prices and cover charges, along with strict dress codes, provide the management with some control over customer demographics. The dancers may be advertised as refined, well-educated women and referred to as entertainers rather than strippers. Sophisticated sound and lighting equipment, multiple video screens, and multimillion-dollar construction budgets help to make the glitzy environment of many contemporary strip clubs into high-tech entertainment centers. This is not to say that smaller or "seedier" clubs have disappeared, however, as they most certainly have not. The clubs in any given area, however, are categorized through their relationships to one another, and this system of relationships helps inform both the leisure experiences of the customers and the work experiences of the dancers.

The proliferation and upscaling of strip clubs during the 1980s needs to be situated in late capitalist consumer culture as well as within a variety of social changes and developments. A commonly noted feature of late capitalism is that more and more forms of entertainment become preoccupied with the commodification of spectacle and experience; certainly, the proliferation of strip clubs can be offered as an example of the profitability of this strategy. The changes in the format of entertainment venues featuring exotic dance, discussed in more detail in the pages that follow, have also followed a pattern of increasing individualization of services and interactions. In many ways it makes sense that strip clubs should have multiplied so wildly in the United States during the past several decades, along with the panic about AIDS and fears about the dissolution of "the family." The process of upscaling in strip clubs, with its promise of "clean" and respectable interactions, could alleviate certain fears about contamination and disease that escalated around prostitution. The fact that sexual activity is not generally expected or offered in strip clubs also fits well with a growing emphasis on monogamy and marriage for heterosexuals after the sexual experimentation (and ensuing disillusionment for many) of the 1970s. There are numerous other social changes that may be influencing this rapid increase in strip clubs in the United States as well: the increased presence of women in the workforce, a continued backlash against feminism and the idea of "political correctness," ongoing and concerted marketing efforts to sexualize and masculinize particular forms of consumption ("sports, beer, and women," for example), changing patterns of mobility that have influenced dating practices and the formation of intimate partnerships, and changes in the nature of work that involve more out-of-town travel for businessmen and thus more anonymous opportunities to purchase commodified sexualized services, to name just a few. To situate the clubs and their customers in such a context, I draw on the idea of the spread of "touristic practices" (Urry 1990) in postmodern consumer culture.

Despite the increase in numbers of clubs and the money being spent in them, however, strip clubs remain a stigmatized entertainment venue, especially for the women who work in them. Dancers may still face prejudice and discrimination when searching for other forms of employment, when interacting with the courts and other bureaucratic agencies, in looking for housing, and in everyday interactions. Leilani Rios, a student at California State University–Fullerton, was asked to either give up her job as an exotic dancer or resign from the school's track team after she was recognized by fellow student athletes while working. As Rios herself noted, the members of the men's baseball team who recognized her were not reprimanded by the college or the coaches for visiting the club (Keichline 2001). Though she was eventually allowed to rejoin the team, her case is yet another example of the stigma strippers regularly face. Over the years, I have heard stories about women working as exotic dancers who have been fired from their other jobs, disowned by their family, and ostracized in their educational institution.

Strip clubs themselves are also often the subject of intense public scrutiny, debate, and regulation and such contention has been part of the history of venues which offer a chance for the eroticized viewing of naked or semi-naked bodies. Efforts to distance strip clubs from their illicit associations in the public imaginary, to bill them as a legitimate form of entertainment, have become increasingly important given the opposition that has arisen with regard to exotic dance in the United States in recent years. Local ordinances have been drafted in cities across the nation to harass, limit, or eradicate venues that feature exotic dance, often citing as justification "adverse secondary effects" such as increased crime and decreased property values in neighborhoods that house such venues. A recent U.S. Supreme Court case, Erie, PA, et al. v. Pap's A.M., et al., upheld the constitutional validity of such regulation despite the often ambiguous and contradictory evidence for these kinds of effects and the previous legal understanding of exotic dance as a form of expression protected by the First Amendment. On an even more conservative note, Justices Scalia and Thompson argued that municipalities had the right to regulate the conduct of their residents through restrictive legislation regardless of whether this impinged on free expression.

Most of the ordinances drafted by local communities, as well as the Justices' decisions in the above case and others, seem to be based on conjectures about just what the men (and women) are up to when they set foot in such a venue. There is endless speculation about drugs, prostitution, and crime—by customers, lawmakers, and people who have never even entered a strip club. Yet my experiences as both an ethnographer of American strip clubs and an exotic dancer did not confirm the worst of these fears. Although these activities surface at times in often scandalous ways, as they do in many industries, I came away from my research with a belief that most of the customers were *in search of* something completely different through their interactions. I also came away with a strong conviction that moralistic regulation about the sex industry is harmful in the long run: not only does it reinstate binary distinctions between good girls and whores, but it tends to penalize and stigmatize women who may be using their most profitable assets to improve their lives and increase their opportunities. That women can earn more money in the sex industry than in many other kinds of work, however, is certainly an issue worthy of much discussion, as are workplace policies and regulations that protect workers' interests in these venues.

Moralistic regulation also seems based on an idea that there is one authentic sexuality that can be legislated and policed: heterosexual, reproductive, serial monogamous (and preferably married) coupling. In fact, I argue that strip clubs remain desirable and become meaningful for their regular customers, in part, *because of* these kinds of sexual policing, not in spite of it. This is not to say that strip clubs, along with other forms of adult entertainment, would disappear if they ceased to be stigmatized and embattled venues; rather, the *meanings* of the interactions and services would change, possibly along with the clientele and the employees. And although there certainly are problems with adult entertainment in the forms in which it exists today, many of which are discussed in this text, these problems are not *intrinsic* to the commodification of sexualized services but are instead related to larger patterns of social inequality.

So what exactly is the appeal of modern strip clubs, in this particular voyeuristic form, for certain groups of late twentieth-century heterosexually identified American men? In the chapters that follow I explore this question through fieldwork in five different strip clubs, located in a large Southern city, referred to as Laurelton in this text, and through a series of in-depth interviews with some of the regular male customers of those clubs. The book is divided into three parts, moving from discussions of seemingly macrosociological considerations—history, geography, social positionings, and cultural ideologies, for example—toward discussions of increasingly microsociological and psychological processes and concerns: identities, fantasies, desire, and intimacy. Throughout the book, however, I return to the idea that personal erotics are deeply intertwined with material social relations and public fantasies, challenging easy distinctions between macro and micro, public and private, personal and cultural, or fantasy and reality.

Part I of this book situates both this study and the strip clubs I am investigating in time and space. In Chapter I, I discuss my methodology, my positionality, and my theoretical approaches. The second chapter establishes striptease as a continually evolving form of entertainment, with the focus on three historical developments that have been particularly influential in shaping the contemporary world of exotic dance: the evolution of public voyeurism as masculinized leisure activity, the intermixing of entertainers and their audiences to produce new types of personalized performances, and the process of upscaling, or of coding particular leisure forms as "respectable." There are certainly other historical developments that are important, such as changes in cultural views on nudity in legitimate performances, the way striptease becomes distinguished from other kinds of entertainment in the cultural imaginary, and the rise of particular forms of technology that intensify modern scopophilia; however, these are the three that most directly inform this project. This chapter also provides a spatial analysis of the strip clubs in Laurelton, along with a closer look at the internal geographies of and popular mythologies about two specific clubs: the upper-tier Diamond Dolls and the lower-tier Tina's Revue.

Exploring the interconnections among masculinity, leisure, and privilege is the work of Part 2 of this book. The way customers discursively understand their visits to strip clubs is the focus of Chapter 3: the clubs are seen as providing a space of relaxation and escape different from work and home, a safe place for transgression and fantasy, and a place to pursue personal and sexual acceptance. These understandings are then linked to discourses of masculinity. Chapter 4 explores embodiment and desire and the way sexual excitement comes to be figured as an authenticating and liberating experience of personal freedom.

Each of the chapters in Part 3 takes up the concept of authenticity, though in different ways. Investigating the various beliefs and fantasies about gender, social class, and race that inform the men's choice of venue and their perceptions of and claims to *authentic* experience is one of the ways I explore the material aspects of erotic fantasy throughout this text. Chapter 5, for example, looks more closely at the way that claims to authentic experience are made by the customers, and Chapter 6 explores the way ideas about class, race, and gender influence the customers' perceptions of authenticity, especially as it is embodied and performed by the dancers.

Finally, the chapters in Part 4 examine authenticity and erotics in wider social and institutional contexts. Chapter 7 examines the relational aspect of the encounters and their place in the everyday life of a specific group of customers involved in long-term relationships outside of the clubs, particularly in relation to a triadic relationship that shapes the meaning of these encounters: that between the customer, the dancer(s), and the "other women" in the customer's life. Here, authenticity appears relative to the meanings that sex, monogamy, and commitment hold for the customers. Chapter 8, the concluding chapter, addresses attempts to discipline and regulate erotic behavior by state and local governments, as well as the need to contest the recent spate of restrictive zoning ordinances being developed around the country that intend to harass or eradicate strip clubs and other forms of adult entertainment.

In addition to the more traditional chapters, I have included several short stories that address the issues raised in the text from the perspective of a dancer. While in the field, I began writing and publishing ethnographic fiction that integrated my experiences, my data, and my theoretical concerns, some of which appeared in local trade magazines and some in more national or scholarly publications. My original impetus for writing these stories was to reflect on my emotions and experiences in the field, as well as to better understand my theoretical questions; the response to the pieces was quite strong and made me aware of the vast potential of different kinds of writing to challenge stereotypes and add complexity to debates about the meaning of the sex industry. It is my hope that readers will come away from this ethnography with a more complex understanding of the forces that shape the meanings of contemporary strip clubs for the customers, of what precisely makes them exciting and erotic entertainment venues for some men, as well as with a different kind of critical eye toward adult entertainment than that often employed by the mainstream media and by both the foes and supporters of modern strip clubs.

Part One

Chapter One

Observing the Observers:

Methods and Themes

This ethnography investigates the motivations and experiences of the regular male customers of strip clubs to explore both the personal and cultural aspects of gender, sexuality, and desire. My decision to focus on the male customers of the clubs rather than the women who dance in them was motivated by both political and theoretical concerns. On hearing that I have conducted research in strip clubs, the most common question people ask me is, "Why do the *women* do it?" Indeed, this was my initial question as well. My original project—and many people who do fieldwork know that one rarely sticks with one's original project— was to focus only on exotic dancers. After all, nearly all of the literature that I could find on strip clubs, both academic and popular, deals with the mythologies that surround the dancers: What kind of "personality" does a woman need to have to become an exotic dancer? How many dancers have been sexually abused or use drugs or alcohol to "make the work bearable"? How did the women go on to have meaningful relationships after transgressing the taboo on mixing money and sexualized encounters and appearing nude in public?

As a student of feminist anthropology, I was interested in the links between power, gender, and sexuality and concerned about the "culture of objectification" that I believed influenced women's experiences in the United States. I was also committed to studying these things anthropologically, by immersing myself in the community that I was studying and by qualitatively exploring what was meaningful to the people there. During an exploratory phase of research I interviewed women who worked in the sex industry—prostitutes, strippers, pornographic actresses, and dominatrixes—and began working myself as a topless entertainer in an upscale table dancing club. Though I had been an anti-pornography feminist many years earlier, while still an undergraduate student at the University of Michigan, my experiences during this early research phase caused me to rethink many of my deeply held assumptions about sex work and the women who engage in it. As I took up an identity as a sex worker, I began to deconstruct my earlier questions: Didn't a focus on the personal problems of strippers derive from the assumption that no one would do sex work unless she were forced, or unless there was something psychologically wrong with her? Didn't my questions show evidence of a preexisting perception of sex work as damaging in and of itself, both to one's "self" and to one's relationships? Didn't these questions sidestep issues of politics and economics in favor of individualistic explanations of deviance and psychopathology? And didn't a focus on the social transgressions of the women—actually, laborers who are providing a service and earning money often unavailable to them in other spheres—normalize the desires that motivated their *customers*, the men who paid them hundreds of dollars each evening to disrobe on stage and to talk to them at their tables?

I began to realize that these basic assumptions about the nature of sex work and sex workers, along with the power differentials that often exist between researchers and their subjects in terms of gender, educational level, economic resources, and cultural capital, were influencing not only the questions that were asked, but also *who* was studied, in what manner, and how the findings were represented. This is not to deny that some dancers have been sexually abused, use drugs or alcohol, or have difficulty forming intimate relationships—just as many secretaries, lawyers, professors, nurses, and housewives do. Rather, it is to point out that the kinds of information sought by researchers and the questions that one asks are in and of themselves political and based on cultural assumptions. An assumption that I make in this text, then, is that the behavior of the male customers of strip clubs needs to be interrogated as a modern form of voyeuristic, gendered leisure practice, rather than unproblematically taken to be an expression of some natural male sexuality.

Though the popular stereotype of anthropologists remains that of studying "primitive tribes," anthropologists have long turned their eyes homeward as well (e.g., Powdermaker 1950; Myerhoff 1978; Moffat 1989; Sanday 1990). However, social scientists, anthropologists included, have tended until relatively recently to "study down," that is, to investigate groups with less social power instead of more dominant groups. Sex workers rather than their customers, for example, have long been the object of inquiry in the social sciences: as individuals working in "deviant" occupations (e.g., Thompson and Harred 1992; McCaghy and Skipper 1969), as examples of deviant, exhibitionistic, or unstable personalities (e.g., Greenwald 1958; Skeen 1991), and, especially in the popular media, as "carriers" of the HIV virus or other sexually transmitted diseases around the world (see Kempadoo and Doezema 1998; Alexander 1987). Dominant forms of sexuality, such as those of heterosexual, middle-class, white males, have only recently become the object of critical analysis (Tiefer 1995: 20), despite the fact that, once interrogated, their practices and beliefs are every bit as theoretically interesting as those of other groups.

Anthropologists and feminist researchers both have paid close attention to the power dynamics inherent in ethnographic research (e.g., Wolf 1992; Stacey 1988). Being a woman and a sex worker studying in my own country and community made the power dynamics inherent in this project quite a bit different from those of studying another culture altogether or from studying more marginalized individuals. As I was studying educated, middle-class men, I was often interviewing from an inferior position in terms of gender, age, and resources as well as from a socially stigmatized position, and this was something that many of the interviewees were aware of and commented on. Studying individuals within my own culture also means that my informants will be able not only to read my text, but to comment on it as well. In fact, several of the interviewees, as well as other sex workers, have already provided comments and criticisms on a previous article (Frank 1998), the chapters here, and the short stories that I have published about the sex industry.

Interestingly, my simultaneous positioning and identification as a sex worker has also led to situations in which I was approached as a research subject, both outside and inside of the clubs. At a pornography conference, for example, I was sitting with a group of sex workers when we were approached by a male psychologist who asked if he could interview us about drug and alcohol use, sexual abuse, and the "problems caused by sex work." Although I had the background and training to respond to him directly with critiques of his methodology (Was he also interviewing women in other occupations to see if they had any of these same problems? Was he going to examine the complexities of the work, many of which had already been presented in sex worker panels at the conference, as well as in the literature?), I also came to feel the frustration that accompanies being targeted by voyeuristic researchers who are not willing to interrogate their own assumptions and ideological beliefs about the population they wish to study. In other situations I spoke with researchers and journalists who were approaching dancers in the clubs while we were working and who did not seem to have any awareness of the problems with this approach ("I'll tell him anything he wants to hear as long as he keeps paying me for my time") or the privileges and assumptions that had led them to seek out strippers as exotic others worthy of study. In working as a dancer while studying the identities and motivations of the male customers, I have attempted, in part, to problematize this assumed relationship between the proper "subjects" and "objects" of social analysis.

After experiencing the financial rewards available to many women working in adult entertainment, as well as the flexibility of schedule that fit so well with my other pursuits, I also came to understand stripping as a type of work—certainly, a type of work deeply intertwined with gendered and sexual positionings and power relations, but as work, nonetheless. As I developed my own core of regular customers at the first club in which I worked, they became extremely interesting to me theoretically: Who were these men willing to spend large sums of money for relatively intangible services, who sought encounters with women that were *sexualized* but uncoupled from direct sexual release, at least in any overt way,[1] who found strip clubs exciting and transgressive (despite the clubs' very controlled and regulated atmosphere)? I came away from this initial research convinced that it was essential to turn the academic gaze on the men who quite literally funded this form of entertainment, especially the men who made regular use of the clubs by visiting monthly, weekly, or even daily. The book, based on additional research in a number of different strip clubs, takes the men's involvement in commodified sexualized entertainment as the primary object of investigation, allowing me to take up questions about desire and fantasy in leisure and consumption practices as well as questions about gender, sexuality, and power.

In the next several sections, my methodology and positionality are explored in more detail, followed by a discussion of the theoretical perspectives and concepts that organize my analysis.

Inside the "Men's Hut"

As a participant-observer, I selected and worked at five different strip clubs in a fairly large Southern city (referred to as Laurelton in this text) intermittently over a period of fourteen months as a nude entertainer.[2] Realizing that my initial experiences and relationships with customers while working in an upscale gentlemen's club could not be simply generalized to those found in a more stereotypical strip bar, I selected a range of different clubs, from the most prestigious clubs in the city to lower-tier "dive" bars. In determining where the clubs fell in relation to one another I looked at reputations, dress codes, cover charges, food and liquor choices, club size and atmosphere, location, and the clientele. The clubs are also given pseudonyms and appear here as Diamond Dolls (upper tier), the Panther Club (upper tier), the Crystal Palace (middle tier), the Pony Lounge (lower-tier dive), and Tina's Revue (lower tier, neighborhood bar). Despite these differences in classiness, the Laurelton clubs chosen all offered nude table dancing. I did not select any clubs that prohibited table dances and relied only on stage dancing, for example, or that prohibited alcohol and offered lap dancing. I also did not choose any clubs that regularly advertised feature dancers (porn stars or well-known dancers who had traveling acts) because of the way such promotions changed the composition of the audience.

Though a few clubs exist in Laurelton that cater to an almost exclusively black clientele, I did not select any of these clubs for my study for two primary reasons: first, my own access to the spaces as a participant observer / dancer was limited by race, and second, as nude dancing is still primarily a white form of entertainment (Meridian 1997), the black clubs are considered a specialized and restricted market by many of the dancers and customers with whom I interacted (even those who prefer them), much like clubs in Laurelton that offer lap dancing from bikini-clad dancers or clubs that rely heavily on feature entertainment. My decision not to focus on these particular sites was a necessary but unfortunate limitation, and there is a great deal more research that can be done on the distinctions and variations among different locations and forms of adult entertainment and on the practices and beliefs of the customers, especially with regard to race.

At each of the selected clubs, I went through the application, audition, and training process as would any new entertainer and worked a variety of shifts to gain access to a range of different customers, employees, and experiences: day shift (11:30 A.M.–8:00 P.M.), midshift (4:00 P.M.–12:00 A.M.), and night shift (8:00 P.M. to close).[3] After being hired I was forthcoming with my managers and coworkers about my research when asked. Some managers and other dancers showed an interest in my project, offering their own insights and observations and suggesting possible interviewees; others seemed to barely take note of my existence, either as a dancer or a researcher.

Engaging in participant observation—in this case, actually working as an exotic dancer—allowed me a perspective on men's behavior in strip clubs and on the exchanges taking place inside that I would have been unable to gain using other methods of data collection. Participant observation offered me the opportunity to interact continually with a variety of male customers, and being involved in thousands of transactions in the clubs irreversibly shaped my theoretical questions and concerns. Further, despite widespread changes in the gendering of the public sphere (and perhaps in part because of those changes), strip clubs and the nuances of the exchanges that take place inside them, are still often off-limits to women in the United States, that is, unless you are the woman dancing on the table.[4] Interactions between dancers and their customers are also semiprivate; the noise of the club and the physical proximity of the participants are such that their conversations are not accessible to a mere observer, male or female. Working as a dancer gave me access to all of the clubs' spaces, allowed me to be involved in dressing room conversations, and required me to learn the tricks of the trade (body disciplines, sales techniques, dealing with the management, negotiating stigma, and so forth). In these respects, working as a dancer and recording my own interactions was essential. Being involved in multiple interactions in the clubs gave me insight into the context and meaning of customer behaviors and desires as well as into the many different ways that other dancers negotiated these interactions.

Though I have attempted to refrain from making too many generalizations about the customers in this text, doing so was commonplace for me while on the job; in fact, it was absolutely necessary to be a successful dancer. I was an employee as well as a researcher, and thus expected to provide entertainment for the club (no sitting in a corner with my notebook) and pay the same house fees and tip-outs at the end of my shift as every other dancer. These fees and tip-outs ranged from $50 to $150, depending on the club and on the shift that was worked. I have not reproduced the "ideal types" that I used while working, as I do not want to reinforce any existing stereotypes of customers or create new ones. Often, however, I had to figure out very quickly what kind of interaction a man was interested in and eventually learned to scan a room, sizing up the customers and making expeditious decisions about how to present myself in our interaction. Thus, although it can certainly be argued that the interviewees, and perhaps even the other customers in the clubs, were reluctant to tell me the whole truth about their motivations and desires in our conversations—indeed, it would have been impossible for them to do so if one accepts the notion of unconscious motivation—I can say with confidence that I do know what men were willing to *pay for* each night. One male academic, for example, argued incessantly with me after a presentation I gave, claiming that the men must have *really* been seeking sexual encounters with the dancers. Yet many customers returned to the clubs night after night and did not receive, or even ask for, such services. Other men might ask for sex or for dates but, again and again, *pay* for talk. This book, then, is an exploration of some of the services that *were* sought and purchased in the clubs and the meanings of those transactions to the men who engaged in them.

This interpretive framework of experience is combined with qualitative interview data. Except for two men who were employees of strip clubs (as well as having been regular customers at one point in their life), all of the men I formally interviewed for this project were customers of clubs in which I worked.[5] While I was working in Laurelton, I spoke with hundreds of male customers about my research and almost always approached those customers as potential interviewees.[6] That is, I was immediately forthcoming about my research purposes whenever possible and provided the customers with a real name (in addition to my required stage name) and information about how to contact me outside of the club for an interview if they showed interest. Even men who did not do formal interviews frequently commented on my research, telling me their reasons for visiting the clubs and discussing their opinions about adult entertainment, commodification, relationships, masculinity, and sexuality. When the men did agree to an interview, I met them at their workplace or at a restaurant or coffee shop in the city for several taperecorded interview sessions.[7]

The primary interviewers ranged in age from twenty-eight to fifty-seven years. All of them identified as heterosexual, had at least some college education, and identified as somewhere in the middle class, despite sometimes significant differences in income and occupation.[8] Of these thirty men, sixteen were married, four were divorced, three were single, and the rest were involved with women at the time of the interviews. Twenty-seven were white Americans, two were African Americans, and one was a white British citizen who frequently traveled to the United States on business and was "entertained" in strip clubs during those visits.[9] All of the men visited strip clubs often enough to consider the visits significant in their own repertoire of sexual practices.[10] These men were not just once-a-year visitors or bachelor party goers, and this is extremely important to the analysis that follows.

Many researchers have noted the difficulty of obtaining data on human sexual behavior (Berk, Abramson, and Okami 1995; Orbuch and Harvey 1991; di Mauro 1995). In addition to difficulties raised by social stigmas and taboos that influence how willing individuals are to talk about their practices, sexual behaviors have a significant fantasy component as well as being shaped by personal history, remembered or not. These difficulties can seem formidable. I recently heard an academic writer on pornography describe herself as "anti-ethnography" because she felt it was impossible to access the truth about why consumers found such productions appealing. Despite her rejection of ethnography, however, she then put forth just such a theory of motivation and pleasure. Although there are complications involved, I believe that it is not necessary or sensible to eschew interview research altogether. As George Devereux suggests, and many others have elaborated, the social scientist must instead scrutinize "the matrix of meanings" in which relevant data are embedded, be reflective about his or her own personal involvement with the material, analyze the "nature and locus of the partition between subject and observer," and both accept and exploit the fact that his or her presence has influenced the event (1967: 6). Further, the point of interviews need not be an attempt to dredge up some ultimate truth about an individual but to explore the ways that people make sense of their experiences and to look for patterns in this process. I thus use the men's talk in the analyses here as an illustration of the way sexual practices and gender identities can be talked about and understood, and about what *conscious* meanings they might have to the participants. Also, as I am interested in the way fantasy and reality are mutually constructed, I then use insights from our conversations and interactions in the clubs, from my observations of their behavior, and from the interview situations, to suggest other possible meanings, motivations, and desires. Wherever possible and relevant in the text I also include information about my interactions with the particular interviewee.[11]

The interviews were transcribed verbatim, but the quotes from the interviewees that appear throughout the text have been edited for clarity and easier reading. Unless they are crucial to understanding the dialogue, verbal tics have been removed when they became repetitive, for example, "um," "uh," "you know," and "you know what I mean." When words were missing, I have often filled them in but placed brackets around them so that my own additions are obvious. I have tried to indicate substantial pauses when they seemed to indicate uncertainty or hesitancy on the part of the interviewee, but have edited out interruptions and irrelevant conversation. My own questions and interjections are included only when they seem relevant to understanding the meaning of the interviewee's comments.

My methodology presented several unique opportunities. First, the interviewees were regular customers of the clubs; that is, they returned to the same clubs several times a week. Thus, I often had the chance to interact with them in a variety of ways and on multiple occasions, as both a dancer and a researcher, both before and after our interviews. The men who ended up interviewing with me were of course different in some ways from the men who chose not to do so; they may have had more free time, more respect for higher education and social science research, or some additional erotic or platonic interest in me, for example. I met most of these men after they had tipped me on the stage, as it is club protocol for dancers to approach men who have already shown an interest in them by tipping and there were always too many customers in the club for me to approach every one. However, my employment brought me into contact with hundreds of men each week and the interviewees do not stand out as especially distinct from other men who placed a significance on regular visits to this kind of venue. Further, as customers were one of the main topics of conversation among dancers in the dressing rooms, I can also be reasonably certain that the interviewees were not altogether unique.

Second, there is a difference when men visit strip clubs as groups and when men visit alone, both in the physical dynamics of the interaction and in the conversation. Because I could never interview an entire group of men at once and because I could certainly never recreate the club setting and interpersonal dynamic, I found it extremely useful to observe the interactions of men in groups in addition to interacting with them individually both inside and outside of the clubs. As their personal narrative accounts often differed from the group interactions I observed,[12] it was invaluable for my research that I had recourse to both of these methodologies.

Third, working in five different Laurelton clubs meant that I sometimes interacted with the same customers in several different locations (much to their surprise!). I was able to observe their behavior in the various settings and to speak with the dancers they went to see at the different clubs. Though each strip club has a significant number of its own regulars, there is also a large amount of traffic among clubs in Laurelton by dancers and customers. Realizing this led me to explore in more detail the fantasies and beliefs that motivated the men to choose one location over another, or to seek one particular *type* of commodified encounter over another.

Finally, I found that norms of social reciprocity worked in my favor; that is, men were extremely forthcoming in our interviews about their practices and desires in part because they interpreted my performances in the club as prior revelations about *myself*. Though the interviews may have taken place several days after our interactions in the clubs, many of the men commented favorably on my willingness to be "vulnerable" to them. Even during encounters that did not lead to interviews, I found that my willingness to disrobe in the club produced an atmosphere in which many men felt comfortable revealing things that they claimed to ordinarily keep secret: particular sexual fantasies and desires, fears of inadequacy, confusion about gender identities, resentment toward women and their demands, and needs for connection and conversation, for example.

Ethnographer, Dancer, Wife

The different roles I filled during my fieldwork influenced both my interactions with the customers and my observations in the clubs. Sociologist Carol Ronai has explored "the difficulty in extricating a researcher self from other selves while involved in participant observation" and writes about the conflicts that she experienced while working as an exotic dancer and collecting data for her master's thesis (1992: 102). Ronai argues that her participant-observer role was "never clearly separated from that of being a dancer, a wife, or the other roles" she enacted (104). At the same time that these roles are not necessarily distinct, however, they may become problematic in relation to each other.[13] Like Ronai, the primary roles that I filled during my fieldwork experience were those of a researcher, a dancer, and a wife, as I was married at the time of my fieldwork. More specifically, these roles were modified by my academic discipline, my appearance, and my own social class and race. Depending on the context, these roles also had different salience and meaning, for both myself and the customers with whom I was interacting. For some highly educated customers, for example, the fact that I was pursuing my doctorate and had chosen such a topic was fascinating. For customers who had not attended college or who did not know (or care) what a dissertation was, this had very little meaning: "Good luck on your school paper," one man said after our conversation in the club. In my interactions with the interviewees, there were times when one role or another took precedence at a given moment in their perception of me as well as times when these roles were intertwined. Men sometimes slipped between thinking of me as a dancer and as a researcher, saying things like "I can tell this to you because you're a dancer" during the interview, or similarly, by commenting on my "difference" from other dancers they met while we were interacting in the club.

There were times while working when my role as a researcher intervened in my interactions with customers and did position me as different from the other dancers around me. Some of the regulars would jokingly call me "Professor" or "Doctor" after they found out about my project, for example. "Watch out for her," a regular once jokingly informed a newcomer whom I was sitting with, "she'll psychoanalyze you!" Occasionally, the DJs would introduce me as a graduate student when they called me to the stage, knowing that this information would make me attractive to particular customers, or would play Van Halen's "Hot for Teacher" as part of my set. On the other hand, the student researcher / sex worker is almost a caricature to some, as evidenced by a fairly recent cartoon in a prominent men's magazine that pictured a well-dressed escort saying good night to one of her customers. "I'll be sure to mention you in my doctoral thesis," she says while getting out of his car. Further, in many of the clubs, I was also working alongside other graduate students, medical students, law students, counselors, business owners, and real estate agents. There were just as many instances, then, when my role as a dancer was more prominent in the interactions than any other. There were some customers and some other dancers in the clubs I worked in who most likely knew me only as another sex worker or who did not believe my story. Yet many of the men who did interview with me did so, in part, *because* I was *both* a dancer and a researcher.

My role as a wife was also often quite salient to the men I interacted with and those I interviewed, and most people would eventually comment on my wedding ring. Both the interviewees and the other customers frequently asked me "What does your *husband* think of this?" Some customers saw my marital status as ruining the illusion: "I can't fall in love with you! You're married!" Other customers saw this as a sign that I was trustworthy and serious: if I was honest enough to wear a wedding ring while working in a strip club (which inevitably resulted in a decrease in profits because of its intrusion into some customers' fantasies), my intentions must be legitimate.

These roles, as identities, also influenced my own experiences of the work and the interactions, as well as how I explored and interpreted my observations theoretically. Just as the men moved back and forth between thinking of me as a dancer and as a researcher, I also move back and forth in this text, sometimes referring to "dancers," sometimes referring to "us." I do this self-consciously, as this kind of reflexivity was essential both on the job and in the writing process. My class and educational privileges necessarily meant that my experiences of working as a dancer were different from those of some of the women I worked with: I was pursuing a "real" career instead of "just stripping" (a mark of distinction in a stigmatized job); I had the opportunity to work at both upper- and lower-tier clubs; and I was sheltered from the economic vicissitudes of the work, to name just a few examples. On a bad night, I could console myself with the knowledge that my employment was temporary. If a customer made a nasty comment, I could write it down and analyze it, distancing myself from the situation.

On the other hand, I went through the same audition procedures and worked by the same rules and regulations as the other dancers, facing the possibility of either acceptance or rejection by the customers each shift and learning the bodily techniques specific to the work. Further, though my academic interest sheltered me somewhat from stigmatization ("Oh, you're only doing this for research"), there were times when I faced much of the same stigma as does any woman (and sometimes man) who labors in the sex industry, even from close friends and relatives. My experiences as a sex worker also politicized me in new and different ways. Actively claiming an identity as a sex worker, for example, rather than using my academic privilege to disavow this aspect of my experience became very important to me over time. My subsequent involvement in the sex workers' rights movement has provided me with the opportunity to make the acquaintance of many brilliant and inspiring women who have helped me to make sense of my experiences.[14] Above all, working in the industry forced me to confront many of my own ideological beliefs about love, money, and power.

It was with regard to the identity of wife that I struggled with the most ambivalence about my research and my dancing. As George Devereux (1967) has pointed out, anthropological data can arouse anxiety in researchers and this anxiety can influence social scientists' observations and their relationship to their data. In retrospect, I realize that I focused more and more on ideas of marriage and monogamy and on the relational aspect of the encounters in strip clubs over time as my own problematic status as a married person in this environment became more evident to me. The men's questions about what my husband thought about my dancing were thus highly significant for me in several ways. First, this appeal as to the feelings of my partner was something that had worried me prior to beginning this project and something that I relentlessly monitored during the course of my fieldwork. Second, it led me to begin asking the men the converse question in return: What does your wife (or partner) think of *your* behavior? I thus began to investigate the way that these men's marriage or long-term partnership influenced the meanings of their visits to the clubs. And third, this query made me question how my participation in these encounters in turn affected the wives or partners of these men. How would these women feel about *me?* How would *I* feel if I found out that *my* husband visited strip clubs several times a week? How would I feel about our marriage, about the dancers he went to see, about the money that he spent?

There were times, then, that I fantasized a continuity between myself and an imaginary, excluded wife rather than between myself and other sex workers or between myself and other feminist researchers. When men made comments during the interviews about no longer being sexually attracted to their wife, for example, my own concerns and anger about aging in a society that highly values youth and beauty in women were sometimes heightened. I say "imaginary" wife, of course, because I have no way of actually knowing whether these men's wives felt excluded or hurt when they learned of their husband's practices or whether they worried about becoming unattractive to their partner. Rather, this was clearly my own imagining of how I might feel in that situation and was a reflection of my own ambivalent understanding of how to manage fidelity, desire, trust, and intimacy in long-term relationships and in a social context where women are often devalued as they age. This anger, however, always coexisted with the emotions spawned by my other identifications: the empathy that I felt for most of the interviewees and customers, the increased feelings of self-awareness and self-efficacy that I experienced while dancing, and the pleasure that I took in my friendships with other sex workers.

It was thus from the interactions and insights that I had while actually working as a dancer, as well as the ways that stripping impacted on other areas of my life, academic and otherwise, that many of my theoretical questions and concerns took shape. My primary focuses in this text derive from my interests in subjectivity, power, and desire, as well as the ways the personal and the cultural are inseparably intertwined. In the next few sections, the major concepts and theories that inform the chapters of this book are discussed.

Theories and Themes

FEMINISM

A great deal of feminist writing on sex work has crystallized around the pornography debates of the past few decades, also known as the feminist sex wars. Predominantly associated with the work of Andrea Dworkin and Catharine MacKinnon, antipornography feminism critiqued male sexual dominance in both the public and the private spheres, conceptualizing it as a hegemonic, totalizing form of oppression. Pornography and other forms of sex work were seen as institutionalized means of buttressing male domination and further alienating women from their sexuality.[15] By collapsing representation and reality (i.e., by arguing that representations of male sexual dominance or abuse are equivalent to actual male sexual dominance or abuse), MacKinnon (1993) argues that pornography is a form of violence that extends to every woman, and works for the benefit of every man, universally.

Other feminist writers have tried to revise this analysis by pointing to sex work as involving more complicated power relationships and interactions. In the past decade or so, a number of feminist works have appeared that have specifically explored the agency of sex workers (e.g., McElroy 1995; Bell 1994; Delacoste and Alexander 1987; Nagle 1997; Chapkis 1997). Shannon Bell, for example, argues that performance artists like Annie Sprinkle and Scarlet Harlot work to mediate debates about female degradation and agency in the sex industry: although both poles exist, neither view can explain by itself why the sex industry exists and what sex workers experience by working in it. There have also been moves to rethink the meaning of commodified sex and pornographic representation, both inside and outside feminism but almost always in conversation with it, in areas such as media and film studies, legal theory, and queer studies. Writers have attempted in different ways to reread pornography in order to look beyond its misogyny and delineate more clearly how various subjects are positioned within the genre, sometimes locating potential pockets of resistance to hegemonic representations of gender or sexuality (e.g., L. Williams 1989; Kipnis 1996). Sex workers have been accepted by some theorists as queers, and radical writers like Pat Califia (1994) and Carol Queen (1997b) have expounded the potential utopia of a "sex-positive" culture (which actually has a long history in feminist thought despite the popular homogenization of all feminists as sex-negative) and positioned sex workers as possible revolutionaries and sexual educators.

In the desire to move beyond the "victim feminism" of the "Mac-Dworkinite" era, however, some feminist writers have begun to worry about losing a critical edge (Dines, Jensen, and Russo 1998; Chancer

1998). Sociologist Lynn Chancer situates the sex debates that have raged in feminism, especially in regard to pornography, as "a particular manifestation of a general social dilemma—the structure versus agency issue that has been troubling social theorists over the last several decades" (4). Chancer does not believe that either side of the debates over pornography and sex work can afford to ignore the other and believes that "sexual pleasure needs to be protected *and* sexism to be challenged" (81). The potential economic and personal rewards that come from sex work for many women, and the radical political potential of mixing money, sexuality, and the public sphere, mean that sex work cannot be dismissed as a possible form of feminist resistance or an exercise of female agency. In this text, I take it for granted that dancers actively respond to the customers, resist the control of the managers and club owners in a variety of ways, and find room to explore and express their own sexualities and desires even in a setting catering to male fantasies. On the other hand, there are certain configurations of power and privilege that situate certain groups of individuals as laborers and others as consumers and that influence the kinds of transactions that are sought and purchased, and these need to be more fully explored.

By shifting the investigative focus from the images of women in pornography to the performances of exotic dancers, and from the sex *workers* to the *consumers,* I hope to slightly reframe the terms of the debate.[16] Male silence on the topic of pornographic consumption, coupled with the prominence of the debates about pornography in public discourse over the past decade, have helped create a dearth of information about how pornographic materials are actually used by customers, which practices are enjoyable, and why (A. Ross 1989: 207). This observation can be extended to knowledge of men's practices of consumption in other arenas of the sex industry as well (e.g., A. Ross 1989; Hart 1994; Chancer 1993; Weitzer 2000), including strip clubs.[17] Though there is some fascinating academic work looking at the male customers of sex workers in specific venues and situations—such as Anne Allison's (1994) ethnography of corporate entertainment in Japanese hostess clubs and Angie Hart's (1998) anthropological look at prostitution in a community in Spain—too often, when men's experiences as customers of sex workers are addressed, they are homogenized and generalized as both similar to each other and to men who do not use the sex industry.

This homogenization certainly occurs in many folk explanations, as when men's desires to engage in different forms of sexualized consumption are seen as simply a result of a natural, animalistic male sexuality (see Tierney 1998). Yet this homogenization also occurs in more political analyses. As Andrea Dworkin writes: "You can't think about prostitution unless you are willing to think about the man who needs to fuck the prostitute. Who is he? What is he doing? What does he want? What does he need? He is everyone . . . Everyone" (1997: 147). Similarly, feminist Susan Edwards proclaims that "the male client in all his guises is the man amongst us" (1993: 102).

Is the male client indeed "the man amongst us"?[18] On a literal level, not all men choose to consume sexual services or even the same *kinds* of sexual services. In the contemporary United States, there has been a proliferation of different sexualized services and products for sale: escort services and street prostitution; strip clubs and peep shows (with and without contact); lingerie parlors (which may allow masturbation on premises); phone sex lines; pornographic movies, books, and magazines; sexual aids; and more. Within each of these categories there are also distinctions that can be made in terms of classiness, accessibility, privacy, and legality that affect consumption practices. Strip clubs, then, must be seen as providing particular types of services that are distinct from other sectors of the sex industry and from other forms of entertainment and leisure—types of services that appeal to some men but not others. To simply equate maleness with clientness in general, then, is to drastically reduce the meanings of such different kinds of consumption and sexual practice.[19] It is to overlook the many differences among men in terms of beliefs and practices, especially the fact that men have disagreed with each other in almost every era about what is offensive or immoral sexual behavior and about the regulation of pornography, prostitution, and female sexuality in general (Segal 1992: 66). During the 1980s, strip clubs along with many other live commercial sex venues were theoretically included in the category of pornography. Even today, striptease is often included with other types of commodified sexualized service as simply part of the sex industry. Sometimes this is an important political and analytical move (and one that I make at particular moments in this text); at other times this generalization occludes the specific motivations and experiences of both the workers and the customers.[20]

Another assumption has been that men are unambiguously motivated to use the sex industry out of a desire for sexual mastery and power over women. In an article that claims to address both the theories and the "realities" of prostitution, for example, Susan Edwards writes: "It is men that we need to study, to understand their desire for power, for sexual mastery. We need to address and confront why it is that men are orgasming to visual images of women's subordination, harm and abuse in pornography, and also to their use and subordination and insult in prostitution. We need to examine the social construction of male sexual arousal and the channeling of sexual arousal into a context of abuse and harm in which women are degraded" (1993: 102). Although I agree with Edwards that it is time to look at the consumer side of the industry to further explore questions of male privilege and motivation, I find the assumption of a straightforward connection between male dominance, masculinity, and male subjectivity to be questionable.

In some ways, strip clubs *as they now exist* are intertwined with certain forms of male privilege. At a macrolevel, most strip clubs are owned and operated by men. Although it is euphemistically called adult entertainment, anyone who has looked for comparable services for heterosexual[21] women has probably noticed that most, though not all, commodified sexual productions (from strip clubs to pornography to erotic massages) are still aimed at male consumers. Many strip clubs featuring female dancers across the country have rules prohibiting women from entering unless escorted by a male (ostensibly for the woman's protection), thereby precluding some women from becoming customers even if they so desire. (Though some cities and clubs offer strip events for women, featuring male and / or female dancers, these venues and events are not nearly as ubiquitous or profitable as those catering to men. Further, due to a number of different factors, women still tend to use these sites quite differently—more for special events and novelty outings than as a significant and frequent leisure destination.) It is also not an infrequent practice for businessmen to visit strip clubs on corporate expense, something for which there is not yet a comparable practice for businesswomen. Privilege is also evident in the distribution of stigma—despite the fact that men experience some stigma and some subjective distress as a result of being customers, men can be customers with relative impunity compared to the women who *work* in the clubs and who may carry the stigma of the sex industry for years afterward. Granted, men potentially face censure from their family (should their family actually find out about their visits) or from acquaintances who do not approve of their practices. The experience clearly does not leave a permanent stain, however, as strip clubs are still routinely used for bachelor parties, outings with coworkers, and other occasions. At the end of the visit the men can, and do, return home. And finally, there are often large discrepancies in earning power between male customers and female sex workers (even though sex workers may do quite well compared to women working in pink-collar or working-class jobs). Customers also often have particular advantages in terms of cultural, educational, and social capital.

But do men *feel* privileged when they partake of the services available to them in the sex industry? If so, when and why? After all, many men publicly claim that sex workers have the upper hand in commodified sexual transactions and very few men unabashedly admit that their visits to strip clubs or their use of other venues is either about personal power or a desire for dominance. Yet what does this denial actually mean? How, precisely, is this particular branch of the sex industry used by its male customers, and to what ends?

MASCULINITY AND SEXUALITY

Though gender has been an object of sociological and anthropological inquiry for some time, the past decade has seen a growing critical literature in both the social sciences and the humanities specifically on masculinity. Masculinity is generally recognized as a "constantly changing collection of meanings" that is both historical and socially constructed (Kimmel 1997: 224). Despite this variability, many writers recognize a "hegemonic masculinity," or a dominant image of the masculinity of those men who hold power and which men must position themselves in relation to (e.g., Connell 2000, 1995; Kimmel 1997; Davis 1997). Even hegemonic masculinity (or hegemonic masculinities) must be seen as existing in tension with competing definitions and understandings. A number of works have explored men's (and women's) different positionings within such competing cultural discourses of masculinity and the ways masculinities are related to other social positionings such as race, class, and sexuality (e.g., Bederman 1995; Cornwall and Lindisfarne 1994; Gutmann 1996; Halberstam 1998).

In *The Men and the Boys,* R. W. Connell suggests that it is possible to talk about "masculinizing practices," practices that are governed by a gender regime, embedded in social relations, and work to produce masculinities in particular settings and by certain institutions (2000: 155). Masculinizing practices may be readily apparent, as in the case of fraternity initiations or boot camp drills that emphasize toughness and physical hierarchy; or they may be much more subtle, involving comportment, dress, sexuality, sport, work, and other everyday or ritualistic practices. "Masculinities," Connell argues, "do not exist prior to social interaction, but come into existence as people act" (218). People's acts, as they become meaningful, link them to larger-scale structures of the gendered order: structures of power relations, production relations (or divisions of labor), relations of cathexis (or emotional relations), and symbolism (59). To say that a practice is masculinizing does not mean that it always or unproblematically constructs a particular stable kind of male subjectivity. Yet, although "men's bodies do not fix patterns of masculinity," their experiences, pleasures, and vulnerabilities are still significant in the constructions and expressions of masculinities (218). Masculinity, like social class, can thus be seen as a process rather than an achievement or a state of being.

Though masculinity is often associated with particular privileged social positions, many writers, both feminist and otherwise, have acknowledged that there is not one monolithic pattern of male dominance that can be exposed and altered. Further, instead of theorizing power as something inherent and fixed, since Foucault (1975) there has been a move toward conceptualizing power as more fluid and dispersed over the social terrain. Class, race, and sexuality, among other categories, exert an impact on individuals' power and privilege, and each individual's ability to influence others and to control his or her environment will vary by situation and context. Thus it is possible to recognize that whereas men as a whole may benefit from particular structures, ideas, or institutions, individual men may not equally reap those benefits or experience their privileges as such. As Susan Bordo writes: "Most men, equally with women, find themselves embedded and implicated in institutions and practices that they as individuals did not create and do not control—and that they frequently feel tyrannized by" (1993: 28). This complexity does not mean that we cannot or should not look critically at particular cultural institutions and practices; as Bordo also points out, men may indeed "have a higher stake in maintaining institutions in which they have historically occupied positions of dominance over women" (29). On the other hand, men can and do change their behaviors and attitudes, and battles over the meanings of gender and the gendered distribution of power are continually fought in the economic, social, and political spheres.

It is important to explore the ways masculinity is constructed and understood discursively; it is also crucial to explore the realm of personal emotional meaning. Masculinity, although linked to power and social position, is more than just a social attribute possessed by an individual. It is also a personal identity that is emotionally experienced, relationally and over the life course of an individual. As feminist psychoanalyst Nancy Chodorow writes: "Meaning—at least about any linguistic or cultural categories that matter to us—is always psychologically particular to the individual" (1995: 517). There are some meanings and experiences of masculinity that are not going to be addressed in cultural critiques and representations and there are some elements of hegemonic masculinity that may be experienced as either (or both) self-constitutive or painfully humiliating for any particular individual. These meanings are also constructed out of and in relation to both conscious and unconscious *fantasy,* which can be a realm of pleasurable wishes as well as a potential domain of anxiety (Cowie 1992: 146).

Part of the reason for men's reluctance to change their behavior and bring it more in line with "feminist" expectations (which admittedly are diverse) may be that on a subjective level, men's experiences do not always fit with the model of masculinity put forth by feminist theorists and social critics. As Michael Kimmel writes: "Men's feelings are not the feelings of the powerful, but of those who see themselves as powerless. These are the feelings that come inevitably from the discontinuity between the social and the psychological, between the aggregate analysis that reveals how men are in power as a group and the psychological fact that they do not feel powerful as individuals. They are the feelings of men who were raised to believe themselves entitled to feel that power, but do not feel it" (1997: 238). Clearly, it is necessary to explore the experiences and subjectivities of men in relation to power, and commodified sexualized services, in more detail (e.g., Cornwall and Lindisfarne 1994; Segal 1990).

For the male customers, I argue, visits to strip clubs are more about sexuality and gender identity than about *sex.* Obviously, by this I mean in part that the men are usually not seeking, or obtaining, sexual contact or release on the premises. However, I also mean to place sexuality as something above and beyond sexual activity. Sexuality is thus conceptualized here as multifaceted: involving social and personal constellations of identities (who or what people think and say they are), ideologies and fantasies (beliefs about what sex is and means; erotics) and practices and prohibitions (what people actually do with their body parts).

The study of sexuality and erotics is a burgeoning and exciting field in anthropology as a result of a strong theoretical interest in subjectivity and an increased willingness in recent years on the part of anthropologists to engage with psychoanalysis as a theory of personal and cultural meaning (e.g., Herdt and Stoller 1990; Sanday 1990; Allison 1996). Though historically some anthropologists have used psychoanalysis, a more general resistance to it followed the critiques of the "culture and personality" school of thought. In an attempt to avoid making reference to a universalized and Westernized theory of the self, many anthropologists have instead pursued the study of subjectivity discursively. Many of these analyses, however, still rely on undertheorized and even unacknowledged universalistic assumptions about the human psyche. What Chodorow describes as an "essentialist culturalism," for example, is an attempt to theorize personal meaning as universally linguistically and culturally constructed rather than psychologically based (1999: 160). My own approach is to draw on some of the basic concepts and processes of psychoanalysis to discuss motivation and personal and cultural meaning (such as ideas of the unconscious, fantasy, desire, and identity and the processes of transference and projection), while leaving some of the more problematic concepts behind (such as a universalized developmental story of the Oedipus complex or the idea that the content of the unconscious is everywhere the same).

Often, the adult entertainment industry is defended as being about fantasy rather than reality. This is an important counter to the idea that the transactions in strip clubs and the stories told in pornography simply reflect the reality of gendered (or classed or raced) interactions. Yet, if fantasy is full of multiple, fluid, and contradictory identifications, why do so many of the same scenarios get replayed and reworked? Why do we so easily "recognize" the schoolgirl, the bad girl, the rich girl, and the bimbo in the scenarios produced in the clubs? Why could I practically control which kind of customer I wanted to interact with on any given night by my *outfit?* Why can any good dancer readily anticipate the desires of a new customer, even though he may be experiencing those desires as deeply personal? Of course, it could be argued, and accurately so, that many of the customers' personal desires do not get represented in the sexual marketplace; they may be too threatening, too unarticulated, or too individualized to garner significant profits. Yet why, then, are other scenarios and stories so lucrative for the dancers and the clubs and so compelling for the customers?

The sex industry and its entrepreneurs and employees—whether they are selling pornography, table dances, or sexual activity—draw on cultural ideologies and culturally and personally defined gender identities to stimulate desire and simultaneously allow for a fluidity of identifications and desires. Thus, although the transactions that take place in the sexual marketplace are certainly infused with some of the same power relations that inform gender identities more generally, these power relations are not always exact reproductions of those found in the social sphere (which are themselves often complex and contradictory). Fantasies, as settings for or mise-en-scènes of desires (Cowie 1992: 137), are not static or determined by one's gender, sexuality, social class, or other identities and social positionings. On the other hand, fantasy *is* rooted in and circumscribed by the everyday through past experiences, beliefs, prohibitions, and patterns of work and social interaction. In *Permitted and Prohibited Desires* Anne Allison views desire as "both real and phantasmic," as something "that segues both into and out of the realities of everyday life," "always interconnected with the paths people assume to make a living, reproduce a community, and move from childhood into adulthood." In other words, she writes, "desire is not reduced or repressed as much as it is actively produced in forms that coordinate with the habits demanded of productive subjects" (1996: xv). Psychoanalytic perspectives, she argues, do not necessarily prohibit us from also studying political, economic, cultural, and historical processes, and it is possible to be "as attentive to relations of power and materiality as to symbolic imaging" (18). In my analysis, I explore the way the men's everyday lives and practices, along with their beliefs and fantasies about different categories of Others, influence their experience of strip clubs as exciting, transgressive, and pleasurable.

Many writers on pornography have drawn on different revisions of Lacanian psychoanalytic theory, feminist and otherwise, to explore questions of subjectivity, power, fantasy, and desire. Although I find much of this work quite interesting, I also find such an emphasis on intrapsychic processes limiting when it comes to examining scenarios that are interactive rather than textual. The Lacanian subject, after all, is always barred from accessing the Other's subjectivity and remains perpetually unfulfilled because of the continual displacement of desire. Instead, I align myself with feminist object-relations theorists and also with selected parts of the work of more traditional psychoanalytic theorists, committing to the exploration of both intrapsychic *and* interpsychic processes.

For thinking about the interactions that take place in strip clubs, for example, the concept of intersubjectivity is useful. The intersubjective mode, feminist psychoanalyst Jessica Benjamin writes, "acknowledges that the other person really exists in the here and now, not merely in the symbolic dimension. What he or she actually does, matters" (1986: 93). Because encounters that take place in strip clubs between dancers and their customers involve a meeting of two subjects, there is always a potential (though not always actualized) for a space of intersubjectivity to be opened up. The ambiguity of the intersubjective space experienced in a strip club has much to do with the range of possible interactions that the customers and dancers are constantly negotiating, and with the different psychodynamic processes involved in this negotiation. Each person brings different needs, goals, and privileges to the situation, and the outcome of the interaction is always to some extent unknown. What the customers end up purchasing, then, is an *experience,* an interactive fantasy through which a variety of different desires are produced and expressed. In exploring these desires, and their accompanying pleasures or discomforts, it is necessary to acknowledge the visual and sensory aspects of the men's experiences and at the same time explore the intersubjective dimensions of the scene.

LOOKING AND LEISURE: FROM
THE MALE GAZE TO TOURISTIC GAZES

The sex industry is one arena where gendered sexual identities and desires explicitly intersect with consumer culture, and the rapid expansion of strip clubs as a form of masculinized leisure in the late twentieth-century United States thus needs to be situated within changing patterns of production and consumption. As mentioned earlier in the text, given the continuing emphasis on leisure, entertainment, and pleasure in the American economy, it is not surprising that the sex industry has grown and diversified quite rapidly, especially in the second half of the twentieth century. Geographer David Harvey argues that late capitalism has seen a shift in the structures of production from Fordism (rigidly organized systems of mass production) to flexible accumulation (small-batch production, speed-up in labor processes, etc.). Such changes in production have been accompanied by accelerations in exchange and consumption. First, the pace of consumption has been sped up "across a wide swathe of life-styles and recreational activities (leisure and sporting habits, pop music styles, video and children's games, and the like)." Second, there has been a shift toward the consumption of "ephemeral" services: "not only personal, business, educational, and health services, but also into entertainments, spectacles, happenings, and distractions" (1990: 285). Strip clubs provide a venue for a very particular kind of modern consumption, one that is based both on spectacle and on the commodification of an extremely ephemeral service—intimate interaction.

The expansion of the sex industry has been accomplished through mass-marketing tactics like those used in other market sectors: advertising, market segmenting, and a specialization of functions; through "recognizing, producing, and proliferating differentiated needs in the service of profitability" (Singer 1993: 38). Market differentiation, for example, has had a tremendous impact on legalized forms of adult entertainment such as strip clubs. The highly profitable discos of the 1970s and early 1980s heralded an intensified focus on the creation of "atmosphere" and luxury in nightclubs, something that the upscale strip clubs have drawn heavily on over the past decade (Bildstein 1996; Haden-Guest 1997). Entrepreneurs began realizing that improving the atmosphere and diversifying the services offered in their entertainment venues would lead to even greater profits, and during the 1980s gentlemen's clubs began appearing in larger U.S. cities in addition to the preexisting neighborhood nudie bars, massage parlors, and pornographic theaters and bookstores. Upscale clubs did not *replace* these other venues; instead, they were designed to appeal to different kinds of customers seeking different kinds of services, especially those men who were experiencing a rise in disposable income due to a strong economy and developing changing attitudes about luxury and leisure (the rise of "yuppie" consumption).

As the century has drawn to a close, the services offered in many strip clubs have become simultaneously more *spectacular* and more *individualized.* Public forums for male voyeurism have long existed, yet the forms and meanings of striptease entertainment have changed over the years, and the services available in modern strip clubs have little in common with the burlesque shows of the turn of the century, the staged comedy routines of the 1950s and 1960s, or even the seedy "champagne hustles" (Bildstein 1996) of the 1970s. Many strip clubs in the 1960s and 1970s featured only a few dancers each night, for example, and these dancers often traveled quite a bit, staying at each venue perhaps only a week performing stage shows (Misty 1973; Ample 1988); other clubs employed regular go-go dancers, prostitutes, and strippers but mixed performances with sexual access and services, often creating difficult work environments for the dancers (Jarrett 1997). Many clubs today, on the other hand, have multiple stages and run enough dancers to have a continuous strip show on each stage in the club, with a new dancer appearing at the end of each two- or three-song set. There may be from ten to a hundred other entertainers circulating among the crowd selling personal dances and attention, depending on the size of the club and the number of stages. On a busy night in the Panther Club or Diamond Dolls, for example, one could look out at a veritable sea of naked women on the stages and the tables, something that customers described as both thrilling and disorienting. No single performer attracts the continuous attention of the crowd in this kind of club; rather, the entire room collaborates in a mass spectacle. There are also numerous opportunities for the customers themselves to become part of the spectacle, either by purchasing their own time on the stage for special events (see Liepe-Levinson 1998, 2002, for a more detailed discussion of such events) or by staging scenes of conspicuous consumption around their tables by spending money and attracting dancers.

In an article written in 1971, Marilyn Salutin described burlesque entertainment, or striptease, as sex "made impersonal." She writes that the dancers "show no affection or emotional response towards the audience" and that their customers are "indistinguishable from one another" (14, 22). Salutin's article highlights a world quite different from that of contemporary gentlemen's clubs, however, although only thirty years have passed. Despite the extension of the spectacle to include the entire room in many modern strip clubs, the services offered have also become much more individualized, an example of the flexibility of the contemporary commodity form. The new individualized form of entertainment offered in the table dance and in the opportunity for one-on-one conversations with the dancers means that one of the most significant services available in some of these clubs is extended *personal* interaction with a dancer. Now a dancer often performs for her customers in a much more flexible manner, perhaps even radically changing her approach from one customer to the next. Most of her income is generated through these private performances rather than her stage dancing. Many of these dancers are fairly steady employees of the clubs ("house dancers") rather than traveling performers ("features"), and there is thus an opportunity for the customers to return again and again to see a particular dancer: not because she is a headliner, but because of the kind of relationship that has developed between them. Certainly, then, the club is a place where women's bodies are displayed and commodified en masse, and usually dancers are hired only if they fit a club's particular marketed image. The interactions that take place inside the club become quite complicated, however, as the dancers are also selling particular versions of their 'selves'—their personality, their attentions, their conversation—in an attempt to generate and sustain these relationships with customers. What the customers end up purchasing is an interactive experience in a voyeuristic leisure space rather than a product or a service whose outcome is completely known in advance.

Interactions between dancers and their customers in the gentlemen's club are thus premised on the commodification of three interrelated elements: bodies made visible in particular ways, identities (public images and personal self-representations), and the production of particular forms of intimate interaction and experience (exposures, conversations, caretaking, mutual constructions of fantasy), a production of what I have elsewhere referred to as the 'commodification of intimacy' (Frank 1998), expanding on Hochschild's (1983) notion of emotional labor. Intimacy has been defined in numerous ways, ranging from bodily contact between two persons to "relationships between loving persons whose lives are deeply intertwined" (Perlman and Fehr 1987, 16–17).[22] At first glance, relationships between dancers and their customers, even their regular customers, may not appear to be intimate as the word is commonly understood. Sexual contact is merely the physical aspect of intimacy, and a fleeting transaction between a dancer and her customer that merely simulates or provides a fantasy of sexual access is certainly not comparable to the relationship of two long-term partners (or even between two parties during a one-night stand). Yet some commodified transactions do involve intimate exchanges, involving trust, revelation, emotional engagement, and even love between the two parties, especially if the relationship is ongoing in the context of the club. Further, even when customers do not desire such ongoing interactions, many do claim to have a desire to be treated as "special" or as "different from the other customers"; providing this service involves complex performances of bodily and emotional revelation on the part of the dancer. The kind of intimate interactions that are sought and purchased in strip clubs, however, are *different* from those available to the customers in other spheres of their lives, and it is through this difference that many of their most important meanings are derived. It is also through a negotiation of such limited, or extended, intimacies that spectacular and individualized elements of their experiences in the clubs are mediated for the customers.

Given these particularities, men's visits to strip clubs can usefully be considered *touristic practices* in addition to masculinizing practices. There are different kinds of strip club customers, of course, as mentioned previously: one-time or first-time visitors, regulars, visitors only on special occasions such as bachelor parties, traveling businessmen, and tourists to Laurelton. Each different kind of customer may have slightly different goals and motivations. Some of the customers are literal travelers, out-of-town businessmen or groups of men passing through Laurelton for other reasons, and these customers often claimed to be drawn to strip clubs while traveling because of the anonymity. The bulk of the customers, however, especially at the smaller neighborhood bars, are local residents of the city. Even locals and regulars, though not *tourists* according to most definitions, can be theorized as engaging in a form of touristic *practice* for several interrelated reasons: the significance of the gaze (in both spectacular and individualized forms) in structuring this form of consumption, the seeking of *experience* through interactions (rather than just a product or a service with a specific outcome), the role of fantasy and mythologies of escape in constructing the clubs as different from work and home, and the temporary nature of the men's visits.

Sociologist John Urry uses the term touristic to highlight the extension of what he calls the "tourist gaze" to a wide range of consumer phenomena (Rojek and Urry 1997).[23] The tourist gaze "in any historical period is constructed in relationship to its opposite, to non-tourist forms of social experience and consciousness . . . The gaze therefore presupposes a system of social activities and signs which locate the particular tourist practices, not in terms of some intrinsic characteristics, but through the contrasts implied with non-tourist social practices, particularly those based within the home and paid work" (1990: 2). He argues that in postmodern culture the tourist gaze "is increasingly bound up with and is partly indistinguishable from all sorts of other social and cultural practices," as almost everywhere "has become a centre of 'spectacle and display' " (93). As tourism declines in specificity, the tourist gaze becomes universalized, "intrinsically part of contemporary experience." The tourist gaze can take two different forms, according to Urry, although there are doubtless other forms of the gaze that can be imagined. The collective form of the gaze involves the presence of other people to create the atmosphere, and it is the presence of such other tourists that lends excitement and glamour to the surroundings (46). The romantic form of the gaze, on the other hand, has an emphasis on solitude, privacy, and a personal, semispiritual relationship with the object of the gaze (45). Both romantic and collective forms of the gaze may be sought, and gratified, in the combination of services (spectacular and individualized) available in modern strip clubs—the difference between the experiences of the guests at a bachelor party, for example, and those of a regular sitting with his favorite dancer.

A focus on visits to strip clubs as touristic practices and on multiple forms of the gaze is useful for several reasons. An important body of feminist work explores the complexities of female objectification under the "male gaze" in male-dominated societies (e.g., J. Berger 1972; Kappeler 1986; Lemoncheck 1985; Bartky 1990). At one time used heavily in film theory and textual readings of pornography, theories of the male gaze employ an analytics of visual power to discuss the relationship between spectator and spectacle, especially as this involves a female object and a male observer. Laura Mulvey, in an influential article about the gaze in film, argued that "pleasure in looking has been split between active / male and passive / female" (1975: 62); this notion was then deployed to discuss the link between gender relations and desire more generally. In a society such as our own where there are distinct gender inequities, male gaze theorists argue, "looking" becomes a form of domination and visibility a form of oppression. The gaze becomes a disciplining force when it is internalized (J. Berger 1972; Bartky 1990); thus women's enjoyment of the gaze becomes a form of narcissistic pleasure, rather than an experience of real sexual agency. Though all women are subjected to an objectifying and disciplining gaze, women who earn their living performing for the gratification of the male gaze, on stage or on film, are situated in an even more problematic position.

Theories of the male gaze have been heavily critiqued for over a decade for ignoring the complexities of fantasy and identification and for precluding multiple readings and gazes in film and pornography, as well as for disallowing for the existence of female sexual agency (e.g., Cowie 1992; L. Williams 1989, 1992). The idea that the gaze could always be male, or that the positions of looker/looked at are always split down gendered lines of "active-'male'-desirer-controller" and "passive-subordinate-'female'-object-of-desire" (Liepe-Levinson 2002: 11) is no longer tenable, and has not been for some time. The challenges have come in a multitude of forums and from many different positions: in feminist theory, especially with regard to pornography, sex work, and s&m (Califia 1994; Allison 1996; Funari 1997; Queen 1997a and b; Reed 1997; Chancer 1998; many others); in social theory; in film theory; by contemporary critics and popular writers (Paglia 1992; Mattson 1995); by cultural icons like Madonna; by popular writers on female and male sexuality; and so forth. With regard to the interactive transactions in strip clubs, theories of a totalizing male gaze and a simplistic gendering of desire have similarly been critiqued for ignoring the various possible positionings of male spectators (Liepe-Levinson 1998, 2002). In a recent article, for example, Katherine Liepe-Levinson notes that "it is virtually impossible for any participant, male or female, to buy control over all the gazes that can occur in a theatrical encounter," such as those found in strip clubs. Theatrical situations cannot constitute spectator gazes, identifications, and differentiations as either completely fluid or "absolutely monolithic, gendered, or classed" (24).

Despite its problems, however, male gaze theory was useful for exploring the notion of observation as power (objectification) and the possibility that such power could be disciplining of its objects. Surveillance, after all, is indeed often used as a mechanism of social power

(Foucault 1975; Bartky 1990), although the shape that power takes is not necessarily *determined* simply by one's positioning as subject or object of that observation. Male gaze theory also addresses the way social positionings can open up particular individuals and groups to more intense scrutiny than others, something that many of its critics would not deny. It is certainly necessary to move beyond the totalizing construction of male gaze theory, yet we need not abandon the idea that voyeurism can be implicated in relations of power and that scopic pleasure can result from the privilege of surveillance at the same time it is experienced by an observer as passive vulnerability or even ambivalence. Perhaps it is time to begin exploring the context and meanings of different kinds of visibility and surveillance, especially those that are commodified: How are particular sights / sites integrated into everyday patterns of work and leisure for their participants? How are different voyeuristic practices situated within broader discourses and understandings of identities, relationships, and consumption? How are these practices (masculinizing, touristic, or otherwise) intertwined with various social positionings?

Approaching men's visits to strip clubs as a form of touristic practice highlights issues of power and privilege, as it implies that the parties to the transactions are coming to the encounters with different purposes (the men for leisure, the women for labor) and thus transgressing different boundaries through their actions. These different purposes and meanings are not rooted in essential gender differences; rather, they are informed by labor relations as well as social positions (including, but not limited to, gender). Certainly these categories are not absolute; customers may conduct business activities at strip clubs, for example, and most customers are also workers in other arenas. Likewise, there may be some dancers for whom stripping feels more like leisure than work, at least on certain days, and a large component of the job involves engaging in practices associated with leisure: drinking alcohol, dining, conversing, flirting, and having fun (or at least appearing to). Yet in the immediacy of the encounter, the money nearly always flows in one direction only: from the customer to the dancer (until later, when the dancer is asked to pay the establishment a cut of her earnings). Further, even though a man may be conducting a form of business on the premises, it is usually precisely because this space is inherently "not work" for him that it has been chosen. Thus, although one or both of the participants to any transaction may be "playing" at any given time, this play is firmly situated within a larger framework of cultural and economic relations.

Further, analyzing the men's visits as touristic practices allows for a focus on consumer aspects of this practice, moving the analysis from the pursuit of sexual satisfaction or domination into the pursuit of gendered services and leisure. This is not to deny the sexualized components of the men's visits, but rather to highlight the ways that sex, entertainment, and leisure are intermingled in a variety of contemporary forms. The sexualization of travel and tourism has previously been an object of social analysis, as has the eroticization of the Other (Curtis and Pajaczkowska 1994). Here, I am also exploring the potential of sexualization and Otherness to be *transporting*—that is, sex or sexualized encounters coming to mean escape, freedom, and transgression to their participants. The men's visits may not require them to travel outside of their national boundaries, or even the boundaries of their hometown (though some men obviously do), yet the meanings of these practices have a great deal to do with ideas about home and away, safety and danger, and the search for Otherness. The idea of touristic practice also links individualized leisure choices and subjective pleasure seeking to the structures and processes that underlie a capitalist economy more generally—that is, the processes of expansion, accumulation, exploitation, and appropriation that situate people and places differently with regard to privilege (positioning some as more likely to serve as "playgrounds" or "servicers") but that implicate nearly everyone in complex relations of labor (the need to work in order to survive, consume, enjoy).

Although I employ the idea of touristic practice to discuss men's patronage of U.S. strip clubs, such practices should not be conflated with sex tourism. A sex tourist travels to particular places around the world seeking "sexual and emotional satisfaction" from "women (to a lesser extent, men) of another ethnicity; often to avoid social and moral consequences in his own culture" (Jokinen and Veijola 1997: 47). Engaging in touristic practices at home is necessarily different from international travel for the purpose of sexual experience, despite the fact that some similar processes may be at work. The visits I discuss may be sexualized, but they do not involve the purchase of sexual release, nor do they necessarily involve this particular pursuit of cultural difference.

Sex tourism has become an industry in itself over the past several decades (arguably longer), promoted by both national economies and transnational corporations in countries such as Thailand, Cuba, and the Dominican Republic (see Kempadoo and Doezema 1998). The connection of the U.S. sex industry to international development, however, is certainly worth exploring, as hierarchies are constructed among forms of sex work and sex workers according to race and ethnicity here as well and sex workers and customers of all kinds move about the globe in search of labor and leisure (a white dancer from an upscale North Carolina club travels to Japan for a working vacation; a Colorado massage parlor is staffed by "all-Asian" employees; college-age backpackers cruise the booths in Amsterdam and return to tell their friends).

AUTHENTICITY: COMMODIFICATION, IDENTITY, AND THE PURSUIT OF REALNESS

The themes discussed above—gender, power, visibility, leisure, and desire—guide my analyses in parts 1 and 2 of the book. Authenticity emerges as a central concept in several different conversations taken up in Parts 3 and 4, especially with regard to commodification, social class, identity, intimacy, and fantasy. The customers I interacted with and interviewed made repeated attempts to secure what they described as authentic or "real" encounters with the dancers in the clubs. They also discussed the physical and behavioral cues that they used to determine whether a dancer was genuine or not; "fake" breasts or bleached hair was perceived as a sign of inauthenticity by some customers, for example, as was the tendency to solicit table dances without the requisite conversational foreplay. Because of this, dancers developed elaborate strategies of authenticating their interactions: providing customers with real names, promising to accompany the men on dates or trips, and even contacting the men outside of the club to "prove" their interest. Several dancers I knew had designated phone lines or cellular phones so that customers could call them and leave messages; the customers often were not even aware that these were work numbers, not those used by friends or lovers.

At the same time, however, visits to strip clubs became meaningful for the customers precisely because the encounters purchased inside were not *really* real, because the clubs offered a fantasy space where the demands and limitations of the everyday could be escaped or transformed, even if briefly. Realness, then, became valued more than the real. Further, perceptions of authenticity were often themselves based on fantasies; for example, beliefs about working-class women as less professional and insincere than middle-class women (or vice versa) sometimes influenced the kinds of clubs that the men chose to visit. Thus, although authenticity emerges as a significant discourse in the men's talk about their visits, the very notion of the real and the *meaning* of authenticity in late capitalist societies and for postmodern consumers must be problematized and explored.

The concept of authenticity has a long history in Western thought.[24] As the concept has meant different things in different times and places, it would be difficult to provide an exhaustive analysis of its meanings. Further, its meanings have overlapped with numerous other concepts, such as alienation and truth. Fundamentally, however, authenticity is always about particular relationships and is necessarily part of a dichotomy and as folklorist Regina Bendix writes, "Identifying some cultural expressions or artifacts as authentic, genuine, trustworthy, or legitimate simultaneously implies that other manifestations are fake, spurious, and even illegitimate" (Bendix 1997: 9). Authenticity is a dialectical and probing "comparison between self and Other, as well as between external and internal states of being" (17).

The connections between authenticity and tourism as a leisure practice in social theory (and in popular thought) also have a long history. Authentic experience, it is sometimes believed, is difficult to come by in modern life, as everyday existence has become thoroughly artificial in urban, capitalist economies. This particular cultural criticism assumes that authentic experience is "available only to those moderns who try to break the bonds of their everyday existence and begin to 'live,'" often through the observation of the supposedly more authentic lives of others (MacCannell 1976: 159). This breaking of the bonds of the everyday could be accomplished by travel in a number of different forms. The flâneur, for example, or the strolling male pedestrian who wanders through the dark corners of the metropolis, has been put forth as an organizing figure of modernity. The flâneur is a man of leisure who seeks to gaze on the dispossessed and the marginal Others of the city, and thus to experience supposedly real authentic life by "engaging with the diverse charms of prostitutes, opium dens, bars, and taverns" (Rojek and Urry 1997: 7). The urban poor, working women, and prostitutes who were gazed on by the flâneur were seen as both fascinating and dangerous, objects of both desire and disgust.

Though sociologist Chris Rojek agrees that under modernity leisure and travel were "seen as spheres of activity in which self-realization could be pursued in a more authentic way than in work and family life" (1993: 6), he also argues that this particular worldview has "decomposed" under postmodernity. People still long to escape the inauthenticity of the everyday, but, he argues, this has become impossible in postmodern societies because leisure has become "not the antithesis of daily life but the continuation of it in dramatized or spectacular form" (213). Other theorists, however, argue that postmodern subjects no longer seek escape or authenticity in their leisure pursuits (Ritzer and Liska 1997) or that the very difference between authenticity and inauthenticity has disappeared (Baudrillard 1981).

In the chapters that follow, authenticity is conceptualized as a psychological preoccupation rather than a concern that will (or could) disappear in a postmodern world. Authentic experience, I argue, may be sought after by the customers for several reasons: as a response to cultural ideologies about the inauthenticity of commodified human interactions, because of the importance of mythologies of escape from everyday roles and responsibilities in structuring their attitudes toward leisure, and because their encounters with dancers draw on sexual self-representations and identities that are simultaneously real and phantasmatic. The ways these fantasy-realities shape the motivations behind leisure practice and the experiences of consumers are explored, in different ways, in Chapters 5, 6, and 7.

A Note on Representation and Authenticity: Experimenting with Ethnographic Writing

At least three different styles of writing are employed in this ethnography: traditional analysis of qualitative data, edited selections from my fieldnotes and interviews or comments based on my experiences as a dancer, and short fiction, which is interspersed with the more traditional chapters. Each style is meant to provide different kinds of information for the reader and to do a different kind of *work* for the analysis as a whole.

The first section of the preface, for example, is an edited version of an interview conducted with Julius, the night DJ from Tina's Revue, during which he performed a typical orientation talk for a new entertainer. I thus heard some version of this lecture twice: when I began dancing at Tina's and in the interview. This edited section along with the italicized comments that I make at certain times in the text situate me as both an entertainer and a researcher, as someone with a complex set of investments and interests in the encounters described.

The inclusion of the short stories, all of which have been published in other forums, is meant to work in two different ways. First, it is a way of problematizing the distinctions between subjectivity and objectification in both ethnographic research and in thinking about strip clubs. The traditional chapters primarily focus on the experiences of and interviews with the male customers. The stories, on the other hand, are all narrated from the perspective of a dancer, providing me with the opportunity to balance what I learned from my interviews with the male customers with what I learned both on the job and in my previous interviews with female sex workers. As a female sex worker / researcher studying men, I attempt to understand how the gaze works in particular situations, playing with the ethnographic objectification of the male "objectifiers" and the narrative subjectification of the female visual "objects." At the same time, I am also trying to disrupt the hegemony of the visual in experience, scientific analysis, and theories of domination (feminism, tourism, etc.) by highlighting the sensory and relational or intersubjective aspects of the job.

Second, the interspersing of fiction and academic writing is an experiment in ethnographic representation. With the postmodernist turn in anthropology since the mid-1980s, there has been a great deal of theorizing about exactly what it means to be an anthropologist "writing culture," and writing itself has emerged as a problematic dimension of anthropological research.[25] The distinction between self and other, between subject and object, for example, has been problematized as a relation of power inherent in traditional styles of representation. Further, critics say, the ethnographer is not merely involved in "translating the reality of others"; rather, an ethnographer may be helping to create that reality through the act of writing—actively inventing, not just merely representing, cultures (Clifford, 1986: 7). Anthropologists have begun to realize that the boundaries between art and science are permeable, and to recognize that even ethnography is at its best a partial truth, consisting of subjective representations and constructions of reality.

Even with this critique in mind, however, most anthropologists do not want to give up on the written representation of culture altogether, and some theorists recommend experimentation with new textual devices (Marcus and Fischer 1986). Fictional devices, although previously used, are becoming more salient in anthropological texts as such a mode of experimentation (see Brown 1991; Wolf 1992). Ethnographically grounded fiction can highlight elements of a practice, experience, or interaction that might be obscured in a more rigid theoretical explication and, as ethnographer Karen McCarthy Brown notes, allows the writer "to tap a reservoir of casual and imagistic knowledge which all people who have done fieldwork have but do not ordinarily get to use" (Brown 1991: 18). The stories included here do both of these things: fleshing out the encounters with details that have no place in the theoretical analyses and, I hope, illustrating some of the complexities of these gendered performances.

Yet, although I have a deep respect for the debates around issues of representation, I maintain a strict boundary between fiction and ethnography here for several reasons. First, I find that my motivations and practices are very different in each form of writing (see Frank 2000). Both ethnographic writing and fiction are creative processes, involve elements of fantasy, and involve the input of numerous others, yet each style is distinct—if not obviously at the level of the text produced, then at least at the level of its production.[26] Second, although I certainly have had to make editorial decisions about what to include from the interviews and what to omit in the traditional ethnographic chapters, I have made the utmost effort to represent the interviewees, their stories, and their words in a manner that is accurate and fair. Third, I see no reason to abandon a distinction between something that happened in space and time and something that did not. The authority of the fiction writer is far more absolute than that of an ethnographer in many ways, for whereas there are multiple potential interpretations of an ethnographic encounter, this is not so for the fictional one: the text may be interpreted in an infinite number of ways, but the characterizations and events underlying it or represented in it can be less easily challenged. The events, relationships, and sensations described in the stories are descriptively true to my fieldwork experiences and to what I learned conducting interviews, yet there are doubtless many, many other stories that could be told, and I make no claim for the generalizability of these particular ones. If authenticity is relative, experiments with representational form do not sidestep the questions of truth or authority raised by the critique of ethnography, though they dramatize these issues in different forms as each style of writing becomes convincing through its own structures of criteria. Instead of conflating fiction and ethnography, then, I wish to preserve a difference between them, as it is in this difference that the possibility for critique remains sharp and the benefits and limitations of each mode of representation become clearer.

Finally, there is a lot of misinformation about exotic dance, and the sex industry more generally, circulating in the public sphere. As I have now spent thousands of hours in both male and female strip clubs across the country as an employee and an observer, there are indeed some things I have learned that I believe are generalizable and may have policy implications, such as the fact that many of the customers who visited table dancing clubs were not seeking access to prostitution. I have relied on specific methodological techniques to obtain and analyze the information I collected, and it thus needs to be distinguished from my more imaginative projects—not in a style that is empiricist (making claims to an objective, overarching Truth), but in one that recognizes the empirical basis of ethnography (see Scheper-Hughes 1992), the existence of patterns of human behavior that can be discerned, systematically reflected on, and analyzed.

Chapter Two

Laurelton and Its Strip Clubs:
The Historical, Physical, and Social Terrain

Contemporary American strip clubs are not the result of a linear history of a dance form called striptease, although the story might be told that way. The story of striptease in the United States might also be told through the narratives of some of its most famous stars, some of whom have written autobiographies, and through the myths and tales that still circulate about their performances: Lydia Thompson and her traveling burlesque troupe; Margie Hart, who wore the infamous panel skirt to "skirt" the threat of indecency charges; Gypsy Rose Lee, with her self-reflexive, sexy, and humorous shows; Ann Corio, Blaze Starr, Lili St. Cyr, Hinda Wassau, and others (see Allen 1991; Jarrett 1997; Others); leading up to the present-day multiple-forum, multimedia stars such as Annie Sprinkle or Danni Ashe. Yet, though it may be tempting (and not altogether incorrect) to see "dancing girls" as a continuously developing form of expressive entertainment—from the story of Salome to the story of Erin Grant in the 1996 Hollywood film *Striptease*—such a trajectory would leave out several important elements of modern interactions. Stage dancing and performances, after all, were only part of what is actually being purchased in the clubs that I studied and worked in. Rather, several strands of sexualized service, leisure activity, and commodified intimate interaction have come together in modern strip clubs to form a type of unique entertainment, as changes in striptease performances are related to changes and innovation in other kinds of entertainments and leisure practices more generally as well. In different decades and different places, performances that feature female nudity and offer sexualized transactions have emerged, raised controversy, been regulated or shut down, and been reopened, upscaled, and transformed. Due to the fact that cities across the nation regulate sexual expression and behavior differently, especially in venues where alcohol is served, geographic regions differ in terms of the kinds of dancing and the amount of nudity and contact allowed today.[1]

In the first section of this chapter three historical developments that have been influential in shaping the contemporary world of exotic dance are explored: the evolution of public voyeurism as a kind of masculinized leisure activity, the intermixing of entertainers and their audiences to produce new types of personalized performances and to generate an erotic charge through "milling" or "slumming," and the process of upscaling, or of coding particular forms of previously stigmatized leisure as "respectable." Other historical developments might certainly be explored as well: for example, changes in cultural views on nudity in socially legitimate performances and corresponding legal regulations, the ways that striptease becomes distinguished from other kinds of entertainment in the cultural imaginary, and the rise of particular forms of technology that intensify modern scopophilic tendencies. I have focused here, however, on the three that most directly inform this project. This history is necessarily brief and incomplete; it would take an entire work of social history, at least, to delineate the nuances of the rise of stripping as a form of entertainment in the United States (and, I hope, one will eventually be written).

The second and third sections delve more deeply into the social geographic particulars of my ethnographic sites in Laurelton. In "Geographies of Consumption," Peter Jackson and Nigel Thrift "herald the coming of the 'ethnographic moment' in geographies of consumption" (1995: 229). They argue that ethnographic studies of consumption must "become rooted in particular places" to "take sufficient account of historical and cultural specificity" and "to pay more than just cursory attention to the voices of consumers 'on the ground'" (230). The geographic specificities of the Laurelton clubs, along with the spatial practices that structure the interactions inside, are essential to understanding the experiences of consumers and the transactions purchased in each different venue. David Harvey writes: "Spatial practices derive their efficacy in social life only through the structure of social relations within which they come into play . . . They take on their meanings under specific social relations of class, gender, community, ethnicity, or race and get 'used up' or 'worked over' in the course of social action"

(1990: 223). To attempt to capture some of this complexity, Harvey draws on Lefebvre's three dimensions of spatial practices: the experienced (material spatial practices), the perceived (representations of space; how spaces are talked about and understood), and the imagined (spaces of representation; mental inventions and symbolic spaces). Loosely drawing on this framework, the social geography of Laurelton is explored as it is experienced, perceived, and imagined in the discourses surrounding strip clubs there. Finally, spatial arrangements and practices in two clubs, Diamond Dolls and Tina's Revue, are examined for the way such arrangements and practices construct consciously marketed pleasures as individualized and enjoyable leisure experiences for some customers.

A Brief History

Many people today erroneously associate striptease with prostitution, despite the fact that the two currently are significantly different as cultural forms. In nineteenth-century cities, striptease shows were often an important part of an encounter with a prostitute in a brothel, both as an additional source of income for the prostitutes and as a way for them to display their talents to potential customers (Gilfoyle 1992: 176). In its current form, however, striptease is a specialized service because it is no longer necessarily coupled with sexual activity; specifically, it is a form of gendered spectacle and an opportunity for public voyeurism—a form of (usually male) sexualized "entertainment." In this way, it has more in common historically with the model artist shows, or tableaux vivants, that became popular during the mid-1800s, than with brothel activity. Model artist shows cloaked female erotic display in the form of "high art" for a male audience. In such shows an " 'actress' assumed a stationary pose dressed in tights, transparent clothing, or nothing at all," changing positions occasionally to allow the audiences different and more risqué views (127). The focus was on immobility rather than movement, though there was a transgressive incident in the 1840s in which "the performers abandoned their stationary pose and proceeded to dance the polka and minuet while completely nude" (127). (Interestingly, when I worked in Laurelton, we were asked to keep moving when nude and were often chastised if we paused too long when taking a tip.)

Public male voyeurism as a form of entertainment was also becoming institutionalized in other forms in the later part of the nineteenth century, especially in the immense popularity of traveling troupes of female burlesque entertainers. In *Horrible Prettiness: Burlesque and American Culture,* media scholar Robert Allen notes that burlesque performers were sexualized for their audiences, yet were also speaking performers, often pushing the socially accepted limits of what women were supposed to wear, say, and do through their productions. Over time, he argues, burlesque metamorphosed from a theatrical form in which female entertainers challenged middle-class norms and values, especially in regard to female sexuality, into a particular kind of spectacle increasingly "centered around female sexual display" (1991: 30). It was the inclusion of the "cooch dance" (belly dance) as a standard feature of burlesque after the 1890s, according to Allen, that dispensed with all pretense that the performances were "about anything other than sexual pleasure" (231). Whether the relative silencing of the performers after this transition meant that middle-class norms of female sexuality were no longer being challenged through burlesque is an arguable point (see Schaefer 1999). These developments, however, did seem to indicate that such performances were becoming more focused on revelations of the female body without explicit narrative excuses or justifications, a trend that continues today in the performances of house dancers.

The cooch dance, what Allen calls the "forerunner of the striptease," was introduced at the Chicago World's Colombian Exposition in 1893, part of an attempt to "introduce the science of anthropology to the American public" (1991: 225). The Exposition was based on turn-of-the-century assumptions about white supremacy and manhood; indeed, the grounds were divided into two racially specific areas: the White City and the Midway Plaisance. Whereas the White City "depicted the millennial advancement of white civilization," the Midway Plaisance "presented the undeveloped barbarism of uncivilized dark races" (Bederman 1995: 31). Even within the Midway, different cultures were presented in a racial hierarchy, as visitors would "first pass the civilized German and Irish villages, proceed past the barbarous Turkish, Arabic, and Chinese villages, and finish by viewing the savage American Indians and Dahomans" (35). The women who did the cooch dance were found on the Midway, of course (Jarrett 1997: 65), and the ensuing spectacle drew on a long history of the eroticization of supposedly primitive female Others.

It also, in turn, influenced history: Lucinda Jarrett, a historian of exotic dance, argues that the cooch dance reinforced and expanded the European vocabulary of the "exotic and erotic" and provided "a catalyst for the birth of striptease in America" (60).

The performances were both immensely popular and hotly contested; indeed, the premier moral reformer at the time, Anthony Comstock himself, even traveled to Chicago in an attempt to close down the shows. Reviewers around the country described the shows as "vulgar," "demoralizing," "too objectionable for people of refined taste to countenance," and "depraved and immoral" (Jarrett 1997: 68). After the Exposition closed, however, cooch dancing spread to New York, drawing hundreds of spectators a day and becoming even more sexualized as it became an important aspect of burlesque shows. Cooch dancing, and burlesque more generally, helped to institutionalize a tradition of male voyeurism without necessarily involving sexual activity as a form of masculinized entertainment and leisure practice. The cooch dance remained disreputable and associated with working-class male entertainment until 1916, when it began to spread to upscale Broadway cabarets (Erenberg 1984: 225).

As industrial capitalism developed in the early 1900s, groups of consumers emerged whose patterns of consumption provided them with a social identity, ways of distinguishing themselves from other social groups (Bocock 1993: 15). As particular kinds of consumption became increasingly a way of performing identity, a process of upscaling ensued in the burgeoning entertainment centers of the turn-of-the-century cities. Already by the end of the nineteenth century articulations of social class centered on the use of moral categories to police the behavior of women, and a discourse of "respectability" became synonymous with one of class (Skeggs 1997: 5).[2] These developments positioned women as both consumers themselves and as objects to be consumed, and as women increasingly entered the workplace and leisure sphere in this context, entertainment styles were transformed. This process was racialized; as historian Kevin Mumford notes, the fact that white women were progressively more able to move about in the public sphere without stigma during this time "was made ideologically possible by the reassignment of the sexual stigma of prostitution to African-American women" (1997: 113).

Historian Lewis Erenberg writes that the turn-of-the-century cabaret evolved into an entertainment form that permitted "respectable" men and women the opportunity to partake in evening entertainment— along with actors, actresses, sporting men, and prostitutes (1984: 139). Significantly, this was not family entertainment such as had been found in vaudeville shows and county fairs, nor even the lower-class, rowdy entertainment that had been offered by burlesque troupes to primarily male audiences. Instead, the cabaret serviced "the fantasies and desires of adult men and women," providing an opportunity for conspicuous consumption in an atmosphere of safety that also imparted an air of excitement and risk (114). In addition to maintaining (and indeed, in order to maintain) the respectability of male and female patrons, up-scale cabarets like the celebrated Ziegfeld's *Follies* also focused on creating a kind of respectability for the performers. Ziegfeld's revue in the early 1900s was modeled on the *Folies Bergere* of Paris and included a repackaging of female sexuality such that "audiences connected the *Follies* not with the working-class sexuality of burlesque but with the cosmopolitan worldliness of Paris" by removing the "markers" of working-class associations. It presented a particular kind of chorus girl to its middle-class, mixed audiences and, in doing so, "brought the female body out of its associations with low, all-male burlesque and beer halls" (214). By coupling the exciting but risqué acts with elegant, fully dressed revues, the value of the women was enhanced: these were *ladies.* They were distinct from the physically larger and bawdier burlesque stars. They were not nearly as Other as the cooch dancers and thus more readily available to fantasize about as potential partners. The Ziegfeld girl embodied the "almost wholesome sexuality of the white middle-class girl next door" (Allen 1991: 246).

In *Ziegfeld Girl,* historian Linda Mizejewski argues that the Ziegfeld girl presented a fantasy of American womanhood and thus "worked as a powerful icon of race, sexuality, class, and consumerist desires" in the early twentieth century (1999: 3). Her body, carefully designated as white and heterosexual through marketing imagery and in the performances at the cabaret, "was conflated with other desires; the body-we-should-want (as male desire, as female ideal) enacts the other things 'we' should want: the society wedding, Anglo blondness, tourism, the Panama Canal." The production of glamour relies on both visibility and inaccessibility, Mizejewski argues, and "the Broadway revue scene was a prominent site among many cultural practices in which glamour—as certain bodies and certain fashionable products—was being developed" (12). Ziegfeld's productions relied on huge budgets with which to produce vast female spectacles with lavish settings, extravagant costuming, and magnificent special effects. There were contentious elements to the figure of the Ziegfeld girl: though she was in part a symbol of a visible, knowable female heterosexuality, she was also positioned so that she might express, in some form or another, her own sexuality and desires. Further, she was also part of a "liberated" group of working women, and there was thus a "tease of an exotic lesbianism" that "may well have been one of the more submerged pleasures of spectatorship" (87). Still, her respectability as an upscale commodity was assured, in part, through the spectacular production of whiteness "and, specifically, its production as glamour" (10) that became meaningful in contrast with other more stigmatized entertainment forms and venues.

In many ways, the contrasting spectacles of the cooch dancers and the chorus girls of the cabarets seem to anticipate many of the same processes that occurred in the 1980s in regard to strip clubs. First, the upscale cabarets of the early century marketed themselves as appropriate entertainment for the middle classes, borrowing forms and themes from existing, "lower" entertainments and reworking them. In doing so, they moved *some* dancing girls out of the vice zones and into areas where respectable men, even those accompanied by their wives, could go to have a drink and "relax."[3] Inside the cabarets, the chorus girls could become symbols of status and wealth, capable of reflecting a man's status (Erenberg 1984: 221). On the other hand, the chorus girls could not stake the same claim to respectability as the female spectators (wives and dates) could, as codes of female virtue were still influential. Through sexualized female spectacle, certain forms of masculinity became wedded to ideas about individuality and consumption, and through the production of glamour or respectability, certain kinds of female bodies became even further imbued with differential value.

Significant also was the rise of a "mingling" between the performers and the audience, a mutual construction of fantasy as both part of a job, for the chorus girls, and part of a commodity, as well as the potential for fantasizing about the lives of the other members of the audience. Performers in the cabarets began to do floor shows in which they moved among the members of the audience, and this lent an exciting air of informality to the performances. The close proximity of entertainers to

audience also meant that the experience was more intimate than previously: "the audience could easily experience the emotion—the gri-
maces, smiles, exultation—of performers at work." Erenberg notes that
audiences were often close enough to touch the performers, "and they
often did so in specially designed numbers and rituals." In this way, he
writes, "the actors were not cardboard figures on a stage; they were
personalities seen in a living, three-dimensional light" (1984: 125). For
middle-class patrons, the breaking of barriers between actors and audience could represent "institutional spontaneity" or "milling": "In
milling . . . one is brought together with others, those who are famous,
who appear glamorous, above the controls of social life, sometimes
even above the law, who seemingly live a life of constant excitement and
danger . . . all in a luxurious setting that gave [the audience] the feeling
of having risked and won. This confirmed the sense of success, occurring as it did in public in front of many other witnesses and in front of
the many mirrors that lined the cabaret" (133). The reason that cabarets
could mediate these different worlds was partly due to the process of
upscaling, of creating more commercial atmospheres that could confer
distinction on their patrons and allow them to engage in the kind of
conspicuous consumption that was generally available only for the very
wealthy. At the same time, it allowed for the possibility of experiencing
the excitement of radical Otherness.

Another way of experiencing radical Otherness was through "slumming," not an altogether different thing from milling but with a slightly
different flavor, as slumming implies not just the mingling between
performers and their audiences, but also a mingling between races and
classes in more marginalized entertainment sites. Slumming, which
Mumford defines as "traveling to 'foreign,' exotic, supposedly inferior
cultures," became popular among such various groups as social re-
formers, intellectuals, sociologists, bohemians, and white urban sophis-
ticates traveling to African American neighborhoods in the early part of
the century (1997: 135). Slummers might be "sympathetic outsiders with
a genuine sense of affinity" or "social superiors temporarily exploiting
people and institutions on the margins, usually for pleasure, leisure, or
sexual adventure." "For the less affluent," Mumford writes, "spending a
night on the town in Harlem might represent the cultural equivalent of
taking a Cunard cruise to Africa, an exciting excursion into another
social world" (143). During the years of Prohibition, Harlem came to be

quite popular with whites who went "to attend clubs, listen to music, and watch dancing they considered uninhibited and natural" (D'Emilio and Freedman 1988: 295). The process of upscaling, then, does not mean that lower-tier venues disappeared or became less desirable; rather, it represents a diversification of leisure sites with different kinds of appeal.

Mingling between audiences and performers (or employees) and between different races and classes also developed in taxi dance halls, a type of entertainment venue that still exists in some areas of the country. Sociologist Paul Cressey distinguishes the taxi dance hall from other types of public dancing establishments and notes that such venues were also called dime-a-dance halls, stag dances, and monkey hops. The women who earned their livelihood by dancing with the customers of the halls were often called nickel-hoppers, as they were employed to dance with patrons on a pay-per-song basis (1932: 17). These halls were generallly closed to female patrons. The customer, Cressey writes, was "interested in securing an attractive young woman with whom he may dance and converse without the formality of an introduction and without many of the responsibilities entailed at other social gatherings" (40). He may also have been interested in securing her sexual favors, though taxi dancers were generally not interested in explicit prostitution, and whether he was successful depended on a number of situational factors (48). Taxi dance halls furthered the development of individualized relationships, sometimes ongoing, between patrons and performers, along with the following of particular "intimacy scripts" or romantic scenarios in the clubs. Voyeurism was still important, but it was the quality of the individualized interactions that held much of the erotic significance for the customers. This is not to imply that such individualized interactions were somehow divorced from other classed, raced, or gendered social patterns; for example, erotic significance was also to be found in the way taxi dance halls "sought to satisfy working-class desire for respectability by creating clubs with the façade of cabarets, dance palaces, or even dance academies" (Mumford 1997: 57). Part of this respectability was based on the attempted exclusion of men of color as customers, who were seen to diminish the appeal of the white dance hostesses as well as to promote "promiscuity and disorganization" (59).

Public masculinized voyeurism, the manipulation of respectability and the erotics of Otherness, and the importance of interaction between performers and their audiences have emerged as important elements of modern strip clubs, and can be found in a variety of antecedent and concurrent entertainments, including the always changing world of burlesque. The Minsky brothers of New York City were the first to *name* the art of striptease (Jarrett 1997: 135), and their first star performer at Minsky's Republic Theater was Gypsy Rose Lee, who debuted in 1931. Significantly, Lee recognized the "seductive potential" of directly addressing her audience and flirted with its individual members (141), something that is an indisputable part of the job in most strip clubs today, albeit in somewhat different, even more personalized, form. Though Allen may have been right in charging that the female burlesque performers lost their theatrical roles as the mounting interest in striptease focused entertainment more and more on female bodily spectacle, increased opportunities for audience-performer mingling meant that bodily display was still being coupled with verbal performances, though this time, the verbal performances were more personalized and the entertainers were playing "themselves."

The story of dancing girls, no matter how it is told, is thoroughly and irrevocably shaped by the history of regulation and the conflicts that surround such sexualized displays and behaviors in American public culture. Antiburlesque campaigns had surfaced almost immediately after the entertainment form arrived in America, and continued to escalate throughout the 1930s. In the 1920s, social class "increasingly became an issue in theatre licensing," whereby upscale cabarets were granted liquor licenses and those venues that featured burlesque for the lower classes were not (Jarrett 1997: 107). During the 1930s, laws against particular kinds of "sexual perversion" meant that "suggestiveness and illusion" were more important than actual nudity in the striptease that was being performed in burlesque theaters, and strippers creatively used net or flesh-colored clothing, special props, body makeup, and stage lighting "alternatively to hide clothing or to hide potentially unlawful nakedness" (Andrea Friedman 1996: 209). Whereas the protests of this time against sexualized entertainment often focused on the sexual depravity or suspected prostitution of the female performers, later campaigns against burlesque, according to historian Andrea Friedman, began to focus on the supposedly dangerous and aggressive sexuality of working-class males. Such campaigns, she argues, "offered an opportunity to articulate deep-seated concerns about male sexual orderliness in a profoundly disorderly world," and such fears of the out-of-control or aggressively sexual male would surface again in the 1950s and 1970s antipornography movements (237). The intricacies of the many battles that were fought in different locales across the country throughout the twentieth century would be impossible to detail here, as would the complexities of the justifications offered for regulating, harassing, shutting down, or allowing venues that offered the display of sexualized female bodies to their patrons.

Despite attempts in every era to regulate theaters that featured the different forms of striptease, however, it continued to thrive and evolve as an entertainment form. In the 1950s, a consumer boom due to an increase in disposable income and production meant that Americans could spend more money on entertainment, and by 1955 stripping was once more a legal form of entertainment, although this time under the euphemism of exotic dance (Jarrett 1997: 167). Jarrett notes that as stereotypes of race and color prevailed during this time, the terms erotic and exotic became synonymous. She writes: "Dancers from other cultures were openly acknowledged as the inspiration for erotic dance, and strippers used costumes of leopard skin and 'jungle themes' and posters of tropical islands to give their acts authenticity" (167). Theaters opened in almost every state, although laws about the allowable combinations of nudity and performance varied. Jarrett writes: "In contrast to dancing, striptease placed its emphasis on the expression of the characters of the performers, their 'personality plus showmanship,' and the elaborate costume and lighting used in each act" (169). Strippers often needed to have a gimmick and an "outsized personality" to distinguish themselves, which meant that by the mid-1950s "strippers became living embodiments of a parody of vital statistics." In a "freakshow" atmosphere, "outsized busts and bottoms made headlines" (173).

During the recession of the 1970s, many women took up employment as strippers to support themselves and their families (Jarrett 1997: 185). The economic squeeze, the association of striptease with drugs and prostitution, the rundown atmosphere of many strip clubs, and the widespread policy of requiring dancers to hustle drinks meant that striptease developed a reputation for being a seedy form of entertainment, which was maintained for some time. During the 1970s there was some interest in the social sciences in stripping as a deviant occupation, and a number of articles were produced on the lives of strippers, the possible psychological reasons for their entry into such a stigmatized occupation, and the hazards of the job (Gonos 1976; McCaghy and Skipper 1969; G. Miller 1978; Salutin 1973), a kind of academic slumming that persists today in some studies of the sex industry.

The importance of Hugh Hefner's *Playboy* empire in these years, and his dream linking a particular kind of desirable masculine identity to the consumption of women and a luxurious lifestyle, cannot be understated in the development of adult entertainment in the United States. Following the phenomenal success of his soft-porn men's magazine in the 1950s, the 1960s saw the advent of the Playboy Clubs, the first of which opened its doors in Chicago. Although these venues did not feature striptease, they did feature scantily clothed women and offered somewhat respectable, upscale, masculinized entertainment that had links to other forms of consumption—a plush atmosphere, steaks, liquor, pornography—and indeed, to a mythologized lifestyle. Though the Playboy Clubs were eventually pushed out of the market, their numbers declining steadily until the last was closed in 1988, many aspects of the clubs later reappeared as strip clubs began the process of upscaling. Many upscale strip clubs, for example, copied elements of the Playboy Clubs: creating their own versions of Bunny Money, which could be spent only on the premises; regulating the behavior and appearance of the dancers to create a particular "type" of female companion; and combining female display with first-rate food and beverage selections to provide a more all-encompassing masculinized leisure experience.

This process of upscaling in strip clubs escalated in the 1980s, and upper-tier gentlemen's clubs now exist in addition to neighborhood bars and run-down, red-light district venues. The number of strip clubs in the United States has been growing rapidly over the past decade, reaching around three thousand venues across the nation in 1998 (Hanna 1998a). This growth has not occurred without the eruption of either national or local conflicts, however, and efforts to distance strip clubs from their illicit associations in the public imaginary have become increasingly important to the club owners given the opposition that has arisen in a number of communities. Because of their working-class associations and the persistent, perhaps erroneous belief that they are indelibly linked to prostitution and crime ("negative secondary effects"), establishments that feature forms of striptease have already been subject to more severe regulations than other kinds of entertainment (Hanna 1999), and some municipalities have attempted to use restrictive regulations to close down the businesses altogether: requiring extremely bright lighting, prohibiting tipping, requiring bikinis or cocktail dresses at all times, stipulating excessive distance rules to separate the entertainers and the customers, and more.[4]

Judith Lynne Hanna, an anthropologist whose early work focused on dance in a cross-cultural perspective, has written more recently on the semiotics of exotic dance in contemporary America and on cultural conflicts that arise with regard to the existence and regulation of strip clubs. Hanna argues that exotic dance is "a form of expressive communication, and within the realms of dance and art," and should be protected under the First Amendment (1998b: 62). She notes the continuities between the stigmatization that exotic dance now carries and way that many other popular dance forms—such as waltz, ragtime, flamenco, rebetika, and tango—have been considered scandalous at times in their history. She also points out that condemnations and unfair regulations of exotic dance venues reflect a class bias: "Nudity can be seen in theaters (e.g., *Mutations, Oh! Calcutta!*) by wine-drinking quiche-eaters but not by beer-drinking pretzel eaters" (1999: 7). Consistently she has argued for the consideration of exotic dance as a serious art form, both theoretically and in the courts, and her work has been a significant intervention in legal, trade, and academic forums (1998a, 1998b, 1999).

My inquiry positions strip clubs first and foremost as continuous with other forms of the sex industry rather than with other theatrical forms, a perspective that is complementary to, but not identical with, an analysis of striptease as a form of stigmatized dance, a kind of "low-cultural" art form. That is, I am primarily concerned with strip clubs as leisure sights and workplaces, and am specifically interested in the varieties of interpersonal interaction being consumed by the patrons (of which dance is an important, but not an exclusive, part). In the clubs in which I worked, most of the dancers' money was earned by selling table dances or through interaction, not while we performed on the stages. In fact, stage performances were referred to as "just advertising" and avoided by the dancers whenever possible. I am also interested in the allure of the *scandalous* itself for the patrons, in the eroticization of this very split between high and low, for if striptease someday takes its place alongside these other popular dance forms, I believe that many of its meanings and its appeal for the customers will also change. This is not to say that there is not a serious expressive element to exotic dance, however, or that it should *not* be considered dance or protected under the First Amendment. Rather, it is simply to point out that this particular project focuses on the political, economic, and psychocultural aspects of men's visits to strip clubs in the contemporary United States. Social class and race (particularly the production of whiteness and fantasies about racialized Others)—coded through the process of upscaling, through social geographies, and through discourses of respectability and authenticity—become an important part of my analysis of this particular gendered form of entertainment.

"That's What You Do in Laurelton!"

Laurelton is a major Southern urban center.[5] As a municipal entity, Laurelton occupies over a hundred square miles and is home to an estimated half million people. As a region, however, Laurelton is made up of several urban core counties, many outlying counties, and over three million inhabitants. Approximately 33 percent of the city's population is African American, about 3 percent is made up of Asian and Latino immigrant populations, and the rest is primarily white.

The city is well-known for its adult entertainment industry, both nationally and locally. For a city of its size it has an extremely large and varied sex industry, leading to its informal nickname of "the Southern Gomorrah." Lacking any natural advantages or tourist attractions to draw visitors, such as beaches, mountains, gambling, or even outstanding cultural activities, Laurelton's high ranking with regard to convention business is deeply connected with the sex industry there—"No beaches, just peaches," reads a local postcard featuring bikini-clad women. In addition to the many sites for commodified sexual services in and around the city (such as massage parlors, lingerie modeling studios, escort services, street prostitution, and pornographic bookstores) there are almost fifty strip clubs in the regional area that feature female performers and nude dancing. These strip clubs have been estimated to generate around $200 million annually and primarily cater to heterosexually identified male customers. Although there are two clubs that feature nude male performers, those clubs are frequented more by gay male customers than by women. As few cities across the country offer the combination of both full nudity and alcohol,[6] the strip clubs of the area are seen as a novelty and a tourist site by some groups of traveling businessmen despite the fact that contact between dancers and customers is almost completely prohibited.[7] The large number of strip clubs and other venues for adult entertainment in Laurelton made it a "buyer's market" in many ways and certainly different from other cities in which I worked as a dancer. There were sometimes more dancers than customers in the clubs, especially the lower-tier clubs, and this meant that there was an added degree of competition among the dancers.

At the time of this research, 1997–1998, Laurelton had three gentlemen's clubs considered high-end because of their atmosphere and services, two of which, the Panther Club and Diamond Dolls, catered very heavily to the convention trade. The city also has dozens of smaller-scale clubs that offer nude dancing and that may have a great deal of local business but do not have the financial backing and national prestige of the larger clubs. Laurelton strip clubs, especially the high-end clubs, are notorious throughout the nation and have been mentioned in the *New York Times, USA Today, Rolling Stone, Playboy, Exotic Dancer Directory of Gentleman's Clubs,* and other widely circulated local and national publications. When one famous rock musician visits the city, for example, he is known to spend a significant amount of time in the strip clubs. When he was asked about this during an interview for a popular entertainment magazine, he replied, "That's what people do in Laurelton!" One of the men I interviewed spoke similarly: "When I first moved here that seemed to be the thing. When you meet somebody they go, oh, you just moved here, let me take you there! And it's . . . not the museums, not the theater. You go to the Panther Lounge, you go to Diamond Dolls."

As one might imagine, the existence of such a large number of strip clubs in Laurelton is cause for a certain amount of ambivalence among the city's residents and politicians, and the clubs have been the focus of much commentary and critique, as well as legal maneuvering and harassment. Strip clubs have become "lightning rods" for community conflicts across the United States (Hanna 1998b), and Laurelton is no exception, especially given regional and local ideas about religion, morality, and monogamy. After his travels to America in 1835, Alexis de Tocqueville wrote, "I think I can see the whole destiny of America contained in the first Puritan who landed on those shores" (1956). Adult entertainment in the United States is certainly part of that destiny and heritage. Indeed, the religious taboos that have long surrounded issues of sex and nudity in the United States have influenced the shape of the sex industry, the services offered, and the attraction and repulsion of particular sites for the customers.

Laurelton is located in the Bible Belt, an extremely religious swath of the country with a population that is publicly quite conservative in many respects. Even as late as the 1960s, for example, laws were still on the books that prohibited dancing on Sundays by *anyone* in the city. Blue laws still exist that prohibit the sale of alcohol in stores on Sundays, with the ironic (unintended or by design?) effect that the local bars, including the strip clubs, are often packed with customers on Sunday afternoons. Further, many people still cling to ideas born of a particular Southern prudery—in *theory*, if not in practice. When it comes to drawing legal and moral lines against particular sexual behaviors, however, many men (and women) are more tolerant of looking than touching, despite religious admonitions against lusting in one's heart or mind. As strip clubs provide live interaction, yet are primarily for looking and fantasizing, they offer a service that is distinct from many other sectors of the industry and are theoretically supportive of heterosexual monogamy in ways that other venues may not be. Further, masturbation is not legally allowed on location in the strip clubs, and thus its place in the encounter (if and when it has one) is easily disavowed. On the other hand, the fact that the clubs feature nudity deems them unacceptable to some of the most conservative and religious residents, regardless of whether any contact takes place.

Legal battles over where culturally stigmatized forms of business should be located, what kinds of services and interactions can be purchased, and which individuals can work or consume in these locations reflect "the struggles that go on over the definition of what exactly is the right time and place for what aspects of social practice" (Harvey 1990: 217). As in most cities around the nation, zoning laws are used to confine strip clubs and other adult-oriented businesses to particular locations in the city. Further, ordinances are used to regulate the behaviors that can take place inside the clubs. The combination of full nudity and alcohol, which is allowed in Laurelton but prohibited in many cities across the country, is one that often comes under attack when residents organize against the clubs. The fact that the clubs bring in significant revenue for the city means that they most likely will not all be closed down permanently by regulation. During the time I was conducting research in Laurelton, however, Tina's Revue (or Tina's), a small club in one of the outlying counties, was fighting a battle to retain its liquor license if it continued to offer nude dancing. The owners were also fighting a law that would raise the minimum age of dancers to twenty-one (it is currently set at eighteen). Further, since this fieldwork was conducted, another club in an outlying county, the middle-tier Crystal Palace, has closed down due to restrictive ordinances prohibiting nudity in venues that serve alcoholic beverages that prevented it from remaining competitive with other clubs in the city.

Zoning laws need to be seen as both exercises in municipal power and as sites of potential struggle where people's ideas and opinions about acceptable public behavior (and business) are expressed and transformed. The laws and regulations, however, also influence the erotic potential of the different sites in a variety of complex ways, delineating the boundaries of acceptable social conduct that then become fodder for fantasies of transgression.

The Social Geography and the Hierarchy of Clubs

For Ruth Frankenberg, geography is "the physical landscape—the home, the street, the neighborhood, the school, parts of town visited or driven through rarely or regularly, places visited on vacation." It is the way physical space is divided and inhabited. Yet this physical space is the product of a social environment. Frankenberg writes: "The notion of a *social* geography suggests that the physical landscape is people and that it is constituted and perceived by means of social rather than natural processes" (1993: 44). In the interviews I conducted with the male customers I always asked the men to hierarchically rank the clubs in Laurelton. This was also a common topic of conversation in the informal interactions I had while working in the clubs. Nearly every conceptualization that I was given by the customers (as well as by dancers and other employees) of the system of clubs in Laurelton was identical. There was thus a very "objective" structure (objective in the sense of agreed upon information): upper tier, the Panther Club and Diamond Dolls; middle tier, the Crystal Palace and the Fantasy Room (which brought in feature performers in addition to the house dancers) and two others; lower tier, the Pony Lounge, Tina's Revue, Rattlers, Kiki's, and the rest of the clubs in the city. Not a single man ever ranked the Pony Lounge or Tina's Revue above the Panther Club or Diamond Dolls, for instance, although certain men put the Panther Club at the top of the hierarchy and other men put Diamond Dolls there. Of the lower-tier clubs, most men ranked Tina's Revue above the Pony Lounge *even if they had never visited Tina's,* simply because of the Pony's location in a well-known red-light district.

There are two red-light districts in Laurelton: a five-mile stretch of road called Chestnut Crossing, located about ten minutes from downtown, and another stretch of road located just south of the city called Lawrence Avenue. The sheer size of the industry in Laurelton, however, means that one passes strip clubs, massage parlors, and pornographic bookstores in a variety of neighborhoods around the city and that the *majority* of clubs are actually located outside of these districts. Of these more concentrated areas, the men I interviewed ranked Lawrence Avenue lower on the hierarchy. This area supposedly was primarily known for its plethora of streetwalkers, its crime, and its high number of African American customers and workers.[8] Chestnut Crossing was more racially mixed and the fairly recent site of "clean-up" attempts by community activists who wanted to see the area known for its shopping and fine restaurants rather than its sex shops. Nevertheless, the Chestnut Crossing area had persisted as a zone of commodified sexuality at the time of my last visit and was the location of one of my fieldwork sites, the Pony Lounge. Some men admitted to visiting these particular districts because the women were assumed to be uneducated and financially stricken, thus their services would be cheaper no matter which type of venue they worked in. Neither of the two highest-ranked clubs were typically associated with these districts by the customers.

Interestingly, even though Diamond Dolls was situated directly on the border of Chestnut Crossing (less than a mile from a club *always* associated with the Crossing), when I asked I was usually told that Diamond Dolls was located in Rockwood, an upscale section of town. Fairly quickly, I noticed that the clubs that were mainly black or working class were often noted as being in "bad areas" of town. As such, these clubs were described as not being very "classy," a designation that implied much more than their location. Because geographies are social it was possible for Diamond Dolls to be technically physically located in

Chestnut Crossing yet still be considered an upscale, safe, and classy club in a "nice area of town."

Beyond slight variations in lists of amenities, a definite shared understanding of the features of an upscale club existed among my interviewees, most of which were related to particular forms of consumption. Nearly everyone agreed, for example, that an upscale club would provide top-shelf liquors and a good wine list, a decent menu, private rooms in addition to the main floor, elegant furnishings, and beautiful, refined women. Elegant furnishings, as well as all the other signs of distinction, were of course relative to the stereotypical "seedy" strip club, with "sticky floors," "poor lighting," and "hidden corners" (where the rules of the club and the city were not enforced). In addition to these standard responses, some men mentioned other distinguishing factors, such as multiple stages, dress codes, tuxedoed bouncers, attendants in the men's room, and valet parking. Some men noted the lack of poles on the stages in the upper-tier clubs in Laurelton; stage shows thus involved strutting and posing rather than skilled gymnastics and stunts. Despite this structural hierarchy, however, not every man *preferred* the more upscale clubs or even the clubs that seemed to match the individual's class status. There were some men who visited particular lower-tier clubs with the belief that the dancers there were under severe financial constraints and would "do anything" (this did not necessarily mean providing sex), including providing services that were illegal in the Laurelton clubs, such as lap dancing. Other men preferred the lower-tier clubs for reasons discussed in Chapter 6, beliefs and fantasies about class, race, and gender that influenced the meanings of their transactions. Classiness and upscaling, then, should not be seen as a process of gradual improvement but as one of market segmentation and differentiation.

Though not explicitly stated, there seemed to be an implicit assumption among the customers that an upscale club was also primarily white. Strip clubs are frequently spoken of in Laurelton as being black or white, as are sections of town and other places of business. In general, the strip club industry is known for being primarily white (Meridian 1997), and there were far more white than black clubs in Laurelton. White clubs remained unmarked; that is, their whiteness was not offered in a description unless race was already being discussed. Frankenberg argues that race and racism "[shape] white people's lives and identities in a way that is inseparable from other facets of daily life" (1993: 6). Although race is socially constructed, she argues, it is *real* "in the sense that it has real, though changing, effects in the world and a real, tangible, and complex impact on individuals' sense of self, experience, and life chances" (11). Part of the way race becomes real is through the organization and meaning given to particular spaces, through the ways those spaces are experienced, perceived, and imagined. Black and white clubs in Laurelton existed in a *nearly* segregated yet hierarchical relationship to each other. Despite the presence of black customers and dancers in every one of the clubs I worked in and visited, for example, none of the highest-ranked clubs in the city were known to be primarily black or were described as black, although one of the primarily black clubs was designated as fairly upscale by some black customers and dancers. Though black and white tended to be the main racial categories used to describe spaces and people in Laurelton, there was also a very small and out-of-the-way club, Chesters, that was described as Hispanic and lower tier. None of the clubs in the city were described as Asian, although some of the massage parlors in town were described this way and Asian dancers were found in both upper- and lower-tier clubs in Laurelton.

In many cases the customers were self-segregating and explained this in spatial terms. Several white men I interviewed, for example, said that they were regulars of the highly ranked (white) club, the Panther Club, because it was the club "closest" to their office. A glance at a city map, however, revealed two other clubs that were closer; these clubs, however, were known as black clubs. Distance, in this example, is clearly racialized. For some white customers, then, the black clubs were perceived as being "too far" or "too out of the way" to serve as desirable sites. Other white men cited the fact that the clubs were located in "dangerous areas of town" as their reason for avoiding them.

Diamond Dolls and Tina's Revue: Experienced,
Perceived, and Imagined Spaces in Two Strip Clubs

"Space and time," writes geographer David Harvey in *The Condition of Postmodernity,* "are basic categories of human existence," often taken for granted and "naturalized through the assignment of common-sense everyday meanings." Spatial and temporal practices can thus "appear as 'realized myth' and so become an essential ideological ingredient to social reproduction" (1990: 203). Both time and space, argues Harvey, are meaningful only in relation to material processes and social relations. He writes that "in money economies in general, and in capitalist society in particular, the intersecting command of money, time, and space forms a substantial nexus of social power that we cannot afford to ignore" (226). "Money," he writes, "can be used to command time (our own or that of others) and space. Conversely, command of time and space can be converted back into command over money" (226).

Geographer Doreen Massey convincingly argues that there are also several other elements that influence our understandings and experiences of space, for instance, gender and ethnicity (1993: 60). After all, she notes, the degree of mobility that individuals have is not simply influenced by capital or time; is it as easy to wander the streets of a city for women as for men, for instance? What Massey terms "power-geometry" is a way of socially differentiating flows and movements in the contemporary era, concerning "not merely the issue of who moves and who doesn't, although that is an important element of it," but "also about power in relation to the flows and the movement" (61). Mobility through space, then, and control over that mobility, both reflect and reinforce the power of particular people and groups (62). Visibility is also related to the formation and maintenance of social power and is implicated in spatial relationships, especially through the distinction between public and private spaces, between who and what is seen where. What can be made visible in the privacy of one's home is often hidden in public; a homeless person urinating in the streets, for example, not only creates a spectacle but should be a blatant reminder of the economic privileges of retreating to private spaces. However, there is more to the interconnection between visibility and privacy than money, time, and space. As Peter Jackson argues, "Our very notions of masculinity and femininity (in all their subtle variations) are actively constituted through distinctions of space and place, public and private, visible and invisible" (1993: 222).[9]

One way strip clubs come to have the power to make experience meaningful is through their inner geographies, through strategies of spatial organization (layout and design, internal regulations, structures of visibility through staging, mirroring, and seating, atmosphere and décor) and representation (as spaces of leisure, freedom, individuality).

In this section, the interior spaces of two particular strip clubs are discussed in more detail as they relate to gender, class, race, money, and time. Diamond Dolls and Tina's Revue were chosen to be analyzed in more depth for their structural relationship to each other and for their long-term presence in the particular neighborhoods in which they are located.[10] Diamond Dolls is an upper-tier club located within the city limits; Tina's Revue is a lower-tier club located just outside of the perimeter of the city. Both clubs had been in existence for at least ten years at their particular sites.

DIAMOND DOLLS

Diamond Dolls was a large, flashy, and notorious club located at the edge of the Rockwood community. Rockwood is Laurelton's most exclusive community and was over 90 percent white at the time of this study, despite the diversity of the city. The average income of families and individuals that reside in Rockwood is double that of anywhere else in the city and the area is known for its high-end restaurants, shopping malls, and entertainment complexes. Despite protests by some segments of the community prior to its opening, Diamond Dolls was able to obtain a liquor license and open for business in Rockwood during the mid-1980s. It was a large windowless building, set back from the road by an extensive parking lot. There was a fountain in front of the entrance, where tuxedoed bouncers and valets waited for the customers to arrive. On most nights there were several limousines parked conspicuously in front of the building. When I began working there, I learned that Diamond Dolls valets parked all of the employees' cars in the front lot and most of the customers' cars in a back lot. This had the effect of making the club always look extremely crowded (even when it was not) and of providing anonymity for the customers if a spouse or acquaintance drove by.

With a national reputation and extensive advertising campaigns, Diamond Dolls was well-known and popular with both the local and the tourist crowds. Like its most significant competitor, the Panther Club, it catered to local and traveling businessmen and advertised in both national and international business publications, gentlemen's magazines, and conference packages.[11] The cover charge and food and beverage prices were quite high at Diamond Dolls, although such charges were consistently waived for frequent customers or celebrities who were known or expected to spend a great deal of money inside. The club explicitly courted sports and entertainment celebrities through such practices, relying on the "Studio 54 effect" to generate interest in the club among the general public. Free passes were also provided at hotels for conferences and conventions and cab drivers received kickbacks to bring tourists to the club. Table dances, however, were set at the same price as at every club in town: $10 per song. In addition to stage performances and tableside private dances, Diamond Dolls offered signature merchandise, nightly skits put on by the dancers, a Folliesesque revue midway through each evening, a distinguished wine and cigar list, fresh sushi and other appetizers, and bathroom attendants. Most of the customers, dancers, and valets were white, although the attendants in the men's room were almost always black.

Diamond Dolls was designed to maximize voyeuristic possibilities and individualized spending. It was a multimillion-dollar building with two levels and four stages, in addition to the amenities listed above. To walk into Diamond Dolls was to be immediately struck by the extravagant atmosphere, the sheer number of dancers (fifty to one hundred on any given night), and the size of the club. Many customers described the environment as one of "sensory overload." The stages were all on the first level, although the main stage had a staircase leading to the upper level. The main stage had a special fan in the floor controlled by the DJ that some dancers used to create special effects (such as the "Marilyn Monroe") and a mirrored wall behind it that extended upward two levels. On the main floor, a digital newsbar displayed headlines, financial information, and sports scores. In true postmodern fashion, work and leisure were blended into a consumer spectacle—though I never noticed much attention being paid to the newsbar and read it more as a way to signify the professional, middle-class status of the patrons. Customers sat in comfortable cloth chairs or on long couches while waitresses wearing leotards, bow ties, jackets, fishnet stockings, and high heels circulated with drinks and appetizers from the kitchen and the sushi bar. On weekend nights the main floor could get so crowded that it was difficult for dancers to even approach the stages when they were called to perform or to move through the masses of men to sell table dances. The cocktail waitresses would often simply abandon their tasks and congregate near the dancers' dressing room.

This particular two-tiered design facilitated a conspicuous display of wealth. On the main floor, the deep cloth chairs were arranged so that rows of men sat facing each other rather than the main stage, an arrangement not found in any of the other clubs in Laurelton. The audience's attention, then, was not necessarily on the dancer moving on the main stage, but on the dozens of dancers circulating among the rows of men or dancing naked in front of their chairs. As the private dances were visible to many of the other customers, some men would group several dancers around their chair to gain attention. Theoretically, the rest of the customers could just sit back and watch other men's dances, given the proximity of the chairs and their arrangement. Such behavior, however, was not encouraged. Dancers would soon ignore groups of men who did not spend enough money buying their own dances, and other customers would verbally reprimand them as well.

The upper level of the club provided semiprivate balcony seating and limited VIP seating for individuals who paid an additional cover charge just to be out of the way of the main floor. For an additional $20 added to their cover charge, men could thus take a position on the balcony and watch not only all of the stages simultaneously, but also all of the private dances occurring on the main floor in addition to purchasing their own. The upper level also had twelve private VIP rooms, called Gem Rooms. Celebrities and famous athletes who wished for privacy were often quickly ushered up to a Gem Room. These were rented hourly by the club to customers at prices ranging from $100 an hour to $500 an hour, depending on the day of the week, the demand, and the customer who wanted the room. Additional fees of around $200 an hour per dancer were charged as well, and all fees could be paid by credit card. The steep prices did not discourage the clientele, however, and on weekend nights there could be up to an hour wait to gain access to a Gem Room. The Gem Rooms were enclosed on only three sides due to legal regulations, but it was extremely difficult to see anything inside the rooms from the main floor. They were furnished with leather couches, adjustable lighting, glass tables, floor-to-ceiling mirrors, and personal waitress service. The rooms offered a feeling of luxury, provided a refuge from the crowds on the main floor, and allowed for more private interaction between dancers and their customers. This did not mean that the main floor was entirely less appealing, however, and many bachelor parties or groups would start out in Gem Rooms and move to the main floor when their financial supply dwindled.

Although the male customers of any club often did not interact with other customers unless they arrived together, they certainly noticed and responded to other men's actions and spending practices and commented on them quite a bit to the dancers. The lights in Diamond Dolls were quite bright and it was one of the few strip clubs where customers were recognizable from across the room. This differentiation was pleasurable for many of the customers, as when Mick, one of the interviewees, told me stories about how he was recognized on sight at Diamond Dolls and let in for free because he was a regular, or when men found themselves surrounded by the most sought after dancers because they were spending money on the main floor. If a customer wanted, the DJ would announce it when he signed up for a Gem Room and turned the attention on the customer and the dancers who were accompanying him up the spiral staircase to the upper level. Seating arrangements could also signify economic standing. Bouncers were more likely to seat known big spenders near the stages; customers who did not spend enough were often asked to leave the club or relinquish their seats to others. Some newcomers earned the laughter of the regulars when they showed a "lack of stamina" and ran out of money quickly.

Inside any club it is expected that customers pay for the dancers' time, directly, through table dances or sitting fees, or indirectly, through purchasing her drinks or food, although how this occurs may be organized differently. Thus, the grouping of several dancers around one man's table, or the prolonged company of a particular dancer, can mark a man as having money. On slow nights, even in Diamond Dolls, less affluent men might be able to sit with a woman between her sets for the price of a single dance or a glass of wine. On a weekend night, however, it could be painfully obvious which men had money and which did not (and this information was often shared among the dancers in the dressing room). For some men, this visibility was disconcerting, and they disliked the fact that not only could they be recognized, but that other customers could see clearly how much they were tipping. Other forms of consumption were also noticed as attempts to mark status. As another interviewee, Ross, said, "Do you order a Budweiser? Or do you order Dom Perignon? If you're really gonna show off for the guys you buy that bottle of Dom." His comment that one shows off for the "guys" rather than the women was echoed by other customers in a variety of ways, especially those men who saw the pursuit of masculinity as competitive and stressful. Some men disliked this competition; after all, one cannot escape the limitations of the everyday in such an atmosphere without enough money. Other men did not feel comfortable in their visibility on the main floor and yet could not afford to move upstairs.

Rumors circulated continuously about the amount of money that was spent on any given night in the club and about which actors, rock stars, or professional athletes had stopped in. The management recognized the appeal that being in the company of (or at least in the same venue as) such prominent Others held for the regular customers and thus courted public figures with free admission and drinks, as well as special opportunities to use the Gem Rooms. Less affluent men sitting on the main floor would ask the dancers if anyone famous was there and how much money he was spending. Other men enjoyed watching customers who were less financially prepared watch *them:* "I'll buy a bunch of table dances when I see the guys next to me don't have any money, just to get things going," one interviewee said. Still other regulars would watch the newcomers or tourists. As one regular told me: "I have a real fascination for these guys . . . they come in there, maybe they have two hundred dollars in their pocket. Maybe they don't even have that. Maybe they got fifty dollars in their pocket. And they got through the door on a freebie card and they get in there and they've got fifty dollars. They're gonna dance a girl a couple of times, buy two or three drinks, and they're out of there because that's all they've got to spend. And that's okay, but . . . it tickles me because they fantasize what's going on upstairs and think there's a whole bunch more going on than really is going on." For the men who could afford to pay the price of a Gem Room this kind of speculation was obviously far less frequent. Indeed, regular customers were pleasant to accompany to the rooms because they did not usually try to bargain for sexual favors. The speculation of the men on the main floor may have added to their feelings of enjoyment and distinction, however, as a man could come back downstairs and have other customers wondering about what clandestine pleasures he had received. That a few extremely prominent athletes admitted to engaging in sexual acts with the dancers, both inside and outside of the club, however, only heightened the fantasies of the other customers.[12]

The spatial arrangements of Diamond Dolls thus means that men with wealth could become differentiated from the crowd, either through staging their own spectacle on the main floor or by becoming invisible in a Gem Room. At the same time, the creation of an enhanced culture of male competition also meant that the owners and managers of the establishment were easily able to more efficiently maximize their profits from the limited space. Paradoxically, the more money you had at Diamond Dolls, the more "invisible" yet renowned you could become—if you so desired. The Gem Rooms were thus subject to a great deal of main floor mythology. The DJ would remind the customers throughout the evening that they could talk to a floorman and take their favorite dancer to a room. Customers who could not afford it would frequently ask what went on upstairs, and there was a tremendous amount of speculation about whether sexual acts occurred (even among some dancers who did not get asked upstairs often). Once, when I mentioned where I worked, a man told me that a friend of his had gone into a Gem Room with two other men and they had each received fellatio for a total price of $1,500. As the hallway adjacent to the Gem Rooms was fairly well patrolled by the security staff, and as I had personal experience working with other dancers in the Gem Rooms, I doubted his story at the time. Regardless of the truth or falsity of his story, however, the fact that a man bragged about paying *three times* the price that oral sex usually costs in the Laurelton sex industry from an upscale escort, as well as the fact that he boasted about paying for it, indicates that he felt this conferred some special status on him (as did his friend who repeated the story).

Determining whether sexual activity occurred in Gem Rooms is made difficult by the privacy expected of such contact in everyday life as well as its illegality. Although strip clubs invert some norms of genital display, they less frequently transgress this boundary of overt sexual activity (except in certain cities).[13] Determining how much sexual activity takes place in any club is made even more difficult by the fact that many dancers played along with customers who asked them for sexual favors in order to maximize their financial gain; for example, telling a customer that you would meet him after work or that you would get "wilder" in the VIP rooms than on the main floor was a common ploy.

Sometimes a dancer would even stage an interaction with a bouncer so that it would look as though it was club rules—and not her own boundaries—that were putting a stop to any further activity (though, as discussed in the following chapters, customers were not always unaware of this element of the performance). Table dances might also get closer the more a customer spent or the heavier the competition in the club on a given night, sometimes just barely staying within the bounds of the legal regulations or slightly exceeding them. Some customers would leave the club thinking that sexual activity had been readily available to them and would endlessly discuss the rumors about where, how much, and with whom. Dancers and regulars, on the other hand, though still susceptible to spreading rumors about the behavior of a particular dancer or club, were much more savvy in their approach to speculating about whether sexual activity was occurring and when.

In my own experience, I never *witnessed* an act of sexual release by a customer on the premises of any of the clubs in Laurelton, though I did hear rumors about such activity from both dancers and customers. None of the interviewees who speculated about sexual activity in the Gem Rooms (nor many of the other customers I spoke with) had personally witnessed such activity, engaged in it, or even attempted to engage in it. Regardless of whether sexual favors were actually sold in the club, then, there was a mythology about the availability of such services that was important to many of the customers, even if they had no intention of participating personally. It is this mythology that interests me here, for despite the salacious stories, Diamond Dolls was still seen as an upscale club, one of the "best in the city." Part of the way it escaped the negative judgments leveled on the lower-tier clubs was through its careful control of the atmosphere (the staging of classiness) and through its control and presentation of its dancers.

If consumption is figured as "a process of communication," or a "social orientation" (Bourdieu 1984: 466), the upscale strip club can be seen as offering a fantasy of distinction for some customers, as well as for the women who work there. The mythology of the supposedly superior beauty of Diamond Dolls dancers was a draw for both the customers and the dancers and was constantly reinforced by the club in advertisements. This reputation was widespread and firmly believed in by both the Laurelton regulars and many of the out-of-town visitors. Although Brett did not like visiting Diamond Dolls personally, for example, he did admit that it was where he would take friends from out of town: "Because it is all nude in Laurelton which is very rare, so you know . . . if you got somebody who thinks he's been around the world and you go, oh, let me show you something. In that regard I would go. To say, oh, yeah, I'm gonna show you something. You've never seen fifty-two naked women, all beautiful, like they do at Diamond Dolls. And let's face it, the women who work at Diamond Dolls are actually gorgeous. You know? They're in the *Penthouse* and the *Playboy*. You know, so, in that regard, I might even do it for business." Many other men spoke similarly. Herb said that it was at Diamond Dolls and the Panther that you find "model types." Indeed, dancers who had shot centerfolds or were interested in moving into feature dancing or still or video pornography often sought out the opportunity to work at the larger, flashier clubs. Their pornographic laurels would be announced by the DJ: "We've got *Playboy* Suzie coming up on the main stage." As the mythology made it a desirable place to work and even conferred some degree of distinction on the dancers themselves, Diamond Dolls was guaranteed a wide selection of dancers and held frequent auditions.

On the other hand, although it was certainly true that it was more difficult to get hired at Diamond Dolls than at Tina's Revue or the other smaller clubs, it was also true that many of the dancers at Diamond Dolls had also worked at other clubs around town at some point. Further, due to the large number of dancers needed on each shift to keep the club running, and the constant rate of turnover, it would have been impossible to hire only dancers who most approximated the ideal of centerfold beauty. As in the other upper-tier clubs in the city, however, Diamond Dolls ran mostly white dancers, featuring only one or two black or Asian dancers a night out of the forty to one hundred house dancers. The management also officially prohibited tattoos (except for small, unobtrusive designs on the ankle or bikini line), nipple, lip, and eyebrow piercings (although in practice, clitoral or tongue piercings turned up rather frequently), and had strict rules regarding weight, makeup, manicures, and costumes. (One of the managers was a particular stickler about the rule of mandatory toenail polish with open-toe heels, and on nights that he worked the dancers hurried to share the same bottle of polish backstage before the shift.) Thus, although a customer was not guaranteed to even *see* a "real" centerfold while visiting Diamond Dolls, much less be able to interact with one, he could be assured that he was going to be in an environment that was primarily white and passably middle class.

TINA'S REVUE

Tina's Revue, often simply referred to as Tina's, was a small, lower-tier club that was frequented mainly by working- to middle-class customers. It was nestled in a strip mall at the edge of Laurelton in DeWeiss County along with a takeout Chinese restaurant, a drycleaner, and a dollar store. Because very few tourists would make the drive outside the city and because cab drivers did not receive the same kickbacks for bringing in customers as from the larger, in-town clubs, the customers were primarily locals. One of the regulars, Robert, told me that he had been coming in five days a week since it opened as a neighborhood pub in the mid-1970s, just for a drink on his way home from work. (On every shift that I worked, Robert was indeed sitting at the bar, and I corroborated his story with an amused manager.) During the early 1980s, when new strip clubs were opening up across the country, Tina's closed suddenly for remodeling. When it reopened a few weeks later with two stages and several nude dancers, Robert was surprised but continued to visit the club every day anyway. "Nothing's really changed," he laughed, "except that now I have company." Indeed, the remodeling was not that extensive and the club still looked much like a neighborhood bar. There was one large central bar remaining in the middle of the space, along with a row of pool tables along one side of the room. The other side of the club was more dimly lit and had a main stage with a pole and a small box stage near the bar. There was one VIP room that was fairly visible from both the central bar and the main floor and that was furnished with an old vinyl couch and a small table. The VIP room was rarely used, despite the fact that the overhead fee to enter the room was only $20.

DeWeiss County was equally racially divided between black and white, though most of the white population lived in the northern part of the county and most of the black population lived in the southern. As Tina's was located just off the expressway that marked the midpoint of the county, it was the most racially mixed club I encountered in Laurelton in terms of both dancers and customers. Upon entry into Tina's, a newcomer would likely be struck by the racial mix, as very few entertainment or recreational spaces in Laurelton can be found with nearly equal numbers of white and black customers and employees in structurally similar positions. Perhaps because there was only one other club in this area of town, Tina's was not usually referred to as a black or a white club. Instead, particular customers might critically remark that the club ws getting *too* black or *too* white, depending on their own race and each shift's lineup of fifteen to twenty dancers or on that evening's clientele.

For the smaller clubs like Tina's, competition with other clubs took place through low-priced Happy Hour buffets, drink specials, and advertising flyers and newsletters directed at locals that featured photographs and articles about particular dancers or special events. Because lower-tier clubs like Tina's depended on local business, the top clubs were not seen as direct competition. The managers of Tina's, for example, were completely accepting of the fact that I would continue working at Diamond Dolls as well. In fact, they proudly informed me that another dancer who worked there did the same and introduced us to each other. Like most lower-tier clubs, they tried to highlight the fact that they offered something different from the upscale clubs, advertising an atmosphere of relaxation away from the "hustling" of the tourist clubs. The busiest time at Tina's was in the early evening after work, during Happy Hour, although it occasionally got busy on weekend nights as well.

In a type of counterdiscourse to the more upscale environments, Tina's capitalized on the fact that it was seen as a working-class, neighborhood bar. The DJ sometimes brought this to the attention of the crowd; while he was waiting for new dancers to take the stage after shift changes or two-for-one dances, for example, he might play selections from Jeff Foxworthy's popular and well-known "You Might Be a Redneck If . . ." CD. This CD brought laughter from white and black customers alike.[14] In a club like Tina's, the presence of a group of men in business suits (called "suits" by the dancers) would be sure to attract a group of dancers, who assumed that they had money, as well as the attention of the regulars and working-class customers. In an upper-tier club like Diamond Dolls, however, suits had less meaning, as anyone on the floor might have money and dressing more casually could even signify a higher-status position.

The fact that Tina's was not organized around conspicuous consumption was important for some customers. Brett, a customer at

Tina's, noted that the residents of Laurelton were unrelentingly focused on social class and that Tina's provided somewhat of a respite from this pressure: "This area's different from anywhere else I've ever been. It's metropolitan but you . . . you go to New York City and there's a hundred different social structures but they all kind of like meld together. Where down here, you know where the lines are drawn . . . and I think the lines are a lot deeper here. It's either you're, you know, a blue-collar guy or you're a white-collar guy. There's no real in between. Where up North, if you're a blue-collar worker but you're working real hard and you're building something up, you're almost white collar." Similarly, Ross said that he preferred Tina's to the upper-tier clubs:

> As opposed to going somewhere like Diamond Dolls, where you have the premium dancers expecting the premium tipping and premium bouncers keeping everybody in line and there's a glass wall somewhere between this and this—between you and the girl—an invisible glass wall and it is an extremely cash transaction. And then the guys there are there to show off their money. It's a very flashy, cashy kind of place . . . you go in and guys, you know, drunk and shoving twenty dollar bills up garter belts just to prove they can do it. And if that's what floats your boat then that's okay . . . I moved beyond that a long time ago. But I also have to admit that I had a period in my life where I did that, so I can understand that. You're one-upping. It has nothing to do with sex. It has really very little to do with the women. You're there to impress, to try to impress the other men. You know, heaven forbid if you have one of the dancers come down and talk to you. Ooh, boy, you've really scored. It's the same thing—it has nothing to do with her. In other words, she's become a totally impersonal pawn. Which is to me—I mean, it's totally depersonalized and I find it totally boring. I prefer a place like, you know, Tina's . . . even if it's in a sense artificial or contrived companionship and friendship in a sense, it's . . . more real. Not just the total artificiality of bells whistling and some lights. All those places like that, it's a deliberate sensory overload.

He said he enjoyed the fact that Tina's was a place "where everybody knows your name," using the phrase in a self-conscious way to refer to the theme song to the popular television show about a local pub, *Cheers*. The name Cheers was mentioned more than once by the regular customers at Tina's.[15] Brett called Tina's "a weird Cheers," where he went to sit at the bar, drink beer, and eat with friends. He disliked Diamond Dolls, preferring the "small pub atmosphere" of Tina's. A Cheers atmosphere was generally assumed to be one that was both comfortable and welcoming.

Both the management and the dancers rigorously policed the type of dancing done at Tina's, and it was generally thought to be an extremely "clean" club. Dancers who moved too close to customers during table dances were quickly reprimanded and even ostracized by the managers and the other dancers. Misbehavior on stage, such as disrobing too quickly, bending over too far, or crawling on the stage, was quickly pointed out by the DJ and even castigated by him over the microphone. Though there were indeed customers who speculated that some of the dancers at Tina's might also work as prostitutes outside of the club (I found such speculation to be the case wherever I worked, regardless of whether it was true), there was a striking absence of rumor about sexual activity inside the club.

Though some dancers sold a lot of table dances, a majority did not actively try to sell private dances and relied on the money they made on the stages and from regulars. Unlike Diamond Dolls, where the sheer number of dancers meant that each might take the stage only once in the evening, Tina's always ran under two dozen dancers. On some nights, this meant that dancers could be on either of the two stages every forty-five minutes. It was easier for the customers to approach the stages to tip the dancers than at Diamond Dolls, as the space was not maximized to fit the greatest number of bodies into the room and the club was almost never uncomfortably crowded. Paul found the spatial arrangements of Tina's less intimidating than at Diamond Dolls, saying that the women at Diamond Dolls were "really objectified" because of their positioning on raised stages and pedestals and the extravagant atmosphere. "That's entertaining, sure," he said, "but it's not as intimate as Tina's . . . It's much more superficial." Although the dancers at Tina's were generally not considered as beautiful as those at Diamond Dolls or the Panther, they were seen as more approachable.

Regardless of the fact that men of both races visited the bar, Tina's could quite quickly become segregated through its spatial layout, especially during the night shift. The nearly complete separation of the pool table area from the main stage meant that at any given time one of these spaces might be almost completely white or black. Some nights were extremely predictable, with the black men tipping the black dancers and the white men tipping the white dancers. Granted, the performance styles of white and black dancers in this environment differed significantly at times, and thus such choices came to be coded in terms of taste. The fact that the dancers chose their own music, for example, also meant that there were logistical considerations that made dancers more likely to dance with those of the same race. As two dancers were on the stages at the same time, this meant that the DJ had to place each dancer with others who would like her music. With the white dancers choosing classic rock or alternative dance music for their sets and the black dancers choosing funk or hip-hop, sometimes to fit the tastes of their regular customers, the sets often alternated between all black and all white.

Men of both races explained their preferences for certain types of dancers in terms of taste. The "bounce" or the "rump-shaker," for example, was allowed at Tina's and practiced there by both white and black dancers alike. This was a move that was popular with black audiences but prohibited at clubs like Diamond Dolls and the Panther Club.[16] Whereas some of the white customers at Tina's certainly found this move enjoyable to watch, others vehemently opposed it and refused to tip dancers who performed it. A white customer might also say that he preferred a particular body type that (supposedly) was found only on the white dancers, and vice versa; for example, several African American men told me that I was too thin to be an exotic dancer. I was also advised to change my working name to something more "exotic" (Princess, Ecstasy, Fawn, and Beauty were all suggested) and wear more elaborate costumes (I almost always wore the same white or black cocktail dress that I wore at Diamond Dolls) if I wanted to be more appealing to black customers.

Just as Diamond Dolls was a site for fantasies about celebrity and high-priced sexual activity, Tina's was a site for fantasies about vice and danger. Paul, for example, pointed out that the mix of people in Tina's was one of its attractions for him, despite the fact that he did not interact with many other customers:

> There are a lot of clubs in town that are really dives and that just are . . . I guess, dismal and dim or something. I don't really know how to describe it. Maybe it has something to do with the clientele. I don't know. To me,

the atmosphere's just not a healthy atmosphere. And Tina's is not all that healthy of an atmosphere, but it has a very divided group. There's a group of guys that sit at the bar that, you know, talk and bullshit and then there's the drug people that come into the place, the heavy drug activity in there. And then there's the regular people who come in and sit at a table and watch a dance or two or three and then leave. So you've got a dichotomy of people that come in. Whereas in the other places, I don't see that same division.

Although he liked to be somewhat close to the danger of a marginal setting, he stayed away from places that had "low, low light," "corners that are very unclean, you know, invisible corners," and where there was a lot of physical contact with the dancers. Alex enjoyed Tina's because of what he felt was a "sinister atmosphere" and because he liked to "watch the scene, the drug pushers and partiers." Kenneth and Ross spoke similarly. On nights when one half of the club—either the side with the pool tables or the side with the stages—was filled with black customers, for example, I frequently heard white customers at the bar discussing the possibility that Tina's was a "drug hangout." "It's an interesting place," one man told me. "You've got the drug crowd on one side and the truck drivers on the other." I did not hear black customers speculating about the occupations or proclivities of the white customers as a group, however. White customers would also talk about white or black dancers who sat with large groups of black men, sometimes suggesting that they were doing so because these men were drug dealers or because the women were also working as prostitutes, even though the more obvious explanation would have been that these were well-paying customers.

Despite the fact that white customers (and some black customers) tended to mention the "underground drug trade" at Tina's, it must have been very underground if it actually existed in any organized form, as I never witnessed any such transactions and spent hundreds of hours observing and working in the club, interacting with a wide variety of customers and dancers. Much like the stories about sexual activity at Diamond Dolls, the idea of drug dealing was more important to the regulars as a fantasy than a reality, lending an air of excitement to an otherwise fairly controlled space. Again, this is not to naïvely say that drugs never exchanged hands or were never used by customers or dancers. But significantly, none of the customers who made the kind of statements above had ever *personally* witnessed a drug trade on the premises, been approached by a drug dealer, or had any proof *at all* that such transactions occurred. Nevertheless, these fantasies lent excitement to the customers' experiences, much in the way that stories about sexual access circulated at Diamond Dolls.

*

Strip clubs are a particular form of public, masculinized, voyeuristic entertainment, drawing some of their appeal from a history of gendered spectacle as leisure practice, a tradition of intermingling between performers and their audiences in both scripted and creative ways, and from their associations with the working classes—associations that are dramatized, but not removed, through the process of upscaling.

Laurelton strip clubs became meaningful within a social geography, a landscape that was raced, classed, and gendered, populated with a variety of Others who lent an air of excitement or danger to the men's experiences (centerfolds, celebrities, prostitutes, or drug dealers). The internal spatial arrangements of Diamond Dolls and Tina's also worked to construct different experiences for the customers and thus became appealing to different kinds of men. In Diamond Dolls there was a clear vertical hierarchy, with the upper tier of the club devoted to VIP seating and the Gem Rooms. Customers purchased time in highly individualized spaces in the club (Gem Rooms, VIP seating, and the chairs on the main floor), thus both conferring distinction on themselves and maximizing profit for the club owners, and money was the ultimate determinant of who moved where inside the club. The experience was more than just one of distinction for the customers, however, as this also permitted a personalized interaction with a dancer imbued with a particular value. Customers could compete on the main floor, as well as in the Gem Rooms, through a variety of forms of luxury consumption, including by surrounding themselves with dancers. Customers could also be relatively (although not absolutely) certain of the racial and class makeup of both the other visitors and the dancers.

In Tina's, the internal spatial arrangements were horizontal, allowing for customers to group themselves in ways that felt comfortable yet also jeopardous, especially given the rarity of a mixed-race setting in

Laurelton. Again, the presence and composition of the other customers were important to the men, leading to both feelings of safety (I'm with "other people like me") and feelings of danger (I'm in the company of others, both men and women, who might "live lives outside the law"). Though there certainly were contacts made between customers and between customers and dancers of different races, talk about different tastes (in music, costumes, etc.) and about different lifestyles (drugs, prostitution) meant that Tina's could also serve as a place in which racial differences were reaffirmed.

That there were relatively few stories about drugs or crime at Diamond Dolls and few stories about sexual activity in Tina's Revue makes sense when the clubs are situated within their respective social geographies. For the men who visited Diamond Dolls, especially those who craved respectability and legitimation, it was stories of possible sexual access that provided the desired transgressive edge to their experiences. The internal design of the club itself, with its provision of private spaces for the men who could afford it, worked to enhance the visibility (or invisibility) and mobility of the patrons and to link them to patterns of conspicuous, sexualized consumption. In a mixed-race setting such as Tina's, the white customers' fantasies focused on the danger of the racialized Others in the club; as a lower-tier venue with a spatial design that did not allow for much privacy, sex inside the club was less appealing to fantasize about than the proclivities and identities of the dancers and the other patrons.

In both clubs, money directly translated into control over space and over the time of the dancers. There is no straightforward way to discuss the different kinds of customers in each club in terms of class or occupation, however, for although Tina's had slightly more construction workers and auto mechanics than Diamond Dolls, I also met lawyers, doctors, and engineers there. Further, although Diamond Dolls was known for its celebrity sightings and for being the haunt of famous athletes, it was also a spot where nervous teens spent their first bewildering night in a strip club and where waiters from the nearby Longhorns Steakhouse visited after work for beer and sushi. Regardless of differences in education, occupation, and upbringing, all of the interviewees firmly believed that they were middle class (and indeed, I could discern no clear demographic pattern to their selection of clubs). On the other hand, attraction to one club or another often had to do with beliefs and fantasies about what is exciting, dangerous, or Other—represented, in part, by stories about illegal sexual activity and drug dealing—as well as with beliefs and fantasies based on ideas about race, class, and gender. These fantasies are explored in more depth in Chapter 6.

Part Two

Interlude

Strawberries

I have just arrived at the club for my shift when the pay phone in the dressing room rings. The house mom answers and then motions to me. "It's James," she says, rolling her eyes.

James tells me that he will be at the club by eight o'clock. "I'd like to help you out tonight," he says. "Oh, and wear the white dress."

"Okay," I tell him. I hang up the phone and smile at myself in the mirror. James is my favorite customer—he always wants the same script. It will be a good night.

I take my white dress out of my locker and begin to get ready for my shift. There is something transcendent about this particular dress—ankle-length white satin, with beaded thin straps. It is slender and form fitting, and as I am naked underneath except for a small white g-string, I can feel the satin caressing my entire body as I move. I wear it with five-inch white heels, which makes me six feet tall in this outfit. Both men and women stop and stare as I pass. I wear a string of pearls, drop pearl earrings, and a pair of elbow-length white satin gloves. As I walk upstairs to the stage, I have to lift the satin skirt a bit to bend my knees. When I let it fall again, the dress is instantly smooth and perfect.

It is over-the-top in its glamour. Where would a girl like me ever wear an outfit like this? It is far too sexy to be married in, at least for my family. It is too white to wear to someone else's wedding. It is too ostentatious to wear to the opera or to a performance—I could never dress it down. It is too flashy, too insistent, to wear to a party. One just can't call that much attention to oneself in many social circles without facing a certain amount of criticism. Too competitive, someone might

Originally published in *Gauntlet,* vol. 17, May 1999. Slightly edited.

say. Who does she think she is? Perhaps if I ever write a best-selling novel, or if I become famous and a benefit is given in my honor—perhaps then it won't matter what I wear. Maybe I will wear this dress.

I remember the day I bought it. It's a beautiful dress, the saleswoman said when she saw me trying it on in my bare feet. But where would you ever wear it? I just smiled and paid her for it in creased dollar bills. Are you a waitress? she asked.

The girls at work call it my princess dress because I move around the dressing room cautiously on nights that I wear it. Don't get makeup on me! I yell, when someone gets too close with a careless tube of lipstick. I put my own makeup on while naked, and then I get dressed right before I am ready to take the floor to prevent accidents. When I come into the dressing room for touch-ups, I take the dress off again. Once, a drunken customer accidentally spilled some bourbon on the dress as I passed. Sorry, he said casually. But I was furious. I made him give me seventy-five dollars for drycleaning, and I took the dress to four successive drycleaners until it was perfect again. I didn't give him a single dance.

The dancers at the club I work at are all required to wear evening dresses. Some of the girls hate this rule about evening wear and whine that they'd rather wear bikinis, but I love it. So what if I have to take the dress off by the second song of my sets? Or to do a ten dollar table dance? The thing that bothers me most is that sometimes I have nowhere to set it down and it ends up on the floor, a sacrilege almost, for such a perfect dress.

Not all of the customers appreciate the dress. You have such nice legs, some tell me. Why don't you get a short dress to show them off?

But the dress draws customers to my stage because the white material glows under the black lights. Sometimes, on the first song, when I am walking out on stage and the lights are flashing and the music is playing and I am strutting around, playing with my gloves, I fantasize about pictures that I've seen of models in Paris or Milan. I raise my arms over my head and cop that faraway look that photographers love. I think that it was Iman who said once that she thought of her homeland when she was modeling. But the Midwest is my homeland. Instead, I pretend I have been transported to somewhere strange, beautiful, and dangerous.

But after the first song, when I strip down to my white gloves and g-string, that's when the money starts coming out. You have a beautiful body, men say, stuffing my garter with money. I wonder sometimes, though, why most men have never learned to appreciate clothes.

James, my regular, appreciates the dress. He finds it elegant, sensuous, and exciting. The first night I met him, he paid me just to sit with him. I don't want you to take that dress off, he said. I put my gloved hand on his leg and we sat together, listening to the music. When he paid me, he didn't want to put the money in my garter like most of the customers. Instead, he slipped it directly inside my white beaded handbag. I carry the handbag to put the money in after my sets instead of leaving it in my garter like some of the girls. I like my line to be smooth, thin. James appreciates this as well. He plays with my long dark hair, and tells me that I am all *length*—my hair, my dress, my legs. I do like feeling myself as length.

James is a middle-aged man, fairly out of shape. He is tall and works as an airline pilot. He tells me that he lives alone and has never been married. Most of my other regulars are married men who want to talk about sex or their wives. James, though, is different. He is shy around women, which is why he prefers to come to the club when he wants company. I do a lot of work for him, though. I don't dance for him much—he prefers talking to table dances. But I listen to his stories about his job. I write down where he is flying for the next week, so that when he returns I can ask him about the various cities that he has been to. This always makes him happy. I pretend to be jealous, and accuse him of having women like me in every city. Of course not, Ella, he says. I remember details about his family—his mother and his sister. I always ask how they are doing. He tells me, I would love my mother to meet you. I answer, I would love to meet her too. Sometimes it is even true. I sense that it would make him happy, and although I don't love him or even consider him a real friend, I do have a respect for his world.

Yet we both know that his mother would not respect my world. I am a stripper. I take off my clothes for money. It's good money, and it's a good job. But it still isn't the kind of job that you put on your résumé.

Sometimes I feel like I should get a desk job. I go to my closet, determined to hit the streets, to find myself a job that pays relatively nothing in green but more in social currency. But the closet is as far as I get.

The clothes! As a secretary I would wear flat shoes. Sensible shoes. Knee-length skirts in earth tones—taupe, beige, moss. I would wear plain jewelry. I would wear pantyhose and a slip, even in the summer, to keep my body reined in. I would look harried and pale. God, I could end up looking pasty like James, like my Aunt Rose, like the women who work at my dentist's office.

No more leopard? No more knee-high patent leather boots? No more white length and glamour? I just can't assign these dreamy items to such a fate yet—to skeletons in my closet. In a few more years, I'll have my journalism degree. It will inevitably happen then.

James shows up on time, as he always does, and waits for me to finish sitting with two customers. I am glad to get away from them, even though they have been buying dances. They have also been talking incessantly about all of the dancers in the club and trying to drag personal details out of me. *What's her real name? Does she have a boyfriend? Are those real boobs? Would you go out to lunch with me?*

"I'm glad to see you," I tell James when I finish my dances.

"What are you drinking tonight?" he asks me. I tell him to get me a glass of Chardonnay and I comment on his suit. He orders from one of the waitresses and she tells us that she will bring it back to the VIP room. James has already arranged with the DJ to remove me from the stage list for two hours so that we can talk. We walk through the crowded club to the VIP room and everyone watches us pass. The girls are jealous because I don't have to dance for two hours. My friend Lana makes a sign to me, signaling that she hopes to get off the list within a set or two. I wink at her. It is a weekend night, and the crowd is rowdy, tough, and loud. I hear two young guys talking about the dancer who is on stage. Look at her tits, one says. The other is in awe, mouth open. As we pass the men look at me, the same shell-shocked expression on their faces. Such short attention spans, I think.

James holds the door to the room open for me. We take a seat on a soft couch in the corner with a low table in front of it. The tables are for dancing as well as for drinks, because our feet are not allowed to touch the ground in this club if our clothes are off. I'm not sure if that makes it any safer for the dancers, but rules are rules. The music is softer in here, the lights are still dim but they are no longer flashing. Instead of glowing, my dress is soft and shimmery. The waitress brings us our drinks, and James decides that he wants to order champagne as well. "What kind do you prefer?" he asks me.

I do not order the most expensive bottle, as I do with some customers, even though I get a percentage of the bill. If I did, James would get suspicious. "I've never tried this kind," I tell him, pointing to the second bottle on the list.

"Wonderful," he says. He begins to tell me about the vineyard, about how and where it is made. James likes to educate me. I don't tell him that I worked in fifteen upscale restaurants before I discovered stripping. Instead I just sip my wine and nod. I've been seeing James weekly for months now and I know what he wants. After a few minutes, he asks for my beaded purse and I give it to him. He slips the money inside and I don't count it because I know that he always give me the right amount, a hundred dollars an hour. "That's just to help you out," he says.

We have strawberries with the champagne. James pops the strawberries into my mouth, because I don't want to touch them with my gloves. They are sliced thin and I remember how many nights I stood in the kitchen of a restaurant, slicing thin strawberries for the customers to have with their champagne, on their cheesecake. Carrying trays full of dirty dishes and lipstick-stained cups on my shoulder back to the bus rack.

I drink the champagne, sip the wine. I decide that I want something sweet so James orders me a dessert. There is a tickle in my head from the alcohol and I lean back on the couch. "You are so perfect," James says. He touches my hair and I close my eyes. He is the only customer that is allowed to touch my hair.

"Where are you flying this week?" I ask him. "Anywhere that I should visit?"

He smiles and begins to tell me his itinerary. He complains about the different airports as much as any passenger and seems to hate traveling. "It just gets old," he says. "Wondering whether the carpet in your hotel room is going to be green or brown. Wondering if there will be pictures of mountains on the walls or pictures of boats." For a moment, I feel sorry for him.

"You should take me along some time," I ask him, as I always do.

"Maybe I will," he says, patting my leg. It's a game we play. I know that I'd never go; he knows that he'd never take me.

He begins to spin tales about what he would show me in each city and whom he would introduce me to. I drift off. I look down at my gloved hand, carefully holding a champagne flute. My beaded purse is tucked carefully into the couch at my side. I cross my legs. I hear myself laugh lightly at one of his jokes and think, I could be anyone. Instead of length, I experience myself as bounty. Cornucopia. The world is full of possibilities, endless opportunities. I feel a strong, sudden emotion for James, for the comforting strangeness of our relationship.

When the two hours are up, a tuxedoed bouncer comes to find me. "You're on main stage in two songs," he tells me.

James looks sad for a moment and I hope that he will buy another hour so that I don't have to return to the floor. Then he stands up and straightens his jacket and I know that he is leaving. I give him a quick hug and he slips another bill into my hand. I don't even look at it because it is always a twenty.

"Have a great flight tomorrow," I say.

"I'll call when I get back," he tells me, and heads quickly for the front doors. Sometimes, I sense that this is the moment that he pays the most highly for.

And then I am back on in the thick of it, a Saturday night on the floor. *Hey, baby, I want a dance, here come here is that a prom dress or something will you go home with me is that your real name?*

Chapter Three

Just Trying to Relax:

Masculinity, Touristic Practice,

and the Idiosyncrasies of Power

I could provide a place where men who faced the increasing stresses of the late twentieth century could escape for a few hours. A place where choices and options are clear-cut, a place where "feminism" was a dirty word, a place where a man could be a man . . . And I knew those men would leave the club each night perfectly content without having had a physical union with the women. For the most part, my clientele were married. They were not as much interested in the physical act as in the mental exercise. This club would be safe for them. They would not catch AIDS, and they could honestly say they were there to watch the ball games . . . the women would be an added attraction. The women would make them feel like the hotshots they knew they were.
—Jay Bildstein (1996: 22, 42), creator of *Scores,* an upscale gentlemen's club in New York City

This chapter focuses on the male customers' spoken motives for visiting strip clubs, as well as on the relationship of these motives to discourses of masculinity, contemporary forms of touristic practice, and social privilege or power. The focus here is specifically on the men's *talk* about their practices. There are, of course, nonverbalized, or less conscious, elements of their experiences that are explored in more depth in the following chapters. Human motivations are not immediately transparent or simply a matter of rationally selecting from the choices presented to us in the social realm, and the customers' visits become meaningful, in part, within a context of competing cultural discourses about gender, sexuality, and consumption that must be explored. As individuals are positioned differently in relation to such discourses, and as individuals create their own gendered meanings out of situations and interactions (Chodorow 1999), not every man is likely to find strip clubs pleasurable, relaxing, or rewarding. This chapter also examines the men's subjective understandings of gendered power and privilege, and argues that although customers' motivations are indeed related to existing power structures and inequalities, their visits are not necessarily experienced as exercises in acquiring or wielding power.

Why Men Become and Remain Customers

Why are some men loyal customers of strip clubs while others find them boring or are contemptuous of their very existence? Significantly, not one man I interviewed said that he went to the clubs for specifically *sexual* release, even in the form of masturbation at a later time. This may be because the Laurelton sex industry is quite large and varied, and men who wanted sexual contact or release had many other venues to choose from in the area. Those few men who did enter the Laurelton clubs expecting sexual release were generally from out of the country or were unfamiliar with the different sectors of the sex industry. That this was not among the main motivations listed is in some ways also specific to Laurelton, for lap dancing and close contact is prohibited in conjunction with the combination of alcohol and full nudity.[1] In other geographic locations, it is likely that different legal regulations will shape customers' motivations somewhat. This does not mean that sexual acts did not sometimes occur in the clubs, however, or that some men did not desire to purchase sexual intimacies from dancers outside of the clubs for one reason or another. This is also not to say that interactions with dancers were not *sexual* in certain respects—some men did describe table dances as "sexual" experiences and found their fantasizing to be exciting and sometimes quite transgressive.

Most men I spoke with, however, also realized that sexual activity was available in other venues of the industry and were explicit about their knowledge of this fact. As Joe said, "It's not a place to go find somebody if you're trying to get sex! You might as well go someplace where you can get sex. There's plenty of them around." Similarly, Steven said, "The bottom line is if you want to get laid, I know where and how and when to get laid." Regular customers often laughed at young, inexperienced, or foreign men who thought that sex was part of the deal being struck between dancers and the customers. As Roger said, "If you're a guy out looking to get a woman, you know, going to the club is passively entertaining for a while but it's not the best way to go out and get laid! It's probably the worst way to do it." Other men pointed out that the fantasy was sometimes more powerful than a physical encounter. Jack said, "Ninety-nine percent of sexuality is in your head . . . a mind fuck can be better than an actual one."

Instead, by far the most prevalent (and usually the first given) *spoken* motivation of the interviewees for visiting strip clubs was a desire to relax. Nearly every man I spoke with gave this response in some form or another:

> I go there to relax and have a good time, get my mind off of work. It does all those things. (Tim)

> It's a business. Where people can just come in and let their hair down, so to speak, and relax. (Herb)

> It's definitely more of a relaxing thing than anything. (William)

I could quote many others. In fact, I heard this off-hand response so many times, from men I interviewed and men I interacted with, that I specifically began to focus on why exactly the men felt that going to a strip club was relaxing. The reasons given fell generally into several different categories: a strip club provided entertainment and leisure, an atmosphere different from both work and home, a relative degree of "safety" as well as "excitement," and an opportunity for both personal and sexual acceptance from women.[2] Although these categories necessarily blend into one another and are not meant to be exhaustive, they also highlight particular themes that ran throughout the interviews. In the following sections, these themes are explored as they relate to several prominent discourses of masculinity in the contemporary United States, as well as to understandings of leisure practice more generally.

Initially, men tended to explain that strip clubs provide relaxation because they are entertainment complexes and leisure spaces, sites that by definition connote relaxation as opposed to responsibility. Several men pointed to entertainment as their main motive for visiting the clubs:

> They're like going to a game arcade . . . you know, it's public . . . go out and have fun in a big bar kind of thing, as opposed to the lingerie [parlors] and the prostitution . . . That's pure sex whereas the other's like a little bit of sex tease with real entertainment. So there's a difference there. My sex life's always been good so it's the entertainment that's more exciting to me. (Mick)

> It's a show really . . . the safeness is being in a club where [nudity] is presented as entertainment. (Herb)

> It's entertainment. Like going to a play or a movie or . . . it's just entertainment. (William)

Yet why a strip club rather than some other entertainment venue? William's statement that "it's just entertainment" highlights the fact that entertainment itself is often seen as a legitimate pursuit, something that should not be held accountable to politics or criticism. As strip clubs have come under fire in religiously conservative communities across the country, the claim that they are a form of entertainment is often one that is used to indicate that leisure is being sold rather than sexual services.[3] In fact, what is often being sold is a *gendered* combination of leisure, entertainment, and service. Visiting a strip club is, after all, significantly different from attending a play or going to the cinema; visiting the clubs means that the male customers will be attended to by women who are young, accepting, usually attractive, hopefully friendly, and whose services (in the form of conversation or dancing) can be purchased for an agreed upon price. It is also a kind of entertainment that men overwhelmingly pursue alone, or with other men, and more rarely in mixed-sex groups. Further, despite the fact that some dancers' appearance, physique, or displays of aggressive sexuality may challenge mainstream middle-class definitions of femininity, I have *never* encountered a performer in a heterosexual strip club that catered to male customers who was not believed to be female or explicitly advertised as otherwise. This may seem either obvious or quite basic; it is, however, extremely important to customers seeking a place where, as Bildstein puts it, "a man could be a man."

"It's Different from Anywhere Else": Searching for Escape

The fascination with *looking* as a form of entertainment is, of course, highly significant in understanding the current attraction of strip clubs. Going to strip clubs obviously presents the opportunity to look at women, and it is this focus on looking in a *public* atmosphere that differentiates the strip club from many other forms of adult entertainment.[4] The desire to see naked women was, as one would expect, intrinsic to the meaning of the experience for the customers. Some men initially explained their desire to visit a strip club with reference to a desire to see women's bodies:

> I'm drawn by the attraction of sexuality. You know, sex sells. Sex and beautiful women are very appealing. And they're very appealing to able-bodied men. And what can I say? You know . . . It's just a fact. (Jim)

> Strip clubs attract me because I love the feminine form. I have a weakness for beautiful women. (Brian)

> I'm an appreciator of female beauty in all forms. (Ross)

> I liked that kind of environment . . . it was pretty cool . . . you know, I mean, who wouldn't like going to watch naked women running around? You know? Who wouldn't like to drink beer and watch naked women running around? I guess—what male wouldn't? That's the way I've always looked at it. (Alex)

Some of these men believed that the desire to look at women's bodies was an expression of natural male biology, a claim explored in more detail in Chapter 4. Whether or not they understood their desire to look at women in this format as a result of biological influences, however, there were always a number of other elements involved that were important to the customers in addition to the visual aspects.

After all, the desire to visit strip clubs is more than just a desire to passively see women's bodies, even for the most scopophilic of customers. There are many ways to potentially see naked women: peeping, viewing pornography, reading medical texts, and developing intimate relationships, for example. Further, men's interactions in strip clubs are with women who look back at them, from the stages ("Remember to make eye contact!" managers would coach), or in individualized interactions at their tables. These visits, then, must be seen as also a desire to have a particular kind of *experience* rooted in the complex network of relationships between home, work, and away. Touristic practices, according to Urry, "involve the notion of 'departure,' of a limited breaking with established routines and practices of everyday life and allowing one's senses to engage with a set of stimuli that contrasts with the everyday and the mundane" (1990: 2). The sights that are gazed on are chosen because they offer "distinctive contrasts" with work and home and also because "there is an anticipation, especially through daydreaming and fantasy, of intense pleasures, either on a different scale or involving different senses from those customarily encountered" (3).[5]

My interviewees, for example, corroborated that these sites / sights are "out of the ordinary," at least initially. For regulars, of course, the experience of just looking at undressed women eventually becomes almost ordinary. ("Almost" because even for the regulars the fact that women were displaying their body meant that this was a very different environment from ordinary spaces like work and home.) Matthew and Steven, for example, spoke about how this became "boring" after a time and that they began to desire other types of interactions, such as intriguing conversations and even ongoing friendships with the dancers. Louis said, "I don't want to go just to watch bodies move around . . . I get to know someone and that makes a difference to me." Several other men who were regular visitors also discussed this process. In all of these cases, what kept the regulars returning to the various clubs was the opportunity to interact with women whom they generally would not meet in their everyday life and to cultivate the relationships they developed with particular dancers and club employees. Thus, although the significance of the dancers' nudity was often minimized by the men in their conversations with me, and was described by the regulars as something that became "routine," it was unquestionably an important and essential part of the encounters in the clubs. Even a man who pays a woman to sit with him and asks her to remain fully clothed, for example, is doing so in an atmosphere in which he simultaneously has the privilege of asking her to *remove* her dress, and the significance of this possibility cannot be underestimated.

For some customers, just to enter a space where nude bodies are readily exhibited is to step into a strange and foreign world. For others, the strip club is but one destination on their daily geographic trajectories: "a good place to stop for a beer." Yet, either way, the club offers a distinctive contrast to other public spheres. For one thing, the behavioral structure of everyday life is indeed inverted for many customers inside the clubs: for example, women do the approaching rather than the men and thus face the possibility of rejection; women "ask" to be looked at naked; and usually "private" performances of sexual desire or sexual display are suddenly made public. Further, although intimate relationships between individuals may be covertly facilitated with money in everyday realms, inside the clubs this facilitation is blatant, immediate, and far less apologetic (though no less complicated in its various enactments). The club is, in the words of one interviewee, "a very different world." Hence, there is an emphasis in men's talk about their visits to strip clubs that these experiences are something that they "don't get at home" (and often don't want at home) and that the visits are somehow intrinsically pleasurable for this reason.

In addition to the display of women's bodies and the provision of their social and emotional services for an agreed upon fee, strip clubs also provide an environment where men, singly or in groups, can engage in traditionally "masculine" activities and forms of consumption often frowned on in other spheres: cigar smoking, drinking, watching sports events, and even being "rowdy," vulgar, or aggressive. Phillip said that in the strip clubs he "sometimes acted like an asshole because I could" and that this was a form of release for him. Alex said that he enjoyed "real bad hole-in-the-wall dive bars" because they were places where he could get "wild" with his male friends. He explained: "We'd do something just to get thrown out. We'd get crazy. We'd get a table dance and like, grab some girl's ass or something like that or just something crazy. We're just—we liked to get rowdy or whatever. Crazy." Alex admitted that he acted differently when he visited the clubs alone, however, and that it was less common for him to go to the clubs with other men at this point in his life. Other men spoke similarly about the release that the clubs offered:

I want to have fun and be relaxed and cut up and laugh and, you know, have a good time. It's a big stress reliever for me. My business is a very high-stress environment and when things get really busy, I can slip out, you know. Stay out for a couple hours and really just let go a little bit and feel better. [In the club] there's something going on that's not normal.

You know, if I just went out to a singles bar, say, then I would know that those girls there are looking to have some kind of relationship beyond what's going to go on just at the bar. But if you go to [Diamond Dolls] you're going there and y'all are entertainers. We're being entertained. And you know, it just takes your mind off things. And of course, guys like to look at girls so . . . it's just so different from any atmosphere you can get anywhere else. It's just for fun and everybody knows what the rules are. (Roger)

You go in and it is so different from the workaday world that I'm in . . . You're immediately going to fantasyland. You don't have to deal with the stress like you do at work . . . You can be real nice to them and you know they're going to be real nice to you. And that does not happen in the workplace. (Beck)

Herb was married to a "very conservative" woman who did not smoke or drink. For him, then, these were pleasures that he could not indulge in at home. At the club, however, "You got your cold beer, you got your shooters, you got your good-looking girls, you got your music, you got your smokes. You can smoke a cigar if you want. And when you're ready to go, you leave it all behind and that stays there and you go home." Herb usually came to the club on his way home from work. Sometimes he came with friends from the office and other times he came alone. Either way, his time in the club was described as "personal" time that was pleasurable because it allowed him to engage in activities that were inappropriate in the other spheres of his life and marked a transition between these spheres. As most of the men I spoke with kept their activities in the clubs a secret from their coworkers and wife or partner, they were careful to remove traces of these visits before returning to the office or home—checking for lipstick on their cheeks (remnants of a thank you peck on the cheek) or perfume on their clothes, for example. Such illicit remains were clearly inappropriate in these other spheres, even more literally marking the separateness of the clubs.

At the same time that strip clubs offer an escape, the temporary nature of the experiences is highly significant. The desire to return to work and home were unquestioned elements of the men's visits and were reflected in the balance between risk and safety that was often being sought. Though some customers expressed the desire for an affair with a dancer or for more "excitement" in their sexual relationships outside of the clubs, very few of them seemed prepared to give up their positions in these other realms to pursue such desires. One customer, for example, spent an entire afternoon telling me his fantasies about visiting a legal brothel in Nevada. He had never used any aspect of the sex industry except for looking at a few pornographic magazines and visiting strip clubs. "I just want to do it once," he said, "and then I want to go home to Mama" (his wife of thirty years). However, he explained, she would never condone it and it was not worth the risk. His hours in the strip club provided him with a transgressive and exciting experience—indeed, provided him an opportunity to share this even more transgressive fantasy and develop it further through our interaction—yet still allowed him to return home.

A touristic practice might be understood as part of a larger process that makes "the habitual desirable as well as making escape from the habits of labor seem possible through everyday practices of consumptive pleasure" (Allison 1996: xv). Not only are the realms of work and leisure still constructed as separate spheres for many individuals (despite the fact that the boundary may be weakening in late capitalist societies), but the (often imaginary) image constructed out of tourist gazes also "serves to validate and legitimize routine experience, domestic and working life, and the social structure within which they are located" (Manderson 1995: 307). Though customers may try to find out information about a dancer's life or ask a dancer out on a date, for example, the creation of the *possibility* of an outside relationship is often more desirable than a real encounter (Frank 1998). Most of the married customers claimed that they were not interested in leaving their wife, and even the men who described their job as "boring," "unfulfilling," or even "intolerable" seemed to have no intention of changing these circumstances. Some men seemed to especially enjoy hearing "hard-luck stories" from the dancers, and seeing other people, customers or dancers, in a state of "extreme desperation" (Alex's description) could serve to make these everyday situations even more appealing.

Part of the reason this distinctiveness from work and home was experienced as relaxing was related to the different kind of relationships that could be developed with women in the clubs. For these customers, everyday relationships with women often were seen as a source of pressure and expectations. Indeed, many men I spoke with described relations between women and men in general in the United States as being "strained," "confused," or "tense." Beck, for example, felt that there was a "chasm" between men and women in modern society in terms of understanding and expectations, and Kenneth referred to the "war between the sexes." Over half of the men I interviewed said that they found the clubs relaxing specifically because they provided an escape from the rules of conduct and the social games involved in entering into interactions with other women in an unregulated setting. If "dating is the institutionalization of romantic encounters without the goal of commitment" (Illouz 1997: 289), relationships formed in strip clubs take this institutionalization a step further: there is no longer a need for pretenses, specific social niceties, elaborate plans, mutual exchanges of personal information, and so on. There is really even no need for romance—romantic props can be used to set a scene or to individualize an interaction, but are not necessary to move the encounter to a sexualized level (involving nudity, erotic conversation, the sharing of fantasies, etc.). At the same time, the encounters were to some extent "predictable." Phillip called his interactions with dancers "relationships of convenience," explaining that he worked so much he could never find the time to meet women outside of the clubs and move through the expected steps of courtship. In a way, the interactions available in the clubs fit perfectly with the sped-up pace of consumption more generally in contemporary late capitalist societies.

Even a simple conversation with a woman in a singles bar or at another location had its own set of rules and expectations that were sometimes experienced by these men as stressful:

> I don't go to a strip club to pick up a woman. This is a way to go be with women, talk to women, even see them naked and not have to worry about playing the social game that is involved if you are trying to pick somebody up. (Matthew)

> For me the club situation is almost a way to relax from the tension of a sexual relationship with a woman. You leave when you want. You don't have to stay. You don't have to get to know the person. (Jim)

As Herb pointed out: "I know why you're there. You know why I'm there." Ross claimed that although he himself did not enjoy the imper-

sonal aspect of the encounters in the clubs, he felt that this was important to many men: "What do the men get out of it? Actually, the advantage of being able to walk away. No mess, no fuss, no big deal. You can
make as much or as little emotional involvement as you want. You can
go in there and shop for a piece of meat, quote unquote, so to speak. I
mean, you want to see a girl, you can see a girl run around naked. Have
her come over, pay her to do a dance or two or three and walk away and
not even ask her her name. Total distancing. Boy . . . I hate to even think
of being able to think like that but you know, I see a lot of people that
way." Soon after he made the above statement, however, he said that he
enjoyed the "female presence without pressure" himself.

Other men discussed their desire to look at women on the street and
their feelings of guilt and frustration about doing so. Saul said that although he still felt slightly uncomfortable looking at dancers in strip
clubs, he considered this preferable to his other options: "I guess I consider [strip clubs] very safe. I would never want to be walking along Main
Street looking at some girl and staring at her and making her feel uneasy.
You know, I don't want anybody to feel creepy or anything. Sure, because I wouldn't want to be a woman where I was on the other shore."
Gary and Paul, both men who described themselves as voyeurs, felt
similarly, saying that they had been called "perverts" by women outside
of the club. "I've undressed girls [with my eyes] from day one," Gary
argued, "so this way, I get to see the final product." He called his voyeurism "a total secret thing," because he knew "for a fact" that he would not
find support with his live-in girlfriend. He had sought psychological help
for his voyeurism and tried several antidepressant drugs that had been
recommended to him by his doctors, yet still desired to visit the clubs.

Interactions with women in the workplace were also often felt to be
constraining. Phillip said that club visits "let frustration out": "With all
of this sexual harassment stuff going around these days, men need
somewhere to go where they can say and act like they want. The worst
that can happen to you is you get thrown out . . . I think that going to a
club is a release." Roger said that in the clubs, "everybody knows what
the rules are." This implies that there are other spaces where the rules
are not so transparent, where the men do not understand exactly what
is going to get them into trouble. Frank pointed out that in the workplace he felt nervous about giving compliments to women for fear that
they would accuse him of sexual harassment:

I think the whole sexual harassment issue is absolutely nuts. I think . . . the pendulum has swung so far the other way . . . they've taken common sense out of it. If I work with you, I should be able to say "You look nice today" without having some separate connotation to that. To say, you know, "That color looks really good on you" is not harassment. To say, "That color really shows off your body," that's a different context. But we've taken all that to be taboo, you know. We've taken all that to be wrong and it's not. Or to put my hand on your shoulder when I'm talking to you or on your arm. That's not harassment because I would do that to a guy . . . I'll go like this if I wanted to make a point . . . but all of a sudden if I do that to you, if I'm standing behind you and I touch you on the shoulder or the arm, it's like, wow. So I think that's gone way overboard and I think it's made males very bitter. That side of it. It's taken some personal side out of it and it's made it [work] a very sterile environment.

Some men, like Gary, explicitly stated a desire to interact with women who were not "feminist" and who still wanted to interact with men in what he felt were more "traditional" ways.

This sentiment was frequently corroborated by other customers I interacted with in the clubs who said that men had to continually "be on guard" against offending women in their everyday lives. Here I do not wish to defend male inability to respect women's demands for comfortable work environments. Indeed, several of the above comments could be analyzed as part of a "backlash" against feminism. Rather, I am highlighting the fact that these men experienced their visits to the clubs (and also, in part, justified them) within such a framework of confusion and frustration rather than simply one of privilege or domination. The rapid increase in the number of strip clubs across the United States in the mid-1980s, after all, was coterminous with a massive increase of women into the workforce and an upsurge of attention paid to issues of sexual harassment, date rape, and the condemnation of the sex industry.

Many of the men I spoke with also discussed their confusion as to what was expected of them as men in relationships with women. Tim said that he felt men were under a good deal of "strain" because wives were also working nowadays, bringing in their own income and thus insisting that they be allowed to take an active part in planning the couple's future: "She's not taking a back seat to decisions about careers and moves, and I think that a lot of men have a hard time dealing with that." Other men complained that they were expected to be strong and assertive, both at home and in their workplace, but at the same time their female partner was interested in greater communication and emotional expression. Joe summed this up very succinctly: "My wife expects me to be strong emotionally, physically, and I expect spiritually too . . . But emotionally, she wants me to be strong but she doesn't want me to be overbearing. Okay? She wants me to cry and be sensitive . . . to be the leader and the rock . . . I'm confused as hell. I wouldn't say that openly in public but I'm definitely confused about what it is to be a man." Zachary, Eric, Kenneth, and Jason made nearly identical comments. Strip clubs offered a temporary respite from both changing definitions of masculinity and requests from women for either instrumental support or reciprocal emotional communication. Beck, for example, described the strip clubs that he visited as places where he felt he was going to be treated "like family" without having to meet any demands or expectations. Some customers even sought advice from dancers on how to negotiate relationships with women outside of the club.

The home, then, was seen as a different sphere with its own set of obligations, commitments, and conflicts. Certainly, the men received a great deal of enjoyment from their family and almost all were adamant that they did not want to change the structure of their private life. The home, however, among these interviewees and for many other men I interacted with, was not necessarily a "haven" from the workplace (Lasch 1977), where the men could simply relax and be themselves. I do not want to imply that somehow a more authentic self was being expressed in the strip club than in the workplace or at home. Rather, a man might have multiple selves, or self-representations, that are experienced in different contexts. Certain self-representations, for example, are expressed in work and marriage, and for many men it is these self-representations that are first invoked to identify themselves. These selves, however, were also often premised on responsibilities and commitments.

Changing expectations about male economic providership and emotional communication in committed relationships may have contributed to some men's experiences of stress and confusion about their gender identity and roles (Levant and Brooks 1997). Arguably, these changes and sentiments may be most intense in the middle classes;

however, nearly all of the men I interviewed identified as such. Some researchers point to what has been called a "crisis in masculinity," which has developed as a "result of the collapse of the basic pattern by which men have traditionally fulfilled the code for masculine role behavior—the good provider role" (9). Such a breakdown of the traditional masculine code has led to situations in which former patterns of success in relationships and work roles are no longer socially elevated. Instead of positing such a crisis in masculine identity arising in different historical situations, Gail Bederman (1995) refers to the circulation of contradictory discourses of hegemonic masculinity. I prefer this approach, as it allows for the existence of contradictions and inconsistencies within each individual's identity and for the recognition that there are always several competing hegemonic discourses of gender identity in relation to which individuals must position themselves. In such cases of competing expectations, a man might find it relaxing to be in an environment such as a strip club, where he does not necessarily have any role to perform except for that of a desiring male (discussed in more depth in Chapter 4).[6] Because the interactions in a strip club (through the gendered performances of both parties) spoke to a male self-representation that was not involved with family or work responsibilities and commitments, the club became an ideal space for some men to access a fantasy of freedom, independence, and idealized masculinity.

The transactions that occur in strip clubs should not be seen as merely providing an escape *from* responsibilities and commitments. As I have argued elsewhere (Frank 1998) and as I discuss in the next sections, some men were also actively seeking an escape *to* a kind of interaction with women that was not available to them in their everyday life. It would also be a mistake to assert that such interactions are only compensatory, whether for the men's alienation as producers or because of an inability to develop intimate relationships with other women. As Andrew Ross points out, such an assertion sees a consumer's pleasure as "organized between, on the one hand, a restricted economy of frustration and oppression, and, on the other, the unlimited utopian haven of fantasy." Such an approach "does not wholly account for the autonomous pleasure offered by the very act of fantasizing, nor does it account for the production of users' fantasies that are neither wholly determined nor neutralized by the form of the containing narrative." Individuals do have independently empowering experiences of fantasy that offer "real satisfactions, and not merely displaced or symbolic solutions to frustrations felt elsewhere" (1989: 206). As emerges in other chapters, the erotics that underlie the men's visits are far more complex than an analysis of compensatory leisure would suggest.

Safety and Excitement

Strip clubs derive some of their appeal from their ability to be both safe and exciting spaces, and when the tension between these boundaries disappears, men may cease to be regular customers. Many of the interviewees discussed their experiences in the language of "variety," "travel," "fun," "escape," and "adventure."[7] One man consistently described himself as a "pioneer," pointing out that he always visited new clubs in Laurelton on their opening night and sought out strip clubs whenever he passed through a new city. Many of the men I spoke with enjoyed sharing tales of their travels to strip clubs in other cities and states: "I could tell stories about the places I've been to for hours," Dan told me and proceeded to do so. Mick told me several stories about the overt sexual activity that he witnessed in clubs in Canada; David discussed the kind of dancing that was done in South Carolina ("They rub their tootie on you . . . it's different there") and the indiscretions that he believed occurred in lower-tier clubs in Laurelton and other cities; Steven and William told descriptive tales of visiting clubs in Florida and Texas. Others, such as Beck, Jim, and Phillip, were interested in keeping an internal checklist of sites they had visited: "I've visited every strip joint in the city"; "If the door is open, I'll go in"; "I've been everywhere in Laurelton." Gary took me on a guided tour of several of his "favorite" clubs during the early phases of my research in Laurelton, discussing the history of the various places and the changes that had taken place over time due to management turnovers, new county regulations, and economic fluctuations. New strip clubs were sometimes referred to as "discoveries," and the men talked about "searching out new places."

Other men described themselves as "hunters," "adventurers," or "explorers." Nick said that strip clubs provided "adventure" and "excitement" to balance out the more mundane "compartments" of his life such as work and home and that such sexualized ventures "make life worth living." Using similar metaphors, Jay Bildstein, the entrepreneur who opened the upscale strip club Scores in New York City, writes of his first experience at an upscale gentlemen's club with a friend of his: "I felt like an adventurer who had just met a grueling challenge. Larry and I were the Sir Edmund Hillary and Admiral Richard Byrd of the gentlemen's club business. Not that a night in Rick's Cabaret was exactly the challenge of a night on the icy slope of Mount Everest, but no man's goal is less important than another's" (1996: 90). Alex also spoke of his visits to strip clubs in terms of extreme masculinized adventure. When I asked him why he went to strip clubs, he answered:

> *Alex:* I like to do bizarre things, you know . . . Wild, crazy stuff. It's like . . . I guess kind of like rock climbing. You know, you've got guys that'll rappel and you've got guys that'll go off the mountain head first.
>
> *KF:* What were some of the extreme types of things you found in strip clubs?
>
> *Alex:* Well, some of the extreme things were like the happy stuff, just the partying and all that. On the other hand, you know, there was a lot of extreme desperation and a lot of loneliness and sadness there. It's just wild, I guess. I don't know if it would be a very good analogy to just call it, you know, getting on the back of a Harley Davidson, you know . . . getting on a Harley Davidson with a shotgun in your hand . . . because there's not any rules, you know?

Despite descriptions of strip clubs as places with "no rules" and as "outside the law," and although customers experience and express feelings of freedom, adventure, or excitement during their excursions to strip clubs, they are actually passing over ground that has been tightly regulated to produce this particular kind of experience. The city has delineated where such clubs can be located and (for the most part) what types of interactions can be had inside. Bouncers physically monitor and control the men's behavior inside the clubs. Other kinds of behaviors are policed by both the dancers and the other customers, such as proper etiquette in regard to watching table dances, tipping procedures, and customer-to-customer interactions. The men also police their own behavior; few bachelors really need their hands to be tied behind a chair during a table dance, and even men who claim to be wild with desire or testosterone are usually found sitting docilely in their chairs. Some of the men's talk about safety, then, can be seen as a derivative of both restrictive interventions on the part of the law and the club and the employees' and their own expectations and boundaries. Their talk about danger and adventure, on the other hand, is connected to historical discourses about masculinity, travel, and encounters with various categories of Others that must be further explored.

Public spaces have long been occupied by men in the cultural imaginary, and although this is changing, the gendered split between public and private spaces is important in thinking about how discourses of travel have been masculinized over time. Indeed, as Eeva Jokinen and Soile Veijola point out, the sociological figures of the tourist, the flâneur, the stranger, and the adventurer are also implicitly masculine metaphors for particular kinds of subjectivities. They describe the nineteenth-century flâneur, or stroller, as the "forerunner of the twentieth century tourist," one who is emblematic of "being seen and recorded and seeing others and recording them." This strolling pedestrian "poetically confronts the 'dark corners' of a town or city, occupied by the dispossessed and the marginal, and experiences supposedly real authentic life" (1997: 26). These spaces in the fast-growing cities were assumed to be dangerous as well as authentic because of their connection with promiscuity, contagion, and contamination. Women who moved about in public spaces and in "dark corners," especially those of different social classes and races, were part of the experience. As Rojek and Urry write: "Some (men) . . . sought out the touch and feel of the other through crossing to the dark side of the city and engaging with the diverse charms of prostitutes, opium dens, bars, and taverns. This was known as 'slumming.' Underprivileged areas and crimogenic zones came to be redefined as tourist sights" (1997: 7). The connection of slumming with privilege means that the figure of the flâneur is also often racialized and classed as well as gendered.

For many customers, the fact that visits to strip clubs often implied a journey into "bad" areas of town was seen as risky and dangerous but also exciting, a form of erotic slumming. Alex said that strip clubs were appealing because they "had that sinister type feel . . . you know, the whole place is just kind of like dark and there's an underground there." He thought I was "very brave" for conducting interviews with the customers, and also admitted that he had fantasized that by meeting me, the "worst-case scenario" would be that "she drugs me and steals all my money." Saul preferred visiting "dive" bars that were located in "seedy areas of town." At the same time, however, he also worried about crime and "getting rolled in the parking lot." For Saul this danger (often fantasized, given the high security of most Laurelton clubs) was an important part of his excursions. Even though we met for our initial interview in a popular coffee shop, for example, he also said that he had been worried about showing up for our meeting. "Who knows?" he said. "I've heard of men being robbed and killed this way." (*At Starbucks?* I was tempted to ask.) He continued: "You never know by looking at somebody . . . I mean, I would never know if you were . . . you know, if you were, like a crack dealer, you know? Or like living day to day? Or somebody that's going to school for your future. When you said you were going for your doctorate, that shocked me." Yet despite his spoken fears, he showed up on time and participated enthusiastically in the interviews. Further, I continued to see him around town occasionally at the various clubs in which I worked.

Mick also enjoyed the idea of strip clubs as marginal places, "on the edge" and somewhat dangerous. He said he even enjoyed the minor fights that occurred among customers in the clubs. In fact, the night that we met at Diamond Dolls he had been influential in helping the bouncers kick out a drunk and rowdy customer who had grabbed at a dancer onstage. After I helped the dancer into the dressing room, Mick called me over to talk excitedly about the incident, as we had both been next to the stage when it happened. During our first interview a few days later, he talked about other altercations he had been in:

> In Texas, Al and I were in a club and Magic Johnson had just left . . . it was one of those clubs, you know, kind of high rollers and some guy spilled my drink and I said a little something to him and he said something back and so we got in a fight. And then there's one in Washington, D.C., where these couple of guys and a couple bouncers got in another fight and I got involved in it. Threw a guy across the tables and that's . . . they're kind of rowdy but the people don't carry guns. So that's a little bit of wild edge . . . you know, you get in a fight and you probably won't get shot. I used to box and maybe most guys wouldn't like that part of it but that's part of the thrill for me. I like to jump in a fight.

The fight was important, but appealing because in this situation it was relatively safe ("you probably won't get shot"). Mick mentioned safety several other times, especially when talking about the risk of disease possible with other forms of adult entertainment, and tended to prefer the more upscale places to the dive bars (the kind of club where a multimillionaire like Magic Johnson just might hang out).

Significantly, then, although strip clubs are relatively safe, they are also *dangerous enough* to be alluring, a bit "less civilized" and rowdier than the places these middle-class customers would ordinarily enter. The importance of race in structuring such fantasies was also quite apparent and was expressed by white customers in worries about visiting the primarily black clubs because of the "aggressive" nature of black dancers, the "rough crowds," and the more "graphic displays" that supposedly were found there. In the end, most men said that they preferred visiting places that were "comfortable" as well as marginal.

Ross said that his visits were exciting because they were "still taboo" and because "good boys don't do that." On the other hand, he also claimed to be interested in how these "other" people lived: "I am sincerely interested in people, in their lives, and I just like to know about everything. I'm kind of omnivorous. I like, you know, to know how other people see this crazy world we're in." He was interested in hearing about the dancers' lives and talking to them about anything, just as he would "talk to drunks on the street." Other men spoke similarly; in fact, many of the more educated men cited a sociological interest in the lives of the women. These customers seemed confident that one could ascertain what a dancer was thinking or feeling simply by observing her performances in the club or by talking to her while she was at work (something that, unfortunately, some researchers also believe is possible). These kinds of comments about taking an academic interest in illicit venues make explicit a connection that is often implicit—between the privileged, roving observer in the form of the flâneur and the social scientist or academic voyeur collecting raw data from marginalized or stigmatized populations, mingling with those who renounce social taboos, all in the name of scientific interest. The legitimacy of research is expected to preserve the boundaries between us and them, between those who are just slumming and those who are full-time residents. That I had crossed this boundary by actually working as a stripper has been extremely upsetting to some scholars that I have encountered, as well as to some of the customers I interacted with and men I interviewed.

The customers often imagined the dancers as living outside of normative social constraints, enjoying immense "sexual freedoms" and a kind of "wild sexuality." The men's ideas about just what it would take to dance naked seemed to bolster this belief that dancers enjoyed a wild, uninhibited sexuality and dancers were also described as brave and adventurous. Jim said, "I think, from the dancer's perspective, it's just like an existence on the edge." (Though Jim several times discussed the "dancer's perspective" during our interviews, he admitted that I was the only dancer he had ever even spoken to more than once.) Male customers also sometimes identified with dancers' perceived sexual freedom. There was constant speculation about the dancers' sex lives and orientations (How many of the dancers are lesbians? Do they sleep with customers? Are they wild in bed?). Even despite our assertions to the contrary, many of the men wanted to believe that we led an exciting and varied sex life and that our choice of workplace was simply to continue this trend. (This was also something that dancers frequently laughed about backstage as we headed to the library to study for the next day's classes or changed into sweat pants and headed home to sleep.)

Some customers projected their anxieties about nudity or exposure onto the women in the clubs. I was frequently asked if I was scared to work in strip clubs, or if I felt the work was dangerous, physically or emotionally. "It must be difficult to take off your clothes in front of people," customers would say. Ross admitted that it was a "fantasy" of his to expose his naked body to the gaze and that the thought was "terrifying." Customers were not usually excited to hear dancers' explanations that nudity was a costume, or that once you've traveled abroad and realized that Americans have some bizarre ideas about the body, stripping becomes just another form of work. Instead, as discussed in later chapters, it was often far more profitable for dancers to agree with the customers' assessments: "Oh yes, I was terrified when I started, and I'm still fairly nervous being naked in front of strangers"; or "I'm an exhibitionist and dancing turns me on"; and so on. When customers talked to me about their experiences with dancers, these kinds of quotes were often offered as proof of dancers' psyches. This is not to imply that these answers did not feel truthful to some of the dancers the men interacted with, some of the time. Rather, these examples are provided to explore how certain kinds of claims became meaningful and exciting for the *customers*.

Excursions into the sex industry are related not only to the allure of bad or dangerous areas of town, or of the individuals who populate those "dark corners," but also to the adventure of sexual discovery. Sexual experiences (not necessarily heterosexual, of course), coupled with travel away from the safety of home, have often been portrayed as a form of masculinized adventure; one only needs to think of Henry Miller, the adventures of Don Juan, stories about Charles Bukowski or Jack Kerouac. For the sociologist Georg Simmel, "the perfect adventure was an amorous one" (in Jokinen and Veijola 1997: 30). Many of the men I spoke with agreed with this idea, even though they were not pursuing sexual contact or release. Steven said:

> Kate, what a guy gets in a men's club, he doesn't get at home any more. My experience was, the first three to six months of every relationship was just outrageous. For many guys, it was almost the quest of meeting and building that trust and building that rapport, to the point where you could bond enough to have sex and whether that happened in one night or it took three months, it's all that excitement leading up and then the exploring and getting to know what you like and what I like . . . So what's happening out there at the men's clubs, as I sit and watch these guys, they're trying to recapture what's not there in their marriage anymore. And just in watching these guys who are so involved in the fantasy that they believe, like I said, that I love you and you're loving me back . . . that, in the back of their minds there's that hope of hopes that maybe I'm gonna ignite another spark again in my life . . . those first days and weeks and months, that unknown, that discovery, that's very exciting. And I think that's part of the attraction of a men's club . . . is that same thing is happening shy of the conquer.

Almost across the board, I found that the men who *preferred* strip clubs and became regular customers often did not claim to visit other venues of the sex industry. For example, although some of the interviewees admitted to periodically reading *Playboy* or renting pornographic videos, such practices were not as significant or enjoyable to them as their experiences in strip clubs. None of the interviewees admitted to regularly using escort services, prostitutes, or massage parlors, nor did many of the men I interacted with on a daily basis in the strip clubs. Several of the interviewees discussed past experiences with prostitutes, yet they did so as experiences that were riddled with much more ambiguity, distaste, or guilt than their visits to strip clubs and none considered this a practice they were likely to take up again.

This may be in part an American phenomenon, related to particular ideas about marriage, monogamy, and consumption, as the boundaries between different venues appear less rigid in many other countries, with stripping becoming blurred with prostitution or with customers alternately visiting venues that offer sexualized conversation, manual or oral release, or actual sex (e.g., Allison 1994; Bishop 1998; Chapkis 1997). This is not to naively claim that the boundaries are never blurred in American venues (especially with regard to lap dancing clubs) or that some American men do not find it exciting to move from one type of venue or service to another; just to point out that there was an identifiable pattern of consumption among men who considered themselves strip club regulars. One realm in which these men claimed that strip clubs provided safety was in relation to marriages or long-term partnerships. Granted, different ideas about the requirement of sexual exclusivity in marriage and relationships exist among individuals in the United States. Regardless of any individual's personal views or practices, however, the predominant representation of marriage is that of lifetime (or, increasingly, serial) monogamy, and one must usually position oneself in relation to this representation. Different men draw their lines in different places as to how far they can explore their desire for others without being unfaithful to their wife or partner. For some men, for example, pornography may be upsetting; for others, it is an unquestioned part of their sexual repertoire. Sites that offer the possibility of live interaction, on-site masturbation, or varying degrees of sexual contact with a woman occupy different slots on a continuum of commodified sexual behavior.[8]

For many of my interviewees, "looking" was the final limit at which they felt comfortable. As strip clubs in most cities in the United States are a legal venue in which no overt sexual acts are supposed to take place, they were thus seen by many of these men as supportive of heterosexual monogamy (though pushing at its borders). Whereas visiting a prostitute, a massage parlor, or a "jack shack" is certainly relaxing for *some* men, it caused conflicts for these *particular* men.[9] The strip club, then, was relaxing because it provided a safe space in which to be both married (or committed) and sexually aroused (or, at least, interacting with other women in a sexualized setting; see Chapter 7). As Beck said, "There's a certain point you just don't want to go past if you want to maintain a marriage." Jim said that he often felt guilty because of the influence of his wife's Roman Catholic beliefs on his own conscience. At the same time, however, the fact that he had to "sneak" around to visit the clubs gave him a thrill. "Stolen watermelons taste better than the ones you buy," he said. He did not believe that his "thoughts and fantasies about breaking a covenant" were the same thing as doing so, however, and he considered himself "faithful" in his twenty-three-year marriage. Similarly, other men said:

> When I'm on the road I know that when I go into a men's club that it's a safe place—from the standpoint of, let's call it, the marriage vows! The temptations are not there for me. They're zero in a men's club . . . I am able to understand that it's entertainment and social interaction. (Steven)

> If you go to a strip club it's safe. Okay? I know why you're there. You know why I'm there, for the most part . . . I have reality at home so I'm going back to that. (Herb)

William said that he got "in more trouble in singles bars than in strip clubs"—trouble not only with his partner, but with himself.

Of course, as strip clubs vary around the country, customers cannot always be certain of the kinds of interactions they will be involved in. My experience in the industry has led me to believe that although men certainly do become accustomed to the services that are offered in their own locale (men who frequented lap dancing clubs in Tampa or San Francisco, for example, often expressed disappointment in the limited interactions available in the Laurelton clubs), there are also many men who set limits to the kinds of commodified sexual contacts that they find acceptable. As Mick said about the dancing in Laurelton, "It's related to it, but not real sex . . . that's why it's okay." What each man defined as "real sex" varied, of course (President Clinton was certainly not alone in his definitions), as did their reasons for not desiring more contact.

When discussing their experiences, several of the interviewees told stories about strip clubs in other cities where they were groped by the dancers or were encouraged to touch the dancers' bodies. William told a story about his discomfort in a club in a city where he and a friend were offered sex by a female employee: "All we could think about was how to get out of there." Steven admitted that he was "no angel," but that a dancer who was too forward or sexually aggressive made him uncomfortable because of his commitments. Mick, Louis, and Dan, (among others) mentioned that a worry about "health concerns" inhibited their enjoyment of greater contact, in addition to concerns about monogamy. Sometimes, even men who were not married or in monogamous relationships preferred that the amount of contact be kept minimal because of fears of AIDS and other sexually transmitted diseases; David, Jason, and Phillip (all single at the time of the interviews) also mentioned that strip clubs that offered lap dancing were not places they enjoyed the most because of the "excessive" contact. David claimed that he even stayed away from lowest-tier clubs because the table dances tended to involve too much contact and overly graphic sexual display. Some men, such as Ross, had a general dislike of commodified sexual contact, and others, such as Tim, had legal concerns. "Maybe in another country I would go for a different kind of entertainment," Tim said, as he was extremely wary of visiting massage parlors or approaching prostitutes in the United States. Though the customers' spoken reasons for discomfort with other kinds of sexualized service were certainly varied—commitments, worries about sexually transmitted diseases, ambivalence about commercialized sexual activities, legal concerns, and so on—the point is that this kind of no-contact strip club offered the customers a "safe" space in which this discomfort was eased.

Personal and Sexual Acceptance / Identity

All of the men I interviewed noted that the interactive nature of the encounters they had in strip clubs was a significant and pleasurable part of the experience, stressing that they especially enjoyed the conversation they could have with the dancers. Certainly, this claim could be dismissed as the men's attempt to justify a sometimes inflammatory practice or defray masturbatory guilt (as when men say they read *Playboy* "for the articles"). However, I believe that the conversations were indeed significant to a large number of customers beyond being a way to legitimate their visits—after all, I was a participant in thousands of these transactions. The men's enjoyment may or may not have been influenced by the *content* of the conversations; for some men, just talking to a beautiful woman about anything was considered to be a pleasure, a luxury. As Beck said, the moment he had some free time "the first place I'd be interested in going to would be someplace where I could talk to a beautiful woman." Jim said that he went to the clubs to have "an idealized social interaction with gorgeous women." Clubs offered an opportunity to talk to women with whom these men generally would not be able to interact, for any number of reasons: a lack of attractiveness, age differences, class differences, proximity, and the women's willingness to interact, for example.

Sometimes, the conversation was valued because it was a kind of interaction that the men felt they had difficulty finding elsewhere, especially in male-dominated workplaces. For a variety of reasons, these men felt that women provided conversation in ways that were significantly different from men:

> Sometimes I go there just to talk because I feel like I can talk to somebody there without any rules. There's no boundaries. I don't necessarily have to talk about sex but I can go there and just talk about anything and sometimes that's kind of nice. You know? It's almost like therapy. You're not there to judge me. (Joe)

> You can open up to women. Women speak. Men don't. Men just—they don't know what their emotions are. How are you doing? Good. Oh really? Come on, I can't take all that information. Come on, say something. You're here, communicate! And it's sad . . . I watched this show the other day and these three guys were driving somewhere and they started to talk intimately. And they couldn't do it . . . this one guy's talking about um . . . how uh . . . he's quick in the sack. And they were trying to console him, they were like, oh, everybody's like that once in a while. "Oh good, it's finally off my chest," you know. And then one of them made a joke about it . . . but that's what men do. Men'll kid about it, you know? But women'll actually listen. Go, "Oh, that's a shame. Well, did you try this?" Men, never. That ego's just too big. Too fragile. (Brett)

Roger said that his male friends were good to talk to about "sports, women, or work," but that he felt more engaged with women in conversation about other things. Similarly, Frank said that he did not engage in a "whole lot of real conversation" with his coworkers and that this is what he sought at strip clubs. He liked to talk about everyday things with the dancers: "About things we have in common, or your husband or wife or kids or whatever." Steven and Matthew pointed out that when they were traveling on business they would usually prefer to have a good conversation with a woman than sit alone in their hotel room. Sociologist Stacey Oliker suggests a possible nonsexual motive for infidelity on the part of men: as men less often develop intimate friendships with other men, sexual affairs with women may be the only route to intimacy that they feel they have (1989: 57). Indeed, strip clubs can be seen as offering similar kinds of releases and connections, without the entanglements, obligations, and repercussions of an affair.

Though the men may have valued the conversation, however, this is not to say that this conversation was always or necessarily based on mutual disclosure or engagement. As a dancer, for example, I often found myself censoring opinions and conversing on topics of interest only to the customers. Further, the customers could still maintain a sense of control over the situation as long as they paid for the dancer's time: how long the conversation would last, what would be discussed, and whether the dancer took off her clothes during the interaction. There was certainly an unspoken understanding that if a dancer was not pleasing, she would not be paid (unless this was a situation being sought after by that individual for a personal reason). Granted, any dancer could walk away from a customer or group if she did not want to engage in a given interaction or found it offensive. Given the sheer number of dancers in each club, however, there was usually someone else willing to take her place, if only for the money.

Some men noted that the interactions they purchased in strip clubs were an ego boost because they provided safe opportunities for close interactions with women without the risk of rejection. Sexuality and sexual conquest, after all, can be experienced as humiliating and stressful for men as well as thrilling. Men with physical disabilities were frequent visitors to the clubs and appreciated the female companionship that was available to them there.[10] Even men who are not impotent, disabled, or unattractive, however, may feel very insecure in interactions with women. Although the desire for an ego boost was almost never the first motivation that men mentioned, it eventually arose in many of the interviews and conversations:

> I guess it is kind of an ego thing too . . . if I haven't been feeling that great about myself and I go in there it doesn't matter if it's real or not, but after a while, it gets in your head, in your memory. (Jason)

You're massaging the man's ego . . . that's what it boils down to. It makes
the man feel good about himself. It's an ego massage . . . giving him the
drinks he wants, the food he wants, the massage he wants, you know,
whatever it takes. (Ross)

There's no way you're going to go in [the strip club] and get the cold
shoulder, that's for sure. It's just absolutely an ego trip because you
go in there and if you're a warthog, bald, and got a pot belly, some
good-looking girl's going to come up and go, "Hey, do you want me to
dance for you?" Seducing women is something all men wish they were
better at, you know? And this seems like you're doing it and it's easy!
(Roger)

David described his visits to a strip club during a failing marriage as
"good for my ego to build me up, to make me feel like I was a man
again." Thus customers were at times seeking an Otherness within
themselves, a sense of escape from those aspects of the self that felt
oppressive in other spheres—old age, ugliness, a lack of social skills, or
intimate failures.

In *The Male Body,* Susan Bordo discusses male anxiety about female
attractiveness and argues: "Just as the beautiful bodies [in cultural repre-
sentations] subject us to women to (generally) unrealizable models of
the kind of female we must *become* in order to be worthy of attention
and love, they also subject men and boys to (generally) unrealizable
models of the kind of female they must *win*—with equally destructive
consequences" (1999: 285). Though most heterosexual men settle for
"inferior fixes," women who may be attractive but do not quite succeed
in approximating the ideal, many men still "remain haunted by the
beauties" (287). Images of female perfection thus "not only shape perception, they also shape sexual desire," and "straight male sexuality is
honed on the images, even fixated on them" (287). That some men
perceive female beauty as being powerful, able to "invade male consciousness and arouse desire and then to reject that desire, leaving the
man humiliated, shamed, frustrated," she argues, may lead some of
them to seek both solace and excitement in pornography (290). In strip
clubs, the "beauties" are there as a live fantasy—young, available, interested, and accepting.

These customers were keenly aware of the fact that competition
among men, not just male bonding, often centered on the struggle to

gain attention from women as well, and they welcomed the opportunity to avoid it:

> Masculinity was the size of your dick and whoever was able to get girlfriends in high school. It was very competitive. And it's interesting, since I was significantly unsuccessful in my quest to be a teenage stud. [With] girlfriends, that is. It was easy to get the sluts. That might have some association today. I can't function in a real bar. I can't pick up a woman. [In the clubs] the pressure's off. I have to be accepted. (Gary)

> I don't get excited about going to your local bars and, you know, just trying to pick up chicks and be the cool suave dude at the bar. I don't like using the lines and I think the competitive nature of that is just sort of silly to me. The girls at the strip joints might be there not only to talk to, they're there because they're working. They have a reason to be there. There's financial considerations pushing that and they'll talk to you whether you're black, you're big, you're fat, you're small, you're forty-six or you're twenty-four. (David)

Conversation took very different forms when it was with a group of men rather than an interaction between a single man and a dancer. With large groups, I found that the talk was often more demeaning of the dancer, her body, or women in general or more sexualized; indeed, the talk became part of this competition at times and this was one of the reasons that many regulars preferred to visit the clubs alone.

Although less directly remarked on than the other motivations, some men were searching not just for personal acceptance of who they are (or fantasize themselves to be) but also for acceptance of their sexual desires. In addition to the customers who enjoyed the everyday conversation about work, current events, their family, or any number of other topics, I also interacted with a number of men who seemed thrilled by the thought of "talking dirty" with a woman about sexual things. When I first began working in strip clubs, I found myself rather frequently telling tales of fictional sexual exploits or verbally creating fantasies for these customers for money.[11] As such conversations and terms are clearly inappropriate between strangers in the everyday world (and even sometimes between lovers), the fact that we could engage in such talk with impunity was relaxing and enjoyable to some.

Male customers also told dancers things they claimed they had never told their wife or lover, usually specific fantasies or experiences that they thought the other women in their life would not appreciate or understand. In this way, my simultaneous positioning as an exotic dancer tremendously benefited my goals as a researcher, as customers told me that they did not feel the need to censor their language or ideas. At times, the desires the customers expressed were simply to look at female anatomy without shame or apology. Many men told me stories about not being allowed to look at their wife's or partner's body this way. Paul, Gary, and Saul all mentioned that they had been made to feel like "perverts" numerous times because of their "voyeuristic" desires to look at women, both at home and on the street.

Other men wanted to express their desires verbally, but not necessarily to act on them. One regular customer was an older married man who considered himself and his wife to be "very Catholic." He enjoyed coming to Diamond Dolls and telling me his sexual fantasies, which he felt he could not share with his wife. His fantasies were fairly standard pornographic fare that I did not personally find upsetting or surprising. Still, he experienced these fantasies as quite deviant and was relieved to find a nonjudgmental ear. At other times, customers had fantasies they wanted to share that had caused extreme reactions in the past from the other women in their life. A man at the Pony Lounge, for example, took me into the VIP room and begged me to anally penetrate him with my high-heeled shoes. When I refused, he became very distraught and told me his wife had left him because she felt that he was a "pervert" because this was what he wanted. Another married man came to the same club several nights in a row, each night offering more money in an attempt to find someone who would have sex with him after work while wearing a strap-on dildo. He told me that he was certain his wife would leave him if he asked her to do so, yet that he still found this fantasy compelling. The dancers may not have accepted his actual offer, and to my knowledge none did, yet the expression of his fantasy did not lead to rejection within the confines of the club and he was provided with information about anal sex in addition to a forum for aural fantasizing.

Many of the customers were also very concerned with seeking women's approval and even enjoyment of the sexual practices they found appealing or the beliefs they held. Certainly, in some cases, the idea that dancers would be more accepting of their sexual fantasies was based on the men's ideas about the ethical inadequacies of women who would dance nude or otherwise work in the sex industry. Joe, for example, said that dancers were less likely to pass judgment than other women because of their stigmatized position: "They're not going to tell you what's right or wrong because here they are, *dancers!*" Gary made several references to dancers as "sluts," the kind of "girls" that he could "get" when other women rejected him. At other times, however, men who were involved in an alternative lifestyle or who had risqué fantasies did not seem to be drawn to dancers by a belief in the dancers' immorality; rather, they genuinely appreciated women who could be open and honest about sex and sexual desire. Swingers[12] sometimes visited the clubs, with or without their partner, as did individuals who had ideas slightly different from the norm about monogamy and heterosexual relationships.

Most of the customers I interacted with did not want to feel as if they were forcing a dancer to do something against her will. Several of the men said that they had left clubs in which they felt the dancers were unhappy or coerced in any way. Charles said, "If the dancers are, or at least appear to be, enjoying the experience, then I will also." Joe said, "It makes it easier to enjoy yourself when you feel like the person is doing it because they want to." Ross told of a "painful" experience when he was the recipient of a new dancer's first, awkward private dance. Though the men usually realized that the women were dancing because of the financial benefits, they did not want to feel as if they were taking advantage of someone or making her feel uncomfortable, and, as mentioned earlier, a belief in the dancer's genuine desire to disrobe in public helped maintain a pleasurable fantasy of sexual transgression.

If there was any effort at all at performing enjoyment on the part of the dancers, however, many customers were readily willing to be convinced, even when there was evidence that the women were financially disadvantaged. There certainly were exceptions, such as Gary, who wanted to see girls who were new to the business and who were especially young, inexperienced, and nervous. There were also men who eroticized the women's poverty, "desperation," or "hard luck." Nevertheless, it would be a mistake to overlook the complexities of the men's desire. In an illuminating passage about pornography, Constance Penley writes: "What's in the hearts of men according to porn? A utopian desire for a world where women aren't socially required to say and believe that they don't like sex as much as men do" (1997: 107). What is in the hearts of men in a strip club? In many instances, a customer would express a desire for women to find him sexually attractive or desirable, along with a desire to have women *want* him to watch. Countless times we were asked, "Does dancing turn you on?" "Are you turned on right now?" Acting turned on, of course, was part of the performance. Certainly, concern about a dancer's enjoyment, and about whether she is "enjoying the experience," can work to alleviate some men's anxiety that might otherwise be directed toward a critique of existing systems of inequality and exploitation in labor markets. Some of this concern, however, may also be seen as a male desire for female sexual freedom, for women's enjoyment of their own body, and for an acceptance of particular male sexual desires and fantasies.[13]

In addition to performing the role of the desiring male, customers also sometimes clearly wanted to be the objects of desire. In an article about men's reactions to women's sexy dressing, Duncan Kennedy writes that some of the male excitement around this practice stems from the fact that "the sexy dresser is doing something that the man would do if he could" (1993: 204). The desire to be looked at with desire and to see another enjoying one's body seemed implicit in many men's experiences and was occasionally made explicit in our conversations. I was constantly asked questions about how it felt to be a dancer, both on the job and in other settings, for instance, and the customers were fascinated with the details of performing. Often the men said things like, "It must be nice to have everybody want you"; "How does it feel to be perfect?"; "Is it fun to be the one up on the pedestal?"; and "I'd trade places with you if I could." The cross-identificatory wishes being expressed in such statements are rooted in complex fantasies of power, exposure, degradation, and idealization, some of which are explored in more depth in the rest of the book.

Customer Anxiety

The men expressed a number of different motivations for their visits to strip clubs; they also experienced a degree of ambivalence about these motivations and about their practices, some of which have been alluded to above. Contrary to the assumptions of writers like Susan Edwards

(1993), who argues that men are straightforwardly seeking power through their use of the sex industry, many men are indeed uneasy about their visits to strip clubs. There are many reasons for this: the cultural shame that often arises for individuals around issues of sex, especially around materials and experiences associated with masturbation (even if masturbation does not actually take place); the social stigma that surrounds the sex industry and its users; moral discomfort, depending on one's religious background and other relationships with women; and political discomfort, given the prominence of certain strands of feminism and ideas about "political correctness" in popular discourse, as well as one's own beliefs about how relationships should be conducted. Some men might also find their desire for commercialized sexual experiences or materials to be an unpleasant compulsion (G. Brooks 1995; Stock 1997). Here we encounter the flipside of the notion that every man is a potential customer: the idea that men who *do* become customers in the sex industry are physically, socially, emotionally, or morally flawed. There is still a forceful stereotype that "sex workers provide sexual relief to society's 'wretched': the old, the unattractive, the unpartnered," instead of to men in a variety of different positions and with varying privileges (Queen 1997b: 130). Some of the interviewees went out of their way to point out to me that their sex life was positive and enjoyable, possibly anticipating and trying to deflect some of this stigma.

Certainly, there are some men who, on some occasions, talk openly and with pride about their visits to strip clubs, perhaps even in a way calculated to make others around them (especially women) uncomfortable. Some visits, such as bachelor parties, are seen as socially legitimate and even as "normal" male behavior. On the other hand, men who visit too often or who talk about using any sector of the sex industry too openly risk censure and ostracism from friends, family, employers, and lovers. Most of the men discussed the need for their visits to be "private entertainment." Alex called his desire not to be seen at the clubs when he visited alone a "healthy paranoia": "Maybe I sound like a hypocrite saying it but I don't mind going to these places, but if I had my choice I wouldn't hang my sign outside, you know. I wouldn't go bragging about it. I wouldn't want somebody I know to drive by and see my truck sitting in the parking lot, you know what I mean? People will have an issue with trusting you or whatever and it puts ideas in people's heads. I keep a low profile." Negative sentiments focus particularly on men who visit strip clubs alone, and for this reason, most of the men I interviewed kept their solitary visits private. Even the men who waltz comfortably through the doors of their favorite strip club several times a week may not wish to disclose this fact to their wife or friends out of fear of angering or upsetting them, being thought of as pathetic, or being taken as a pervert. Gary and Dan had been in relationships that were terminated by the woman because of this behavior.

Even when visiting the clubs for socially sanctioned occasions, the men may not necessarily experience this as a positive exercise of power on a subjective level. Whereas talk about women's bodies is often a means of bonding with other men, it may be laden with conflicting personal emotional meaning. Many men felt guilty, for example, because they knew their wife or girlfriend would disapprove of their visits to strip clubs, even as they enjoyed the male camaraderie and the sexualized nature of the encounters. (The complexities of some of the men's visits to the clubs in terms of their outside relationships and commitments are discussed in more detail in Chapter 7.)

Finally, visits to strip clubs were usually premised on the ability to spend significant amounts of money on tips, private dances, conversations, drinks, and cover charges. Although some men might visit a club and spend only a few dollars on tips, men who desired longer or more personal interactions were expected to pay (sometimes quite a lot) for a dancer's time. Visits to strip clubs, then, could serve both (or either) to enhance a man's feelings of financial power and status—and thus, for some men, feelings of masculinity—and/or to function as reminders of his need for continued (or future) monetary success.

Conflicting conceptions of masculinity interact with ideas of clienthood itself to create anxiety for some male customers. There are times, for example, in which availing oneself of commodified sexual services is seen as a deficit in one's masculinity; that is, having to "pay for it" is demeaning if other men can (presumably) get the same female attention for free. Increasing commodification and concerns about authenticity (a concept further discussed in Chapter 5) are in conflict in consumer cultures more generally as well, intensifying the potential for uneasiness with such transactions. Is a customer just a dupe being tricked out of his money and receiving nothing in return? Becoming and remaining a customer, then, is a complicated process that is rife with ambivalence.

*

Not surprisingly, not a single man I interviewed claimed that he visited strip clubs explicitly out of a desire to exercise power over women. Men have many different motivations for visiting strip clubs that, although related to male social power, clearly complicate this connection as well. Granted, a man buying table dances for his friends or business associates may indeed be expressing a particular gendered form of power, especially if his female coworkers have been excluded. A man who returns to a strip club again and again may indeed have some problems relating to women in his life or have a desire to degrade or dominate the women with whom he interacts in any sphere. But then again, he may not. Instead, he may be looking for any number of other services and consolations. These different motivations influence which arenas male customers choose to visit and which services they seek. Men who visit strip clubs, for example, *often* are doing so with an understanding that they are going to look and to fantasize rather than to participate in a sexual act. The choice of venue, such as a strip club over an escort service, is filtered through regional, religious, cultural, and personal ideas about morality, consumption, and gender. Men's consumption practices in strip clubs are thus premised on a range of desires, such as a desire to publicly display a particular "masculine" self free of obligations and commitments, a desire for "adventure" by mingling with Others who are seen as "wild" or visiting spaces believed to be "dangerous," a desire to feel desirable (at least in fantasy), or a desire to have a *sexualized* interaction with a woman that does not involve the vulnerability of actual sexual activity.

Some of the services and consolations a man may seek in the sex industry, and in strip clubs in particular, are necessary *because* of his privileged position in society. Ideas about stoic masculinity, for example, are idealized in the workplace, and most individuals with powerful positions are expected to mask their emotions. Stoic masculinity often pervades other areas of men's lives, however, and can prevent emotional sharing in male friendships. When a man needs someone to turn to for emotional support, often it is a woman. Many dancers, for example, spend a great deal of their time with regulars discussing the man's wife and family and both his difficulties and joys in relation to them. Many sex workers also frequently joke about really being "therapists" and understand their jobs to be about boosting a man's ego by convincing him that he is desirable, masculine, and successful. As Brett pointed out, male egos are not experienced simply as "big," but also as potentially "fragile."

Unfortunately, there are many times when viewing or encountering the Other is simply a means to assure oneself of the significance of one's own projects, a phenomenon that unfortunately underlies many forms of touristic practice more generally. Customers tended to make sense of their visits by drawing on particular masculine traditions and on dominant cultural ideologies of sex and gender. Though they may visit spaces that pose certain challenges to dominant ideas—places that display public nudity, for example, or in which female sexuality can be expressed almost aggressively—they also move through these spaces with unquestionable privilege and are seldom "marked" by those visits. Further, male practices of consumption in strip clubs, and the sex industry more generally, can also serve to maintain imbalanced power dynamics in personal relationships with women, especially when they are used to shame or anger a wife or partner. These practices may also draw on negative racial stereotypes or on a potentially destructive bifurcation of women into madonnas and whores for their individual or collective erotic charge.

On a microlevel of interaction, the transactions that take place in a strip club may also be intertwined with male privilege. Male power need not necessarily be expressed in physically dominating a woman, and male social dominance can be (and often is) maintained regardless of whether any man actually feels his privilege. As mentioned earlier, simply being in the presence of a beautiful woman who appears to be genuinely interested can boost a man's ego and restore his security in his masculinity.[14] Such a systematic appropriation by men of women's emotional labor can indirectly support male dominance at a societal level (Bartky 1990). Men who visit strip clubs often are not asked to challenge their views; even if a dancer shuns a customer because of his sexist or racist opinions, for example, there will almost always be another woman who will tolerate his views simply for the financial gain. If men do end up questioning their sexuality or their desires, they may look for other forms of entertainment or develop other sexual practices. Certainly, when experiences in the clubs fail for some reason to validate customers' everyday existence, the men may develop a critical lens through which to view their life. There were indeed men whom I met in the clubs who were questioning their heterosexuality or cultural ideologies about gender and relationships. Yet because part of the fantasy sold in strip clubs involves convincing men of the importance of their own projects, these challenges are posed only rarely. When such challenges are posed, and taken seriously, strip clubs may lose their appeal for the customer.

Such an analysis of male privilege should not be seen as discounting women's experiences of empowerment while working in the sex industry. To say that social privileges influence the men's interpretation of their experiences and the meanings of their visits does not mean that dancers do not exercise agency in the transactions in the clubs or are not themselves situated in complex and fluctuating networks of privilege. This is also not to imply that commodified sexual exchanges are *inherently* about the preservation and reproduction of male power. Rather, it is to point out that structural inequalities between men and women and between different classes of laborers, as well as cultural beliefs and expectations and personal understandings of gender, influence the conditions under which such transactions are carried out.

Chapter Four

The Pursuit of the Fantasy Penis:
Bodies, Desires, and Ambiguities

In "The Popularity of Pornography," Andrew Ross argues that getting men to talk about their pleasurable consumption of pornographic materials would tell us "how capitalism's production of marketed pleasure is variously rearticulated through people's own imaginary relations to the daily round of work and leisure," as well as "how people variously respond to the invitation to think of their bodies as a potential source of achieved freedom, rather than a prison house of troublesome bodily functions or a pliant tool for the profitable use of others, whether patriarchs or capitalists" (1989: 207). Chapter 3 interrogated the spoken motivations of the regular male customers and the relation of those motivations to work, leisure, ideas of escape, and discourses of masculinity; this chapter more specifically examines issues that were alluded to in the men's talk about their visits but not always consciously developed: the way sexual arousal, a lack of sexual arousal, or, at times, fantasies of sexual arousal, become a meaningful aspect of visits to strip clubs for some of the customers. Strip clubs obviously are designed to cause bodily responses in their patrons through loud powerful music, colored lights and strobes, the availability of alcoholic beverages, public nudity, the staging and experience of desire, and the possibility of sexual arousal. What is the connection between physicality and the discourses of masculinity discussed in Chapter 3 that are drawn on by the men to make sense of their visits? How are bodily responses to the dancers' performances, or the lack of those responses, experienced and interpreted by the customers? After all, despite all the talk about relaxation, the regular customers' focus on conversation in their interactions with the dancers, the prohibitions against sexual release in the clubs, and the fact that the customers were *not* pursuing sexual activity through their visits, there was still an edge to the encounters they sought and purchased from the female dancers that was very clearly sexual.[1] Further, the visits were still intertwined with the men's understandings of sexuality, and masculinity, more broadly.

This chapter builds on the discussion of touristic practices and masculinity to explore the various bodily experiences, pleasures, and vulnerabilities that emerge through the men's commodified interactions with the dancers. The first section argues against pop-sociobiological understandings of strip clubs as an outgrowth of natural (ahistorical, precultural) aggressive male sexuality as enough of an explanation to make sense of this form of consumer behavior. The second section, however, explores the ways that male customers draw on this pop discourse to explain their visits, even when their own narrated experiences contradicted its fundamental claims about male desire, along with the reasons that such a discourse about natural desire becomes important. The final sections explore issues of gender, sexuality, and power along with the men's own performances of desire, taking up issues of visibility, virility, youthfulness, and commodification.

It's All in the Biology?

At the same time that many theorists point to the socially constructed nature of sexuality (to different degrees, of course), there are still many scientific and popular claims made to both essential differences between the sexes and to the evolutionary underpinnings of modern forms of sexual desire. Though "all but the most radical theorists concede that both nature and nurture shape human behavior" (G. Brooks 1995: 71), in the years that I have been studying sexuality I have found it far more difficult to get people to interrogate the cultural aspects of their experiences than the supposedly natural aspects. I find many of the sociobiological and evolutionary psychological arguments to be of relatively little use in answering the specific questions that interest me theoretically, yet their hold on the popular imagination is so strong that they must be briefly addressed. It should be made absolutely clear, however, that there are many interpretations of and variations in these theories. Sociobiologists, behavioral ecologists, and evolutionary psychologists (all slightly different) cannot be unproblematically homogenized any more than feminists or philosophers can be, and there are numerous points of difference in belief and argument among and within the different camps. As with other kinds of complicated theories, the nuances of many of these arguments can be lost as they work their way into the mainstream press or into television journalism, resulting in an unfortunately simplified *pop*-sociobiological or folk view of human sexuality.

While working on this project, I encountered many individuals who believe quite strongly that there are biological explanations for the attraction of strip clubs, for example, and who argue that an investigation of this particular form of consumption needs to go no further. Men are naturally predisposed to desire variety in women, I was told, and that is why they frequent strip clubs. As males are genetically programmed to spread their seed and produce as many offspring as possible, the argument typically proceeds, they thus have a greater interest in multiple sexual encounters than do women and have greater difficulty being monogamous. Men desire not just variety, however, but also youth and beauty in their female partners. In an academic version of this argument, sociobiologist Donald Symons argues that "human psychological adaptations were shaped over vast periods of time to solve the recurrent information-processing problems that our ancestors faced" (1995: 86). One of those problems was mate choice, he argues, and males have been "selected to be sexually attracted by cues of good health, good design, and developmental stability" in women. Human males have evolved to "selectively detect and respond to certain specific characteristics" in women, many of which are related to age: smooth skin, bilateral symmetry, a low waist-to-hip ratio, and lighter than average skin color, for example. He writes: "Who men actually mate with depends on many things (such as opportunity and risk) in addition to sexual attraction. Few fifty-year-old American men will ever mate, short-term or long-term, with a twenty-year-old woman, but . . . *Playboy* magazine does not need to publish a special edition for older men featuring photographs of older women" (1995: 88).

Strip clubs, with their insistence that women meet certain standards of attractiveness, could thus be seen as merely tapping into these primal needs and desires for both variety and particular kinds of women. It makes sense in evolutionary terms, people have argued to me, using folk versions of these arguments, that men, especially those with an aging wife, would seek out younger, more nubile women, and one place where they are easily found is in the various venues of the sex industry. The customers, then, are acting out of an anachronistic impulse that does not need to end in sexual activity to be pleasurable. Yet, if everything argued by sociobiologists like Symons were true, men who use the sex industry could potentially be the very lowest on the scale of well-adapted humans at this point in time. Strip clubs, after all, are a means of making money for both men and women. Through female (and male) artifice, the customers would be seen as duped into wasting their resources on women with whom they have extremely little chance of actually copulating. As many, many dancers support their children and family through this form of work, male customers would be seen as tricked into supporting other men's offspring. Further, as in many cases actual sexual activity and release is available in close proximity to a strip club—in massage parlors or from prostitutes or escorts, for example—the men who choose to spend their hard-earned resources on voyeurism alone would also be making a foolhardy decision genetically and financially. But the customers were aware of the fact that sexual release would not be offered on the premises, and except in very rare cases, chose these sites from an array of other possibilities. I thus prefer to think that they usually know what they are doing (i.e., spending resources on a woman who is unavailable to them in some ways) and that they are doing, at least in part, what they want to do. Why this is something that is desirable, however, is another question—a *cultural* and *psychological* question.

Why would a fifty-year-old man rather spend his resources on the pictures or on the three-minute-long nude dances of a twenty-year-old woman than on trying to *mate* with one, if that is the ultimate goal or underlying urge? Why not just seek sex with these kinds of partners? If the answer hinges on the immorality or illegality of prostitution, or the desirability of monogamous marriage in the contemporary United States, we have already entered the cultural realm and need to ask further questions to understand differences in behavior. And why are other forms of pornography besides centerfolds popular as well, such as videos of many men having sex with a single woman? Why would men want to watch other *men* have sex with women that they found attractive (or disgusting)? A response to this for those committed to biological explanations might still be: looking at naked women is the next best thing to actually having sex with them; therefore, the men are still exercising their biological or evolutionary imperatives when they visit strip clubs. Yet if men choose the *"next* best thing," we need to begin asking questions about cultural influences (something with which most biologists would agree). How might we explain variation in men: why some men prefer prostitutes, strip clubs, pornography, or a more private looking (or even touching) in a massage parlor or lingerie shop?[2] Or why other men, such as former Mayor Rudolph Giuliani of New York City, spend much of their time trying to eradicate such possibilities altogether?

Another proposed pop-sociobiological answer to men's practices of consumption in strip clubs has been to see such behaviors as related to the effects of sex hormones, particularly testosterone. In 1998, an article in the *New York Times* suggested a connection between strip clubs and testosterone based on a study of rhesus monkeys. When two male monkeys at Yerkes Primate Center in Atlanta competed for status in a contest over a female monkey, the author explained, testosterone levels "rose in the winner and fell dramatically in the loser." When the defeated male saw another sexually receptive female monkey, however, his testosterone levels rose again—even if she was unattainable. One implication of this, pointed out one of the psychologists affiliated with the Yerkes Center, "is that strip bars are popular because male losers can retreat there to raise their testosterone levels" (in Tierney 1998). Despite the somewhat tongue-in-cheek tone of this article, it was quoted to me or alluded to rather frequently during discussions of my research in a variety of different forums. Again, it is important to stress that strip clubs have not always existed in their current form, do not exist everywhere around the world, and do not appeal to all men (or even to all men with low testosterone levels, most likely, though my research does not allow me to make suggestions on this front). Why should strip clubs ever have arisen to meet this need for compensatory testosterone raising, if that is indeed something that they could do, rather than some other, equally arbitrary form of compensatory activity? Even if such a theory could be tested and proven, there would still be numerous questions that would need to be answered.

In *The Centerfold Syndrome,* psychologist Gary Brooks critiques this kind of evolutionary approach to sexual desire on several grounds: that such theories cannot be proven; that they cannot account for change; that evolutionary researchers (and their fans in the general populace) too often and too readily generalize from animals to humans; that these arguments rely on essentialist and universalistic assumptions that do not hold up under careful scrutiny; and that certain behaviors may not be "functional" at all but rather the product of "random genetic events" (1995: 87). Such theories problematically suggest, he argues, that "our tastes, in terms of what 'turns us on,' whether in food or in objects of sexual desire, are a product of our adaptive history" (85). Even for behavioral ecologists, theories about contemporary sexual behavior that rely on ideas of selection or adaptation can seem shaky; after all, the rapid extension of the human life span means that there may be little we can predict about the sexual behavior of a contemporary fifty-year-old human anyway—there simply has not been enough time for selection to work. Because of this, and because of the fact that not every behavior or feature of an organism's ecology is subject to strong selection, non-reproductive sexual behavior is subject to "drift" and one may see a high level of variance in behavior and response.[3]

This is not to say that hormones do not affect sexual desire or influence human sexual behavior to some extent. It is also not to say that an exploration of the evolutionary roots of human behaviors is not a worthwhile endeavor, perhaps indispensable when attempting to answer certain questions. Rather, it is to point out that such theories lack explanatory power when applied to complex patterns of consumption and sexual practice, developed during relatively recent time periods and reliant on numerous technologies for their effects. In somewhat of a rapprochement between biological determinists and cultural constructionists, feminist philosopher Susan Bordo sides with primatologists Richard Wrangham and Dale Peterson in recognizing "that our biological inheritance itself allows for a great deal of creativity and intelligence both in adapting to new environments and in adapting environments to new goals." There are always "repertoires of possibilities, never single paths," and the paths that have been taken by some individuals in any given society thus must be studied in context and in comparison to others (1999: 263). Different researchers, of course, depending on their personal interests and their disciplinary leanings, will ask different questions and explore diverse parts of this problem.

What I turn to in the next section, though, are the ways that a folk theory of natural male sexuality becomes meaningful to the customers themselves, and why.

"Men Are Dogs": Customers' Understandings of Biology and the Body

Despite the fact that appeals to a reductionist biology may not have much explanatory power when it comes to understanding some men's pleasurable experiences of consumption in modern strip clubs, or in explaining the differences among men, *these kinds of explanations* were often drawn on at some point by the male customers to explain their desires, both to me and to themselves—even when such biological explanations contradicted their other statements. Many of the customers made reference to a "natural" male sexuality, for example, a sexuality that was aggressive and even difficult to control. Some invoked images of men as "hunters" or "predators" as they did so:

> I think men are born hunters. And [going to strip clubs] is just another aspect of hunting. (Herb)

> My honest opinion is, men are dogs. If it wasn't for society saying they should have to be with one partner all the time and that . . . stereotype, it'd be open season. (Joe)

Other men discussed male sex drives as overpowering and the "mating instinct" as something that underlay their desires to visit strip clubs:

> I do believe there's a stronger biological drive in a man to be [promiscuous] . . . I've read about all the monkey studies they've done . . . playing with the hormones of the animals and making the woman in heat. The monkeys like her. After she mates, they don't anymore. They actually run away from her. They bring a new monkey in, the male monkeys are back on it again . . . I think that there's a biological component for males to be more interested in the next person, the next female. (Jason)

> I think we're pretty silly. I think we're just men and I think . . . we think a lot more with our pricks than with our heads. (David)

> Men think only with their hormones . . . Must be some type of residual mating instinct [that makes the clubs appealing] . . . Stripping is animalistic inspiration. (Brian)

Beck said, "It's just the biology" of men that makes them react so strongly to "attractive" women. Some women, said Herb, bring out the "animalistic lust" in him more than others. Jack said that men in general would do almost anything to sleep with women: "[Men are] hoping that they're going to put you in a place where they can take advantage of you. That's basically what it is. And guys have done that all their lives. Guys have gone and slain dragons for women. They've gone and killed other men for women. They've gone and brought home bear skins, tiger skins, whatever the woman wanted. Just to impress the female." Ross said that strip clubs took "our society's relationship between men and women down to that ur level, as in ultimate beginning, most basic."

For Roger, the desire to visit strip clubs was natural in that he believed that this desire to look at a variety of women was biologically driven. Repeatedly during the interview, he stressed that "all men like to look" and that this was an "instinctive" behavior. Further, all men were seen as naturally desiring multiple partners, an idea that he justified by mentioning several times the "hundreds of partners" that he believed homosexual men had: "Men are sexual predators . . . They always are. And as much as the homosexual community wants to tout the fact that they have stable relationships, the only thing that has caused stable relationships in the homosexual world has been AIDS. Period. Before that—I mean, Laurelton was full of gay bathhouses and . . . it was, how many could you do. Every night. And they've always been that way and when they say they're not it's bull. By far and away the majority of homosexual men, now I'm not talking about women, but homosexual men have hundreds of partners. Not twenty or thirty . . . hundreds." On the other hand, he claimed that long-term, monogamous heterosexual partnerships were really the "only natural option" for humans, thus also using homosexuals several times as an example of men who had "rejected nature." Paul also at times invoked a universal and necessary sexuality for men, even those who differed in object choice, arguing that if men do not have enough contact with women "they go rigorously gay," as "in the military and prison." Further, he argued, "A lot of males choose it [homosexuality] because they can't deal with a female and communicating with a female. It's just easier to communicate with a male who already knows what a male wants."

Theorist and AIDS activist Simon Watney has noted that lesbians and gay men are often seen by pop evolutionary commentators as exhibiting " 'pure' sexual and gender characteristics" because they do not have to meet the expectations of, or compromise with, the desires of the opposite sex: "In this version of the world, gay men supposedly inhabit some kind of no-woman's land, completely untouched by, and unconscious of, the opposite sex. Dismissed on the one hand as 'failed' heterosexuals, we are restored on the other as ideal demonstrations of unadulterated masculine and feminine sex-drives" (1987: 52). Paul's and Roger's comments illustrate the fact that Watney's observations are relevant for individuals outside of academia or journalism as well. Strip clubs have proliferated over the past two decades, a time when few men could fail to be aware of the existence of the politics of sexual identity or of what has sometimes been termed in the popular press the gay lifestyle. Gays and lesbians (along with bisexuals, transsexuals, transgendered individuals, pansexuals, etc.) have become steadily more visible in American public culture during this time in a number of different and important ways. During the early years of the AIDS crisis, however, there was an unrelenting focus in the media on sexual promiscuity among gay men, and for many of the men I interviewed, this promiscuity was still the core feature of what they saw as men "rejecting heterosexuality." Indeed, several other interviewees and customers also expressed fantasies about homosexuality as a lifestyle in which a man could have unlimited partners and sex without commitment, identifying with this supposed freedom at a certain level at the same time that they disavowed a same-sex object choice for themselves.

Regardless of the fact that these customers had explained their desire to visit strip clubs in relation to an insatiable male desire, however, a desire that could be observed in other men, even those who were homosexual, they also explicitly narrated experiences of their own that contradicted ideas about a homogeneous male sexuality or an unflagging desire unstimulated by the market. Even though David claimed that men "think more with our pricks than with our heads," for example, he also personally carefully avoided all sexual contact in the clubs and told stories about the physically platonic relationships that he had developed with dancers over the years. Likewise, even as Paul made comments that seemed to imply a natural continuity among men, he told me that his own past sexual desires (his tendency to engage in peeping tom behavior, for example, that would sometimes lead to solitary masturbation but no attempts to make contact with the objects of his visual quests) would make him an "outlier" in my study, different from the majority of men with whom I would be speaking. And despite his invocations of nature and universal laws of masculinity, Roger also pointed to cultural and historical reasons for American male scopophilia during our conversations:

> *Roger:* The desire to look at women is in all heterosexual men . . . if somebody's showing it we're going to look . . . It's like if a girl bends over in a short skirt in a restaurant and there's a dozen guys sitting there and they all go "ooh" . . . They're all gonna look. But they've got the excuse. They didn't plan that. They didn't mean to. It was just there, you know?
>
> *KF:* Why do you think they like to look?
>
> *Roger:* I think it's part of the physiology . . . that causes us to procreate all the time.

However, when I then mentioned that people in different parts of the world cover up in different ways, suddenly our conversation changed:

> Yeah, I've traveled in Europe and on the beaches there girls go topless all the time and nobody thinks it's bad . . . I think a lot of that is created in this culture, you know, because of the Puritanical upbringings that we have in our history . . . There's no doubt that the fascination with women's breasts in America was created by *Playboy*. Period. I mean, before Hugh Hefner and his pinups and foldouts, it wasn't such a big deal. But it is certainly a big deal now! A billion-dollar business to make boobs out of silicone. You know? So I think that's a very cultural thing and . . . you go to Europe and there's girls lying around on the beaches and nobody . . . you stand there and talk to them and nobody thinks anything of it!

Like most of the other customers, Roger also claimed that he went to the clubs because they were "relaxing," provided a form of entertainment that allowed him to briefly escape the pressures of work and home, and because he was in a long-term relationship in which he desired to remain faithful (all issues taken up in different sections of this book).

Similarly, Beck spoke about how men "only want one thing" and how this drove them to participate as customers in the sex industry. He told me about the advice he gave his daughters: "Men are all alike. They'll see a good-looking woman . . . the blood leaves the brain, goes to the penis, nothing but sex, and that's all. And that is literally a fact and it's just the way it is! You know? I don't care whether they're rocket scientists or . . . dirt farmers or whatever but it's just the biology. And as long as they [his daughters] know that, they know all they need to know about men." At times during the interview, Beck identified excitedly with this perspective, mentioning that he often felt drawn to look at young women when they passed by him and that this desire had even motivated him to show up for the interview with me. On the other hand, he also said that in the strip clubs he was "not interested" in the sex part of it and that he just liked to sit and talk, "listening to one fascinating story after another." Beck made friends with the waitresses, the bartenders, and a few of the dancers, but these relationships, according to him, were not fueled by sexual tension. As we had interacted at length in the club on several occasions and I knew his "friends" as my coworkers, these statements seemed accurate. In fact, he also claimed that sex was one of the "last things" on his mind due to his age and to serious stomach problems that required him to take heavy medication. The contradictions between his own experiences and his explanation of male desire were not necessarily experienced as problematic to him until I asked about the disjunction between them. "Maybe when I was younger I acted more like these other men," he answered, pointing out that he was "just not very interested in sex anymore." When he was younger, however, he admitted that he had rarely gone to strip clubs.

After we discussed the contradiction, Beck had a few critical comments to make about the male sexuality that he had previously invoked: "I also think maybe in a hundred years or ten years or a thousand years, we will be advanced enough to look upon this whole thing as being kind of silly. Which it is, kind of, you know? It really is. I remember reading in [the local paper] about some woman who came from France and I don't know whether she was a porn star or a dancer or a stripper. But she said that she couldn't make a living because it was a normal part of human life [there] . . . And here we just build up all of this crap around it so then we satisfy the need by having places like the Crystal Palace and the rest of them!" He continued to say that the prohibitions of and stigma against nudity (as well as against the spaces in which one could view it in the United States) were part of what made it exciting to visit the clubs: "That's what makes it interesting and enticing. When you can't see it, you want to go see it. That's the whole point!"

In a similar manner, Mick initially stated that going to strip clubs was "just something all guys do." As a market researcher, however, Mick also knew that this was not accurate according to his own information about advertising and marketing. A few minutes after making this statement he noted, "It seems like a thing that older people do more," but explained this first as simply a financial matter: "Older men have more money." Later on in the interview, however, he pointed out that he believed the "market" was really "shaping people's desires," that women would eventually be persuaded to go to male strip clubs as regulars if such venues and services were readily available to them, customized to their needs, and less stigmatized. As the behavior that he was trying to explain became more and more distant from his own identity (i.e., as when speaking about the behavior of potential women customers, for example), Mick saw it as increasingly socially constructed through the marketplace.

So why are these appeals to an essential biological nature important to the men, and why do they continue to be drawn on even when contradictions between the men's experiences and beliefs become apparent? First, appealing to a natural or universal male sexuality could absolve the men of responsibility for engaging in behaviors that are sometimes considered inappropriate by a wife, partner, or friends; after all, what is explained as "natural" is often also deemed to be justifiable, excusable, or inevitable. Roger's desires to visit the clubs caused him a certain amount of stress due to his religious upbringing, for example, stress that was somewhat relieved when he reminded himself that he was simply acting the way "all men" did because of biological reasons. He explained quite explicitly: "I've just come to the decision that looking is not cheating . . . for me. But my brother-in-law pastors, they'd just freaking go crazy . . . it would kill 'em . . . I mean, if they went to Diamond Dolls they'd come home and just feel horrible . . . But since all men like to look, and that's their nature, that's instinctive, you can't fault men for failing when they want to do that. I guess that's where I get my rationalization in." Likewise, Gary was pleased when he was given an explanation for his desires to visit strip clubs, desires that he sometimes found distracting or embarrassing, by an expert who placed the source of his thoughts and behaviors outside of his conscious control: "I take Prozac and I have a prescribing psychiatrist that I have to go to every three months to renew the prescription. And I asked him the other day, 'Why do I live with a woman who I have no . . . literally no desire to have sex with or very infrequently, but then I lust after all these other women whether in a mall or in a strip club?' And he did say it has something to do with the seratonin level and so he increased my dosage . . . And number two, he also said that it's the way I'm wired! Which I found very significant."

Second, for some men, this appeal to natural male desires seemed to deflect, at least in part, anxiety about clienthood and about the com-modification of sexualized services. If the desire to go to strip clubs is not inherent and natural in male bodies or the "animalistic" recesses of their brains, and is instead constructed by the marketplace, the customers could simply be the dupes of advertisers, marketers, and both male and female sexual entrepreneurs. If men were homogeneous as a category, the reason that some men went to strip clubs and others did not was simply circumstantial (financial, regional, because of their relationships, because of their religious beliefs, etc.). The logic of capitalism, after all, has always worked its magic through the perpetual creation of new needs and desires, and through the ideological or discursive rendering of those needs and desires as natural. At the same time, critiques of capital-ism and commodification have seeped far enough into public awareness that, as mentioned in the previous chapter, many of the customers realized that paying for it, whether it be female attention, conversation, or sexualized services, would at best be seen as inauthentic (and perhaps pathetic) and at worst as perverted or exploitative. Though Alex was often worried about being recognized in strip clubs by people he knew, for example, he also felt that he was acting more naturally than people who would not visit the clubs: "Let's say you stood up and took off all your clothes. Now what man, unless he's gay or something, wouldn't look and probably be thrilled to death? You know, it would be unnatural in society to do that but when it gets down to basic human nature, it's only natural to look . . . you know, and to enjoy what you are seeing." Alex thought of himself as a modern rebel of sorts (think of his Harley Davidson metaphor in Chapter 3), and part of the attraction of the clubs for him was the way they allowed him to access a feeling of being outside the law, resisting socialization despite the fact that he was engaged in acts of consumption facilitated and organized by the market.

Third, sexual desire, and / or sexual arousal, whether actual or fan-tasized, was emotionally meaningful for the customers. The discourse of natural male sexuality provided them with a means of talking about their desires and experiences that allowed them to pleasurably express, explore, remember, develop, fantasize about, or temporarily experience aspects of themselves that did not necessarily emerge in the other spheres of their lives. As part of each customer's repertoire of "masculinizing practices" (Connell 2000), for obviously the men did not necessarily share with each other work or home environments or other patterns of leisure and social engagement, visits to strip clubs offered the men opportunities to think of their body not as a prison house or working machine, but as a source of desire and freedom. The next several sections explore these opportunities in more depth.

Nudity, Gender, and Power

Strip clubs are designed to appeal to the customers on a sensory level, not limited to the visual but also including the tactile, olfactory, and auditory. Despite the strict rules against most forms of contact, for example, there were varying amounts of nongenital touching involved, initiated by both the customers and the dancers. The rules were more relaxed when dancers were clothed, and while seated, dancers might sit quite close to the customers, thigh to thigh, and touch the men on the arms or legs or whisper in their ear. It was not unusual for dancers to greet regulars with a kiss on the cheek, or to thank tippers in the same way. Hugging, though not officially allowed, was also a common form of physical contact. During personal table dances, "accidental" contact might be made as well, and some dancers became quite skilled at such "mistakes." Sometimes a man's shoulders or legs could be used to balance, for example, or a dancer could grab a man's hands and hold them during the dance—ostensibly to keep him from touching her and getting them both in trouble but often also as a way to make physical contact. Though it cannot be legislated against or regulated, eye contact was also a way for a dancer to engage the customers in a more intense sensory experience, directing her gaze, communicating desire (even if performed), and sometimes signaling with a facial expression when additional physical contact might be made. It was possible to use long hair almost like a limb, allowing it to brush a man's face, chest, or lap while performing. Perfumes and body lotions were used by most of the dancers, and the scents could be left on the customers' clothes even if the physical contact was limited. A dancer could move close to a customer, though backing away quickly before any rules were officially and visibly broken, so that he could smell her skin and hair. Cigarette smoke, alcohol, and sweat were some of the other most obvious and visceral scents, sometimes differentiating the dancers from the other women in the customer's life who would not visit such venues or collect such *public* scents on their bodies. Dancers could also use the pitch and tone of their voices to sensually arouse the customers—whispers, coos, throaty commands, innocent giggles, and so forth—especially during table dances.

Nonstop music was used to enhance the mood and the atmosphere and was selected to be sexy or fun (though employees sometimes disagreed about which songs fit these designations). Music, as Gilbert and Pearson point out in their analysis of the pleasures and politics of contemporary rave cultures, is constituted by vibrating waves of sound, waves that are registered throughout the body, not simply in the brain (1999: 44). Though they argue that the "interactions between sounds and our bodies will always be in part a result of learned responses, of personal and / or cultural dispositions" (48), significantly, in strip clubs the male customers themselves are often prohibited by club rules and the social norms of the environment from responsive bodily movements such as dancing. Though the men's desires to dance or move to the music vary, the fact remains that they are watching someone else's movement and subjected to the same auditory stimuli.

Though the regular customers downplayed the importance of nudity, no matter what kinds of interactions a male customer sought in the clubs—watching the stages from afar, buying multiple table dances, having in-depth conversations with a variety of women, paying for repeated and extended interactions with one particular dancer—the fact remains that in the club a customer could, at any time, ask the entertainer with whom he was interacting to disrobe. Though the degree of nudity varies in strip clubs around the country, Laurelton laws allowed the dancers to strip completely (though regulations governed the kinds of movements the women could do while undressed, the types of poses they could strike, how much pubic hair they needed to have, and a number of other elements related to their performances). Depending on the rules and layout of the club, the dancer might disrobe on a customer's table so that he could view her from below, on the floor between his legs while he was seated, or in front of his chair on a slightly raised platform. Nudity has an assortment of sometimes conflicting meanings in the contemporary United States and can at different times (and to different observers) signify a variety of things: naturalness, authenticity, vulnerability, sexual power, revelation of one's inner self, humiliation, degradation, a lack of self-respect, as well as sexual accessibility and a prelude to sexual activity. Customers also brought their own beliefs about nudity to the interactions, as well as their own sexual history. There were some men, for example, who claimed that they were never allowed to look at the body of their wife or partner, even during sex; in these cases, nudity might be fascinating, awe-inspiring, or even upsetting.

Public nudity is embedded in a host of additional symbolic and emotional meanings, often ambivalent and frequently revolving around issues of power and control. Even for those men who did have access to private revelations, the fact that they were paying for live, public performances meant that there were additional emotional layers wrapping their interpretations of their encounters: mixtures of shame, anxiety, excitement, and desire. If it is true that "there is no apprehension of the body of the other without a corresponding (re)vision of one's own" (Phelan 1993: 171), some of the pleasure in these commodified encounters arises from complicated, and coterminous, fantasies of security (rooted in the ritualized performances of sexual difference that unfold in the clubs) and fantasies of rupture or transgression (rooted in the feelings of degradation, vulnerability, and freedom that many of the customers felt would accompany their own public nudity).[4]

For first-time or irregular visitors, the spectacle created in strip clubs around female nudity can be overwhelming, especially in the larger clubs with multiple, elaborately mirrored stages and high numbers of dancers. Yet only men who were infrequent visitors mentioned feeling this kind of intense stimulation from the nude bodies alone; for the regulars, nudity becomes, though not something associated with the everyday, a backdrop to a larger scene of gendered and sexualized interactions. Many authors have noted the increasingly sexualized nature of advertising (e.g., Williamson 1980; Bordo 1993, 1999) and consumer culture more generally, and scandals arise each year about the overt and brazen links being drawn between sex and commodities (just think of the furor over the "rec-room" Calvin Klein ads or the criticisms of portrayals of naked young frolickers in the 2001 Abercrombie and Fitch catalogue). Nudity in this kind of no-contact club in some ways becomes more of a prelude to a moment of purchase than to a moment of sexual release, much as it does in commodity culture more generally, though this time the purchase of a gendered and sexualized interaction or service. As Carl said of being a long-term regular of strip clubs: "Every time I see a woman go onstage, I think, yippee, she's going to get naked! But seeing a woman undress is no longer a part of sex. It used to be really important, but now it's not." Alex and I had a similar exchange:

> *KF:* So does looking [at the nude dancers] make you respond with a desire for sex?
>
> *Alex:* Oh, it may sound off the wall, or whatever, but I guess it's kind of like going and looking at cars. You know? You see a really hot awesome car and you want to drive it. You'd like to, anyway, and that's the first thought. But if it really came down to it, would you or not? That's a whole new thing.

The pleasure in viewing in some ways can become desirable in and of itself, though always in the context of larger patterns of gendered interaction. Gary claimed, "I don't get erections in strip clubs." He talked quite a bit, however, about how he was interested in "young dancers" with "no cellulite" who were naïve, untarnished, and innocent. His desire for younger women, however, was not physical: "I come off as a higher standard to them." As he had experienced difficulties attracting women ever since he had begun dating, he felt that these younger, inexperienced dancers would look up to him and be more likely to pay him attention.

Some social theorists have argued that in late capitalist societies sex, and the goal of desire, have become transformed: "The aim is not the relaxation or tranquility that comes with sexual satisfaction—that seems more of a nightmare—but a never-ending supply of excitement and stimulation" (Schmidt 1998: 237). The sex industry often has been used as an example of a place where such contemporary, alienated, and bleak sensation seeking occurs (Schur 1988; Stock 1997). As psychologist Wendy Stock writes: "Were it not for our desensitized tolerance towards the marketing of sex, the very term [sex industry] would shout an alarm to us, revealing the dismembering of sexuality from potentially intimate, mutually vulnerable, human eroticism to a preprogrammed dance of mannequins, interacting as if the only value was the execution of the sex act itself . . . the sex industry sells men a limited and often alienating form of sexuality" (100). Sociologist Gunter Schmidt believes that this trend of seemingly increasing commercialization of sexual products and encounters, and the concomitant desensitivity that supposedly accompanies it (what has been called by some the "postmodernization of sex"), are actually more prevalent in *discourses* on sexuality than in the real sex lives of men and women," as sex surveys seem to show almost all sexual activity between men and women restricted to those in "steady relationships" (237). In fact, he sees "a grotesque discrepancy between people's desexualized lives and the outside world, overflowing with garish stimuli" (231). He writes: "The Victorians, it is recounted, were entranced by the sight of a naked piano leg, whereas in our blatantly nude world naked bodies leave us cold" (231). Schmidt does not believe that sex will disappear along with the sexual taboos that once structured it; rather, he believes that heterosexuals have begun to take "part of their sex lives elsewhere," especially into masturbatory activity, as a way of escaping from the obligations and negotiations of contemporary relationships (232). Certainly, social norms and expectations around sexuality and sexual satisfaction have changed, and regular customers did express some desensitization to female nudity ("it gets boring") and a propensity for particular kinds of sensation seeking in their leisure practice (touristic practice); yet, it was actually the intersubjective nature of their encounters with the dancers that most of the customers felt made the experience erotic, at least for those who preferred strip clubs. It was not just the presence of nudity or other forms of sensory stimulation, nor just the presence of talk, but the presence of all of these that allowed for the mutual creation of fantasy—a fantasy that was both relaxing and stimulating.

It is essential to recognize that the dancers are not the only performers in these venues; the customers, sometimes consciously and sometimes not, are also part of the scene / seen, intricately involved in performances of identity, sexuality, and desire that generate meaning and pleasure out of their interactions. As theatrical scholar Katherine Liepe-Levinson points out, male spectators of female strip shows sometimes pay for their own opportunity to be in the spotlight, "to participate in highly regulated rituals about sex and desire both as viewers and performers" (1998: 31; see also 2002). In the Laurelton clubs, such special opportunities were presented through bachelor dances, shower dances, or feature acts in which the male customers were brought up onto the stages and became the focus not only of a dancer's attention but of the whole audience's. At Diamond Dolls and the Crystal Palace, bachelors were sometimes stripped down to their underwear by a group of entertainers in front of the crowd, for example. Customers could also create spectacles around their tables by purchasing the attentions of several dancers or buying table dances, and the DJ might point out big spenders. At all times, however, even when simply watching the dancers perform on stage, the men were visible to the dancers and, unless they were in a VIP room, to other customers in the room. Though the regulars, in my experience, rarely took advantage of such onstage theatrical opportunities, the fact that they engaged in sexualized encounters with the dancers in a public place, in the presence of a live audience, was certainly significant to the meanings of the experiences.

In strip clubs, performances of gender can become public performances of sex, both in the sense of sexual difference and in the sense of sexual arousal or desire. Sexual difference, in this setting, is affirmed by the dancers' nudity and, simultaneously, the men's clothing. As the exposure of male genitals was prohibited in the strip clubs that I selected for this research, there was no recourse to a penis to authenticate sexual difference. Genitals and secondary sexual characteristics become authenticating accessories for the dancers, or "revelations," and henceforth, *her genitals* become authenticating for the customers as well. Women's bodies of course differ, in breast size and shape, the size and shape of the labia, body type and structure, facial appearance, skin and muscle tone, and so on. Such differences, however, are generally contained in a strip club; there likely will be no one performing with genitals or secondary sexual characteristics that do not conform to expectations of a "woman": there will be no one lacking one or both breasts, no one sporting an obvious beard or a mustache (though amounts of leg and pubic hair vary), no one with ambiguous genitalia. Though this is true in most venues and regions, it is especially so in Laurelton. Of course, New Orleans, San Francisco, and other cities that boast a wide and varied sex industry may feature transsexual dancers (pre- and postoperative) or genitally ambiguous dancers. Often, however, these differences will themselves be advertised and highlighted for the customers, perhaps even distinguished spatially inside the club (women in the first room, men in the second, "others" in the third, for example).

Pressing up against normative boundaries and expectations of gender, of course, can at times generate excitement. Ronnie was a dancer at the Crystal Palace, a female bodybuilder who was nearly indistinguishable from a man in certain costumes and when viewed from behind. She had short hair, an extremely muscular build, very small breasts, a square jaw, and masculine features, which she accessorized with a man's watch, no jewelry, minimal makeup, and masculine movements (flexing her muscles; simulating a man's thrusting movements in sex during her dances). As Ronnie stripped, the masculine reading of her gender was disrupted as she was shown, repeatedly over the course of a night, to not really be a man. This experience was unsettling for many customers. As it is common for bachelor parties to concoct scenes that will unnerve or humiliate the bachelor, Ronnie was a favorite at such occasions. This is not to say that Ronnie did not have a number of customers who eroticized her appearance, just that her masculine appearance and behaviors were also used to induce an uncomfortable tension in others: Should the bachelor show desire for her, the way that he believed he should feign or express desire for a stripper? If he did so, what did that mean? Was he gay or straight? What would a "normal" man do?

Ronnie's masculine appearance and performance style was an exception to the norm, at least in the Laurelton clubs, yet there were other, much more subtle, ways that these boundaries between sexual difference and sexual desire were both upset and reaffirmed. Some dancers took male names, such as Tommi, Frankie, Ryan, and Joey, for practical reasons (there were few "sexy" girls' names left to choose from at some of the larger clubs, where dancers were not allowed to share names and many dancers wanted to steer clear of "everyday" names to avoid calling to mind a customer's wife or daughter) as well as for the purpose of creative contrast. Dancers also engaged in cross-dressing in some of the clubs, stripping out of a man's shirt and tie or a policeman's uniform, for example. These contrasts, however, no matter how disquieting for some men, were always neutralized by the revelation of the female body by the end of the third song of a stage set or within the first few seconds of a private dance. Thus, any gender ambiguity on the part of the dancers was carefully and profitably managed and kept within certain boundaries: customers knew exactly when, and how (by paying money), to put an end to it.

Liepe-Levinson argues that strip shows both transgress and rein-scribe dominant myths about sex and gender through the theatrical aspects of the shows themselves (the social and geographic locations of strip clubs; the exterior and interior designs of the venues; the costumes, choreography, and behavior of the dancers) and through the behaviors of the spectators (2002: 8). She writes, "Within the transgressive 'po-etics' of the strip show, depictions of female and male sexual interests (as in 'real life') take the form of active, dialogic conversations with the cultural imposition of sexual 'normalcy'" (15). Female strippers, for example, may exhibit an aggressive, and hence transgressive, sexuality in their movements and performances (in addition to hyperfemininity), as well as appearing nude and miming auto-erotic pleasure in public (113). In the Laurelton clubs, female dancers were not only sometimes quite aggressive in their stage performances but were also allowing the men opportunities to look closely at body parts often reserved for the most private of interactions (and sometimes not even revealed then). Yet, although the performances of the dancers and the customers do disrupt some cultural assumptions about public and private, passive and active, masculine and feminine, and reality and fantasy, they do not usually result in a total subversion of any of these boundaries. The ritualized aspects of the encounter—the fact that dancers would dis-robe in particular ways in specified places, that a table dance would end after one song and the dancer would re-dress, that cash could either send an entertainer away or signal her to stay, that there were some preset roles available for both parties to adopt (whether or not they actually did so)—thus helped to stabilize any ambiguity or discomfort beyond that which produced erotic tension. Further, the most funda-mental assumption of the congruence between a particular gender identity and a corresponding sexual desire for an "appropriate" object—heterosexuality itself—is rarely overtly challenged, and is in fact often elaborated on in the clubs, especially for men.

Performing Desire

The fact that sexual desire for women could be performed publicly through their interactions with the dancers but did not need to be "proven" (indeed, couldn't legally be proven) is highly significant in understanding the gendered and sexualized performances given by both the patrons and the entertainers in strip clubs and the meanings of those performances. The specter of homosexuality was omnipresent in many different ways in the clubs and in the men's talk about the meanings of their visits, as mentioned earlier. As Judith Butler has argued, the normalization of heterosexuality is instituted by a logic of repudiation: "Identification is implicated in what it excludes" (1993: 119); just think of the paradoxical statement: "I'd never even think about having sex with a man"). Heterosexual relations can be homosocial; that is, interactions with women may be used to create and express emotional bonds among men (Sedgwick 1985); in strip clubs this is something that many of the managers and dancers are aware of, as well as some of the customers (especially those who use the clubs to conduct business or to interact with clients or employees). For many customers, then, heterosexuality could be comfortably secured, at least temporarily or in fantasy, through a public performance of desire for an obvious woman.

During bachelor parties and other group functions, a dancer's job, in part, is to ease the customers through what Eve Sedgwick calls a coercive double bind in a culture that refuses to recognize the continuum of possible emotional bonds between men—a man's need to distinguish being a "man's man" from a "homosexual." The performers' nakedness and the men's desire for her (real or performed) serves as a kind of proof that this line has not been crossed. In this sense she functions as a "real live hetero-safety precaution" (Frank 2002). Further, the experience or performance of sexual desire could in turn serve as an affirmation of gender identity to oneself as well as to others (although sexual desire can feel quite different from or independent of gender, it can also serve to reinforce ideas of oneself as masculine or feminine).

This is not to say that all of the transactions that occur in heterosexual strip clubs are straight, for they most definitely are not. There are also many bisexual and lesbian women who work as dancers, performing desire for men for financial remuneration, or who visit such clubs as customers, as well as women who have sex with women or women who enjoy looking at other women's bodies. Not all of the customers are necessarily straight either. In fact, I had several regular customers tell me that they were bisexual or had fantasies about other men. Two older men told similar stories about "the 1970s" and their sexual encounters with other men during those "experimental years." One extremely generous regular at an upper-tier club I worked in explicitly identified as a gay man, and preferred to engage in high-dollar consumption practices—purchasing expensive bottles of champagne and buying women off of the stage rotations to drink it with him, for example—rather than watch the dancing. There were men who wanted advice and information about anal penetration and felt that they could not ask anyone they were close to about it for fear of being accused of being gay.[5] There are also certainly men who enjoy watching other men in the clubs for a variety of other reasons, and there are any number of potential desiring gazes. At times, customers visited the clubs seeking gratification of certain fetishes, such as the desire to interact with a dominant woman or to experience public humiliation or pain. On the other hand, although strip clubs may construct heterosexual desire as problematic in some ways—as dirty, illegitimate, or artificial, for example (Liepe-Levinson 2002)—and although the desires of the customers were not neatly contained within heteronormative standards or stereotypical positions, the transactions did not overtly question the connection of heterosexuality to normative patterns of masculinity and this was a significant part of their appeal to the regulars. As venues offering public, sexualized, cross-sex interactions, strip clubs offer an opportunity for men to "pass" or perform as straight for their friends and themselves, as well as offering ways for male customers to think about their sexuality as transgressive or liberating, especially from the constraints and responsibilities of work and home, no matter what their conscious or unconscious object choices.

The position of desiring male was one that many of the customers found enjoyable to express or perform, though this is not to say that such a position was stable, uncomplicated, or the only option. For example, popular discourses and myths about male sexuality and masculinity may result in incompatible visions of male fulfillment. As Gary Brooks points out, male competitive trophyism encourages men to compete for women as sexual conquests during adolescence (and sometimes later). This behavior comes into conflict with certain developmental and societal expectations of men in later life, when they are expected to "settle down" and prove their success in a long-term marriage (1997: 34). Strip clubs provide a momentary and pleasurable resolution to this contradiction, as men are allowed to express a desire for many different women, publicly and explicitly, without breaking their commitment to the other woman in their life. In this way, the public nature of the strip club is quite important: others may see the men desiring, but they also see them just looking. The men also observe *themselves* desiring, something that may be quite important to them as they age and develop insecurities about their sexual potency or attractiveness. These observations take place literally, in the mirrored walls of the clubs, and more figuratively, in the sense of self-reflection and fantasy.

The customers' interactions with the dancers provided a fantasy not just of heterosexual identity then, but also of sexual competence (I refer to it as a fantasy not because their identity might not match their practices, but simply because stable identities are themselves a fantasy). A strip club offers a certain protection from vulnerability that other arenas, including the bedroom at home, may not. Significantly, the men remain clothed during the interactions and are rarely physically exposed or expected to perform.[6] Ejaculation, after all, is not really necessary to enhance a man's feelings of masculinity, especially in a commodified encounter. As Anne Allison writes of male patrons of hostess clubs in Japan, when a man desires to feel good about himself as a man, "it is less sex as an act of penetration and release than a talk about sex" that is effective in these settings, specifically, a talk about sex with a woman who indulges him and does not counter his assertions (1993: 12). Indeed, when sexual action never occurs, the man is far less vulnerable. He can fantasize about his prowess and about sexual contact with a woman, yet he is not responsible for actually performing or providing pleasure to her. He is also prohibited from revealing his naked body to the dancers, which in itself can provide another form of refuge from judgment.[7] Some of the talk about the relaxing aspects of strip clubs must certainly be understood in this context, as interconnected with the experiences, pleasures, and vulnerabilities of the body.

The clubs thus provided some customers with a space in which a disjunction between desire and bodily performance could be negotiated. Some of the men with whom I interviewed and interacted had experienced difficulties with sexual performance in their intimate relationships, for example. During our second extended interview, Ross explained that his marriage had become "asexual" in recent years because of his inability to get erections. Yet he had slept with a number of women before marriage and said, "My work and my sexual identity are the lynchpins of who I am." He linked this to the fact that no matter what he did as a youth, his physically and emotionally abusive father repeatedly called him a "faggot" and told him that he would amount to nothing. When Ross began experiencing problems with his sexual performance in his mid-thirties he desperately sought medical help. Several years before Viagra hit the markets, he had undergone numerous surgeries to help regain his erectile functioning, one of which had left him "a eunuch" due to a disastrous surgical error. Ross was one of the few men who mentioned a desire to end his primary relationship, in which he claimed that he was remaining only because of his child. In strip clubs, Ross could watch and interact with the dancers, express his desire for them verbally, and be witnessed doing so by others. In this way, visits to the clubs allowed him to access the body he remembered from his youth, a fantasy body that could respond and perform when bidden, that needed not to be explained in a new sexual encounter, along with a "real" identity (or, to put it slightly differently, *access* to a self-representation that was already experienced as real or original).

I had a fascinating and similar encounter with a business traveler who returned to one of the upscale clubs two nights in a row, buying a number of personal table dances from me on each visit. On the first night, after several hours of interaction, he excused himself to go to the restroom, paid for one more dance when he returned, and then announced that he had to leave. He asked if he could hug me before he left and I allowed him to. As he hugged me, he pressed his groin against my leg. "See what you do to me?" he asked, smiling. The next night when he returned, he again bought several dances in a row from me. When I finished dancing and sat down again, he told me that he had a confession to make. He explained that when he had gone to the restroom the previous night he had given himself an injection, a process that, due to an injury, he goes through each time he wants to attain an erection. "But that doesn't mean I wasn't really turned on by you," he said. "I was so turned on by you that I had to have the shot." But why even confess? The erection, followed in this case by his confession, I would argue, worked to make the interaction pleasurable and complete for him because the confession, in part, outed his desire as "real" (necessitating an action) and not just one that was being consciously performed for the benefit of either of us.

Of course, by mentioning some men's impotence or anxieties about sexual performance, I do not want to reify stereotypes about the sexual inadequacies of men who might use the sex industry. There are, after all, many, many men who visit strip clubs whose body is agreeable to them and for whom sexual functioning is not an issue. Rather, my argument is that part of what strip clubs provide for their customers is the fantasy of the "perfect penis" (Tiefer 1995) without needing to prove it either visually or through their sexual performance. The fantasy of the perfect penis, of course, is connected to power and to hegemonic ideologies of an aggressive male sexuality, the penis as a "power tool" (Bordo 1999), but has some of its roots in feelings of vulnerability as well. After all, as Leonore Tiefer argues, "sexual competence is part—some would say the central part—of contemporary masculinity," despite the variety of differences in how masculinity is understood and expressed by individual men (142). Though increasingly there are ways to be masculine without relying on physical validation, she argues, the growing importance of sexuality in contemporary relationships has meant that "there seems to be no apparent reduction in the male sexual focus on physical performance" (152). This emphasis on sexual performance remains high in the social context of changes in the expectations of intimate relationships (increasing expectations that intimate relationships will provide psychological support and gratification), in the reasons individuals enter into relationships (for companionship rather than economic need or familial duty), the increasing importance of sexuality in consumer culture, and changes in the meanings of sexuality (such as a growing acceptance of the idea that sexuality will provide "ever-increasing rewards and personal meanings"; 153).

There are certainly times when the customers become physically aroused and are able to make the dancers aware of their erections, even in a strictly controlled environment. To show, or ask a dancer to feel, an erection, as some customers did (in either clandestine or blatantly illegal ways), is not simply proof of sexual responsiveness; it can also be proof that desire, self-presentation, and body are in alignment with each other, that a man is heterosexual, that he is still capable of responding as youthful, virile.

Youthfulness, in fact, was an issue that emerged quite frequently in conversations and interactions I had in the clubs. Strip clubs, in some respects, offer a synchronic experience of male sexuality that can serve to boost egos and restore a sense of masculinity by providing an atmosphere reminiscent of young adulthood. Many men limit their visits to strip clubs to the more socially "legitimate" occasions, such as bachelor parties and fraternity outings. I spoke with men during the course of this research who had gone to a club only once on just such an occasion, usually during their early twenties. Similarly, most of the men I interviewed had originally visited a strip club at some point during college. Later on in their lives, however, different circumstances sent them once again into a club and this time they were motivated to return on their own for additional visits. Indeed, the majority of the regular customers were men middle-aged or older. This is in some ways an interesting and complicated return to a site of adolescent fantasy. Though the music changes over the years, some of it is replayed in the clubs; some fashions and styles change, some reworked in the dancers' costumes and appearance to appeal to a particular age group of men. The dancers are still young and beautiful inside the club, just as the man may remember them. Except this time, he can afford to keep their attention.

Psychologists Good and Sherrod argue that men frequently seek to "maintain grandiose self-images" as part of their gender identity. They discuss the heightened importance of these images in middle age: "They want to perceive themselves as powerful and in charge. However, occasionally men glimpse their very mortal (and unacceptably deflated) real selves. During such times, men may attempt to restore their self-image through redoubling their efforts to gain power over others. These efforts may include familiar coping strategies that already had deleterious aspects to them such as displays of power over others at work or workaholism, purchasing a sports car (displays of financial / physical power), and having affairs or dating younger women (displays of sexual potence)" (1997: 194). Good and Sherrod also point out that during midlife men may sometimes reengage in the kind of nonrelational sex, or sex that does not necessarily require the context of an intimate relationship to be desirable, that they had in their adolescent years to reclaim a fading sense of strength and influence (198). Some men may not have experienced a sense of strength and influence in their everyday lives even during their adolescent years, yet feel that they *should have*. For these men who are willing and able to pay for it, the discovery of the type of female attention available in a contemporary strip club can be a monumental experience. Although these authors' reliance on the notion of the real self is potentially problematic, the idea that such behaviors take on intensified importance in middle age is both widespread and potentially illuminating in regard to strip clubs. One of the DJs at Tina's Revue spoke about how he needed to try to match the music he played to the average age of the crowd to facilitate this fantasy of youthfulness: "When I play Lynyrd Skynyrd's 'Sweet Home Alabama,' they're remembering driving around in the back roads, smoking dope and having fun drinking whiskey. 'This is the first time I drank Jack Daniels! Oh my god, we went to a hog race afterward! I must have thrown up for two hours! Oh god, it was so much fun' . . . well, the man's changed, but in his mind's eye he can go back." Another DJ told me that if the music was right, "you become that girl he wanted in high school and didn't get, or that one he let get away."

Youthfulness was clearly something that the men desired for themselves and not simply in the bodies they chose to view in the clubs, though it was obviously the youthfulness of the women that helped facilitate the fantasy. "These places keep me young," a customer told me during a table dance, "because you're so young." For others, effortless sexual response (though not necessarily desire) was something that was associated with youth. Some of the older men, for example, expressed difficulties becoming aroused by their wife or long-term partner at the same time that they claimed they wanted to be able to be excited by them. As Joe said:

> I feel like the older I get . . . you know . . . when a man is twenty years old . . . he's a walking erection. Any port in a storm. I think as you get older, though, you need to be excited a little bit more. It takes a little bit more stimulation. And the variety is what actually does that. At least, from my perspective. The same thing over and over, you kind of get desensitized to it. You know? You still get sexually stimulated but . . . it's almost as if you have to have a little something a little different, you know, to have that stimulation. And my current wife . . . we can have sex anytime, you know. Morning, noon, night. Three times a day. It doesn't matter. She would have sex, okay? Which is pretty special, if you think about it. And I know that I love my wife's body. I get turned on by my wife. Extremely turned on. But I find that the older I get, I can be turned on but still not have an erection. And there's almost not a direct correlation between the two. But I can still have a good time anyways. I can

certainly try and give her pleasure. That turns me on but I don't necessarily have to have an orgasm from it and . . . I think I've finally got my wife to understand that . . . but yet there's this stigma that women think that if a man doesn't have an orgasm he didn't have a good time.

The stigma that Joe alludes to underlay some of the furor in the United States during the late 1990s over the release of Viagra, the scores of men who begged their doctors for prescriptions, who began taking the drug recreationally, who claimed that it changed their life. As many commentators and researchers have noted, the word impotent "is used to describe the man who does not get an erection, not just the penis" (Tiefer 1995: 141; see Bordo 1999). Joe was not the only regular who discussed the stigma carried by a lack of appropriate physical response.

Some men also expressed difficulties responding to their wife as a sexual object as they both aged and became more used to each other over time. Jim said:

It's something that's difficult to convey to my wife—that it's improving our sexual relationship for me to go to a club and get, kind of, sexually turned on and then, you know, come home. And maybe part of it is, I think she wants herself to be the focal point of our sexual relationship. And she is. But she doesn't want to share that with a fantasy that I might have of having, you know, a pleasurable memory. And I don't know whether she has fantasies and pleasurable memories of people other than me. I think she probably does. Maybe she just doesn't want to admit it at this point. I think that's cause for perhaps some difference in philosophy between my wife and myself on that. But at the same time, here I am, you know, I'm forty-eight years old and I try to stay in shape. I do some running and keep physically active and try not to let my belly hang over my belt. Try to stay outside a little bit and, you know, be sexually appealing to women, not just necessarily my wife, but certainly, she's the object of my life.

Jim's wife had attempted to seduce him at one point when she found out that he frequented strip clubs—doing a striptease for him at home—but he had been unable to respond, something for which he felt guilty and slightly defensive.

The customers discussed the difficulties that their wife or partner had with "losing beauty and youth" and with "not wanting to be reminded that it was still out there" by their husband's visits to strip clubs. They also cautiously discussed the importance to themselves of their wife's loss of youth and beauty, sometimes explicitly comparing the bodies of the dancers to that of their wife. I have quoted these particular men at length, however, to point out that this reference to women's bodies was not simply an exercise in male privilege or misogyny. These men's visits could quite possibly have contributed to their wife's or partner's insecurities (and several interviewees explicitly stated that they believed there were connections), and it is certainly the case that the ability to purchase the attentions of others to make oneself feel younger and more desirable is a privileged position (and one their wife might not be able to occupy); yet the visits were also intertwined with the men's own insecurities about losing a youthful and healthy body, an attractive body, a body that would and could perform sexually when the opportunity or need arose, especially in the context of an ongoing intimate relationship. One of my regulars began visiting strip clubs frequently when his wife was diagnosed with breast cancer, and we occasionally discussed his emotional reactions to her illness, her imminent death, and his struggles to "be there for her" at the same time as he wanted to simply indulge himself in his own grief (and, at other times, his guilty enjoyment of his own health and desire). While there is obviously a great deal more to this complicated story and relationship, my point here is that the fantasies purchased by the regulars were not just part of an isolated game, played out "just for fun," but should also be seen as intertwined with everyday hopes, dreams, fears, and intimacies. The relationship between the dancer's body, their customers' partner's body, and their own body and sexual and emotional performances was thus complex and multifaceted; some of the emotional complexities of this relationship are discussed in more detail in Chapter 7.

To claim that interactions in the clubs improved their sexual relationship at home or were related to their ideas about sexual performance was not a universal response, however, and other men claimed to compartmentalize their fantasy encounters in the clubs and their "real" intimacies. As Steven said, "It's not like I'm making love to my wife and fantasizing about a dancer or something." Herb, Kenneth, Brett, Nick, Roger, and Tim spoke similarly, as did many other customers I spoke with informally in the clubs. In addition to arguing that their encounters in the clubs did not affect their sexual relationships, other men also argued that their commodified interactions did not affect their *body*. In fact, the number of times that I heard men say "This doesn't affect me physically" exceeded the number of times that the interviewees explicitly claimed a physical response or a desire for a physical response. "I don't get hard-ons while I'm watching dancers or anything," Carl said when I asked him about how he responded to table dances, for example. Whether a given man did or did not get erections or did or did not feel sexually aroused (which, as the men pointed out, is not necessarily the same thing) in any given interaction on any given day is less important, however, than ways that the specter of obvious or out-of-control bodily response (when one's body does not respond to a situation in ways that are appropriate, expected, or desired) affected their interpretations of their encounters and the pleasure that they took in these particular acts of consumption.

Ambivalence and Commodification

Despite the sexualized environment, then, there was a certain ambivalence about sexual arousal in these venues. One of the more interesting things I discovered as a dancer was just how "civilized" the men actually were in the clubs, even when they were consuming alcohol and "getting rowdy." Of course, there were some instances when a man made inappropriate comments or tried to touch a dancer, but these instances were very few and far between and, in general, the men were exceedingly polite, restrained, and respectful. Again, some of this might be attributed to the fact that these were table dancing clubs where all activity was publicly visible and the employees stringently enforced the no-contact rules; dancers do sometimes narrate drastically different experiences in other cities. Nevertheless, there are indeed particular public social codes and rituals that are usually followed by the customers. Part of this social code, at times, involves a sustained, conscious performance of "uncontrollable" desire; during bachelor parties, for example, it is common for the bachelor to have his hands or body restrained in some way and to be given a dance by one or more women. In these situations bachelors might struggle against their bonds, yet the performative aspects of the struggles are often clear to most observers as well as to the bachelor himself. After all, any serious struggle would probably have resulted all too quickly in the bachelor's freedom. During bachelor dances or during shower dances (where a customer was stripped down to his underwear and tied to a chair in an onstage shower with a dancer or two), for example, a man might whisper, "This is mostly for my friends." As Liepe-Levinson writes about the performative dynamics of table dances in male and female strip clubs: "Table-dance activities produce numerous subgroups of female and male patrons who sigh together, shake their heads in unison, collectively roll their eyeballs, giggle, and pretend to slide under the tables or off their chairs. As they perform for one another, the spectators murmur or exclaim statements such as: 'I can't stand it!' 'I can't take it!' 'I don't believe this is happening.' Yet, they continue to engage more 'up close and no-touch,' 'bound massages,' 'air kissing,' and 'clothing rack' [where the dancer's garments are placed on the man's body] scenes for themselves and their friends" (1998: 19). Liepe-Levinson argues that this controlled desire is a result of surrendering to the rules of the game at hand, of "the spectators' wish to play at being sexually overwhelmed or to play at jeopardizing *self-control*" (19). Certainly, surrendering to the stimulations at hand and to the expectations of others is something required of many different varieties of leisure experience and ritual engagement.

The controlled displays of desire are related also, I believe, to ambivalence about sexual arousal that has to do with the commodified underpinnings of the transactions. Displaying too much desire, or actual sexual arousal, after all, would also be a source of embarrassment for many customers, especially those who visit the clubs alone. A customer, then, might be performing a lack of desire or arousal rather than the opposite. Some customers seemed to believe, consciously or unconsciously, that their expressions of desire could easily slide into making them appear ridiculous, and indeed, men who became visibly aroused were sometimes mocked by their friends or by other customers in the club. For single customers, the poker-face or impassive expression is the social norm for the table dance, though the men might converse with the dancer about her effects on their physical state (saying things like "Do you know how much you turn me on?"; "I can't believe what you do to me"; "You drive me crazy"). With regulars, conscious performances could be more sustained; a regular might provide the dancers with information about himself that was more or less true, for example, or pretend that he was interested in developing a sexual relationship with a dancer outside of the club. At the same time, regulars might worry about being taken advantage of or being "led on" (similar, in some ways, to individuals in noncommodified relationships).

This ambivalence about the expression of desire was tied to notions of dignity and authenticity. The ability to command a woman to take off her clothes in public, whether or not it was exercised, was certainly seen as a powerful position by some men, and one that could be lost if they became too engrossed in the interaction or too aroused (physically or emotionally) by the dancers. Some customers, for example, saw the dancers' need and desire for money, and their willingness to disrobe to obtain it, as part of a power game that disadvantaged the dancers. Gary said, "The men have a power over the dancers that's very vivid. There's a tremendous . . . separation of powers there. It's more subservience. A master / servant type of thing. The dancer's the servant and the man's the master. And he's got the money so he's the boss." Ross claimed that there was a pleasure in knowing that you had "control over the dancers," that they took their clothes off when you gave them money and that the customer could "walk away" whenever he liked. Jason said that in the clubs "if you want someone to hang out with or not, there's a little more control in it"; that is, he could ask a dancer to leave if he tired of her company and he could always find someone to sit with if he felt lonely on a given evening.

On the other hand, the fact remains that the dancer must be paid for her performances.[8] Many of the customers I interviewed claimed that the dancers often had the upper hand in transactions in the clubs because of their ability to capture the man's interest, desire, and the contents of his wallet. Steven argued, for example, "Men might think they're being dominant or macho, but if the woman is pretending to be subservient and then walks away with his money, who has the power in the situation? I've seen big domineering businessmen walk into a strip club and turn into jelly." Customers expressed worries that they would be "hustled" or that they would seem "weak" by spending money on particular dancers. To stay in bodily control of one's responses was also to stay in financial control of the situation. At the same time, to feel, imagine, or perform a bodily response could lend the interaction authenticity and could feel exciting, liberating, and transgressive. Finding the balance between these states was tricky, yet successful dancers could help to do so through their self-presentations and interactions—through their productions and expressions of their body, behaviors, identities, and conversations. Through the skilled labor of the women, a delicate and pleasurable equilibrium could be struck for the customer between a loss of self-control and the maintenance of self-composure, between the desire to be the object or the subject of the gazes, between the desire to desire (to *spend*, to consume) and the desire *not to*.

The issue of power in commodified sexualized transactions is complex, and is thus not simply a matter of one party or the other "having" more power naturally, physically, financially, or emotionally. Subjectively, there are situations when both parties claim to have it, situations when one or the other makes this claim, and situations when both parties claim powerlessness. At the same time, there *are* links between slippery fantasies and desires and more intractable power relationships, though these links may not be straightforward or even experienced on a subjective level, and it is these links that I turn to in parts 3 and 4.

*

Whether or not men have an aggressive, explosive, or uncontrollable sexuality has been endlessly debated in academic literature, courts of law, and popular culture, to name just a few sites of this discussion, and in regard to issues of rape, the sex industry, sexual harassment, women in the military, and many others. My argument here is not meant to support, deny, or try to draw out the bases for the existence or expression of male sexual aggression or particular desires (for youth, beauty, variety, etc.). Nor am I attempting to argue that men are *really* vulnerable sexually or that they are simply led by the marketplace to desire certain kinds of partners or interactions. Rather, this chapter has been concerned with the ways that beliefs and fantasies about sexuality and sexual arousal figured in the meanings of the men's visits and connected with social discourses of masculinity more broadly. As practices that can be considered both touristic and masculinizing, the transactions taking place in these venues are more complicated than a discourse of natural aggressive male sexuality allows for, whether this discourse is being presented by sociobiologists, antipornography activists, or the male customers themselves.

In a recent article, antiprostitution activists and feminist researchers Melissa Farley and V. Kelly quoted and interpreted Herb's statement about men's "hunting" as evidence of the male sexual aggression against women that takes place in the sex industry (2000: 54). Yet to interpret the quote this way is to take literally what should be seen, in my opinion, as a metaphor—a way that Herb was attempting to make sense of his behavior by linking it with supposedly scientific or historical understandings of human nature. Herb's "hunting," after all, when read in the context of his other comments (a context that Farley and Kelly conveniently overlooked), was about searching for someone to talk to and laugh with, about finding someone who might "smoke the same bad cigarettes or drink the same beer or something." Certainly, the use of such a metaphor is problematic in some ways and should catch our attention—but the problem is in attributing an intrinsically aggressive, predatory, or destructive sexuality to men (something done by both Herb and Farley and Kelly here, consciously or not), not necessarily in commodified sexual practices or services in and of themselves. Now, obviously, the transactions that occur in the sex industry, in all of their various permutations, do *sometimes* involve the expression of aggression against women (though this was not my experience with the regular customers) verbally, physically, or in representations. But it is of course also the case that aggression against women also occurs in marriages, in boardrooms, in locker rooms, and in any number of other spaces, venues, representations, and modes of transaction, financial or emotional. Further, commodified interactions, especially those sought and purchased by regulars, can sometimes involve emotional exchanges, intimate moments, mutual respect, and displays of affection, just as more legitimate relationships are expected to (Frank 1998). Finally, the customers were often seeking transactions that are not adequately explained by a pop-sociobiological discourse of natural male sexuality, as should have become clear through my analysis in this chapter.

As part of a range of masculinizing practices, men's consumption in strip clubs offers a means to experience their body in pleasurable ways: as young, as virile, as attractive, as independent; sometimes as powerful, sometimes as vulnerable. Strip clubs also offer a venue where gender difference, along with heterosexual desire, is consciously performed and affirmed. Such performances, of course, are evidence of the instability of all identity and sexual desire, yet at the same time, the men I interviewed and interacted with generally used the clubs and their encounters in them as a way to reassure themselves, to make themselves more comfortable, to *relax* in a variety of different ways. Though we should not overlook the transgressive (and perhaps even transformative) aspects of public nudity and the commodified and ritualized performances of sexual desire by both patrons and entertainers, it is also the case that transgression may be more exciting because of the rigidities of everyday life. After all, as is discussed in the next several chapters, fantasies of race, class, and gender influence erotic experience and interpretations, and these fantasies about various categories of others are often rooted in material inequalities and deep-seated psychological fears and anxieties.

Part Three

Interlude

Fakes

When I get home from class, I see my housemate Chris leaning intently over a photograph at the kitchen table. There is a magnifying glass in his hand. As we both study photography, I lean over closer and set my backpack down on a chair. "What's that?" I ask, hoping to learn something. After all, I am only in my first year of coursework and Chris is almost finished with his degree.

Before he can answer, I see that it is a photograph of one of the blonde Baywatch girls. She is naked and is giving a blowjob to a skinny white guy. "Oh great," I say. "Now you're into Pam Anderson? Why don't you just go buy the video if you want to see her with Tommy?"

He laughs. "It's for a project."

"Yeah, sure. I think I'm going to do my next class project on Brad Pitt. But I'll try to find better-quality photos."

"No, really," he says. "This is the rage. Naked celebrity photos. They're all over the Internet. But some are real and some are faked. Here's an awful one from a local Web site," he says, and pulls out a picture of Teri Hatcher in a nun's habit with her breasts exposed. They are tremendous. "See how there is a fuzzy line across her neck? It just obviously doesn't fit. And this body couldn't be hers. But this one I'm not sure about." Using a magnifying glass, he continues scanning the photograph.

"And this is supposed to teach you about photography?" I laugh.

"No! This is going to make me some money. If I can become really quick at identifying fakes, don't you think that will be useful?"

Originally published in *Vixen,* June 1998. Slightly edited.

"I've got to get to work," I say, trying not to sound too doubtful. "It's my first night dancing since I moved here."

"Okay," he says disinterestedly. "I think this is real, though. I think this really is Pam Anderson! Maybe it's worth something if it's real."

*

Big-breasted women on billboards. Naked women in the movies. Girls, Girls, Girls. All Nude. All the time.

Dreamgirls. Showgirls. xxx. Cheap.

*

I am in the dressing room getting ready for my first shift at the new club. Methodically, I begin to go through my routine. First, I set my hair in large rollers. It is quite curly naturally and the large rollers tame it down so I don't look like anyone's kid sister. Then I begin to put on my face makeup. Mascara, eye shadow, eyeliner that curls up along the sides of my lashes. Concealer, blush, lip liner, lipstick. As I check my bikini line for stray hairs, I listen to the other girls talking and miss my friends at the club I used to work at out West. It is hard to be the new girl, in a new city, but I don't have many options. I had to move here for photography school and I have to work four nights a week to make enough money for tuition and supplies.

I keep to myself as I am getting dressed, as I find this time to be relaxing, almost transformative. For now, I do not have to be anyone but me. I begin to rub body glitter onto my butt and torso, something that I always do toward the end of my routine because it tends to get all over everything if I do not wash my hands right away afterward. I glance around the dressing room, trying to figure out what to wear. I don't want to be dressed too much like another dancer or the customers will get us confused. I make a mental note that the girls wear knee socks and plaid skirts here, something that we didn't do at my last club in Colorado. What is it about the schoolgirl look that Southern men like so much? I wonder.

I also notice that the dancers wear far fewer clothes than we were required to at my last club. Maybe because it is the South. It is hot here. Plus, regular girls are wearing such skimpy outfits to the mall! Somewhat disconcerted, I look at the three little dresses that I brought to wear. They suddenly look very conservative. Shit, I think. I'm going to look like a librarian in here. I make another mental note to get to the costume shop before my next shift to buy some more revealing clothes to work in.

"Where are you from?" a blonde girl asks, glancing sideways at me as she strokes on her lip liner. She is wearing a leopard bikini and I notice that she has a small tattoo on her inner thigh.

"Pennsylvania," I say. It is the first state that comes to mind, although I could name countless others.

"Oh, I got my boobs done in Pennsylvania," she says. "I know, I should have done it here or in Florida where there's a plastic surgeon for every hundred girls. I just didn't want everyone to know back then. Now I don't care. After all, my income doubled." She laughs and then scowls as she looks over at my butt. "We don't wear glitter here," she says.

"It's not allowed? Or people just don't do it?"

"It's cheesy," she says. "This is a classy club."

I nod and turn away, moving toward the bathroom sink to wash the excess glitter off my hands. Good, I think to myself. I'll stand out somehow. I move back to my station and begin to get dressed. A dancer begins to slowly spray a fruity perfume down her legs and I move away from her so that it doesn't mix with my scent. Working my way over bags of clothes and piles of shoes, I find another spot to stand. I pull on my orange t-back and check it in the mirror.

"Uh oh, you can't wear that," the house mom says, coming up behind me. She is a large woman with red hair piled high on her head.

"Why not?" I ask, beginning to get frustrated.

"You can't bend over to take it off or you'll break the law! You have to wear bottoms that snap away like these," she says, holding up a strange looking piece of material with two dangling plastic clips. "See, I'm turning these into break-away panties for that other new dancer. I'll get you something." She disappears for a moment and returns with a pair of red bottoms that snap at each hip. "Remember to never leave your bottoms on the stage or let the customers get near them. They'll steal them as soon as you turn your back."

"Why?" I ask.

"They want to sniff them," she says. She holds the piece of material up to her nose and pretends to inhale deeply.

"I'm not used to dancing totally nude, I guess," I say. "The rules are a bit different here."

"Oh yeah," she says. "Do we have rules. Come sit down when you're ready and we'll go over them. Do you have a name yet?"

"I've been dancing in Colorado as Sara," I say.

"I'm Sara," a girl calls from the mirror.

"Pick something else," the house mom says. "Just so you know, we already have an Alex, a Tyler, and a Nikki."

"Of course," I say. "Everyone does." I suggest some alternative names: Kristi, Shannon, Paula. All taken. She hands me a list of names from the baby book and the schedule and I begin to flip through it. I am really frustrated now, as I have been Sara for two years. It's such a nice, plain name that dancers don't usually use it. My real name, Elizabeth, has never made me feel sexy. Lori? Taken. Samantha? Taken. Jessie? Sorry.

Ugh. The night has begun.

*

Big-breasted women on the covers of magazines. Naked women inside. Magnets in the shape of women's torsos. Women wrapped in bows, showing long, tanned legs.

Exotic. Erotic. Playmates. Pets.

All these beautiful women to look at. Where do they keep coming from?

*

No touching the customers. No touching your breasts or genitals. No bending over or spreading. No sitting on laps. No flashing on the first song. Smile.

There is no specific rule as to when we take off our clothes, as long as we are naked by the end of the set. Generally, though, the house mom explained, girls take off their tops when they make three to five dollars, and go totally nude when they make eight to ten dollars. I am allowed to get naked on the first song if the customers tip enough, something that was specifically against the rules at my last club.

Before going onstage for the first time at a new club I am always nervous. Well, of course, friends say. They think that I should worry about being naked, or about falling down in my heels, or about seeing someone I know. But those are things that I don't worry about at all.

Instead, I worry about not being able to get my bottoms unsnapped gracefully, not knowing what the DJ is going to play for me, not knowing which dance moves are really allowed and which are not. I've danced in clubs where you couldn't touch any part of your body to the floor and I've danced in clubs where rolling around on the floor was expected. No matter how many times they go over the rules, nothing matters until you see it all in practice.

The DJ plays an eighties song for my first set of the night and introduces me as Claire, a name that I finally settled on with the house mom. Claire: how am I going to remember that? I think to myself. But then I am moving around the stage and the lights are warm on my skin. My dress feels floaty and light. I have to remind myself that I am a stripper, not a dancer. Sometimes, when I hear the music, I just want to be up there dancing and I forget to take off my clothes.

I dance the first song in my dress and no one comes up to tip me. Oh well, I think. I'm not wearing a bikini. Not sexy enough—even though my dress barely covers my butt and pushes my cleavage up on top. Okay, I just won't expect any tips on the first song tonight. When the second song starts, I peel the dress off quickly, so that I am topless with my new bottoms on. Still, no one comes up to tip me. I turn around and flip my hair so that it splashes on my butt. That is always guaranteed to send a customer up! I see some nods in the audience, but no one rises. I kick a leg around the pole and lean back in a half backbend. I press up against the mirrors. Nothing.

Weird, I think. Maybe I'm not smiling. I smile, making eye contact with several of the men in the audience. They smile back. It is beginning to seem like I have been onstage forever. Shit, I think. The dress? The glitter? Maybe they really do think that glitter is cheesy here. It could be my name, I realize. I remember trying to dance with the name Jenny before. After the third man told me that his wife's name was Jenny, I realized that I needed to change it. A man doesn't want to be fantasizing about someone who has the same name as his wife. It gets just a little too close to home.

I check my image in the mirror. I look the same as I always do when I'm dancing. More makeup than usual, large curls in my hair. Five-inch heels. I look okay. What is it? I wonder. I glance at the DJ. He seems unconcerned.

Finally, the third song starts. I debate getting off the stage and running to the dressing room. This has never, ever happened to me before. Feeling teary-eyed, I decide to just stand there on the stage, barely moving, in a kind of protest. Why expend all of this energy for free?

"This song, you'll see Claire nude! Totally nude!" the DJ says. "And remember, this is her *first* night!" I glare at him. He motions for me to take off my bottoms. I shake my head. He motions again, more insistently, so I unsnap the bottoms and tie them around my arm. I begin to move a little bit just so that I don't feel foolish.

Suddenly, there are five men at the stage. I see a few other men rising, reaching in their pockets for money. All at once, everyone in the room seems to be standing there waving their dollars. As I move to take my dollar from a man on the end of the stage, he smiles and says, "No one wants to waste their dollar before they can see the pussy."

*

Women sell cellular phones—smiling, wearing skintight dresses. Women sell bubble gum—smiling, wearing short miniskirts. Women sell contact lenses—smiling, wearing low-cut shirts.

Here, we sell "woman" in all different shapes and sizes. Why bother hawking a product at all when we all know what it really is that people want to buy?

Or do we?

*

Table dances are cheap in this city, so I find myself dancing more than I am used to over the course of the evening. I notice that some girls flash on the first song of their sets, as that seems to be the only way to avoid a mad rush of customers to the stage during the third song. After a few sets and some quick dances, I sit down at the bar to get my bearings.

A man approaches me. "Are you new?" he asks. I nod. "What's your name?"

"Claire," I say.

"That's not your real name," he says, motioning for the bartender.

"Do you want a drink?" I order a cranberry juice and vodka and he orders a beer. "What's your real name?"

"Sara," I lie.

"You look like a Sara," he says happily. "You're beautiful, Sara." He looks at my chest. "You have real breasts, don't you?" he says, as if he had made a sneaky discovery. I nod. "Don't ever get implants," he says. "Stay natural."

We talk for a bit and then he buys a table dance. "Are you turned on right now, Sara?" he asks as I take off my dress.

"Of course," I say. "I'm an exhibitionist." Men always like to hear that women are exhibitionists, I think to myself.

"You're not nervous?" he asks.

I shake my head no. "I enjoy dancing."

He looks disappointed. "But I thought it was your first night."

"In this club!" I say.

"Oh," he says sadly. "You're a professional."

I put my dress back on and make my way through the club again, laughing to myself. Sometimes I feel like I am giving people exactly what they want. Other times, though, I just can't even figure out what that is.

A table of men waves me over. Two of them are in their fifties and one looks like a teenage boy. They ask for a dance and so when a new song starts I take off my dress. I dance in front of all of their chairs, switching my attention from one to another and reminding myself to keep smiling. Sometimes I start thinking about other things—how my feet hurt, how much more money I need to make for tip-out, what my boyfriend is doing that night—and I get an expression on my face that can be mistaken for a scowl.

"What's your real name, Claire?" the youngest guy asks. He looks directly in my eyes, refusing to look at my body when I am in front of him.

"I can't tell you my real name," I say, trying a different approach. I turn around trying to get him to look at my butt and to forget about trying to talk.

"Why not?" he asks.

"Because it's mine," I say. I turn my attentions to the next man, putting my hands on his shoulders and looking down at his face. He keeps looking directly between my legs, never meeting my eyes.

"Who's your barber?" the man asks loudly. "Looks like all you girls have the same barber." The other men laugh. I smile.

I move over to the third man. "I like the glitter," he says. "Just don't get it on my clothes. I don't want my wife to know where I've been." The other men laugh. I smile again.

"Is tonight really your first night?" the youngest asks excitedly. I nod. "Are you nervous?" he asks.

"A little," I lie. I am beginning to realize that everyone wants a new girl here. "I've been having a few drinks to get myself through it."

He smiles. "You're doing a wonderful job," he says. "But are you sure you want to be a dancer?"

"I think so," I say. He looks at me with sympathy in his eyes.

Another of the men says, "Looks like you're cold, Claire." I look down at my nipples. "Well, they keep it cold so that you girls look good. If you know what I mean. Get used to being cold if you're gonna be a dancer." The other men laugh. I smile.

At the end of the song, I tell them that it will be ten dollars. The youngest man pulls out thirty dollars and as I lean down to take it, he grabs my arm. "Please tell me your real name," he says in my ear.

"Allison," I say softly. "Please don't tell everyone."

"Oh, I won't. I won't. My name is Jack. Would you go out to lunch with me tomorrow?"

"I'll think about it," I say.

As I move away from the table into the crowd I hear him say, "She told me her real name!"

✻

Here is an arm; there a leg. Here is a woman's torso, the same shape as a perfume bottle. Here is a skirt—you can almost see the panties underneath if you look up, up, up. Here is an eye, a glimpse of a smile.

What is it that makes us want to look? What is it that we're looking for?

✻

Midway through our shift, the DJ puts me onstage with the blonde girl who didn't like my glitter. Her stage name is Blair and the DJ seems to think that it is funny to keep saying our names over and over because they rhyme. I motion for him to shut up. Blair has changed her outfit, and now she is wearing a see-through purple dress. The dancers change their clothes a lot here, I think. In Colorado, the clubs were a lot busier and we never had time to change our clothes. I resolve to bring a few more outfits with me for my next shift.

We each take one end of the stage and basically ignore each other. A man waves at me from her end of the stage and so we switch sides after one song. I bend down and pull my garter out so that he can put a dollar in. He has the name Buck embroidered on the pocket of his shirt. "She has bigger tits than you," Buck tells me happily, looking at Blair. "But your legs are better."

I smile at him. What am I supposed to say? It always seems strange to me that some customers seem to want to give you a play-by-play run-down on their opinions.

"Are her tits fake?" he asks me.

"I wouldn't know that," I say, "but my legs aren't." After a few moments I move away toward another customer, a young guy in a baseball hat. He holds out a dollar and I dance in front of him for a few moments. "Who's your barber?" he asks, laughing. "Are you taking applications?" I smile and hold open my garter. He is trying to be witty, I think to myself. Does he have any idea how many customers make the same comments?

"Oh no," he says. "I want to see you work for it."

I smile, let the garter snap back on my leg and move to the other side of the stage, switching places with Blair again. For the first time, she smiles at me. "Did he ask you to work for it?" she says. "He's always in here." I nod and laugh.

During the last few seconds of the set, Jack approaches the stage, quite drunk. He slips a napkin and a dollar into my garter. "I love you Claire," he says through heavy-lidded eyes. He is slurring his words. "Call me. I'll buy you lunch."

"Okay, Jack," I say. He is pleased that I remembered his name.

After our set, Blair and I walk down the stairs to the dressing room holding our clothes. "If there's anything I can't stand," she says, "it's guys who think that a dollar entitles them to some kind of erotic aerobic workout. A buck's a look. It's just the economics of it. A dollar says 'thanks.' Now, a ten or a twenty onstage is different. That's saying something, you know?"

I sit in the dressing room for a few minutes, listening to the other dancers talk about boyfriends, kids, and customers. I touch up my makeup and put my dress back on.

When I go back out on the floor, I approach a man who waves me over. He introduces himself as Scott and I notice that he has a large black binder on the table. "What's that?" I ask.

He acts a bit nervous and I wonder if I should sit with someone else. "Well . . ." he hesitates.

"Well I'm not going to sit here if you're looking at kiddie porn or something," I say jokingly. We make small talk for a few minutes and I tell him that I study photography in college. His face lights up.

"Okay, sit," he finally says. He pulls out a grainy photograph that looks familiar. It is the same picture of Pam Anderson that Chris had been examining and I laugh. "Why are you laughing?" he asks, but then does not wait for an answer before he continues. "What I do is work with these nude celebrity photos that you find on the Internet."

"Really?" I say.

"See, this one is a fake." He points to her head. "Her head is a bit too large for her body. That's the first clue. But the most important thing is this. Here." He pulls out a magnifying glass and holds it over the photo. In the dim light of the club I can barely see anything.

"I don't really see anything," I say.

"Look here. The real Pam Anderson has a tattoo on her finger. This one doesn't!" He pulls out a picture of her from a tabloid magazine and points out the tattoo. He sits back looking quite pleased with himself.

"That's interesting," I say. "How do you remember such details about her?" Wait until I tell Chris, I think to myself.

Scott snatches the photo from me and places it back inside the binder. "You've got to keep your eyes open, girl. You've got to *look*."

*

Breast men. Leg men. So many parts to look at that, after a while, you can look beyond the obvious. "I love the nape of a woman's neck," a man might say. Or, "I love navels." "Would you believe that I love the underside of a woman's wrist?"

The eyes, the eyes, the eyes. Some just want to look in the eyes. "That's where it really is. It's in the eyes," they say.

Giant eyes, rimmed with black mascara, gazing frozen off the side of a city bus.

Hello, I say.

✳

I do a table dance with a girl named Tracy for a man in a business suit. "How many girls here are lesbians?" the guy asks us. "I know a lot of you girls are lesbians." He sounds titillated, like a little boy.

We look at each other. "We're girlfriends," she says. "We don't see anyone else."

"We're exclusive," I say. "But sometimes we like to bring a man home with us."

We flirt with him and he buys three dances from each of us on his credit card. His cell phone rings twice and both times he answers it. "Real lesbians," he tells someone on the phone. "Oh, I guess they could be faking. But they do look good together!" He winks at me.

Next I sit down with a much older man in the corner. He is wearing an old threadbare shirt and polyester pants. He smells like cigarettes and second-hand stores. "I don't want a dance," he says. "Will you just sit here for a moment if I pay you for a dance anyway?"

"Sure," I say. He takes out a ten and slips it in my garter.

"I'm Terry," he says.

"I'm Claire."

"You look like my wife did," he says.

"Really?"

"When she was young, of course. You remind me of her." He looks sad and I put my hand on his leg.

"Tell me about her," I say.

"Oh, you don't want to hear all that from an old man. You're a pretty young girl. Other people can tell you better stories."

"No, really," I say. "Tell me about her. Did she have obnoxious curly hair like I do?"

He laughs. "Actually, she was blonde. Short hair. But it was something in her eyes. Something in your eyes reminds me of hers."

We order drinks and he pays me for ten dances over the next hour. I don't take off my clothes and we just spend the time talking. He tells me stories about how he and his wife met, how he hitchhiked to Santa Fe to visit her at school, how they raised four kids together. He tells me how she died of cancer a year ago and how he wanders around the house with nothing to do. He asks me a few questions and I tell him my usual mix of truths and lies. I tell him about my sister, who is two years younger and my best friend. I tell him about my Golden Retriever puppy, and how he chewed through all of my furniture in one week. I tell him that I'm a student in town. Those are the truths. I also tell him that I don't have a boyfriend and that I still live with my parents. Those are the lies. Necessary lies—you don't want customers to be able to track you down if they decide to freak out on you. You also don't want to ruin a fantasy by telling someone that you are attached or even that you date around. "I just don't understand why it is," a guy once said to me. "All you beautiful girls and you're all single!" We had laughed about that one for a while in the dressing room.

Terry is a very polite and sweet man. I feel his loneliness and I am glad that I can talk to him for a while. He orders me some French fries and a bottled water. I don't want to drink any more alcohol so that I can pass my breathalyzer test. When I go onstage, he tips me during my first song instead of waiting until the third. Finally, it is almost time for the club to close. "You can dance this last song for me," Terry says, and I do. As he is watching me, I feel very close to him, like I want to protect him. I put my hands on his shoulders and they feel tight, tense. I feel him relax a bit under my hands. I smile.

After the song, he pays me for two dances instead of one. "I really had a nice time with you, Claire," he says. "A pretty girl is just another pretty girl. You know? There's got to be something more." He stops for a minute. "But you're very special. I had a really nice time."

"I did too," I say. "I really did."

"Oh, you don't have to say that. I know this is your job."

"No, really," I say. "I did."

"Oh, Claire," he says. "That's probably not even your real name."

"No, it's not. My real name is Elizabeth," I say. This time, I do want to give him something from me. Something to tell him that I really did enjoy hearing his stories.

"Okay, Elizabeth. Let's do this again." I give him a hug and head toward the dressing room, looking back over my shoulder at him. He waves and heads toward the door.

I do hope I see him again, I think. I picture him returning alone to a house cluttered with old lamps and musty bookshelves. I can almost see him climbing into bed, a bed that he shared for forty years that now seems too big, too open. I can feel the deep impression of her body in the mattress.

As I walk toward the dressing room, I feel a hand on my back. I turn around and it is Scott. He presses a business card into my hand. "Here's my card, Claire," he says. "And it gives an address for the Web site I manage—Great Nude Celebrity Fakes. We could maybe use you."

I look at the card and the Web site name confuses me. "So what do you do? Your job is to weed out the fakes? How could you use me?" My manager motions for me to get in the back and the lights in the club come on, bright and disrupting. Sometimes it is quite difficult to get customers to leave the club at closing time.

Scott looks at me in disbelief. "No," he says, shaking his head. "You don't get it, do you? My job is to put together the composites! I get a nude model and I put these things together. There is some great technology out there. I try to make them flawless, much better than that sloppy photo I showed you. But everyone knows they're fakes. That's beside the point." He shakes his head again and says, "Oh well. Call me if you want." He clutches his black binder underneath his arm and heads for the door.

I gather up my things in the locker room and change out of my heels into sneakers. I fold my money, count out my tip-outs and set them aside, and stuff the rest of the bills in my purse. Poor Chris, I think with a smile as I prepare to leave, actually believing that someone might pay him to *weed out* fakes in this crazy postmodern world.

✳

Girls on film. Girls on stage. Girls on television. Images, essences, art?

Oh, the possibilities. Didn't you ever put Skipper's head on Barbie's body? Ken's? Looking . . . looking.

There is always something, something else . . . just out of sight.

Chapter Five

"I'm Not Like the Other Guys":
Claims to Authentic Experience

It was the weirdest thing ever, Kate. I met a girl there . . . I thought she was a
very beautiful girl and we sat down and started talking and she became very
interested in me and she gave me her phone number, like, after we'd only been
talking like five minutes! And oh man, I was like, oh shit, man! I'm doing good,
and I'm . . . you know, this is . . . this is really happening to me? I'm forty-seven
years old and this girl's interested in me? Goddamn.
—David

When you come to work you need to put everything else out of your mind
except the reason that you're here. And the reason that you're here, it's to sell
an illusion. We create an illusion for money. We try to create the fact that
they're here with you and they're going to end up going home with you, falling
in love with you, whatever their fantasy is at the time. You've got to create that
illusion, but that's all it is. It's a business.
—Night manager, Pony Lounge

The short story "Fakes" was written in early 1998 as an attempt to think
through some of the complex demands for authenticity made by the
customers of strip clubs. This chapter continues this inquiry, using the
talk of the interviewees, in addition to my experiences in the clubs, to
explore the interconnections among customer experiences, pleasure,
and a discourse of authenticity, or "realness." Elsewhere I have examined the issue of realness in regard to dancers' relationships with their
regular customers and discussed the strategies used by dancers to authenticate these interactions (Frank 1998). Realness is not important

only in ongoing relationships with regulars, however, even though it has a specific and important place there. It was also an element in many men's experiences of pleasure or satisfaction in their visits to strip clubs even if they did not develop longer-term relationships with particular dancers. This was evidenced by the pride with which customers spoke about certain kinds of pleasurable encounters and about the concern, voiced repeatedly in interviews and interactions, that they were somehow being hustled or misled into paying for a faked or an unsatisfying performance.

Many men, of course, understand their visits to strip clubs to be about "entertainment," "fantasy," and "fun" rather than *reality* (see Chapter 3). As Herb said, "You keep fantasy and reality apart." Some men also consciously choose to interact with the dancers with the most oversized breasts and the most outrageous makeup and costumes (accoutrements associated with inauthenticity, as will be discussed), especially at bachelor parties and on other group occasions. Other men are happy enough to spend time with known hustlers if they find the dancers attractive. Judging someone to be sincere or fake is not the only way to discern the value of an interaction, as there are times in which "the ability to pull off a role with spirit" is more important (Abrahams 1986: 66). I was sent away from a table one night, for example, because one of the men in the group thought I was "too serious" and he "didn't want to have to think"; I had mentioned that I was a graduate student. As in other chapters, I am not trying to generalize here about *every* customer or *every* interaction. On the other hand, concerns about realness, at some level, were salient in the *majority* of the interactions that I had and surfaced in every one of the interviews in one form or another.[1]

Because of the inherent difficulty in interviewing individuals about fantasy and desire (conscious and unconscious), I often asked the interviewees broad, general questions about their visits to strip clubs and let them talk as long as possible without interrupting them to redirect the questioning. I also allowed the men to ask me any questions that occurred to them during the interviews. Many of the comments about realness that appear in this chapter were offered spontaneously in response to questions about what was particularly enjoyable about visiting strip clubs or in these extended dialogic exchanges.

Authenticity and Touristic Practice

The question of authenticity has long been an issue in the literature on tourism and tourist motivation, both academic and popular. Early on, tourism was opposed to travel and exploration and associated with "packaged" and "largely inauthentic" experiences (Curtis and Pajacz-kowska 1994: 202). The traveler, then, supposedly seeks and gains self-realization through his[2] journeys, his "raw and meaningful encounters," whereas the tourist is interested in "guarantees—itineraries, insurance, and secure destinations." Though these assumptions about exploration and travel are questionable, this opposition has also been highly signifi-cant in structuring the discourse on motivation and pleasure in tourism and touristic practice and certainly arose in the many ways that cus-tomers narrated their experiences (203). Some authors have theorized a concern with authenticity as a result of the alienating conditions of modernity; others have postulated it as the result of a desire for distinc-tion, as an experience that grants a form of symbolic capital to the discerning individual, "more a marker of taste than of alienation in modern society" (Tucker 1997: 115).

Daniel Boorstin, an early writer on the phenomenon of mass tour-ism, was quite critical of tourists, arguing that contemporary American mass tourists "cannot experience 'reality' directly but thrive on 'pseudo-events'" (in Urry 1990: 7), gullibly satisfied with contrived events and finding *pleasure* in them despite their inauthenticity. Sociologist Dean MacCannell challenged Boorstin's position, noting that this kind of critique of tourists is couched in a "rhetoric of moral superiority" (Oth-ers are tourists and I am not) and that tourists are often reproached not for their desire to leave home but "for being *satisfied* with superficial experiences of other people and other places" (MacCannell 1976: 10; emphasis added). He also noted that such moral pronouncements were not merely the provision of the social theorist, as even "tourists dislike tourists" (9). Such a critique of society, couched in what MacCannell terms a "dialectics of authenticity," "assumes the inauthenticity of everyday life in the modern world" (147).

MacCannell, on the other hand, sees tourists as "contemporary pil-grims," "seeking authenticity in other 'times' and other 'places away from that person's everyday life'" (in Urry 1990: 8). In this search, particular fascination comes to be shown by tourists in the "real lives" of others, making a "production" and a fetish of urban street life, rural village life, and traditional (thus authentic) domestic relations. Tourists may sometimes be allowed to peer into some of the "back regions" of societies they visit, or they may either purposefully or accidentally stumble on what they perceive as such an experience of real life (Mac-Cannell 1976: 97). Because the tourist gaze becomes obtrusive to the hosts over time, however, tourist spaces may come to be organized around what MacCannell terms "staged authenticity," such that they *appear* to offer an entry into "back" regions (98).[3] The knowledge that authenticity may be staged leads to a fundamental uncertainty in the tourist, as "often it is very difficult to know for sure if the experience is in fact authentic." It is always possible, MacCannell argues, "that what is taken to be entry into a back region is really entry into a front region that has been totally set up in advance for touristic visitation" (101). He sees a continuum of stages, from front to back regions, and notes that "adventuresome tourists may progress from stage to stage," courting authentic experience in an incremental manner (106). MacCannell realizes that, although the tourist may indeed encounter inauthentic scenarios, this results from the social relations of tourism and not necessarily from "an individualistic search for the inauthentic" through the consumption of pseudo-events (in Urry 1990: 9). The tourist may also potentially come away from the experience dissatisfied with the outcome of his quest.

MacCannell's construction of tourist experience has been as widely critiqued as it has been influential.[4] Philip Crang, for example, critiques MacCannell's division of tourist spaces into regions, arguing that the "contemporary spatial restructurings of tourism-related interactional settings do not all follow the trend of staged back regions" and that the oppositions of authenticity / inauthenticity and truth / falsity cannot be thus so simply discussed in these terms. He also writes: "Simple associations of front-stage with a 'put on' performance, and back-stage with 'natural behavior,' are stultifying to critical analysis. They lead to a replication of the 'tragic' narrative of lost authenticity, in which the real is destroyed by whoever seeks it at the moment of its discovery" (1997: 149). Using Arlie Hochschild's (1983) notion of emotional labor I have also challenged a simplistic reading of performed emotion as inauthentic, arguing that even commodified relationships may involve a high level of emotional involvement and that "natural" intimate relationships may rely on manufactured intimacies (Frank 1998).[5]

Some writers have also questioned whether individuals even still seek authenticity in touristic experience and practice in postindustrial capitalist societies. The idea of the post-tourist was originally proposed in response to this question about motivation (Feifer 1986). The post-tourist is self-reflexive, recognizes tourism as a "game," and enjoys pseudo-events or staged performances for being "exactly what they are" (Urry 1990: 100).[6] In a different formulation, sociologist John Urry has argued that rather than the search for authenticity, a key feature of tourism has become the "difference between one's normal place of residence / work and the object of the tourist gaze."[7] Authenticity is thus important only insofar as it provides a "contrast with everyday experiences" (11). In providing a contrasting scene, touristic practice also serves to legitimize the tourist's everyday life. Urry draws on Colin Campbell's (1987) idea of the "imaginative hedonism" that underlies modern consumption to argue that tourism also "necessarily involves daydreaming and anticipation." Instead of consuming for distinction or for identity, Urry argues, people may "seek to experience 'in reality' the pleasurable dramas they have already experienced in their imagination." They may end up disillusioned, however, as " 'reality' can never provide the perfected pleasures encountered in daydreams" (13). Although tourists may still seek authenticity, then, they may actually derive more pleasure from the anticipation than the realization of their daydreams. Urry's focus on the relativity of authenticity with regard to the everyday is a significant move toward understanding people's diverse motivations and pleasures in particular forms of leisure consumption. What is needed, however, is a deeper understanding of the way that the everyday is itself informed by fantasy.

Sociologists George Ritzer and Allan Liska, on the other hand, argue in a recent article that there is evidence that "people increasingly travel to other locales in order to experience much of what they experience in their day-to-day lives." That is, instead of desiring an "out of the ordinary" adventure or even an escape, people are in search of highly predictable, highly efficient, highly calculable, and highly controlled ("McDisneyized") experiences (99). Ritzer and Liska draw on Baudrillard's notion of simulacra to discuss tourism and propose yet another tourist motivation: that "many tourists today are actually in search of *inauthenticity,"* or perfect simulacra. As an illustration of this, they note that the caves of Lescaux in France have been closed for preservation but that an exact replica of them, a simulation, has been built nearby and opened to the public (107). Yet, if Ritzer and Liska are correct, what then could account for tourist dissatisfaction with particular experiences? Simply unpredictable events, or a lack of efficiency? And how would tourists distinguish among sites / sights? Why would one *desire* to visit any given destination over another?

In arguing that tourists actively *seek* the inauthentic, Ritzer and Liska are actually departing from Baudrillard, for whom this dichotomy no longer exists. Indeed, for Baudrillard, simulation is different from something that is *faked*: "Pretending, or dissimulating, leaves the principle of reality intact: the difference is always clear, it is simply masked, whereas simulation threatens the difference between the 'true' and the 'false,' the 'real' and the 'imaginary'" (1981: 3). The era of simulation, he writes, has been "inaugurated by a liquidation of all referentials" and has seen "their artificial resurrection in the systems of signs." The search for the real is "no longer a question of imitation, nor duplication, nor even parody." Rather, "it is a question of substituting the signs of the real for the real" (2). When Baudrillard himself discusses the caves of Lescaux, for example, he concludes that there is *no difference* between the original caves and the replica: "the duplication suffices to render both artificial" (9).[8]

Certainly, technology has advanced to the point at which such near perfect replication is a distinct possibility, and this has significant consequences for consumption and tourism. As geographer David Harvey notes, it is possible to "replicate ancient buildings with such exactitude that authenticity or origins can be put into doubt." Antiques and art objects can be manufactured, even forged, and images can be transformed into material simulacra "indistinguishable from the originals" (1990: 290). In the age of simulations, a self-conscious search for the inauthentic would be just as meaningless and futile as a search for the authentic. Tourists must then either abandon the search altogether or always remain profoundly dissatisfied. In looking at strip clubs we are seeing the production of images, identities, and experiences rather than material objects. How does a dialectics of authenticity play out in regard to this particular form of touristic practice and consumption?

Do the customers really seek authenticity in their interactions with the dancers, or is authenticity disappearing as a concern, as some of the above theorists suggest? And finally, how does a discourse of authenticity influence the pleasure that consumers take in these interactions?

Visiting a strip club like Diamond Dolls, one would find, at first glance, a confirmation of Baudrillard's theories of simulacra and hyperreality. After all, in Diamond Dolls up to a hundred women a night impersonate decontextualized and dehistoricized images: the schoolgirl, the dominatrix, the blonde, the athlete, the exotic Asian, the cowgirl. Each may be a stranger, yet "someone we recognize, or think we recognize," images that are a condensation of social narratives about the already "over-represented" female body (Phelan 1993: 62).[9] Sometimes this procession of images takes the form of self-conscious masquerades; often not. For many dancers, silicone or saline breast implants have become the ultimate accessories, as real breasts are increasingly found to be lacking in aesthetic perfection by the customers. Indeed, some customers may not even remember (or know) that there once was a difference between natural and surgically enhanced breasts, as unmodified breasts have disappeared from many of the cultural representations of women's bodies.[10] (*"Oh, and there's a new surgery to standardize your labia, to make sure the lips are tucked like Barbie, have you heard?"*) Hundreds of smiles are offered as examples of "Southern hospitality" (Does anyone remember which women worked to make everything so hospitable for white men in the Old South?), meant "just for you" but directed at the crowd. And several times a night every dancer in the club disrobes simultaneously in a prearranged, much anticipated spectacle—momentarily proving sexual and gender difference to be obvious, inarguable. "In post-modern terms," Gamman and Makinen write, "gender is the perfect simulacrum—the exact copy of something that never existed in the first place" (1994: 217).

Yet despite its seductiveness, such an analysis of the strip club falls short of the actual complexity of the customers' experiences. And despite claims that the search for authenticity as a motivating force for leisure or touristic practices is diminished in postmodern societies, the issue of authenticity remains and continues to be interrogated by the customers themselves.

Claims to Authenticity

The customers made a variety of different claims to authenticity in their relationships in the clubs, despite the fact that most of them also claimed that their encounters there were about fantasy. Though claims to authenticity were made in a number of different ways, the men most frequently tended to draw on the following narratives to support those claims: friendship, cynicism, comparisons between commodified and legitimate relationships, and comparisons to other forms of adult entertainment.

FRIENDSHIP: "GETTING BACKSTAGE"

Many of the men I interviewed who considered themselves to be regular customers of particular clubs referred to their relationships with the dancers they visited as primarily that of "friends." These men pointed out that they knew significant details about the dancers' lives: where the women lived, whether they had a boyfriend or partner, the names of their children, their history, and so on. These men also claimed that these relationships were symbiotic and pleasurable, highlighting their platonic aspects and stressing that they returned for the conversation, the friendship, and the atmosphere of the club rather than out of any prurient interest in the dancers. Beck referred to his favorite strip clubs as being "like Cheers," making reference to the neighborhood pub featured in the television show of the same name. Indeed, this reference to "Cheers," a popular television series about a neighborhood bar where "everybody knows your name," also turned up quite frequently in my informal conversations at the various clubs, both upper and lower tier. Beck claimed to be friends not only with the dancers, but also with bartenders, waitresses, and other employees of the clubs.

Some of the men also pointed out that they did favors for the dancers out of this sense of friendship. When I first began dancing, for example, one of my regulars used to buy me off the stage rotation several nights a week, paying a hundred dollars an hour for my time while we sat together in the club as "friends." The monetary exchange was never done as a direct transaction for the time I spent with him, however. Rather, he would say, "I'd like to help you out, Kate," and then pull out the exact amount of money that he owed me according to the rules of the club. Customers also brought gifts to the dancers or provided them with aid in the form of rent, car, or credit card payments instead of in direct cash transactions. Instead of giving me extra money, for example, another regular bought me a cellular phone and offered to pay for my calls. Mick told me proudly that he was often involved in providing legal advice to the dancers he was friends with and had helped several of them through divorces and other legal proceedings. Roger pointed out that he had provided financial information to dancers, helping them choose good investments and teaching them about the stock market. Other men offered to fix things around the dancers' apartments, pay for their breast implants or other plastic surgeries, landscape their yard, help them find "real" jobs outside of the industry, or prepare their tax forms.

Many of the men I spoke with also expressed an interest in getting backstage, to know what happens in the dressing room, after work, or in the dancers' private life. This was something that was assumed to happen when one became friends with the dancers, of course. It was also, however, an aspect of the visits that such men courted even during brief encounters. The dancers' life (or stories of their life) thus also become part of the performance and part of the experience being sought. Ross and Beck, for example, claimed to enjoy talking to any of the dancers, not just the ones they saw regularly, "getting to know them as people" and hearing "one fascinating story after another." Matthew said that he first started going to strip clubs when he was in a fraternity during his college years: "I think the fraternity was just sort of interested in going and seeing naked women. But as I said, at some point you sort of get bored with that. There's only so many you can see. And at some point, I don't remember when it first started, but someone sat down and started talking. And then I started thinking about social views about sexuality and nudity and started trying to get into [the dancers'] heads about how they do it." Similarly, Jason said, "I'm interested in the culture, the subculture stuff that goes on. It's always interesting to me to hear the stories and watch." Jack, a regular customer turned manager of a strip club, said, "I fell in love with the psyche of dancers and I've been in love with it all my life . . . just to find out how they got into it and how far left or right or whatever . . . how these girls work. Or some of the problems they have in life." Alex said that he enjoyed "just watching people, everybody," and "knowing what's going on." Similarly, several times during our interactions in the club and during the interview,

Roger referred to himself as "a kind of anthropologist, like you."[11] To have an anthropological or sociological interest in the interactions, it seemed, was to express not only a more refined understanding of the events that unfolded in the clubs but also to justify one's own presence there (participant observation?). In some ways, then, my presence as an anthropological observer could thus be used by some of the customers to legitimize their visits even further.

Many of these men asked me a number of questions about what it was like to be a dancer (Do you enjoy dancing? Are you ever nervous?), whether the stereotypes were true (Have most of the dancers been sexually abused? Are many of them lesbians?), and most important to them, how I / we felt about the customers (Do you hate the men?). They also tended to report to me at length, both on the floor of the strip club and in the interviews, on what dancers in other clubs had told them about work, boyfriends, parents, and school. Interestingly, these men also felt very individualistic in their desires for authenticity, repeatedly making generalizations about other men and saying things such as "I *know* I'm not like other guys"; "Other guys just want to look at T&A"; and "I'm not going there for the nudity."

Another way of getting backstage would be to actually date a dancer. Although none of the interviewees explicitly drew on this claim, there were other men with whom I talked who maintained that their inter-actions in the clubs were more authentic than those of the other customers because they had actually had an intimate relationship with a dancer at one time.

RECOGNIZING PERFORMANCE: THE POST-TOURISTS

Another way the men established themselves as different from the other customers and as the recipients of genuine interactions was by claiming the ability to see through staged performances in the clubs with the cynicism of a post-tourist. There were some men who claimed that at the most basic level they "didn't care" whether an interaction was genuine, because they understood that most of the encounters would involve as much fiction as truth. At the same time, however, these men also made claims to be able to tell if the interaction was faked and offered examples of their ability to discern the truthful aspects of it. Tim claimed that he could look out at the floor and tell which dancers were "hustlers": "That one, that one, that one, and that one—they're just here to make money." This ability to discern the truth, for these customers, becomes a way of supposedly distinguishing oneself from the masses who are so easily duped by the inevitable performances.

Several men, for example, commented directly that they enjoyed watching the other customers become entranced in an inauthentic exchange. Roger said that he would sometimes set up such a scene: "This is what I like to do, like what I did last night. I'll go in there and spend a bunch of money with guys who don't have any money or don't have as much as I do, or whatever. You know, or don't want to spend it for whatever reason. And I like to cut up and get people up and just have a good time with them and see what they'll say if I buy them dances and stuff like that. And I like to watch the interaction, like you do . . . I'll be sitting at a table with some guy and he'll say, you know, 'I brought three hundred dollars with me, I'll see if I can get that girl to go home with me.' And I'm like, uh huh, yeah . . . that always tickles me." Though Roger is the one who paid for the interactions he felt a sense of superiority because he also felt that he really understood how this world works. He was adamant that he "understood strip clubs as a business," and laughed at (less wealthy) men who thought the dancers were really attracted to them: "I mean, I'm sure most of these girls like their customers so-so, or at least to a certain degree just like in any other atmosphere. You're going to like some people you meet and not going to like some people you meet. So it can go either way. But the idea that this is a singles bar and that you're gonna pick these girls up and take them somewhere else . . . it just isn't going to happen. It just doesn't work that way." "It amuses me," he said, "to see these men so captivated that they really think they have a chance with the dancers."

Steven had been visiting strip clubs for many years, both on business and for pleasure when he was traveling. His comments were similar: "I think most guys realize it's a fantasy. Yet, many of them get caught up in the fantasy. I don't know how many times I've laughed with my business associates about the guy at the next table . . . he's just sitting, totally looking at the girl in adorement and is starstruck and he's just falling in love with her. And she's good! She's falling in love back, right? And he's buying it! [laughs] To me, it's like you want to go over and knock on his head. Hello? Hello! She isn't going to marry you after the night's over!" Here Steven's unintended double meaning of "buying"—that of both purchasing and believing—is striking. Doubting the dancers' stories and

performances is, in part, a way of reasserting control over a commodified situation (I may be *buying* her time, but I'm not *buying* her performance). Unlike other men who were "suckered" into believing that
their interactions were genuine, Steven believed that he was able to
separate the performances from the real encounters. He explained:

> I am not fooled by the dancer who hands me a phone number at the end
> of the night in a club . . . this just happened last month in Dallas. "Oh
> God, I really need to meet some new people who really have their head
> on their shoulders and, you know, people who are working profes-
> sionals such as yourself!" "Ooh, I would love to go to lunch and get to
> know you!" I did not walk away thinking it was sincere. I walked away
> thinking me and my two associates spent some good money and she
> would like to see us come back and make sure we spend it on her again.
> That's all it was about from my perspective. The number was on a
> napkin that is somewhere in a garbage can.

Despite Steven's cynicism, however, he also mentioned that he had
made several "very good friends" in the Panther over the years he had
been visiting the club and that he returned to see them each time he
came to town.

Paradoxically, sometimes the men's cynicism kept them from believing things that were actually true, such as when I told customers that I
danced under my real name (as I did whenever possible)[12], that I was
doing research for my dissertation, or that I enjoyed a particular man's
company. One customer doubted that I was really married even though
I wore a wedding ring; he thought this was a ploy I was using to make
myself seem unavailable. For some men, such cynicism also meant that
many of their interactions were dissatisfying. Others, like Steven, found
pleasure in the experiences as entertaining even as they doubted the
veracity of everyone's interactions (and also derived pleasure from the
ability to point out others' gullibility). In many ways, however, such a
post-tourist's mentality is not very different from that of someone seeking authenticity. After all, the cynic is once again the one who perceives
the "real nature" of things—even though, in this case, it is an essential
fakedness that in the end is revealed to be the truth. The discerning
individual, then, is once again able to one-up his peers. By claiming to
understand the rules of the game, the customers were also claiming the
authority to be able to judge their own encounters as genuine or not.

SOCIAL CRITIQUE: "IT AIN'T NEVER BEEN FREE!"

Another claim to authenticity took the form of a social critique of relationships between men and women more generally. Some of the customers pointed out that the explicit commodification underlying relationships in strip clubs made the interactions there *more* authentic than their relationships in other spheres, for example. The absence of gendered "games" was noted positively by many of the men (see Chapter 3). In other relationships, such as dating or marriage, these men felt they had to pretend that money was not involved in the considerations of both parties. Yet, as Herb noted, "It ain't never been free, darling!" Gary compared the relationships that he developed both inside and outside the clubs to each other, speaking of them both as "investments" and situations of "trade." Ross compared the brief relationship between a dancer and a customer to a "marriage contract" where both parties could potentially "have their needs met." Like two of the other married men, Louis and Tim, Ross felt that his own marriage was based, in part, on such economic considerations.

These interviewees explained that the monetary exchange was instrumental, not necessarily a barrier to an authentic interaction. As Herb said, "Paying the money gets you to where you want to be without all the other trappings of having to go through a typical courting-type relationship. Where it's like, okay, you're pretty, I'd love to see you naked. I want to have a situation where I can have that happen and then we can move on. I mean, I'd love to have it happen without the money but it's probably not going to!" Similarly, Ross said:

> You're massaging the man's ego. That's what it boils down to. It's what makes the man feel good about himself. It's an ego massage, by giving him the drinks he wants, the food he wants, the massage he wants, you know, whatever it takes, it's in return for—value for value. I mean, since we're not in a barter economy it's one thing that to me takes the sting out of money. I look at it as just a method of transference. It comes across as cold-hearted cash, but we're talking about giving somebody ten dollars and on the one hand . . . I can look at it as x amount of what I did, you know, just reduce it to something I can carry around . . . The whole point is people can't carry cows and pigs on their arms and you've got something you can shove in your wallet . . . it's like, I take out this little unit that came from what I did, and in return I want you to do

something for me. That's barter. People see money as more impersonal than I do, I guess. It is, but it's not . . . I mean, you put something into that money! It's like, I'm giving her part of my life and my work. I'm not sure many people realize that when they make cash. You earned that money. That means it's part of the time of your life and everything of your life put into that money.

Ross felt that his relationship with his wife was in some ways more impersonal than his interactions with dancers, as he and his wife no longer had sex and were staying together (in his opinion) only because of their son.

Though feminist theorists have made similar critiques over the years about the economic underpinnings of heterosexual relationships, none of these men identified as feminist. Rather, their critique seemed to stem from a desire to defend their practices against those who would say they were being conned out of their money by a manipulative female.

"REAL" LIVE NUDE GIRLS

Claims to authenticity were also made through the assertion that strip clubs offered a more "real," and thus a more desirable form of adult entertainment than pornography, prostitution, and lingerie parlors. As I noted earlier, most of the American men I encountered who considered themselves *regular* customers of strip clubs did not find other forms of adult entertainment especially enjoyable. This was partly due to beliefs and concerns about safety, monogamy, and commitment. To some extent it also involved their ideas about commodification and about what constituted an acceptable exchange. Jason, for example, said that he never used escorts:

There's probably a spectrum of comfort in regard to what you're getting and what you're paying for and all that. I guess it's not much of a stretch to go from a strip club to an escort if you rationalize it. But the thing is, with an escort you're paying by the hour . . . So to me, you know for sure by definition that they're not with you in any way, any time they're in there, just to be with you. And you can rationalize it . . . I mean, anyone could. They could say, "Well, yeah, but they like me better than the other people that are paying them." And at a strip club you can hang out with people who you don't give that many dances to. Or even none. I mean, some of the girls I've got along with the best and hung out with the most, just because of the time involved, they've started feeling bad about it. The good ones, the nice ones. They've actually started feeling . . . That becomes less of a transaction and more quality time.

Ross felt similarly about escorts and prostitutes, as he believed that sex should be accompanied by a "real" connection:

Ross: I have a very strong abhorrence to money for sex . . . my entire life, I paid for sex once. Just because I had to, to see what it was like. It was disastrous.

KF: Before you were married?

Ross: Yeah. Disastrous. Didn't even consummate it. I couldn't. It was just so abhorrent to me. And she was, you know, it was a nicer lady of the evening. It was not a street prostitute. But even so . . . when I slept with a lot of people when I was younger, it was never, "Hi, what's your name, let's go back to my room." It was somebody that I liked and you'd talk and well, some of the talking was very short but it still was not, you know . . . most of that time, I tried to stay with relationships. Even if it was a casual encounter, I didn't go, I'm gonna get laid tonight . . . I mean, we'd go through the whole courtship ritual, so to speak. It was not a meat market approach. It was, you know, I'm looking for somebody to spend the night with and feel that sense of connectedness. I just could not look myself in the mirror going totally for paid sex. To me, that makes it so mechanical and such a transaction. Dancing is one thing, I guess, in a sense because it's um . . . [long pause] I have to give that some thought. I really do.

The financial transactions that took place in the strip clubs were less direct and less mandatory for Jason than in other commodified sexualized arrangements. For Ross, the exchange with dancers was more acceptable because it did not involve actual sexual release, something that he thought should not be a "mechanical" transaction. Phillip recounted "horror stories" of his experience in a Laurelton jack shack, saying that his visit was "an anomaly," contrived and "completely unerotic," and that he would never return.

Other men spoke negatively about pornography, arguing that it was too far removed from the real world of heterosexual interaction to be worthwhile. Louis said, "Why would you sit at home and look at pornography when you can go out and talk to a real woman? I don't like being aroused without something behind it." Gary was adamant about this as well, saying, "I'm very antiporn. It's not a turn-on to me . . . I'm not into x-rated films. I'm not into watching other guys getting sucked off. It's just not my idea of a good time." In the past, he had looked at pornographic magazines, however: "I always had a level of decency because I found *Hustler* to be really trashy and disgusting. I never got into *Hustler.* Then I got into the ones with the amateurs in there. I've always been into the amateurs. Like *Gallery* magazine. The girl next door." But, he added, "once you see them in a picture, now you want to see them in person." His comments point to an authenticity of presence that was important to other men as well. David said, "I can't talk to a book. I can't talk to a video. You can get aroused, and dream about it, but that becomes very selfish to focus on yourself. Why not share that with someone?" That this "shared" encounter involved a potential performance was a risk David was willing to take; as evidenced by his quote at the beginning of this chapter, however, he was also not one of the men who tended to automatically doubt every transaction. Steven said that "porn was good when you were twelve" but that he was no longer interested in it. His comment is interesting because it connects certain sexual practices to the issue of maturity. For heterosexuals there is certainly a strong push toward taking up a monogamous partnership as one matures; this is also part of the definition of maturity given in psychoanalytic theory.[13]

Interestingly, men I spoke with who did *not* enjoy strip clubs also often drew on these same kinds of arguments. One man referred to strip clubs as "refusing to deliver the real thing" (sexual release), for example. Glen, a former customer who had decided that he no longer liked strip clubs, said that the clubs were "just a tease" and that the women were "exploitative"—unlike the women on the pages of a porn magazine who did not keep demanding to be paid directly for their bodily revelations. Similarly, Brett said, "Why would you want to just sit there and stare at a woman? I just don't—that's what I don't understand. I mean, I would rather go out and interact and meet somebody and hope to get to stare at her later on like that in the privacy of my home or her home. But to just sit there all night and just say, here's my money, here's my money. I don't get that." Brett found it "insulting" when he felt that a dancer was being insincere. Although he was an occasional customer of Tina's Revue, he stated that he only went with friends and was "more interested in the food" than in watching the dancers. At the same time, however, he did have a desire to "get backstage," and spent time when he was in the club asking the dancers questions about their lives.

"Whether It's Real or Not": Alienation, Taste, and Identity

Claims to authenticity, then, were ubiquitous as the men narrated their experiences in strip clubs. This does not mean that the men were *not* actually friends with the dancers, were *not* really interested in getting backstage information (or were *not* able to do so), could *not* tell the difference between genuine encounters and perfunctory exchanges, or did *not* believe that their interactions in the strip clubs really were more "real" than those offered in other kinds of male-female relationships or in other forms of adult entertainment. Rather, the *claims* to authenticity were important to the men themselves in understanding and narrating their experiences and in shaping the pleasure that they did take in these commodified encounters. So why are these claims so important?

Some theorists argue that the emphasis on authentic interaction is due to the alienation brought about by the spread of commodification to human relationships. As Arlie Hochschild points out in *The Managed Heart*, in a society in which the growth of the service sector has meant an increase in the commercialization of feeling and the need for "emotional labor," there has been a corresponding increase in the value of authenticity in interaction. She writes: "All of us who know the commercialization of human feeling at one remove—as witness, consumer, or critic—have become adept at recognizing and discounting commercialized feeling: 'Oh, they have to be friendly, that's their job.' This enables us to ferret out the remaining gestures of a private gift exchange: 'Now *that* smile she really meant just for me.' We subtract the commercial motive and collect the personal reminders matter-of-factly, almost automatically, so ordinary has the commercialization of human feeling become" (1983: 190). This "private gift exchange" in a strip club can take the form of a man paying money to the dancer who is most convincing in her performance of authentic engagement. Certainly, there were some men for whom this analysis would ring true, who discussed the "depersonalization" of the work world and their desire to "just connect with another human being." Yet, as will become clear, their claims to authenticity were more complicated than this.

Jason, a regular customer at Diamond Dolls and one of the youngest interviewees, said: "Some [dancers] will trick you but [with friends] it's not tricking. We both know what they're supposed to be doing, I guess. You're just good friends. Once a girl makes the money [from other customers], then she'll come back and hang out. And I like to make them feel okay while they're hanging out with me and I'll throw some dance stuff in there. Because I understand they've got to make money. There's a couple of cool girls that I can hang out with there that are doing it not so much to make money but to hang out. That's the ones I like best. [pause] Whether it's real or not." Clearly, Jason's statement needs to be unpacked. As a dancer at Diamond Dolls, I can honestly say that I never met a dancer who fit his description of "not doing it so much to make money but to hang out." Hanging out, playing, and partying, however, were all important and interconnected aspects of the job itself, as in other kinds of tourism employment. Jason's comment that this was important to him "whether it's real or not" highlights this idea of a private gift exchange and the fact that for some men it is the *performance* of authenticity that needs to be the most engaging.

Jason admitted that he could not always tell who was sincere: "Sometimes I make a mistake because someone'll look like they're friendly and you know, they do a dance for you and they're not . . . you give them the money and they go away." He said that he appreciated it when a dancer sat with him without asking for table dances, and in these instances, he would often pay her anyway for a dance or two. Because of the emphasis that Jason placed on this proof of friendly sincerity, however, he was often dissatisfied with the attention that he received from dancers. He would make a dancer wait four songs before paying her for one ten-dollar dance, and the financial constraints of high club tip-outs and stiff competition meant that few dancers could wait that long, regardless of whether we enjoyed his company. Those of us who knew him, then, often would avoid his table unless the club was nearly empty and there was no other money to be made.

As Jason's comments indicate, customers often are not unaware when the pleasantries of an interaction have been purchased, and such commodified relationships are always threatened by a possibly explosive contradiction rooted in common ideologies surrounding intimacy and companionship: real relationships are not supposed to be based on lies or performances, and though money can buy a lot of things, it *should not be able* to buy love, companionship, friendship, or happiness. The difficulty in mediating this contradiction was evident to many regular customers. Zachary said, for example, "About once a week I stop in the Panther and, you know, eat lunch. Coming in there once a week, you get to meet people and everything. You meet some of the girls and you know some of them you are friendly with and you like and you become friends with. I walk in there now for lunch and it's like, you know, a bunch of the girls recognize me and everything and they're like, 'Hey, that's Zach!' And they'll come over they'll sit with me and hang." Although he had originally gone in because of curiosity, he claimed that it was the relationships that he developed that kept him going back. Yet he was often concerned about the genuineness of these relationships: "You just don't like to think that if they had the opportunity . . . [pause] you almost have to say to yourself, if they had the opportunity to take all my money and disappear, would they? How bad would this person screw me over?" He spoke at length about encounters where this *had* happened and about the disillusionment he felt later.

The payment of money thus has the potential to unsettle an interaction because its symbolic value is one that is ideologically incommensurable with romantic love or true friendship. Herein lies an important contradiction: if a dancer's performance is believable enough, the relationship between dancer and customer seems genuine; an exchange of money during the interaction, then, undermines that authenticity. It is the exchange of money, however, that always facilitated the interaction in the first place. In addition to legitimating (both to others and to oneself) visits to strip clubs that might otherwise be stigmatized, an emphasis on developing a "real" relationship may help mitigate the psychological dissonance caused by the commodification of interpersonal interaction. In relationships with regulars, gifts came to take on a specific importance as they mediated and *personalized* the relationships, simply because they were not in the form of money. Many customers also preferred to buy dancers cocktails instead of table dances, because the dancer would have to sit with him to drink it and it made the payment of money less direct.

Over the years that I have been studying strip clubs, I have had the opportunity to speak informally with many people outside of the clubs about my research in addition to conducting the more formal interviews. Early on in the process I noticed an interesting pattern among many men with whom I spoke. Some, of course, were threatened by my work; others thought that it could not possibly count as anthropological research. A few vehemently denied *ever* visiting strip clubs. Some, however, quickly began to tell me about their last visit to such a club. "I'm not your average customer," these men would say. "And you know, the dancers could tell. Why, last time I was in a club the women were telling me their real names, and saying that they really enjoyed hanging out with me. Some of them even gave me their phone numbers!" The men would look quite pleased and wait for my reaction. This same type of exchange also happened during the interviews, as evidenced by the quote from David at the beginning of this chapter.

Of course, as a dancer, I know how many countless times each night I would give that particular line (Oh, if only I didn't have to make my tip-out I would *love* to just sit here with you all night! I just don't meet many men like *you*). I also know that I, and many other dancers I knew, would reveal our real names strategically to just those customers who needed to feel that they were different or special, sometimes also divulging other supposedly "private" (and sometimes fictional) information to keep them interested.[14] Finding out things about a dancer, to a certain extent, made her seem more genuine and, in turn, made the entire encounter seem more real, as well as more individualized and special. Ironically, it was often not the truth that was significant so much as the discovery, the access to more supposedly private information. For example, when I first began working as a dancer I found that when I used my real name as my stage name and shared this with my customers they seemed disappointed. Thereafter I learned that I could make up a fake-real name to give them when they pleaded for it. This seemed to please them; they believed they found out something about me as a person and something that possibly few other people in the room knew.[15]

The focus on names is in part based on the idea that a name reveals, or is attached to, a true self. That one would not call a friend or lover by his or her first name is unheard of among most middle-class Americans. At the same time, the fantasy of sex with a stranger is often rendered as sex without any verbal exchange: I didn't even get her name. In this way, the fact that dancers use stage names, and the emphasis placed on finding out a real name, is an erotic game in itself: one might be able to really find out her name (and thus have access to a genuine encounter); one might also be given just another fake name (sexually exciting, as it ensures again the fantasy of sexual access without commitment). Customers, of course, might also give fake names to the dancers, disguising or elaborating on their identities.

Yet, were the customers looking for something that was *really* real? After all, though a discourse of authenticity is indeed important to the male customers of strip clubs, "real*ness*" was often more highly valued than what was actually "real." In fact, the commodification of these encounters was also an essential, desirable aspect of them. We cannot make the mistake of believing that the men were actually seeking uncommodified relationships, as most men (and all regulars) knew that they would be expected to pay for certain services before they even entered the club—at some level, this situation was desirable.

Saul, for example, enjoyed visiting lower-tier clubs and "listening to the dancers' hard luck stories." He would go when he "had extra money" and find someone that he "felt a little sorry for" to sit with in the club. Yet he had never spoken to any of these women twice and said that it "just depends on what mood I'm in" as to whether he felt like listening on any given day. Ross said that he was "sincerely interested in people, in their lives," and that he enjoyed his interactions in the clubs when the women would tell him about their problems and "sit and make a human connection." The sharing of personal troubles made this connection seem more tangible. Ross attributed his desire for that connection to the impersonal nature of contemporary life:

> You get that boost to your ego. Even if you know that you paid that woman for the attention and you got her dancing for you, smiling at you, before and after the dance, coming up to you and she'll put her hand on your shoulder and be talking to you. Even if it's total B.S. and fundamentally you both know it. Our society is a, unfortunately, a very impersonal society. Our bonds as individuals are very superficial, in the main. We don't have the sense of place and continuity of even fifty years ago. Twenty, thirty years ago . . . you don't have the personal interactions. You don't, you know, walk down to the corner store and talk to so and so . . . you drive into the Quickie Mart and the minimum-wage employee of the month is there. Your circle of interactions is both widened and more shallow. You see a lot of people that interface at this very, very superficial level. And so anything that smacks of a deeper humanity, you'd be into that.

At the same time, however, Ross also said that the clubs were enjoyable to him because "you can leave when you want, just walk away."

The payment of money was also a desirable way for the customers to flaunt their social status—either to themselves or to others. To be able to pay a lot of money for an intangible service is, to some extent, a mark of wealth and esteem. The payment of money also could serve to stabilize an interaction for a customer and to redress any possible power imbalances brought out by the exchange. The financial underpinning of the interaction offers an easy escape; after all, a man simply has to leave the club (or stop paying) to be free of his commitments. Or, if a man having a conversation with a dancer suddenly feels vulnerable, he can pay her for a private dance, positioning her once again as "just a stripper" or a fantasy and reminding them both of their contextual obligations to each other.

Clearly, negative cultural ideas about commodification, especially the commodification of feeling, influenced the men's claims to authentic experiences. One of the reasons some customers *talk about* authenticity, then, is to some extent to combat the feeling (or the perception of others) that they are being taken advantage of or being duped into wasting their money. There are a variety of discourses regarding masculinity, maleness, and clienthood that inform men's understandings of their involvement in the sex industry. One of those discourses in the United States, as mentioned in Chapters 3 and 4, is that men who frequent strip clubs (except on "legitimate" occasions such as a bachelor party) are pathetic because they "have to pay for it," that is, because they are *purchasing* female companionship that other men can obtain without providing direct financial compensation to the woman. Although they dealt with the stigma in different ways, all of the men in some way had to position themselves in relation to this discourse.[16] The sincerity of the dancers' gestures, then, could also mean that the customers were getting *more* than they paid for and possibly more than the other male customers in the room. These men knew the exchange was a commercialized display of feeling, yet they also wanted an interaction that went beyond this (authenticity=value). Authentic experience can thus be a form of symbolic capital, as mentioned earlier.

A discourse of authenticity was also important to the customers because of the ways it articulated with their personal identities. Relationships in strip clubs between dancers and their customers take place within a larger gendered and heterosexualized network of power relations. Further, these relationships are based on an exchange of sexual self-identities and, as such, involve a complex entanglement of fantasy and reality. They must be interpreted, then, within a psychoanalytic framework that allows fantasy and reality to be conceptualized as irrevocably intertwined, as mutually constitutive. In a strip club, a man most likely will be denied sexual access to the women. A fantasy of sexual possibility, identity, and interpersonal intimacy is cultivated, however, and the combination of these elements may make it an attractive atmosphere for some customers. The suspension of the real, in many ways, underlies the very existence of strip clubs, and the performances given there were often more desirable than an outside relationship: in the clubs, men were granted safety from the struggle to attract "real" women, from the necessity to form "real" commitments, and from the demands of those real women on their time and emotions. Further, behaviors that were unacceptable in the "real" world, such as an obvious appraisal of women's bodies, were allowed in the club, even encouraged by the women themselves (Want to buy a table dance?) (Frank 1998).

This notion of the real clearly needs to be problematized. Certainly, one of the verbalized goals of a customer who *frequents* a strip club is escape from the real world. This may mean several different things, however. There are, of course, regulars who do have commitments to women outside the club, women who are making demands on their time and emotions and for whom the club provides an escape *from*. There were many other men, however, who were actively seeking an escape *to,* searching for an intimacy that was clearly not available to them in that outside world: men who were recently divorced, who had few social skills, who had physical handicaps, and others. Repeatedly, I listened to men who claimed that they "didn't know how to talk to women," " had difficulty meeting people," or just "didn't have the time to develop a relationship." These men paid the dancers to listen to their work stories, laugh at their jokes, and eat dinner with them. In these strip clubs, real*ness* was thus more highly valued, or at least more realistically expected, than what was actually real.[17]

Consequently, there is a fetishization that underlies the provision of sexual services. In *Nightwork,* Anne Allison writes that in paying money for a sexual service "men are not only buying a commodity but putting themselves into the commodity too. That is, there is a fetishization of subject (man) as much as of object (woman), and the customer is not only purchasing one thing or an *other* but is also paying to become one other as well. He seeks to be relieved of his everyday persona—the one to which various expectations are attached—and given a new script in which he plays a different role" (1994: 22). Thus, although the man might know that it is a fantasy persona, its realness makes it all the more desirable. There are also several imaginary relationships involved in such a transaction. The dancer, as an employee of the club, is produced as a particular commodity, a body that can be viewed on demand (payment) and that is infused with prefabricated meanings (classy, trashy, sexy, etc.). The special lighting, the costumes, and the makeup all combine to make her physical body imaginary, something that would not be exactly reproducible outside of the club or in a different venue. Through the physical presence of the dancer, the male customer is visible as a heterosexual man who desires women.[18] This is a live, *specular* image: other dancers and customers are witnesses to the transaction (this witnessing is a crucial element: if a man were not looking for a public encounter, he most likely would not have chosen a strip club). Further, while the dancer herself is also manufacturing or presenting a particular identity, a public *image,* in her interaction with the customer, she is simultaneously involved in the production of particular male subjectivities for her customers, one of which is that of "a male who can pay a female to service him" (Allison 1994: 204). The man's private *images,* his self-representations, are thus also involved.

As any individual in the club can be provided with such a service, however, as long as he can afford it, a "genuine" interaction, no matter how brief, becomes a mark of distinction. Insofar as all interactions in the club are mediated by money, these interactions are thus also always open to the suspicion of being false, as mentioned earlier. In her interactions with a customer, then, and with regulars in particular, a dancer is also trying to produce for him the subjectivity of a man who is worth being listened to *regardless* of the money he pays her. This subjectivity may already be experienced by the man as a real one, however, in which case it becomes the realness of the dancer's identity and the interaction they have that affirms his own identity. Peggy Phelan, using psychoanalytic theory to discuss performance, writes: "As a representation of the real the image is always, partially, phantasmatic. In doubting the authenticity of the image, one questions as well the veracity of she who makes and describes it. To doubt the subject seized by the eye is to doubt the subjectivity of the seeing 'I' " (1993: 1). Self-identity, according to Phelan, fails to secure belief because our own origins are both real and imagined. Identity needs to be "continually reproduced and reassured," because we prefer to see ourselves as "more or less securely situated," our beliefs as secure and coherent (5).

In a discussion of realness in performance, Judith Butler writes that realness is a standard used to judge any given performance, "yet what determines the effect of realness is the ability to compel belief, to produce the naturalized effect."[19] The performance that works, then, is that which effects realness such that "what appears and what it means coincide" (1993: 129). All the while, however, this "passing" is the effect of a realness based on the performance of a recognizably impossible ideal. The dancers in the club, then, were selling their selves, their identities, and a particular experience to the customers. The realness that was performed was important not so much for its details or its truth value as for its ability to "compel belief" in the entire interaction, and, significantly, in the man's own fantasized identities. In a number of highly complicated ways, then, a commodified relationship can both assuage doubt and redouble it.

The Absolute Fake?

Exotic dancer and filmmaker Vicki Funari notes with uncomfortable amusement the male customers' desire at the peepshow in which she worked:

> I keep wondering: Why are men willing to put money down for what is so clearly faked? The only answer that seems to work is that the men aren't interested in the truth of women's experiences. The porn customer's truth is one of paying for services; that's the only power he can claim in this interaction. But is that what gets him hard? His buying power? Why then are we advertised as seductresses and paid to simulate our own desire? Our performance of female desire is a simple reversal of the truth: the mainstream porn industry, of which the peepshow is one

facet, exists to fulfill men's desires, not women's. Why does the hetero-sexual porn customer need the fiction of female desire to sustain his erection, instead of just naked female bodies? (1997: 26)

She notes that this "fiction" is part of an unacknowledged economy of desire, "an integral part" of the customer's excitement.

Paradoxically, the customers who worried the most about authen-ticity, who approached their encounters with endless questioning and staunch skepticism, were the most likely to end up dissatisfied with their visits. Joe, for example, visited only lower-tier clubs, believing that the women there were more likely to spend quality time with each customer. He was very worried about being taken advantage of by dancers, however, and, like Jason, was cynical to the point that it af-fected his interactions. He continually watched other men to judge the realness of their interactions and compare it to his own: "I spend a lot of time watching the people. I don't know if that's normal or not but I spend a lot of time watching the other people and seeing how some of the guys interact with the girls and stuff. I've often wondered, well, does she just know him? Or did he come in here because he knows her? Or is she with him because he's spending a lot of money on her?" He also said that he was very careful about spending money in the clubs: "I enjoy the table dances but I don't feel like ten dollars for one song is reasonable. It's too much . . . any time I've ever paid for a table dance, I felt a little cheated. So I don't care to get table dances unless it's a two-for-one. Then I may do it. Or if I feel a particular interest in a girl, for whatever reason, a table dance is okay because I can get a closer look. It's more intimate, you know."

Joe would not tip the dancers on the stages because he wanted to remain anonymous to the other customers, a face in the crowd, and because he was not interested in tipping dancers who were not attrac-tive (or "attracted") to him. He said that when he did approach the stages, it helped if he felt that the money was not very important to the dancers:

Now when I go up there, a lot of it has to do with how the girl is dancing . . . some girls, it's just a quickie little thing and here's my garter strap and I don't want you, give me your money. Other ones are true exhibitionists and it doesn't matter if you weren't giving them a dime, they were going to dance for you . . . and I feel like when a girl's doing that I enjoy it more because now it's not a sense of I'm paying for this service. It's more of, "I'm doing something for you because I want to do it. And I'm really enjoying myself." Therefore, I can enjoy myself . . . it doesn't feel so anonymous and private, you know . . . It's more open and relaxed and . . . and yeah, you feel more comfortable about spending the money. There's a portion of it that's all about the money. There really is a portion of it. And of course, I haven't delved into it that much but without the money a lot of it wouldn't happen, okay? That's just how it's set up. But it makes it easier . . . to enjoy yourself when you feel like the person is doing it because they want to and not because of the money.

Joe's caution and lack of tipping, however, meant that he was often frustrated in his visits because the dancers paid him very little attention. He clearly *wanted* to believe in the interactions, despite his realization that it was "all about the money." Indeed, he seemed to believe many of the things that he'd been told by dancers in the past, lines that I immediately recognized. During the interview, for example, he said that he went to the clubs to "enjoy myself," "just like you [dancers] go to the club to enjoy yourself." *I do? And all along I thought I was working! But then again, the money does sometimes make it enjoyable* . . . Besides noting that some of the dancers were "true exhibitionists," Joe also commented that he enjoyed only interactions in the clubs that were based on "some sort of minor mutual attraction." *But every dancer knows that if you don't feign (feel?) attraction for a customer, you'll never make any money!*

Again, the boundaries of work and leisure, of authenticity and inauthenticity, and of real and manufactured emotion become blurred through the workers' performances.[20] As Philip Crang argues about tourist work, in such settings "not only does work involve being surrounded by other people consuming and having fun, but having fun can also become the work itself" (1997: 151). Dancers know that enjoying their job is *part of* their job. In clubs that serve alcohol, dancers often drink with the customers to create an atmosphere of leisure rather than work (alcohol also is associated with *access,* authenticity). Further, the most successful dancers learn how to use physical cues to signal "mutual" attraction and pleasure—through touch, posture, attention, and gaze, for example. Yet, although some dancers definitely enjoy their work more than others, there is no way for the strip club *not* to be a workplace for a dancer. After all, she is still on the clock, being watched by the management, and expected to pay out some of her earnings at the end of the night. And though some dancers may even consider themselves exhibitionists and thus find the work enjoyable (and may certainly refer to themselves as such when asked in the clubs), it is imperative to be extremely cautious about using psychological labels to describe someone's performance while on the job. Most dancers would not fit the clinical definition of exhibitionism set forth in the *Diagnostic and Statistical Manual of Mental Disorders*. Obviously, public and private desires overlap for some dancers, just as for workers in other occupations. However, the constant interrogation of a dancer's desire means that this type of labor is somewhat distinct.[21]

Umberto Eco writes: "The American imagination demands the real thing and, to attain it, must fabricate the absolute fake" (1986: 8). Paradoxically, certain demands can be met only through fabrication, no matter how sincerely one wants to meet another's expectations. In an essay about camp, for example, Andrew Travers argues that camp is based on an "ambivalent sincerity, from which it provides no exit," that it is "a mordant consciousness of commodified human relations" (1993: 127). As an example of camp he uses the sincerity and authenticity of the orgasm, writing that "a faked orgasm is often more real than a real one" (137). He notes that a faked orgasm may indeed be the result of a sincere desire to please one's partner, even though it may actually *"look more sincere when it is faked"* (138):

> (The lover faking an orgasm can do a better job of seeming sincere because he or she, unlike the one losing himself or herself in the act, has a surplus of attention—and repression—to devote to improving on nature.) The possibility of insincerity then corrupts the sincere desire to please, because now the desire to please must contend with the possibility of its being seen as such in an apparent absence of its involuntary desire, and so must begin to calculate . . . That is, it must *depart from its sincerity on behalf of sincerity,* in the direction of feigning, a little louder here, a little more thrusting there, catapulted by itself into Goffman's hyper-rituality (1979) and Baudrillard's hyper-reality (1983). (138)

The orgasm thus becomes theatrical, Travers argues, the "paradigm face-to-face interaction, if interaction is a moral order policed by the selves it constitutes" (139). To desire the absolute fake is to doubt the real to such an extent that false proof is more satisfying than truth: the performance becomes more convincing and desirable than the real.

This problem has been posited by some thinkers as a product of the social relations of modernity, one that has only intensified in postmodern societies. In *Ways of Escape,* Chris Rojek provides an interesting example of the Batuan Frog Dance, a popular ritual that is staged for tourists to the South Seas and that has been invented by tour operators to satisfy the desires of the visitors (1993: 204). There are many examples of such authentic fabrications in the tourism literature, as well as in the work of theorists of the postmodern.[22] But rather than seeing such fabrications as "perfect simulacra," as "absolute fakes," or even as paradigmatic of human relationships and desires in late capitalist societies, we should be focusing on what it is that individuals themselves bring to the sights / sites, and how these fantasies and beliefs have different material and psychological results—leading one tourist to come away with "proof," another to see camp and laugh, and yet another to doubt.

What, after all, are we *expecting* our experiences to tell us? What fictions are they sustaining? And what power relations are they supporting or eliding?

*

Talk about authenticity remains a concern of individuals engaged in this particular kind of voyeuristic, interactive touristic practice. A discourse of authenticity is indeed important to the male customers of strip clubs, regardless of whether their interactions in the club are actually real and sometimes even *because of* the fact that they are *not* real. Real*ness,* on the other hand, is highly valued for several reasons: for assuaging doubts about the commodification of interaction and for compelling belief in a man's fantasized identities. The paradox is that the incessant demands of some customers / tourists to make experiences speak the truth leads directly to the possibility that such demands might remain ultimately unfulfilled.

Authenticity cannot really be found in a place, an object, or an experience—it is a psychological process, derived from the interaction between self and Other (imagined or actual). Unlike some theorists of postmodernity, I do not believe that a concern with authenticity is disappearing, although the terms within which it is understood may mutate over time. The concern with authenticity will not disappear among those engaged in touristic practice, along with other kinds of social interactions, because authenticity is ultimately a *relational* problem. Concern about the authenticity or inauthenticity of experience emanates from several points. First, it is a result of the instabilities of holding relative privilege in a classed, capitalist society. Second, individuals attempt to use authentic experience as a confirmation of the possibility of escape—from work, from home, from aspects of the self that are seen as oppressive (or *to* those very same realms). And third, authenticity is important in securing self-identity (which is both real and imaginary) and is implicated in any relationship between self and Other. There are thus multiple fantasies around and through which a discourse of authenticity becomes enfolded, and authentic experiences can offer, among other things, proof and hope. The next chapter probes more of the intricacies of this relationship, particularly the ways the customers perceived authenticity as embodied and performed by the dancers.

Chapter Six

Hustlers, Pros, and the Girl Next Door:
Social Class, Race, and the Consumption
of the Authentic Female Body

In "Disgust and Desire: *Hustler* Magazine," film theorist Laura Kipnis raises the issue of class in the critical reading of pornography, taking Larry Flynt's infamous publication as an object of analysis. She argues that *Hustler* magazine represents "anarchistic, antiestablishment, working-class politics," and portrays the unromanticized, grotesque, and vulgar body, violating the taboos of more "classy" magazines such as *Playboy* (1996: 137). *Hustler* presents two kinds of women in its pages for its male readers, she suggests: the "standard men's magazine fantasy bimbette" and the "haughty, superior, rejecting, upper-class bitch goddess" (150). The frustration and resentment expressed in relation to the upper-class women in the pages of the magazine, according to Kipnis, "reeks of disenfranchisement." "The fantasy life here," she writes, "is animated by cultural disempowerment in relation to a sexual caste system and a social class system" (151). *Hustler,* then, is read by Kipnis as a working-class version of the more airbrushed, mannerly, and middle-class *Playboy* or *Penthouse* magazines.

However, consumption practices are not so easily read off of social texts, and in a footnote Kipnis notes that the demographics for *Hustler* are actually quite complicated: in 1976, 40 percent of its readers had attended college, 23 percent were professionals, and 59 percent had an income above the national mean. One man's analysis of these findings was that it was "more accurate to say that *Hustler* appeals to what people would like to label a blue-collar urge, an urge most American men seem to share," than that it appeals to a blue-collar customer base

(Kipnis 1996: 218). A demographic profile conducted for *Hustler* in 1998 showed an average income of $41,500 for its readers.[1] Similarly, *Playboy's* image of upper- and middle-class consumption is also a somewhat idealized one. As Dines points out, the 1995 *Playboy* demographic profile puts the median income for readers at $26,000 for single men and $41,000 for married men. Further, it shows that only 50 percent of the readers have been to college (1998: 56). These figures had not changed much by spring 2001: still just a little over half reported attending any college and about 50 percent made under $50,000. Clearly, desire itself does not divide neatly down class lines. But what might underlie the differences in taste and practices? And precisely how does social class influence erotics?

In Laurelton, I selected five different strip clubs occupying different positions on the class hierarchy in an attempt to explore this very question. Although some men I spoke with said that they felt "more comfortable" at clubs that catered to their own class status (working-class / lower-tier clubs; professional or white-collar / upper-tier clubs), and although I could reasonably anticipate more "suits" at the Panther Club than at Tina's Revue, social class was not an accurate predictor of which clubs customers preferred across the board.[2] There were class distinctions between clubs, but there was also a great deal of traffic between the different strata and comparisons and preferences were made between them for reasons related to social class but not determined by it. This is not to say that social class was not intertwined with customer preferences and erotics; in fact, a man's *fantasies* about class, gender, and race influenced both what he felt to be an authentic encounter and his pleasure in the interaction.

Realness, as discussed in Chapter 5, is highly valued by regular customers for several reasons, especially for assuaging doubts about purchasing women's sexualized services and for compelling belief in a man's fantasized sexual self-representation and identities. In the next several sections I turn to the ways that personal and cultural fantasies about class, race, and gender influenced the customers' *perceptions* of this authenticity, especially as it is embodied and performed by the dancers. Two salient discourses that emerged during the interviews and interactions are discussed in relation to existing social distinctions and inequalities: those of professionalism and propriety. Finally, the concept of social transgression in the sex industry is taken up through a discussion of the obscene body and through customer fantasies of defilement and purity.

Signs / Perceptions of Authenticity

Because the expectation in a strip club is that *all* interactions (unless perhaps they are between dancers and long-term regulars) are motivated *immediately* by self-interest (would you like to *buy* a table dance?), the point at which a dancer is asked to "prove" her disinterestedness in financial gain or be labeled a hustler comes quite early on in the interaction. Significantly, as mentioned in Chapter 5, even men who knew that they would be paying for their interactions in the clubs and who desired this state of affairs often sought signs of a dancer's sincerity before they interacted with her.

Sometimes this proof was seen to emanate from the dancer's physical appearance and demeanor before any encounter occurred; a "fake" body, for example, could imply an inauthentic presentation of self. A great deal of the commentary of my interviewees (as well as of other customers I interacted with in the clubs) centered on breast implants, which were often taken to signify insincerity:

> I'm very against boob jobs so I have big problems with the modern-day dancers anyways because there's so many of them. I usually don't even tip them. I don't like anything synthetic, artificial. Like that girl-next-door fantasy but I want the real thing. I don't want someone who's doing this just to make money. (Gary)[3]

> A lot of times those that have spent money on their body . . . this may be my opinion . . . they're not as sincere. I like the ones with natural beauty. (Tim)

Zachary said that he would not even tip dancers with "big fake boobs" and that he felt that these women were seeking inordinate amounts of money or attention. "I'm not real big into like giant breasts and stuff," Frank said. He noted that he enjoyed dancers who "worked" on their bodies, but not if they crossed the line into surgically altering them. It was not uncommon for breast implants to be referred to derogatorily as "Tupperware" or "plastic" by some customers. The stated distaste for implants among these particular interviewees also most likely influenced their decision to interview with me, having already judged me sincere by my appearance in the club.

Regardless of the stated distaste for implants among my interviewees, however, it was a well-known fact that a dancer's income would significantly increase once she had breast implants. For one, men were quite easily convinced that the dancer's breasts were "real" even if they were not. In Laurelton there were a number of dancers who had specifically requested natural implants, done with smaller cup sizes and the incision placed under the armpit instead of under the breast so that it is nearly undetectable. In some of these cases, the fact that they had even had surgery at all was carefully concealed from the customers and sometimes even from other dancers. Further, an increase in postimplant income was also due to the fact that men in groups often selected women who fit a particular centerfold ideal; bachelor parties, for example, tended to choose blonde-haired, large-breasted, tan women ("real *strippers*"), and those of us who did not fit these descriptions often chose Saturday as our night off. The men who desired a "genuine" encounter in their personal interactions might not have the same criteria in selecting a dancer to please their friends or business associates.[4] There were also customers who wanted to stay as far away as possible from women who reminded them of their wife, partner, or daughter, and thus someone who looked more like a pin-up girl than the girl next door was far more desirable to interact with in the club.[5]

The signs taken to signify sincerity are also relative, and not every man interprets breast implants as detracting from a woman's ability to provide a real and satisfying fantasy encounter. There are also men who feel that surgically enhanced breasts are more attractive than natural breasts and interpret a dancer's willingness to invest in her body this way as a legitimate form of "self-improvement" (a discourse certainly related to social class) or simply as sexually alluring because they perfect the female body. Nevertheless, *whichever* position the customer took, a dancer's breasts were often taken as a sign to be read directly off her body, used to set particular standards and expectations for the interaction.

"Bleached blonde hair," "too much makeup," and even "too much hairspray and perfume" were also mentioned as immediate indicators of insincerity; significantly, these were also bodily inscriptions of social class. In some clubs, for example, there were very beautiful dancers who were able to successfully pull off a Pamela Anderson look—breast implants, collagen lip implants, dyed platinum hair (or wigs), and thick makeup—with no complaints from the customers. "Bad" surgeries or dye jobs, however, were sometimes interpreted as signs of inauthenticity or "laziness." Sociologist Beverly Skeggs notes that although physical attractiveness may work as a form of "corporeal capital," it is also often a form of class privilege (1997: 102). Some dancers at every club enhanced their appearance through a variety of techniques, such as hair extensions, plastic surgeries (on breasts, stomach, face, and hips), or year-round tanning. Access to such techniques, as well as the quality of the results, was often connected to social class and economic assets, however. Even the application of stage makeup and accessorizing one's costume carried with it certain kinds of cultural capital as well as learned skill and financial flexibility: knowing how to put together colors or fabrics, where to buy makeup that would not cake or streak (M.A.C., a kind of professional stage makeup, was a favorite in the upper-tier clubs), when to wear gloves with a gown, and what kind of costume jewelry would come off as hopelessly fake or tacky and which would look sophisticated.

Despite the fact that they sometimes disagreed with each other, customers thus continually made distinctions between dancers who were beautiful and glamorous and dancers who were trying unsuccessfully to effect a particular look and came off as "cheesy" or "trashy." In a fascinating ethnographic study of white English working-class women, Skeggs explores the centrality of ideas about respectability in signifying social class and argues that glamour "is a way of holding together sexuality and respectability." Glamour is also a way of producing "coded displays of sexuality that could generate value" (1997: 110). Of course, such displays of sexuality in strip clubs are necessarily more exaggerated than those produced by women in most other realms: makeup can be overdone, necklines can plunge and hemlines can rise, bodily movements can be aggressively suggestive. Yet when the dancers failed to negotiate these exaggerated signs in ways that the customers recognized, they were often seen as insincere, as trying to hustle them.

The customers also said that they focused on a dancer's comportment and behavior as a sign that she was sincere:

> It has to do with a combination of personality . . . and approachableness and not feeling like it's too much of a business. You know, there are some

of those girls in there that make you feel like you're just there to give them the money and . . . It just feels too business. (Roger)

You might see someone that's really pretty but it's just like, what good's a Porsche if it doesn't run? You know, I guess it's just somebody's attitude . . . if they have a tendency to smile. (Alex)

I like real people. Um, real . . . from a guy's standpoint, you want people who appear to be genuine, you know? You like women that smile at you, but only if it's what you perceive to be a genuine smile. It may or may not be, but if you perceive it to be a real genuine smile then you appreciate that . . . You can look across the bar and see a woman and say, that woman is so plastic . . . If she sits there and primps her hair or looks like she's disinterested, like she just doesn't want to be there, like she is there because she has to be. (Frank)

Remembering a man's name and information about his life when he returned to the club a second time was an extremely successful strategy for demonstrating one's sincerity as a dancer, something analogous to what Urry has referred to as a "moment of truth" (1990: 71). Several men told stories about having long conversations with a dancer and then returning to the club on a later date only to find that the dancer had forgotten them entirely. (In this I was benefited by the careful fieldnotes that I recorded each night about my interactions with particular customers.)

Some of this ability to appear genuine is certainly related to cultural or educational capital: the ability to conform to certain middle-class patterns of social interaction or the ability to converse on subjects of interest to the men such as law, politics, philosophy, or finances, for example. Though the initial stages of romantic bonds are motivated by self-interest for many middle-class American individuals (i.e., people choose a partner based on his or her social, cultural, and economic assets), these choices often are talked about in terms of "creativity," "values," or "curiosity" (Illouz 1997: 228). The tendency for middle-class customers to talk about the "personality," "attitude," and "interest" of the dancers, I believe, reflects some of this same deflection of material differences. Brian said that he looked for "intelligent and interesting women," and Charles said that he enjoyed the Panther because "the girls are not only extremely beautiful, but smart too," providing "fascinating conversation" rather than just trying to sell private dances.

Nervousness or awkwardness would also signal the fact that a dancer was genuine, more like a "real girl," as did *mistakes* (sometimes carefully crafted) in performance or attire. During my first shift working the pool at the Crystal Palace, for example, I had accidentally brought the wrong kind of bathing suit to wear. Laurelton regulations about exposure meant dancers could not bend over (even slightly) to remove their bottoms; we thus wore g-strings that snapped at the hips. Because the bathing suit could not be altered so that the bottoms would snap away, I had to step awkwardly out of it in my five-inch heels, balanced precariously on the rim of the pool and keeping my knees locked together to avoid breaking any laws. More than one customer tipped me afterwards, commenting on the fact that this made me seem more like "the girl next door" than a dancer. Similarly, the night I met Kenneth, one of the interviewees, he tipped me onstage and pointed out that he could tell I was new because I was "wearing the wrong kind of shoes," three-inch heels instead of the typical five-inch heels (for which I had already been reprimanded by the management). I also frequently listened to interviewees and other customers tell stories about encounters with dancers on their first night: "Her hands were shaking during the table dance"; "She asked me if she could keep her bottoms on because she wasn't quite ready"; "I bought her a glass of wine so that she'd be able to go on stage." At some clubs it was a common ploy for a seasoned dancer who was having a bad night to suddenly become a nervous "new girl" halfway through her shift. The lack of "professionalism" exhibited by dancers new to the business implied to some men that they would not be as skilled at manipulating them out of their money. To others, it seemed to provide a balance between purity and defilement that was particularly exciting.

In a piece on Parisian striptease, semiotician Roland Barthes writes that striptease is based on the fundamental contradiction that woman is "desexualized at the very moment when she is stripped naked" (1972: 84). The classic props used in striptease, he argues—costumes, feathers, furs, stockings, jewels, and gloves—ensure that the nakedness that follows the woman's act is "no longer a part of a further, genuine undressing." Instead, it "remains itself unreal, smooth and enclosed like a beautiful slippery object" (1972: 85). The dance routine is also a barrier to the true erotic, as through a series of ritualistic gestures it hides the very nudity that it is supposed to reveal. Professional stripteasers can "wrap themselves in the miraculous ease which constantly clothes them, makes them remote, gives them the icy indifference of skillful practitioners, haughtily taking refuge in the sureness of their technique" (1972: 86). Barthes notes, however, that eroticism resurfaces in the amateur contest: "There, 'beginners' undress in front of a few hundred spectators without resorting or resorting very clumsily to magic, which unquestionably restores to the spectacle its erotic power. Here we find . . . no feathers or furs (sensible suits, ordinary coats), few disguises as a starting point—gauche steps, unsatisfactory dancing, girls constantly threatened by immobility, and above all by a 'technical' awkwardness (the resistance of briefs, dress, or bra) which gives to the gestures of unveiling an unexpected importance, denying the woman the alibi of art and the refuge of being an object" (86). Barthes, of course, is discussing striptease that took the form of elaborate costuming and lengthy stage shows, a type of performance that is quite rare in contemporary strip clubs but that is sometimes talked about nostalgically by both dancers and customers. In this type of stage show, the entire audience shares the view of the performer and there is little "private" or individualized contact between the stripper and the members of the audience. Nevertheless, the popularity of amateur contests in contemporary strip clubs, the allure of "new girls," and the customers' dislike of professionalism all support Barthes's contentions. What Barthes perhaps did not realize, or what has perhaps changed since he wrote, is that some dancers have themselves become mythologists of sorts, self-consciously fashioning ways to produce an illusion of unveiling. (*Don't you think little bunny earrings make me look innocent and virginal? If I wear full underpants instead of a thong, the customers think I just walked in off the street!*) Such a strategy, of course, does not work for every woman, nor does every woman need or want to use it. As will become clear in the next section, however, a discourse of professionalism does arise in the customers' talk about their experiences and is related to both social positionings and erotics.

Professionalism and Authenticity

In addition to distinguishing among *individual dancers* in terms of sincerity, men also quite readily distinguished among whole classes of women and clubs, often contradicting each other in their judgments as to which clubs offered the most authentic and pleasurable encounters. Physical and behavioral differences were thus also used to distinguish between upper- and lower-tier clubs and were linked to both classiness and realness. As Jason said, "I don't go to sleaze pits. You know, nasty places. I'm not into that. I like girls that look classy. Not the girls that look rough, like they've been riding on the back of a Harley or something for a week straight, you know? I like real girls. Not the ones with big fake double DS and bleached blonde hair." For Jason, *real* women were women of a particular social class and appearance. Similarly, Phillip said that "the girls at the lower-class clubs have no respect for themselves . . . I don't like all that rough stuff. I like sensual dancers."

William claimed that the "look is totally different" in a lower-tier club: "A club like that has fifteen girls there and maybe two or three of them are what I would consider attractive." He commented that the dancers at lower-tier clubs tend to be "out of shape," "unhealthy," and dressed in "trashy" outfits. *Trashy outfits? We're strippers, after all . . .* But distinguishing among different types of lingerie has become big business—just think of the supposed difference between Frederick's of Hollywood and Victoria's Secret (and the relativity of this difference when compared to expensive, hand-made lingerie). Judgments of classiness and trashiness become issues of taste in the talk of the interviewees rather than issues of social positioning. Taste is a word that has been abstracted from its original meaning of a physical sensation to mean more generally "a matter of acquiring certain habits and rules" (R. Williams 1976: 313). Taste also comes to influence perceptions of authenticity. As MacCannell writes: "The dialectic of authenticity is at the heart of the development of all modern social structure. It is manifest in concerns for ecology and front, in attacks on what is phony, pseudo, tacky, in bad taste, mere show, tawdry and gaudy. These concerns conserve a solidarity at the level of the total society, a collective agreement that reality and truth exist somewhere in society, and that we ought to be trying to find them and refine them" (1976: 155). Yet, though there clearly are different kinds of outfits that dancers wear (ranging from thong bikinis to cocktail dresses to evening gowns in Laurelton), judgments about what was trashy more closely adhered to the *body* of the particular dancers than to the outfits themselves. In fact, I saw many of the same outfits at both the upper- and lower-tier, black and white clubs. However, those bodies that were "out of shape," "unhealthy," even "*too* tanned" or "*too* pale" were consistently seen as trashy and lower class. Further, bodies and outfits that were viewed in different contexts were interpreted in different ways: a very thin and pale dancer at the Pony Lounge was shunned by certain customers as being sick even if they knew nothing about her life ("She looks like she has AIDS"; "She must be a drug addict"), but the same look taken up at the Panther by a woman who called herself Monique and spoke fluent French was seen as erotic. Dancers also made these kinds of judgments about each other and about themselves: "trashy" women "belonged" at lower-tier clubs because of their bad taste, unsophisticated behavior, and poor decision making, for example.

Other men distinguished between the upper- and lower-tier clubs by the amount of cultural or educational capital they imagined the dancers to have, and this was in turn related back to both the sincerity of the dancers and the potential realness of the exchange. Matthew, for instance, preferred the upper-tier clubs because he believed that the women there were not just after the money but were interested in other things as well. He enjoyed the fact that the women at the Panther were often well educated and had career aspirations. Even within the upper-tier clubs, however, he found that some dancers put him more at ease during the interactions than others, specifically, dancers who claimed to have fairly mainstream goals and career aspirations. These women were not out to hustle a man out of his money, he believed; rather, they were employing a legitimate American strategy of self-improvement through their work. In the upper-tier clubs, he said, "You've got women who are there temporarily and view this as a temporary situation. They're putting themselves through college and grad school. They're looking to make a lot of money very quickly and then they're going to go do something else . . . And then you've got other women who just . . . this is it! This is where they are. They have no great aspirations to do anything other than this . . . it's pretty much a job and, 'Okay, we've chatted for three minutes, are you ready for a table dance?' " Similarly, David said that he enjoyed the upper-tier clubs because "The girls in the seedier places, for lack of a better term . . . seem to be there to just get your money and don't really want to develop a relationship with you . . . don't really care what you've got to say or anything. They're there to do dances and, you know, you'll pay a lot."

Professionalism, of course, had both negative and positive connotations depending on the customer and the context. To the men who referred to the upper-tier clubs as more professional or businesslike, this signaled polite and enjoyable service. As many of the upper-tier clubs had rules against hustling for table dances, the men felt that they were not being manipulated out of their money. Tim, for example, said he felt "more comfortable" in this kind of club because the women would not "hassle" the customers and were more professional and polite: "The reason I pick the Panther is because it's more of a business club. I try to stay away from the blue-collar kind of clubs because I feel a little bit uncomfortable and I'd rather be in a more upscale place . . . It's much easier to be relaxed and comfortable and plus the service is good. The girls are attractive."

To other men, however, professionalism implied a standardized and emotionless atmosphere where the dancers were only out to make a profit. Saul, for example, told me that he preferred the lower-tier clubs because the women were "less likely to be professionals," were less "slick." When I asked him, "What signals 'slickness'?" he responded, "Nothing makes them uncomfortable and I could talk about something and I get the impression that they talk to five thousand guys a day and pretend the same interest to each one of them. And I don't care if they're interested in me or not. But it's almost scripted." Saul enjoyed listening to the "hard-luck stories" of the dancers he met in the lower-tier clubs and spent much of his time just talking to the dancers. Similarly, Paul preferred the lower-tier clubs because, although the upper-tier clubs were "entertaining," they were "not as intimate as Tina's." "Real intimacy," he believed, was more likely in a lower-tier club, because the dancers were less likely to be "hustlers."[6] Ross also believed he was more likely to have a genuine encounter at a lower-tier club and spoke at length about the reasons for this: "It's not very extreme, which to me is like you can get to know everybody there and it's much less of a barrier there. Even the dancers . . . because I always like to look at people as people, I can get to know them. And you can sit and well, know that so and so has such and such problem, so and so has problems with her roommate and we can sit and make a human connection."

Likewise, Gary said that he preferred the Pony Lounge (a lower-tier club) to Diamond Dolls (an upper-tier club) because at Diamond Dolls the women were too perfect, "pure objects," "not human," and "professionals." "They take away some of the humanness," he said, "and the women there are more of a fantasy than a reality." In addition to visiting lower-tier clubs, Gary liked to go to amateur contests in search of "young, nubile, and untarnished" dancers, although he noted with distaste that in recent years the supposed amateurs were "all turning out to be professionals" or seasoned dancers from other clubs: "I especially like the new ones. I mean, I like freshness, innocence. Not hardened, pro hustler types." As quoted earlier, he also believed that the breast implants many of the women had at the upper-tier clubs ruined this illusion. The emphasis on youth was interesting, for youth itself could sometimes signal genuineness through naïveté or innocence, regardless of class differences. On the other hand, younger dancers were seen by other men as too flighty, inexperienced, or self-absorbed to provide satisfying and authentic exchanges. Age is relative here, of course, as I did not often find dancers past their late twenties working in Laurelton, even in the lower-tier clubs.

Some of the men were also interested in "saving" the dancers who worked in the lower-tier clubs; this was a motivating fantasy of Gary's, something that he pursued whenever he found someone suitable for whom to become a "sugar-daddy." He had developed several of these relationships in the past, but none had lasted longer than a year. Customers sometimes provided financial support for "improvements" such as breast implants or other kinds of plastic surgery, expensive wardrobe items, or job training.

Propriety: Gender, Race, and Class and the Boundaries of the Erotic

The men I interviewed, as well as many of those with whom I interacted, repeatedly expressed concerns about comfort and safety, as well as these preferences for particular kinds of dancers and clubs. Nearly all of the men discussed their desire to visit a "comfortable" club, for example, yet which kinds of clubs and encounters they felt provided this varied. Customers also discussed their feelings of comfort or discomfort in certain clubs in terms of propriety in addition to authenticity—the propriety of the spaces themselves (their furnishings, internal spatial arrangements, and modes of surveillance) and of the women (referring to the behavior and appearance of the other customers and the dancers in the clubs). In addition to framing the meaning of strip clubs as a form of touristic leisure practice, concerns about comfort, safety, and propriety can be seen, in part, as coded ways for talking about social positionings such as social class, race, and gender. These concerns are important in thinking about the attraction that different spaces hold for consumers as well as the way inequalities are bolstered and reproduced through notions of authenticity, taste, and erotic attraction.

Women who work in different venues are imbued with different values as dancers, and one way this plays out is through customer talk about beauty. On a national level, Laurelton is acclaimed for its large numbers of attractive, unattached females. Many times I heard men from out of town discuss Southern women (and Southern dancers) as more attractive and attentive to men than women in other parts of the country. Southern women were said to "take better care of their bodies," to be less likely to be "feminist," and to embrace traditional values. Gary said, for example, "Southern women are totally different." When I asked him how they were different, he said that the "Southern belle type" has been "trained or conditioned in the chauvinistic, old-fashioned type of approach, so they come off very sweet." Humorously, at times my own supposedly superior value as a "Southern woman" was even discussed by the customers in front of me, an ironic occurrence given that I am originally from the Midwest (and had often informed the customers of this). The mythology and the fantasy of Southern womanhood sometimes took precedence over any more objective indicators of desirability.

Men who chose the higher-end strip clubs in Laurelton often claimed they did so simply because "the women were prettier." Businessmen would draw on these constructions when choosing where to take clients. "You don't take clients to the Pony Lounge or Tina's Revue," one businessman told me. "You want them to be in the company of ladies who are a step above all that." When I asked him to explain, he linked lower-tier clubs to prostitution and cited them as having dancers who were "overweight, tattooed, not very bright." The dancers at the Pony Lounge were sometimes referred to in a derogatory way as "the whores of Chestnut Crossing." Men who were traveling or visiting with business associates would also often choose the Panther or Diamond Dolls because of their reputations for beautiful women (reputations earned through vigorous marketing and timely photo spreads in magazines like *Playboy's Guide to Men's Clubs*). These clubs were referred to as "touristy" and were seen as providing the best opportunity to impress friends or clients. I constantly overheard or participated in conversations about which clubs had prettier women simply because of my standard questions about why a man had chosen one club over another on any given occasion. The beauty of the women in the upper-tier clubs was thus secured through expectations and fantasies and, in fact, was even discussed as truth by men and women who admit to never having set foot in the Laurelton clubs.

Beauty was connected to propriety, in part, through an appeal to aesthetic value. One frequently given justification for men's visits to strip clubs is that "all men like to look at beautiful women" or that "women's bodies are works of art." The appreciation of female beauty, then, was sometimes given as a justification for visiting the upper-tier clubs: "What man wouldn't want to visit Diamond Dolls or the Panther?" For women, investments in beauty are investments in femininity, and thus in middle-class respectability (Skeggs 1997: 111). As symbols of conspicuous consumption in the clubs, beautiful women could also maintain the respectability and class status of the *men* who spent time with them. In *The Female Nude: Art, Obscenity and Sexuality,* art historian Lynda Nead argues that the female nude "should be recognized as a particularly significant motif within western art and aesthetics," as it "symbolizes the transformation of the base matter of nature into the elevated forms of culture and the spirit." Nonart, or obscenity, "is representation that moves and arouses the viewer rather than bringing about stillness and wholeness" (1992: 2). Just as the differentiation of a high-art nude from a centerfold in aesthetic terms can sometimes differentiate the *consumers* of each, an encounter with a beautiful woman could serve to partly legitimize a stigmatized behavior in the strip club. If a woman was beautiful, or recognized as such by others, a man could claim to be enjoying her in a purely aesthetic manner, which is generally seen as more respectable than looking at her for the purpose of pornographic (masturbatory) fantasy. This claim, however, is often made to balance out the "obscene" body with which a customer is also faced in such a scenario, a point taken up in the next section.

Though the men spoke about beauty as if it were inherent in the dancers, the clubs themselves actually created these bodies in different ways, through advertising and through such special effects as staging arrangements, lighting systems, fans set in the stage floors, smoke, and strobe lights. My body at the upper-tier Panther looked extremely different from how it looked at the Pony Lounge, for example. At the Panther, the height of the stages perfected the breast line of the dancers, as the customers were always positioned such that they had to look up at the nude bodies of the women. The lighting was exquisite, making one's skin look tanned and flawless. At the Pony Lounge, however, the lighting was harsh and the smoke was released from a visible pipe over the head of the dancer on the main stage, instead of misting from the floor the way it did at some of the upper-tier clubs. In addition to associating the lower-tier clubs with "unattractive dancers," Phillip, Brian, Charles, and David all associated these kinds of clubs with impropriety: "rough stuff" and "grinding," for example. This again is a perception that the upper-tier clubs helped in part to create, through staffing attentive bouncers, policing the dancers' private and stage dances, and by asking rowdy customers to leave. It is also, however, related to the ways that respectability is gendered and classed.

Perceptions of comfort, safety, and propriety were also entangled with fantasies about racial differences in Laurelton, and my interviewees, both black and white, expressed a preference for white clubs.[7] Louis, for example, is an African American man who said that he felt "uncomfortable" in the primarily black clubs in these areas and cautioned me against visiting them:

> My opinion is there's another level of black culture in clubs. There's another level. I don't think in Kiki's—I've been three times now, and maybe I've seen one white, maybe, I'm not even positive. So if that gives you an idea. I am not comfortable there and that's probably funny to say. I'm not comfortable being with any one particular predominant race. All black, all white, anything. I'm not comfortable there. I'm comfortable with a mix. Kiki's is not only all black to my knowledge, it may as well be, but it's the type of clientele I'm not comfortable with. I feel . . . I . . . and I shouldn't say this . . . I can handle it if I want to, but I'm not comfortable on the inside. It's almost a reflection of what I came up in and I'm not comfortable with it. There's just a type of clientele that are drawn there. And that's not to say that you can't have any troubles in any club, but I . . . I do believe that you're going to have more in particular areas depending on the social status and how they're, you know, coming up. So I'm not comfortable with that. Not at all.

Similarly, Paul noted that although he enjoyed visiting Tina's Revue, there was "a limit" to "how low of a club" he would visit and that he found the black clubs in town to be too graphic, making him "uncomfortable." He wanted "at least some sense of modesty or appropriateness" and "not just pornographic stuff." The women in the black clubs, Paul said, did not "value themselves enough," performing "gynecological" shows for their tips. Later in the interview, however, Paul discussed his enjoyment of an upscale club in Israel where "anything goes" and the (white?) women put their genitals just inches from his nose. Jim also mentioned the "graphic interaction" in the black clubs and said that he had "the impression that black dancers are more aggressive," despite the fact that he could not remember the last time he had visited a black club in the city. As noted in Chapter 2 and in numerous works on race and sexuality, (white) representations of black women historically have often portrayed them as being hypersexual, aggressive, and even pathological or diseased.

Whereas very few men noted the economic factors underlying the supposed differences in behavior in these bars, Herb, an African American man, did point out that he felt different financial constraints influenced the transactions and that he preferred to go to white clubs rather than black clubs as a "safety mechanism." "The fact that I make the kind of money I do, if I do decide to spend two, three hundred bucks, you're going to take that better than one of the ladies at the black clubs. If I spend two or three hundred bucks, then there's expectations. I mean, I may get a phone number even if I don't want it. I guess that may be socioeconomic. Black women don't have as many chances at, you know, a guy who can afford to spend that kind of money." Being given a phone number, then, comes to be read as aggressive in this particular situation, perhaps because Herb felt that her desire for an actual phone call was more real. Although all of these men had actually visited the black clubs at some time, similar comments were made by individuals who refused to do so.

The negotiation of racial differences became quite complicated in the transactions that occurred in the white or mixed-race clubs. African American dancers working in the white clubs often spoke about the potential racism or ignorance of the customers, as well as the way particular racial and ethnic stereotypes could either "sell" or curtail their earnings in different spaces. One dancer in the lower-tier Pony Lounge, for example, always wore leopard- or zebra-patterned costumes, consciously playing on the animalistic jungle theme that customers often expected from her. In the lower-tier clubs like Tina's and the Pony Lounge, black dancers performed to rap music as well as rock and dance music. In Diamond Dolls, the Crystal Palace, and the Panther, however, the black dancers were more concerned with looking as Caucasian as possible to make the customers "comfortable." Tommi, a dancer at the Panther, wore a long straight black wig and told the customers that she was half Cherokee or half Filipina in addition to African American, "depending on my mood." "Guys want you to be anything but all black," she said. Dia, one of the two African American dancers working at Diamond Dolls while I was there, noted that she would not receive tips from white men if she chose to dance to hip-hop or funk music. She also laughed as she told me about the amazement of white customers when they saw that she had tan lines ("Black women can tan?"). Other dancers told stories of being shunned by groups of men who seemed to be "afraid" of them or who would blatantly refuse to tip black dancers or even look at them on stage. Of course, these women's experiences must be contextualized, and Laurelton, as a Southern city, has a history of racism and segregation. Yet, women of color in other locations and other sectors of the sex industry have pointed out the need to fight ethnic and racial stereotypes in their workplace and the way that racism shapes these transactions, at the same time that they recognize that such stereotypes have erotic force for some of their customers (S. Brooks 1997; Nagle 1997).

In a cover story in *Exotic Dancer Bulletin* (a trade journal for the industry) on why there are so few black feature dancers, columnist and dancer Reese Meridian puts forth several hypotheses. So far, Meridian notes, strip clubs do not seem to have as much of a draw for black customers. Further, racism plays a role in both "discouraging African-American women who would like to dance from pursuing a career in the mainstream clubs" (read, white clubs), and in discouraging club owners from hiring black features and dancers out of a fear that their clientele will be unhappy. Though there are a few primarily black clubs across the country, such as those in Laurelton, they are still currently seen to represent a specialized market and generally do not draw a mixed clientele. In these clubs the music is sometimes different (rap and R&B rather than rock and roll) and the dancers are expected to move differently ("White girls prance; black girls dance"; 1997: 53).

Interestingly, some of the successful black feature dancers quoted in Meridian's piece draw on discourses of propriety to claim an ability to draw customers on either side of the color line. Safire Blue, an African American entertainer, said, "The bottom line is that a beautiful woman in a breathtaking gown crosses color boundaries" (1997: 51). Her clothes and her beauty are seen as having the power to elevate her above the status of the purely sexual and to potentially overcome racism. Similarly, Brazil, a mixed-race entertainer, was quoted as saying, "The bottom line is that if you act like a lady, you are treated like one—color doesn't have anything to do with that" (54). Here, race becomes class ("breathtaking gown") becomes gender ("a beautiful woman" who "acts like a lady"), and the material and symbolic boundaries that have been constructed through years of inequality and racism become reduced to personal issues of taste and conduct, for both the customers and the dancers.

The Obscene Body

Talk about beauty, professionalism, and propriety should not mislead us into thinking that the customers all preferred "respectable" to "disreputable" venues, or that their differences in consumption were actually related just to differences in taste ("I'm turned on by middle-class women"; "I'm turned on by working-class women"). Male customers move between different kinds of venues (upper tier to lower tier and vice versa) and between different kinds of women (the woman at home; the public woman), and these movements and contrasts also have erotic potential. There is an interesting story about the supermodel Jerry Hall boasting that her rock star husband Mick Jagger would be faithful to her while on the road because of her beauty and style: "Why go out for hamburger when you can have steak at home?" she reportedly said. Mick's reply, as the story goes, was: "Well, sometimes everyone enjoys a greasy hamburger." Whether or not this is a true conversation, it highlights erotic issues that also surfaced in public discourse when actor Hugh Grant was arrested after paying for oral sex with an African American Los Angeles street prostitute named Divine Brown, cheating on his own supermodel girlfriend, Elizabeth Hurley. (How could he be interested in Divine when he had *Liz?* people asked.)

Sexualization, erotics, and social class are tangled together in complicated patterns of both cultural and personal fantasy. Despite the distinctions made between dancers and clubs in terms of classiness, for instance, exotic dancing is still stigmatized, and women who choose to transgress these boundaries of private and public will always be considered "trash" in some circles. In *Imperial Leather*, Anne McClintock notes that though the figures of the nineteenth-century traveler, the urban explorer, or the flâneur were generally masculine, lower-class women working as prostitutes, maids, and streetsellers were an important and sexualized part of the city landscape. Their social ambiguities, however, and the challenges they might pose to dominant constructions of gender are neutralized through their production as spectacle for an upper- or middle-class male observer (1995: 82). Even today, women who occupy certain public spaces (either geographically in the city or psychologically through class status) are the source of middle-class male fascination, identification, desire, and disgust. These women, in fact, are part of the very adventure of urban exploration because of their difference from women who would not transgress these boundaries.[8]

Rojek and Urry note that in slumming there are two dichotomies that work together: "gaze / touch" and "desire / contamination" (1997: 7). Walking the fine line between fascination and the fear of pollution cannot be discounted as an element of the customers' experiences of pleasure and authenticity. "Sometimes men go to strip clubs to see women that they wouldn't date, wouldn't even talk to," Jason said. His quote can be read two ways: these women would not be available for the men to talk to or date because their supposed social class, attractiveness, or morality was either much higher or (more likely) much lower than his own.

A few men said that they preferred the lower-tier clubs because they believed that the dancers there were more likely to engage in illegal behaviors. Whether or not the men themselves were interested in actually purchasing sexual activity (if it could even be negotiated), just being in such an atmosphere lent an air of authenticity to their experience. Nick said that he preferred lower-tier clubs because he believed the dancers who worked in them might be more likely to involve themselves in a real sexual encounter. At the same time, however, he found most of the dancers in the lower-tier clubs "too unattractive to even consider." As with the other men who expressed an interest in sexual activity, Nick seemed to foreclose the possibility of such activity ever occurring—courting both danger and safety at the same time.

Some customers told me in whispered tones about scenes of possible prostitution they believed they had witnessed in the lower-tier clubs. David told me that in one of the lower-tier clubs he had visited in Laurelton:

> There's a room that has beads on the door and you can sit at the regular bar but these people that go back to do these couch dances . . . I mean, you can actually see people in there performing . . . [pause; voice drops to a whisper] sexual acts . . . the guys . . . are actually either masturbating or being given oral sex of some sort or something like that. I don't know why that's not stopped, but I mean . . . I haven't been in there! [laughs] No desire to. No desire to go in there. Because I'm not sure what kind of fluids you might run into . . . so when you see someone that doesn't seem to value themselves any more than that, I don't know, but it seems to take a little bit off of it.

Though David said that he now preferred upper-tier clubs, and we met at the Panther, the lower-tier clubs had a hold on his imagination, and our conversation repeatedly returned to these scenes of supposedly semipublic female impropriety.

Jim, a customer at the Panther, said of one of the lower-tier clubs located in the basement of a hotel: "I think the hotel is known for having um . . . women of the street, occupying rooms, or temporarily occupying rooms. It used to be kind of a trashy neighborhood and I think it's just . . . it seems to be in decline. I think if you went in there, and the lights were on and you saw the condition of the carpeting and, you know, the . . . the real look of women, you'd probably want to never go back! It seems like a place where you could easily get yourself involved in . . . you know, AIDS and all kinds of sexually transmitted diseases. The dancers are not beautiful and I think they may tend to go beyond the limits of what legally you're allowed to do." Similarly, Alex said that the lower-tier clubs were "pretty wild": "I wasn't getting in on it . . . But you know, what went on . . . they had different rooms and stuff and what went on in there was, you know, out of sight, out of mind kind of thing. You know, there's a lot of heads that look the other way. A lot of that. I think. I don't know, but I think pretty much anything goes on in there. If you wanted to do whatever you wanted to do, there was a price for it. I didn't go back there, but just . . . [pause] the atmosphere." Though Alex had no firsthand experience of any sexual activity, and did not even know anyone who had participated in this, he enjoyed believing that it was available if he so desired, as did Jim. For Alex, part of the thrill of going to strip clubs was being in an "atmosphere" that was "wild" and "sinister," and he believed this was most likely to be found in a lower-tier club with women who had no moral qualms about engaging in such behavior.

Paul's earlier comment that the women in the black clubs did not "value themselves enough" and gave performances that were too graphic, coupled with some of the comments made by men who felt that the lower-tier clubs were inappropriate and uncomfortable, illustrate the delicate boundary between desire and contamination. The performances, for these men, had suddenly become a bit *too* authentic. Certainly the customers also wondered about whether or not sexual activity had occurred in the Gem Rooms of the upscale Diamond Dolls, and some hypothesized that it had. However, and significantly, these customers also figured that the dancers who engaged in sexual activity in the Gem Rooms "valued themselves" higher than the "whores of Chestnut Crossing." Yet in all of these cases, the men were not talking about real but conjectured encounters: no money had been seen changing hands, no confessions had been made to them by dancers, no prices had been requested or quoted, and no sexual acts had been engaged in personally *by these customers.* By framing their judgments in terms of how the women valued themselves, however, these men effectively obscured the fact that the customers were already valuing certain women differently.

As has been well argued elsewhere, madonna / whore categorizations of women are often split down class lines.[9] Freud's argument about the "split" desire in some (white, Western) men was set forth in his theory of love, which was based on two currents of feeling: the affectionate (originating in early relations with the mother) and the sensual (more sexual; originating in puberty). Romantic love was the synthesis of these two currents directed toward a nonfamilial object. In an ideal situation, then, it would be possible to feel passion and tenderness for the same individual. But this does not always happen, and the result is a psychopathological state in which a man's feelings become bifurcated: "Where they love they do not desire and where they desire they can not love" (Freud 1950: 207). This bifurcation serves the purpose of making the real, or original, object choice (mother) unavailable, as "the sensual feelings are diverted from their desired object choice . . . by the barrier of the incest taboo and the disgust, shame, and morality that sanction it" (W. Miller 1997: 128).

For William Miller, a scholar who has written extensively on disgust, Freud's account is about social class more than anything else (1997: 130). The madonna / whore split takes on class connotations for the (middle-class) man: "Those who remind him of mother and sister, that is, women of his own (respectable) social class, will be loved tenderly but not sensually; those who are nothing like mother will get sensuality devoid of tenderness" (128). The pleasures of sex, he argues, come from violating disgust prohibitions. "Freud's story," he writes, "is of men who seek women who are morally and socially contemptible, not physically disgusting" (although physical disgust can also potentially play a part for some men, especially in the sex industry). Lower-class women, who "will do and suffer things respectable women won't," thus become sexually alluring. Miller notes that disgust, associated with the " 'social deformities' of low-class taste and vulgarity," thus works to both attract and repel (130).

Several of the men I interviewed discussed a tension between feelings of sexual desire and feelings of friendship or tenderness for women. Beck said, "That's something I've noticed in me and it's really weird. And I think it probably has to do maybe with a Puritan upbringing . . . I tend to do this and I guess some guys do. They're going to look upon somebody either as a friend, somebody they really care about, or a sex object. And that's a real weird dichotomy. And I have . . . nothing to say about that. I just don't understand it at all. But that's a fact." He said that he felt his wife was "much more of a friend now" than a sex object. He also said that since we had done an interview, he would no longer be able to see me in the club, explaining that this happened whenever he got to know a dancer: "Once you start the friendship thing, if you've had them separate your whole life, it's hard to look upon them as friends and sex objects too." Jim and Joe, as well as a number of other men I spoke with in the clubs, echoed these concerns. Jim said about his wife:

I want her to be attracted to me and I want to be attracted to her . . . she takes good care of herself too. I think she tends to think of herself as less of a sexual object and she got upset one time when she tried to . . . basically, dance and seduce me with, like a T-shirt with you know, holes cut out for the nipples and . . . she thought that when I kind of felt embarrassed about it or, you know, laughed a little, she thought I was laughing at her and it was really kind of an embarrassment type . . . I don't know . . . it's my own psychological discomfort, I guess, that I wasn't able to feel relaxed with her trying to be, you know, my private dancer. And I think she tried to do that and she felt that maybe I've not lived up to my part of the deal in getting turned on and stuff like that.

Dancers were often caught in the middle of this tension between attraction and repulsion, sometimes quite self-consciously. They were not only presenting themselves as beautiful or sexually alluring, as acceptable and sometimes idealized sexual objects,[10] but also as defiled by their public nudity and their acceptance of financial compensation for sexualized companionship and the voyeuristic pleasures of the customers. This aspect of the men's experiences became evident in statements they made about the lowness of dancers in comparison to their wife, girlfriend, or daughter, as well as in the ways negotiations were made inside the clubs.

Although the interactions that I am discussing do not involve sexual activity, they do involve viewing the female genitals—publicly and sometimes at close range. Some men, in fact, admitted that they rarely viewed female genitalia. Other men did not admit it but gave me many reasons to assume that this was the case, such as a complete lack of anatomical understanding, nervousness and discomfort, or an inability to look. Despite the fact that the male customers often insisted that "the female body is beautiful to me," for a man who is used to having sex in the dark (and even one who isn't), cultural and religious devaluations of the female body, especially the genitals, may play an important and exciting part in his experiences in strip clubs.

At the Panther, the women dance on tables that are illuminated from below, right above the customers' food and drinks (we joked about the fact that we were still required to wear shoes by the Health Department and told the customers that they were lucky we waxed off most of our pubic hair). Certainly, the genitals are a reminder of the "abject" (urine, feces, the unclean, the impure), as they mark a boundary between inside and outside, forming the margins of the body (Nead 1992: 32). In Laurelton, where the dancing is completely nude, the man may find himself gazing up not only at a woman's labia during a table dance, but also at the anus—the "essence of lowness, of untouchability" (W. Miller 1997: 100). The surfaces of the genitals may be cosmetically enhanced through stage makeup or waxing, but the threat of contamination is omnipresent: *What do you do if your tampon string comes untucked? What if you haven't wiped properly? What if you get wet? What if you fart? Is this power—to know how quickly you could ruin his day?* Indeed, as one moves into other realms of the sex industry these boundaries are redrawn, and a customer may come closer to, or further away from, such bodily thresholds.[11]

Body fluids, of course, have social and cultural meaning, and are often seen as contaminating or dangerous (Douglas 1966; Kristeva 1982). The very fact that body fluids have been seen as contaminating, however, can also be a source of erotic excitement for some individuals, a fact that has long fueled pornography and erotica. Some customers told stories about witnessing a slipped tampon string or a trail of blood on a woman's leg while she was dancing, a piece of toilet paper stuck to someone's genitals that glowed under the black lights, or women working in lower-tier clubs whom they suspected of having engaged in sexual relations before performing on stage, who "dripped." Other customers told stories about these kinds of events that they'd heard second- or third-hand, and such stories circulated in both upper- and lower-tier clubs almost like urban legends. The narratives and possibility alone held a fascination for some of the storytellers; for certain others, there was possibly even a hope that one might spontaneously observe such "leakages."

The anus, which was prominently displayed by the dancers in particular positions and angles, is also figured as a locus of possible homosexual activity; after all, it is the possible erasure of sexual difference, the only part of the genital area that is similar to look at on both sexes. Given that identifications are multiple, fluid, and even contradictory in fantasy life, and given that some of the men clearly saw themselves in the position of the "being desired," by the dancer or *as* the dancer, the fantasy of having one's anus seen (perhaps by a man) certainly has some complicated erotic potential.

For some men, then, ideas about defilement and purity—of or by either the dancer *or* themselves—play a role in their experience of certain encounters as more authentic (although getting *too close* to the real becomes uncomfortable). The line between disgust and arousal, fascination and repulsion is fine indeed. This is not to say that the same emotions and psychic barriers motivate every man when he visits a strip club. Rather, it is to point out that beneath the talk of authenticity lies a complex world of fantasy about class, race, sexuality, and gender that influences some of the pleasure men take in these experiences and the decisions they make about where to spend their leisure time and money. These decisions and pleasures are not inherently about the reproduction of social inequalities or stigmas, though they do derive some of their power from the hierarchical ordering of differences.

*

Fantasy has a conservative side. This does not mean that fantasies should be condemned, disciplined, or ignored; indeed, this would just cause them to reemerge in other fashions and forms. It is not, after all, only in the sex industry that fantasies refuse to be tamed into "politically correct" or comfortable scenarios. Rather, there is a need for ethnographic explorations of how cultural products and representations become meaningful to consumers at this level before attempting to ascertain their place in the social order. Despite the fact that stripping does potentially involve some important social transgressions, especially that of middle-class feminine modesty, I found the customers to be quite conservative. Those I interacted with and interviewed were generally not interested in political transgressions (though that could have made the work a lot more fun) or challenging dominant ideologies—they were interested in *pleasure.* And the search for pleasure required walking a fine line between safety and danger, excitement and relaxation, adventure and leisure, escape and return, desire and disgust.

Certainly, multiple identifications are possible in any scenario, and psychic fluidities are undeniably complex and unpredictable. But there are also a lot of stabilities and repetitions. *It's a good thing, or dancers would never be able to figure out how to make money.* Conceptualizing fantasy and reality as always already intertwined, then, we can see how fantasies about class, race, and gender influenced the customers' perceptions of authenticity as well as the pleasure they took in particular encounters. The customers repeatedly stressed concerns about comfort, safety, and propriety in their choice of clubs and in the interactions they purchased, at the same time that they purposefully sought encounters that bumped up against these boundaries, encounters that were just authentic enough to be compelling. The men distinguished among dancers (and indeed, whole clubs) based on sincerity or authenticity that was both embodied and performed and related to social positions and inequalities. For the consumers, the dancers' bodies became flexible symbols of desire and disgust, beauty and abjection, forms of cultural capital and forms of lower-class obscenity.

Significantly, the pleasure and use of fantasy is not just in playing with transgressing social boundaries and escaping the everyday; rather, the pleasure of fantasy for individuals, especially the kind of interactive, co-constructed, public fantasy that one finds in this particular kind of strip club, lies in its simultaneous ability to make other fantasy-realities more real, less threatening (*Here I am with a "real" low-class whore—I'm a man who can flirt with danger; Here I am with a "real" girl, not just a stripper—she enjoys talking to me because I am an interesting, desirable, stimulating man; Here I am relaxing in an obviously commodified environment—I'm a man who can see through manipulation and seduction; etc.*). The next chapter turns to the way fantasy articulates with everyday practices, especially, in this case, to the ways that the men's long-term relationships with women outside of the clubs influence the pleasure they experience in their encounters with dancers.

Part Four

The Management of Hunger

I am pulling a gold knit dress carefully over the rollers in my hair when my friend Maya enters the dressing room of the strip club where we work. She is still in her street clothes and looks like a young boy—a baseball cap, baggy jeans, and a T-shirt. She has a duffel bag slung over her shoulder and is carrying her hair attachment in one hand, a long, shiny black ponytail.

She throws something at me and it hits me lightly on the arm. "Hey, Kenzie," she says, "one for me, one for you." I bend down and pick a small stuffed animal off the floor. It is a kangaroo Beanie Baby, with a baby kangaroo tucked into its pouch.

"How cute," I say. "From the Doctor?"

"Of course," she says. "One of the door girls was on her way back to give them to us and I saved her the trouble. I think he's early." She sets her bag heavily down on a chair and lays the ponytail carefully on top of it.

I check the clock and it is 6:15. "Thanks," I say. "I'm almost ready anyway." Every Friday night, the Doctor and I have a dinner date at 6:30, and though my shift doesn't actually start until 7 I am always dressed and ready to go when he arrives. He has to be home by 8:30 or his wife gets suspicious.

The club that I work in has a main room with four stages, a VIP room with couches, and a dining room where the customers can take dancers to dinner or for drinks. Most dancers charge a hundred dollars an hour

This short story first appeared as part of an article: Frank, K. "The Management of Hunger: Using Fiction in Writing Anthropology," *Qualitative Inquiry* 6(4), December 2000.

to go to dinner with a customer, and I am no exception. Seeing the Doctor early on Fridays means that I still have a chance to try to get someone else to take me to dinner after he leaves, before the restaurant section closes at 11.

I spray some perfume into the air and walk through it, careful not to get too much on my skin. Then I check my makeup, take out the rollers in my hair, and brush it so the ends curl under. I arrange the kangaroo on the top shelf of my locker with the other stuffed beanbag animals that the Doctor has given me—a Siamese cat, a giraffe, the tie-dyed Garcia bear (worth some money, he tells me), a bat, and a multicolored snake. A sequined t-back falls off the shelf and I kick it back into the pile of costumes at the bottom of my locker. Then I dig through the pile of multicolored thongs, dresses, and shoes that crowd the narrow space until I find a pair of matching gold stilettos.

Maya sets the other kangaroo on top of her makeup case and begins to strip off her street clothes. "I'd rather have the five bucks than a dumb Beanie Baby," she says. She takes out a bottle of lotion and begins to rub it on her deeply tanned body. Maya looks like she is wearing a bathing suit even when she is naked because her tan lines are so stark. It completely baffles some of the white guys to see an African American woman with tan lines. She is the only black dancer in the club and sometimes tells customers that she is part Fillipina, so that the hair extension is more believable. Other times she tells them that she was born in Mauritius and that she is really part French. White fraternity boys are often scared of her no matter what she tells them, and she says that she can see them hesitating in the audience while she is on stage performing, holding their limp dollars in sweaty hands. Because of this, her regulars are all older men.

"Do you want to come to dinner with us tonight?" I ask her. Though the Doctor has been taking me to dinner weekly for over six months, he thinks that Maya and I are roommates and often asks her to join us. As with most of the customers, I could never tell him that I really live with my boyfriend, Seth. Maya and I are very convincing at being roommates, though, sometimes even staging fights about dirty dishes or borrowed clothes to seem more realistic. Several times the Doctor has given us grocery money after we've described the sorry state of our refrigerator to him—imaginary baby carrot sticks, sour milk, ketchup, and Slim Fast. We always split that money evenly.

"Not tonight," she says. "I think I'll make more than a hundred an hour working the floor." Then she pauses, "I shouldn't say that—I might jinx myself and end up with the Plague." I laugh, having experienced "the Plague" myself as often as any other dancer. Some nights everyone in the club thinks that you are ravishing. Other nights, the exact same look and moves can't turn a single head. A bout with the Plague has sent many a dancer home empty-handed at the end of a long shift after paying out the mandatory taxes, tips, and house fees. But empty pockets are an occasional job hazard—just like swollen knees, razor bumps, and periodic cynicism. When I started dancing I learned quickly never to spend my money before it was earned, to put bags of frozen peas on my knees after particularly busy nights (works better than ice to calm the swelling), and to rub Secret deodorant on my bikini line to make unsightly razor rash recede. I have not yet, however, found a remedy for the cynicism. Perhaps that is best.

"Well, at least come do some dances with me," I say, and she nods. Sitting down on the floor, I fasten the ankle straps on my high heels. Then I take one of my small sequined evening bags out of my locker and slip a lipstick in it. Besides the lipstick, the purse is completely empty to leave room for my money. This was one of the things I found most amusing about dancing when I first started—walking into a nightclub at the beginning of the evening with an empty purse and leaving at the end with a roll of smoky cash.

The club is still nearly empty and I immediately spot the Doctor at the bar. He is drinking a gin and tonic and talking to the bartender, who he's known for years. He turns to look at me as I approach. "You look great, Kenzie," he says, using my real name instead of my stage name. I've been letting him call me Kenzie for several months now at Maya's suggestion.

I give him a quick hug. "Thanks for the kangaroo."

"Sure. Can I get you a drink?" he asks. "Or would you like to go to dinner?"

"Dinner," I say. "Can we have wine at the table?" He nods and picks up his glass. We make our way through the club to the dining room and I wave at a few of the dancers showing up for the night shift.

This early in the evening there are only a few couples in the dining area. This section is lush and intimate—mostly tables for two or semi-circular booths, decorated with candles and freshcut flowers. The tables are wide enough to do table dances on, which is also just wide enough to make the geometry of the room seem odd. Though the dancers wear long gowns, their "dates" are sometimes wearing shorts, also making the scene peculiar to the eye. A brunette dancer that I don't recognize sways high above the breadbasket and centerpiece on one of the tables, naked except for her high heels. Because we serve food, high heels, strangely enough, are required at all times by the health department. The two customers staring up at her barely notice us enter the room.

The hostess recognizes the Doctor and leads us to our usual table in the corner. As we slide into the booth, I make sure that he is sitting on my right side, my better side. We sit close together and I ask him about his week. He tells me stories about work, absently drumming a finger on the table. Unlike some of the customers, he makes no attempt to hide his wedding band. The waitress takes our order—grilled mahi-mahi for me, rare steak for the Doctor. The irony of a doctor ordering red meat is not lost on him, and he has told me that this is the only place where he doesn't have to worry about reproach. He picks out a bottle of Merlot from the wine list and orders another gin and tonic. The Doctor always spends over a hundred dollars on our food and drinks, and some nights I wish that he would just give me the money or let me dance for it instead. But that isn't how our relationship works, and with the stiff competition for good customers here, I don't complain out loud to anyone, much less to him.

When the waitress brings our drinks, she leaves a basket of bread on the table with a small crock of herbed butter. I sip the wine but don't yet touch the bread. The Doctor likes to see me eat, but I have to be careful and not get too full. It is hard to dance on a full stomach; also, if my plan to go to dinner again later works out, I don't want to be stuck ordering a salad or wasting my food. The waitresses and managers frown if you don't order a whole meal, understandably, and if you order an expensive meal but don't make a show of eating, the customers get suspicious.

Some of the dancers who go to dinner with customers frequently have elaborate strategies of food management. Carrie dines three times on Wednesday nights, as she has been at the club for several years and has a number of good regulars. She is quite thin and eats very lightly, picking at the food they buy her. Styrofoam containers with half-eaten portions of steaks, salads, and pastas get stacked up in the kitchen with her name scratched across them. Ally drinks too much champagne to boost her appetite, then eats too much food to sober up. She can't seem to learn moderation. Jessie only pretends to be eating, slipping pieces of overpriced fish under the table to an invisible dog.

I sense that the Doctor is in a melancholy mood tonight, and try to cheer him up by talking nonstop about things we might do together if he ever takes a vacation. I suggest swing dancing, horseback riding, and the beach. I tell him that if he takes me to the beach I'll make him get up every morning at 5 A.M. and go jogging with me. He laughs and looks down at his softening abdomen. I tell him that in the afternoon I'll bring him piña coladas by the pool and walk around in a thong, making all of the other men at the pool jealous and the women mad. I show him that I am wearing a gold t-back that matches my shoes, trying to get him to relax by being silly and childlike.

But nothing is working tonight and I worry that he has lost interest in me. I've heard that the Doctor gets sick of dancers after a while—one day he'll just show up and choose someone new to spend his money on. That's how it happened when we first began sitting together, and the dancer who used to sit with him got so angry that I had stolen her regular that she left the club for three weeks, until the managers talked her into coming back. Now she refuses to speak to me if we end up on the same shift.

"Let me dance for you," I say finally, and he helps me to the table.

I take off my dress and dance two songs for him to the smell of our dinners cooking in the kitchen. This early in the evening, the room is cold and goose bumps rise on my legs and arms, making me feel exposed. I never feel naked unless my body doesn't cooperate with my plans for it. During my second dance, Maya weaves her way over to our table and kisses the Doctor on the cheek. She is completely transformed, wearing a floor-length blue dress and black velvet gloves. Her hair is slicked back into the luxurious ponytail attachment, which swings behind her as she walks. "Thank you for the kangaroo, Tom," she says sweetly. "It's adorable." Then she wipes the lipstick off his cheek with a gloved finger. "Don't want to get anyone in trouble," she says dramatically. The Doctor stiffens and from my precarious stance on the table I give her a dirty look. Maya always forgets that the Doctor hates to be reminded that our dates are clandestine.

He motions for her to get on the table and we dance for him to-gether—black and blonde, a contrast he likes—placing our feet carefully around the bread plates and wine glasses with each move. We are so close together on the small table that when she turns her back to me her fake hair whisks across my stomach. Then we turn in the other direction and she steadies me by putting her hands on my hips. The table rocks slightly as we move back and forth.

"Why don't you ever wear your hair down?" the Doctor asks her.

"It's too thick," she lies with a smile. "It looks more glamorous up."

When she leaves with several twenties folded into her garter, I dance one more song. Then he helps me back down onto the bench and hands me his snakeskin wallet like he always does. I take the money out for my dances, twenty dollars each, and for the time we will spend at dinner in advance. He knows I won't cheat him. *We need to trust each other,* he told me the first night that we were together in the club. *That's the only way these relationships work.*

He still seems too serious.

"What can I do to cheer you up?" I ask, sliding the wallet back to him.

"I would love to cook dinner for you sometime," the Doctor says, ignoring my question and continuing to slowly drum the table top with his fingers. "Maybe at my summer home in the mountains."

"Any time," I say brightly, knowing that all of our plans are safely impossible. Though I am glad to get him daydreaming, I am surprised that he mentions one of his houses. Usually we just talk about being together in public places, faraway or exotic travel spots.

The Doctor, after all, is married with two daughters nearly my age, Lisha and Kaila. Though they are both attending the same college and are far from being children, I know that he buys them Beanie Babies like he does for Maya and me. Once when I was taking money out of his wallet, I came across a picture of Lisha in her dorm room that was clearly taken just for him. Blonde and tan, just like me, she was sitting on the side of her bed and wearing a red sundress with small white flowers on it. She was smiling and pointing to a pile of stuffed animals on her bed, many of them the same Beanie Babies that I have in my locker—the Siamese cat, the snake, the floppy orange giraffe. I remember the photo and picture him at the cash register of a kiosk in the mall, four identical little animals in his hands—two that will be shipped off to Auburn University in a small brown box, two that will be hand-delivered to the Sin City Cabaret.

The Doctor always talks very protectively of his daughters. I know so much about Lisha and Kaila—I've heard about their majors, their grades, their sorority, their propensity to date boys that the Doctor thinks have no promise. Sometimes I feel like a Peeping Tom, someone that looks periodically into their lives while always remaining hidden in the shadows.

He talks less about his wife, but I know that they've been together for twenty-seven years, longer than I've been alive. I wonder whether she knows or suspects how he spends his Friday nights. There are only so many "meetings" one can attend, only so many nights of working late that seem believable. Perhaps she no longer cares how he spends his evenings, or perhaps it no longer crosses her mind that he might be interested in the theatrics of romance, in candlelit dinners, in pursuing and being pursued. Or maybe he won't let her give him any of those things, ignoring her when she puts on a silky negligee or scrap of a thong, unable to see her as anything but a mother, a friend, a roommate.

That experience is not unfamiliar to me, I realize. There are nights that I arrive home from work with my head still full of whispers of praise and passionate promises from my customers, my body still electrified with the beat of the dance music and the thrill of the money. *You smell like smoke,* Seth says flatly from our bed, even before he can see me or smell me. He is annoyed that I have awoken him from his dreams. *You need to shower or you'll get that goddamn glitter all over the sheets.*

"I don't cook much anymore," the Doctor says, breaking my reverie. "I can't remember why I stopped. No time, I guess."

While we wait for our dinner to arrive, the Doctor begins to tell me stories of food that he will cook for me if I join him in the mountains, describing dishes that he used to make during his bachelor days. He had actually considered culinary school instead of medical school at one point in his life, but knew that there was no money in it. Now, in this place where he feels beyond reproach for his decisions, he freely dreams up plates of linguini with pesto and chicken, fresh boiled lobsters with melted butter, elaborate salads with melon and walnuts.

"I can't watch you boil a lobster," I say.

"Oh, they don't feel pain," he says. He makes a motion with his hand, dunking an invisible kicking lobster into a kettle. "That kicking is a reflex."

In his fantasy kitchen the Doctor prepares regions, ethnicities, whole countries—Northern and Southern, French and Greek, Italian and Indian, Thai and Japanese. He bakes for me—cooking up visions of banana bread, zucchini bread, foccacia with olives and onions. He puts me to work in the kitchen chopping, grating, and washing, and pictures me fresh-faced and ponytailed, wearing flat sandals instead of stilettos. He talks of fresh crushed spices, of garlic and cumin, cayenne and ginger—each with its own objective and attitude. He pours Chiantis and Cabernets, sweet wine from Sauternes and miniature glasses of port. And desserts, of course—he'll serve cheesecake with raspberries, a light tiramisu, carrot cake with thick sweet frosting, homemade baklava layered and brushed with pounds of butter.

"You'll make me fat," I say, smiling and patting my stomach.

"Of course," he says. "Did you know that in Tibet some mothers rub their babies with butter twice a day? Pure hedonism, no?" I shake my head. I didn't know about the babies, but I remember hearing a dancer talk backstage about how to naturally enlarge your breasts by rubbing them each with a full stick of butter every night until it is gone. The fat molecules, she told us, are absorbed by your skin and become part of your body. Maya and I had vowed to try it but gave up after one night because it took so long to make a stick of butter dissolve.

The Doctor butters a piece of bread, slowly and thickly, and sets it on my plate. I look down at my body in the clingy gold dress, at my tan legs, my long thin arms. His eyes follow mine and I fantasize that we see the same thing—my flesh, growing and puffing over the bones, becoming taut and engorged, not in bulges, but everywhere evenly blossoming, ballooning, voluptuously inflating. My small breasts become larger, rounder, even stretching the fabric of my dress.

He touches the emergent fatness of my thigh, the newly fleshy outlines of my body, looking amused. Despite my protests, he continues to feed me pizzas with four kinds of cheese and sundried tomatoes, fluffy slices of broccoli quiche, a stir-fry made with red, green, orange, and yellow peppers. I roll on the couch of his airy mountain home, side-to-side, front and back. *I'm too full,* I say, laughing, helpless and unable to stand. But he ignores me and heats up a messy chocolate fondue for strawberries and oranges, licking my enormous bloated fingers after I eat.

When the waitress finally sets our dinner plates down in front of us, the smell of the real food makes me deflate. My stomach growls but the portions are small, less colorful and less appealing than the meals we have already cooked and eaten together. I pull a piece of wilted lettuce off my plate and set it on the white tablecloth, which is still puckered from my high heels. We look at each other and laugh.

He isn't tired of me, yet. He asks me to do four more table dances as we eat our meal, pointing to the places where the food has settled in my stomach. There. And there. And there. *Really?* I say, running my hands over my flat stomach. We taunt each other. A modern-day Persephone, I know what he is looking for. Only so much, I think. Only so much.

But it's just dinner, after all, and this isn't his mountain home or his home in the city. We are still on safe ground, exactly where we both want to be. And when he returns home and his wife asks, *What did you have for dinner, dear?* it will only be the bloody tangibility of the steak that will weigh on his conscience.

At 8:15 I walk the Doctor to the front door of the club and give him a quick hug good-bye. "I'll see you on Friday if I'm hungry," he says, and I smile at him, sliding my purse underneath one arm. I know that he'll be here.

I move back out onto the main floor, hoping to stir up another dinner date or a couple of table dances before I have to go onstage. As I prepare to transform myself into whatever the next customer is looking for, I remind myself that my value here lies in what I am *not* as much as in what I am. Not a lover, not a wife. Not a daughter. Never a daughter.

A feast without food, a paradox of sustenance.

Chapter Seven

The Crowded Bedroom:

Marriage, Monogamy, and Fantasy

Everyone has secrets.

—Tim

In contemporary America, marriage and monogamy have deep ideological and psychological meanings. Despite the fact that individuals may arrange their own relationships in a variety of ways, and may even choose not to marry, they still must position themselves in relation to dominant discourses about heterosexuality, monogamy, and marriage.[1] In many popular representations—films, books, songs, and everyday conversation—marriage is portrayed as a site of ambivalence, sometimes figuring as a source of life's richest and most important fulfillments, sometimes as a trap, as that which ties a worker ever more tightly to the need to work, either (or both) on the relationship and / or to provide for one's family. In spite of such ambivalence, there is evidence that many Americans share certain ideals about marriage as well: valuing sharing in marriages, "lastingness" of commitment, and the personal fulfillment of both partners (Quinn 1997: 190).

This chapter explores how men's beliefs about marriage and monogamy, as well as the ways that they practice marriage, influence their desire to visit strip clubs and the pleasure they take in doing so. The idea of practice emphasizes the fact that marriage is more than just the beliefs and commitment of two individuals; it is also the enactment of those beliefs and commitments on a day-to-day basis. Thus, whereas many people may hold the same beliefs about marriage, they may practice it differently, as beliefs do not necessarily translate into behavior. Even among people who are unfaithful to their partner, monogamy is often a strongly held moral ideal (Blumstein and Schwartz 1983: 271). Precisely how does these men's relationship with their wife or long-term partner influence the pleasure or excitement they experience in their interactions with dancers? The focus here is on a triadic relationship among certain customers, the dancer(s), and the other women in the customers' life that shapes the meaning of their encounters.

Marriage and the Sex Industry

The relation of marriage to the sex industry has been approached in three primary ways: commodified sexualized relationships have been theorized as similar to those found in marriage, as necessary for the maintenance of the institution, or as inimical to it. This first approach is often taken by theorists wishing to critique marriage as an institution of gender oppression or inequality. Many early feminists, such as Mary Wollstonecraft, Emma Goldman, Cicely Hamilton, and Simone de Beauvoir, among others, noted the similarities between the institutions of prostitution and marriage, arguing that whether a woman sold herself to one man or to many, it was "merely a question of degree" and of duration (Pateman 1988: 190).[2] This metaphoric comparison still emerges at times in feminist discourse, fostering debates about the meanings of female bodies in the various positions of worker, wife, and prostitute (S. Bell 1994). That marriage could not even exist without prostitution has also been suggested. Pat Califia argues, for example, that "the opportunity for paid infidelity (as long as it is hidden and stigmatized) makes monogamous marriage a believable institution" (1994: 243). Many other writers, however, have taken the third approach and drawn on cultural ideas about love and intimacy to critique the sex industry instead, and to portray the exchanges purchased in the industry as inimical to "real" and ideal intimate relationships (e.g., Reisman 1991; Stock 1997). Judith Reisman has written a nonfeminist, antipornography tract that blames the sex industry for nearly every possible problem in modern marriages. Reisman even suggests that men come to prefer centerfold images or sex workers to the real women with whom they are involved.

Despite the fact that marriage has been discussed in literature focused on the sex industry, there is little direct note taken of the influence and specter of the sex industry in the copious academic literature on marital relationships. As commodified sexual services and images (both legal and illegal) make up a multibillion-dollar-a-year industry (Schlosser 1997), and as many of the customers in each sector are married men, this absence is striking. In two large research studies of the sexual practices and beliefs of Americans, for example, commodified sexualized services are barely even noted (Blumstein and Schwartz 1983; Michael, Gagnon, Laumann, and Kolata 1994). Further, in much of the literature on love and intimacy, commodified sexual encounters are conspicuously absent from discussions of relationships that are not seen as in jeopardy.

When the use of commodified sexual services is discussed, it may be invoked to say something about the male partner's inability to develop a "healthy" intimacy with his wife. As psychologist Wendy Stock writes in a book on male sexuality: "The predominant effect of the sex indus-try on men is through the alienation from self, an impaired ability to relate intimately to romantic / sexual partners, and an increased likeli-hood of inflicting emotional and physical harm on female romantic / sexual partners and on children" (1997: 111). Stock draws on the idea of nonrelational sexuality, defined by psychologist Ronald Levant as "the tendency to experience sex as lust without any requirements for rela-tional intimacy, or even for more than a minimal connection with the object of one's desires" (Levant and Brooks 1997: 10). Stock admits that "nonrelational sex is not inherently bad" and that both sexes report positive experiences when it is engaged in as an optional practice. She argues, however, that in our culture traditional male socialization has elevated nonrelational sex to "the most desirable form of sex" and sometimes "the only option in men's sexual repertoires" (100). The uses of any sector of the sex industry by men, according to Stock, is an example of a problematic nonrelational sexual practice.

As mentioned throughout this text, men go to strip clubs for a vari-ety of reasons and with varying frequency throughout their life. This chapter focuses on a particular group of men I encountered. Sixty-three percent of the thirty men I interviewed (and approximately the same number of those with whom I interacted on a daily basis) fit a specific pattern of beliefs and practices.[3] These men visited strip clubs on a regular basis, varying from several times a week to several times a month. Although they occasionally visited the clubs with friends or business associates, they differed from men who visited *only* in groups because they also visited alone. Regardless of how often they visited a strip club, they considered these visits meaningful enough to be counted as part of a repertoire of personal practices. These men were either married to, divorced from, or planning on being married to women whom they described as "conservative." This conservative designation was invoked with regard to issues of morality and sexuality; for example, the men described themselves as "weaker" or "lazier" than their wife or partner in terms of moral resolve and also consistently portrayed themselves as more "sexually adventurous" and "interested in sex." The men claimed to be committed to monogamy, for the most part, and chose strip clubs because they believed they would not be expected or tempted to have sexual contact with the women.[4] At the same time, they admitted that their ideas about what exactly constituted monogamy sometimes differed from their partner's ideas. Nevertheless, they saw their relationship as stable and caring; that is, they expected to remain committed to this partner in the future and believed that she felt the same. These interviewees believed their marriage would be considered "successful" to an outsider, and they described themselves as "reasonably satisfied" with their relationships to "very much in love" with their wife.[5] This fairly positive view of their marriage is consistent with the expressed beliefs of many of the customers discussed by other sex workers (e.g., French 1988; Nagle 1997). Even the men who expressed interest in an extramarital affair often did so in ways that precluded its realization, as will be discussed.

Although they enjoyed visiting strip clubs, these men did not consider themselves to be consumers of other forms of adult entertainment. They described pornography as "too impersonal," "boring," and "unrealistic," for example, and prostitution as either "cheating," "too dangerous," or "too direct of a financial exchange."[6] All of these men also preferred strip clubs in which lap dancing was *not* allowed. To some degree, this preference is because we met in a city in which this type of contact was forbidden, yet most of the men had traveled widely and experienced other types of clubs.

Finally, and quite significantly, for these particular men, visits to strip clubs were kept almost completely clandestine. They might occasionally visit a club with a group of men, but their solitary visits were secret from their family and from most of their friends. They were aware that their visits to strip clubs affected their wife or partner, and expressed concern about that fact. Both in the clubs and during the interviews, the men often broke into extended monologues on this topic, offering stories and examples of how their behavior was perceived by their spouse. Many times they provided extended, recreated conversations, arguments, and confrontations with their partner. The wives' responses ranged from "going ballistic" to mild displays of anger when they found out about such visits. The men offered justifications and rationalizations for their behavior; at the same time, they often admitted to feelings of empathy for their wife's pain. However, despite admissions of empathy and guilt, this knowledge of their wife's disapproval or dismay did not result in a change of practice. Sometimes, they explained, it resulted in a kind of "don't ask, don't tell" agreement with their wife about the behavior.[7] At other times, the men tried their best to keep their visits secret, sometimes "getting away with it" and sometimes "getting caught." Either way, their situations were similar in that the wives knew that they were interested in visiting strip clubs and might do so, but were never sure when this might happen or if it actually did.

This pattern complicates existing ideas about the place of commodified sexual services in long-term marriages. Although the concept of nonrelational sexuality is useful for discussing the inequities and problems in some marital relationships, as well as for investigating the relationship between discourses of masculinity and processes of male socialization, it is not adequate to discuss the variety of encounters being sought in the sex industry—especially the complex pattern of consumption discussed above. Granted, some men experience their sexual desires and practices (especially those connected with the sex industry) as compulsive, addictive, and disruptive to their long-term relationships (e.g., G. Brooks 1995, 1997; Stock 1997). Further, there is no doubt that even as the husbands described themselves as satisfied, in certain cases the wives may have felt that their own needs for intimacy were not being met (seemingly a common complaint among women in heterosexual relationships more generally). Marriage, after all, may yield different sorts of pleasures and dissatisfactions for men and women. Some of the men I spoke with also expressed sexist sentiments or a distaste for their partner's body based on cultural ideals: "I wish my wife had nicer breasts"; "tried to dress sexier"; "had a better hip-to-waist ratio." Many men indeed have unrealistic expectations of what women's bodies look like because of the way women are represented in popular culture, and have difficulty accepting their wife's body as she ages. There are also men for whom certain kinds of intimacy may feel unachievable or threatening.[8] I would agree, then, with those who argue that there are certain cultural and social configurations of gender and power that work against the possibility of marital relationships that are egalitarian and satisfying (physically and emotionally) for some individuals. All the same, we should not assume a particular kind of ideal intimacy in long-term marital relationships that can be simply opposed to commodified relationships. Indeed, many long-term marriages and partnerships involve forms of deception, some of which are based in the psychodynamics of interpersonal relationships and some that are perhaps crucial to "lasting" marriages.

It is important to explore the ways that visits to strip clubs became exciting for these men because of the beliefs they held about marriage, monogamy, and intimacy, the ways in which they practiced marriage, and the relationship that they had with their wife. In the next several sections, I argue that the men's use of commodified sexualized services is not necessarily a result of an inability to be intimate, but rather, is a means of dealing with one of the psychic side effects of love and intimacy in traditional relationships: aggression.

Secrecy and Transgression

The encounters that were purchased by these particular interviewees in strip clubs were exciting and desirable to them for two primary reasons: they were *secret* and they were interactive, *sexualized* (but not sexual) encounters seen as outside of their primary committed relationship. Normative patterns of intimate activity require that sex be kept hidden from those who are not directly involved, and so secrecy (slipping off together, not letting other individuals in on things that are said and done during sexual encounters, developing behavioral and linguistic codes as a couple) is necessarily a part of erotic activity. But both of these—secrecy and sexualized relationships outside of the primary bond—often are believed to be destructive of intimacy, and thus of the marital bond, by one or the other partner. Except for two men who identified themselves as swingers, I never met a regular customer who said that his wife approved of his behavior.[9] The ideas of deception and sexual excitement are linked, however, as expressed in the many forms of popular culture—films, novels, television—that eroticize forbidden relationships, especially relationships outside of marriage. Some writers have posed an "inescapable conflict between passion and marriage in the West, with adultery nearly synonymous with passion" (Richardson 1989: 109). Yet, why? Is this simply because our culture has failed to provide us with positive representations of passionate marital sex? Or is there something more going on?

Many men got around their wife's suspicion by visiting the clubs during working hours or by inventing evening meetings and work-related events. Other men chose times when their wife was busy and not likely to notice their absences. Around Christmas, it was a joke at Diamond Dolls that the men had dropped off their wives at the nearby mall to shop or that they were supposed to be out shopping for holiday gifts themselves. One older retiree visited the Panther on Mondays and Wednesdays and the Crystal Palace on Tuesdays and Thursdays, bringing the dancers freshly baked breads in the afternoon.[10] His wife worked on those days, he explained, and she did not even know that he left the house while she was gone. He always made at least one loaf of bread to keep at home, however, as proof of his time spent baking. Interestingly, in addition to being secretive about their visits to the strip clubs, these particular interviewees also hid from their wives the fact that they were interviewing with me. In fact, several of the men discussed the interview situation itself as transgressive and thus explicitly or implicitly sexualized the encounter, despite the fact that I chose public locations (coffee shops, restaurants), dressed conservatively, and came equipped with my tape recorder, consent forms, and briefcase.[11]

The important thing about this behavior was not just that it was secretive but that it felt transgressive through its sexualization (though without sexual contact or release) and its proscription, and sexualized through its transgressiveness. Few men described their visits as absolutely forbidden by their wife, but it was clearly not something that these "conservative" women condoned. (Doubtless, however, there were other sexual behaviors that would have been *absolutely* forbidden that they did not choose to engage in, such as visiting prostitutes illegally or having a mistress.) Anne Allison writes, "Desire is something that is constructed both as part of our everyday work worlds (hence, permission) and as something that takes us beyond to a place that feels refreshingly transgressive (prohibition, often staged)" (1996: xxiii). Indeed, these encounters were staged and were often spoken of as "safe" (as opposed to prostitution or adultery) at the same time that they were discussed as potentially disruptive to relationships.

Roger, for example, had been married for twenty years at the time of our interview, and was a successful independent businessman. His wife was a stay-at-home mother for their two kids. He had no desire to end a relationship that he regarded as "successful" and as a "model" for his children. On the other hand, he secretly frequented the upscale Diamond Dolls several times a month, sometimes returning to see the same dancer several times in a row. At times, he had even exchanged phone numbers with dancers, but this had not led to anything but a few lunch dates around the city. Like most of these men, he had not told his wife that he was participating in the interview with me. At one point during our interview at a local coffee shop, Roger recognized a friend of his wife's in the store and became nervous. "If she approaches us," he coached me, "just tell her that you work in real estate."

> KF: Does your wife know when you go to clubs? Do you keep it to yourself, or—
>
> Roger: I'm sure she knows but it's not something that we discuss. She doesn't like it. So it's sort of a "don't ask, don't tell" relationship on that. You know, don't tell me what you're going to do and I'm not going to bother you about whether you went to [a sports bar] or Diamond Dolls. I don't care, you're just out with the guys.

Later in the interview, however, the issue of secrecy came up again. Roger said that his wife felt it was "degrading to her" when he visited the clubs, that she felt it "shouldn't be done," and that it was certain to cause an argument between them if he was caught. Further, his wife's attempts to find out where he had been indicated that she certainly did seem to "care," and our conversation on this topic is worth quoting at length:

> KF: So how does this affect your relationship with your wife?
>
> Roger: Um . . . It's a different compartment altogether. I don't, you know . . . Nothing about going to the clubs attaches to my own self. It just, you know . . .
>
> KF: So even the positive things don't carry over? The fantasy part?
>
> Roger: Oh . . . you know, I guess some of that does, but I'm not fantasizing about some dancer while I'm doing it with my wife or anything

like that. You know? No. No, it doesn't . . . it's really very compart-mentalized.

KF: So when you go, do you go usually from work on your way home?

Roger: Yeah. See, it's not something I can just call up and say "Well, I'm not going to be in tonight, I'm going to Diamond Dolls." It's gotta be something, "Well, I'm going to such and such meeting and I'll be home late." Or . . . you know, like last night, you know, I told her I was going to work late and then go meet some friends of mine to watch Monday night football. So, you know, she's in bed and asleep by the time I get home. She doesn't have a clue where I've been or what I've been doing. It does upset her if she finds out that I've been to Dia-mond Dolls, and every once in a while she figures it out or something gets said or you know . . . for whatever reason, you know . . .

KF: With friends, you mean?

Roger: She'll just know . . . I've got so much communication here. I've got a pager and a cell phone, you know? A radio and all this stuff. She'll just figure out what area of town I'm in, you know, by where I've been or what I'm doing and she'll say, "Well, you know, I know that meeting had to have been over by eight and you didn't get home until ten." You know? "And you went right by Diamond Dolls." So I'm not going to lie to her if she says, "Did you go there?" If she asks me . . . let's just say she heard an ad for the Miss Diamond Dolls contest on the radio. Which they did run. And then she says, "Did you go to that?" And I'd tell her, "Yeah." You know? She'd be mad for a little while and I'd be in the doghouse and then she'd get over it after a while. And we'd go on about our business. But she also knows the line I draw about that. You know, I've never had any kind of intercourse or oral sex or anything with any other woman but her. I mean, you and I have had as much sexual contact as I've had with any dancer in the whole world. So . . . that's pretty limited! [laughs] And she believes that and knows that and she knows how I feel about that. So I don't think she's sure I'm out trying to have an affair or anything like that. Because I'm not. So she doesn't get upset about it that way, but again, she just feels like that shouldn't be done.

Several times, Roger expressed his belief that he was being faithful to his wife. He said, "You know, I'm married and I'm not going to go out and cheat on my wife. I've just come to the decision that looking is not cheating." Despite this stated desire to remain monogamous, however, Roger also commented that he had not been presented with any opportunities to actually have sex with any of the dancers he met and suggested that he might be interested:

> I'm not saying that if you told me right now, "Well, let's go back to my house," you know, I wouldn't go! But nobody's ever asked and I've never pursued anything like that. You know, because I understand, or I feel like I understand, that that's the way it works. I mean, you know, particularly with girls at upscale clubs like Diamond Dolls. You all are all stunningly beautiful girls. To even consider . . . that you all are running around without male companionship outside the club is sort of ridiculous. You know? . . . It would be hard to believe that a dancer can't find a date some other way than pulling one out of the club.

Roger enjoyed fantasies of himself both as a man who would remain committed to his wife and as a man who might potentially embark on an extramarital erotic encounter with a dancer from an upper-tier club if she asked. He thus indicated his availability for sex and then immediately acknowledged that he understood that this was not generally going to result from a visit to a strip club, especially (in his eyes) in the kind of upscale club that he preferred. His fantasy of the *possibility* of a further transgression was expressed in other ways, however. For example, several times he commented on rumors about the extent of sexual activity that could be purchased at Diamond Dolls, especially in the upstairs, private VIP rooms (or Gem Rooms):

> I started going down to the Panther and just got to be a regular down there. Then a dancer at the Panther told me that one of her girlfriends had gone back to Diamond Dolls to work and she just railed on these Gem Rooms. "I can't believe what's going on up there. They get away with all this stuff." So, I said, Well, I'll go find out what's going on! . . . You know, it's a little more over the line, you know? And I was fascinated about what really would go on in these Gem Rooms too because of everything all these people tell me, you know? I mean, you can sit down there [on the main floor] and talk to guys and to dancers in there and they'll go, "You know, I know so and so goes up there and they do so and so." And I go, "Really? I've never done that and I've been coming here a lot!"

Once or twice he had gone upstairs to a Gem Room. He described an instance in which he thought he heard sexual noises coming from an adjoining room, but he had not engaged in any sexual activity himself or found any proof that it occurred. Despite his fascination, then, he not only failed to seek out such activity but set himself as opposed to it:

> I have a high disposable income. If I want to go in there and spend ten thousand dollars, I'm going to go in there and spend ten thousand dollars . . . I guess if you really pumped money into it you could . . . you could find the right woman to do just about anything you wanted . . . But I never approach it from that attitude so I never get approached about it. I'm not looking to do that so it's probably not going to happen to me. It's in a box, you know? It's over here and I know that it's a fantasy and you go do it and it's kind of fun and you have a good time. It's not something that I'm sitting at work going, "I really wish I could get that dancer and have my way with her," you know. As soon as the door closes, you're gone. You're back in the real world again. Get the cell phone, start dialing numbers, and go back to work.

For Roger, the fantasy, and the potential of crossing this line, was in some ways far more compelling than actually crossing it.

Other men had similar stories about keeping their behavior secret, to some extent, from their wife. Beck, for example, had been married for twenty-seven years, had two daughters, and portrayed his family life as pleasant and enjoyable. He described his relationship with his wife as "friendly" but without passion:

> *KF:* Have you been going to the clubs the whole time that you've been married basically?
> *Beck:* Off and on. Much more so since I've been in Laurelton . . .
> *KF:* And is it something that you talk about with her [his wife] or is it just all on your own?
> *Beck:* I'm on my own. She would go absolutely nuts. I know what she thinks of them. She thinks they're all hidings for prostitution or something so . . . who knows what she thinks.
> *KF:* So you've had enough conversations that you know she would be displeased?
> *Beck:* Um hmm . . . she thinks I'm being unfaithful.

KF: And so do you think you have a different understanding, then, of what faithful is than she does?

Beck: No, I think she objects based on her imagination.

KF: Her imagination of what you're doing?

Beck: Of what . . . yeah. And I told her that, you know, if the door is open, I'll go in. If it's a bar or a nightclub or a strip joint or whatever it is . . . that's me. And it doesn't mean I'm having sex with anybody. And that's just the way I am! So she doesn't ask me and I don't tell her and most of the time, you know, I'm working late and I'm working a lot of hours or something and I just stop in some place for a little while. It's not like I spend hours and hours in a wild drunken orgy or anything, you know? [laughs]

As with Roger, these encounters were also important for Beck because they were *sexualized* yet did not involve direct sexual activity. Actual sexual activity, he said, was not even important to him anymore because of health problems and his age.

Jim had been married for twenty-three years and said that he went to clubs "on the sneak." He did not go to the clubs before he was married; the visits started afterwards. "Stolen watermelons taste better than the ones you buy," he said, describing his reason for enjoying the secrecy. Toward the end of our first interview he asked: "Does it feel like you're sneaking around right now, Kate?" "No," I answered, "why?" He laughed. "By helping me sneak around!" Soon after telling me that part of his motivation for coming to the interview was the thought of a potential sexual relationship with me (indeed, he expressed surprise that I had brought a tape recorder and a consent form, saying, "You really *are* going to interview me!"), he noted that he considered himself a faithful and attentive husband. Jim's comments might be interpreted as examples of predatory behavior or a lack of intimacy with his wife. On the other hand, despite his spoken desire for a possible "real" sexual encounter, he admitted that this was not something that he actively pursued. Through a series of stories, he painted a picture of himself as a man who was interested in the "thrill" of sexual adventure, but not in actual sexual release outside of his marriage. Further, he admitted that he knew about other available sexual services in the city yet did not actively seek these out.

Pain and Retribution

Like the men discussed above, Jim knew his wife objected to his behavior and that her objections were based on her fantasies of what actually happened in the clubs. Although the secretive nature of their encounters made these men's visits to strip clubs meaningful, this must also be seen in the context of relationships in which a conservative woman would find this behavior upsetting. These men believed (usually from past experience) that their wife would feel betrayed or hurt by their activities in the clubs. Strip clubs were transgressive, then, because of their connection with sexual behavior—for example, men noted their wife's concerns about "nudity" and "big breasts and prostitution"—and because they had the potential to affect the couple's relationship in an adverse way. The men's recitation of disagreements with their wife about strip clubs was evidence that they had been "caught" in the past and that the possibility that they might visit again was a specter in the relationship.

Some of the women objected to their visits, the men said, because it made them feel insecure in the relationship. Herb said that his wife felt insecure about her appearance and attractiveness when she found out that he had been to a strip club: "She doesn't like it. Obviously because of the implications of it, that I may actually meet somebody or something. The thing that really gets her, I think, is the nudity. The fact that you get to see a little and then, in your mind, she believes that of course you're comparing these younger . . . she imagines more beautiful women to her. And perhaps preferring them or whatever. And lusting after them and so forth. And my wife is cute as a button! I mean, that's not why I'm there. I'm not there because I don't adore my wife." When I asked him why he *was* there, he answered: "Going to strip clubs is a way to relax. It's almost like a searching situation . . . kind of like you're searching for a friend . . . I think men are born hunters. And that's just another aspect of hunting, when you find what you're looking for in a dancer, in terms of personality as well as physical attractiveness. The ability to sit and talk and laugh and maybe for some reason you smoke the same bad cigarettes or drink the same beer or something . . . Just a connection with another human being." The multiple meanings of relaxation have been explored elsewhere (see Chapters 3 and 4). What is significant here is that although Herb felt that his behavior was upsetting to his conservative wife, he still desired to visit the clubs, especially for the interactive component. Other men felt similarly. Nick said that if his wife found out about any of his involvements with other women, including his visits to strip clubs, it "would break her heart." Likewise, Jim said, "I think she is upset about it because she feels like maybe that means she isn't satisfying me enough and therefore, you know, that means she's less of a woman . . . and that's why it upsets her. And I guess it bothers me too, that she feels that way."

The men's partners also expressed concerns about monogamy. Jason said that his partner did not like it when he went to strip clubs. He did not cease his visits, although he defended his fidelity:

> She pretty much told me—don't do it. "I don't ever want to hear about you doing it and please don't go." She said, "It's not that I don't trust you so much that . . . I just don't want some girl trying to work her ways on you and you thinking about it, you know? I don't even want you think-ing about it." . . . I told her straight up, I say, "You know, this doesn't really have any effect on me" . . . I said, "to give you an example, You know, I wouldn't care if five of the top supermodels . . . I walked in a room and they were all in a room there waiting for me, wearing lingerie or something and they all, you know, took off their clothes and they were all telling how much they wanted me!" And she's like, "Oh, that's a dream, isn't it?" You know, like that! [laughs] And I said, "Just let me finish! Just let me finish!" And I told her, I said, I said . . . "I wouldn't care if there were five supermodels there or whatever." I said, "I told you that I'm not gonna screw around and I'm not gonna screw around" . . . I told her, "Now I'm not saying that I'm not seeing them and I'm not saying that I couldn't enjoy their beauty," you know, but I said, "yeah and probably looking at them, it might kinda turn me on a little bit!" You know? It might make me horny or something. Five supermodels, hey . . . I said, "But you don't have anything to worry about because I'm gonna come back to you and you're gonna be the one who's getting it anyway." That kind of made her feel better but she was kind of insecure with herself and she was like, "Well, that's nice and I'm glad you wouldn't sleep with them or whatever," but she said, "I don't want you getting turned on by somebody else!" This was her big thing. She said, "I don't want you getting turned on by somebody else. Looking at somebody else's body and then coming to me."

Joe said: "I know in my own heart I'm not going to do anything. I may flirt a little bit but it's really harmless." Still, his wife was very concerned about his visits and he knew it would always "hurt her feelings." Beck's wife, as mentioned above, was overtly concerned about the possibility of prostitution in the clubs, and thus potential infidelity, as were the wives and partners of Mick, Brian, William, and Jim.

Other women saw the seeking of female companionship itself as a form of infidelity and were worried about betrayal through emotional involvement. David, for example, said that although he mainly "sought companionship" at strip clubs, his wife saw this as a breach of trust: "Tina's so strongly dogmatic, strictly by the Bible book, that you don't seek any companionship because all you're doing then is taking that energy away from your relationship and spending it on someone else. And that's a valid point. If you have everything that you need to fulfill you with your spouse then you don't ever need to expend that energy with someone else. But I'm not sure that ever exists. There's not necessarily just one person."

That strip clubs were meaningful in terms of the relationship that a man had with his partner was also expressed in the periodic nature of these men's visits. For many of these men, visiting the clubs was consciously related to how their relationship with their wife or partner was going. When David's marriage was teetering on the brink of divorce, for example, he began going to the Panther weekly to visit a particular dancer. Similarly, when I asked Mick how often he went to clubs, he said that when his marriage of four years was "going better," he went in less. His wife had some drinking problems and he found that he went to the clubs most often when her drinking was heaviest. "You know, you've got to get the other person back," he said. Significantly, this was important to him even if his wife did not find out about the visits.

Jim said that he visits a club twice a month, though more frequently if he is having difficulties with his wife. He spoke about the times when he was a weekly customer:

> *Jim:* I feel in my own mind that I probably went to these clubs because I felt like my wife would not listen to me and maybe I used it as an excuse, and said, well, if she's not going to be pleasing to me then I'll go to a place where the pleasing occurs automatically and there's no commitment involved. And you know, take it for what it's worth

and enjoy it for the temporary feeling, good feeling that it is and that's it. But then there was still the guilt feeling of having done that that probably caused additional strain in the relationship with my wife.

KF: And you didn't tell her but you would know and you'd have that feeling?

Jim: I think sometimes she could tell . . . she could tell that I had gone to a place and would use that later, saying, "Well, when you came in the other day I could smell cigarettes on your clothes and so you must have been out to one of these places."

After a "heated argument" with his second wife, Joe abruptly left the house and went to a strip club, returning home later with lipstick on his cheek. Another fight ensued, and his wife eventually dowsed him with a wine cooler because she was so upset by his behavior. Being "caught" is something that he is careful of now. He checks for lipstick and other signs that he has been to a club before he returns home: "Now if I ever go, that's the first thing I do . . . See, I don't smoke. And my wife doesn't smoke and if you go in one of those places it just sucks to your body . . . So, it's like, well, you're going to get caught. If your wife doesn't like it, you're going to get caught."

Though he described her as conservative, he noted that his wife was open-minded about some aspects of sexuality if she thought it would please him:

Joe: You see, she would go with me if I wanted to go but she doesn't want me to go by myself. But that's not the same thing—going with your wife. It's not the same thing. I have suggested that with some other couples, that we go to one of the male-female strip clubs. And my wife was all for it, okay, so long as it was okay for her too she didn't have a problem with it. And my wife is very committed to our marriage. She's very committed to me. And she definitely doesn't believe in extramarital affairs and she doesn't really care for erotic videos or anything like that. But she would go . . . But, if she knew I went by myself she would get her feelings hurt. She would really get her feelings hurt. It would almost be . . . a betrayal of her . . . whatever the reason may be, she would feel betrayed. You know? So if I ever go I don't say nothing to her. I'd rather not. But usually the reason I go is out of spite. And I've noticed that. I went when I was upset at her. And

I found that almost every time I've gone, it's usually because I'm upset at her. It's just my way of rebelling, I guess.

KF: Rebelling without her ever knowing? It feels like rebellion even though you never tell her?

Joe: Right, right, right.

KF: Why do you think that is?

Joe: I don't know . . . I've thought about it. I don't know. It's almost like saying, well, I know she doesn't appreciate it . . . usually when I'm upset at her it's because she's done something that I didn't appreciate and . . . and this is the best I can do. You know?

Joe said that his wife "knows she has to keep me satisfied sexually" so that he will not seek sexual pleasure elsewhere. Because of this, he said, his wife would have sex any time he wanted and he felt this did not justify looking for sexual activity outside of the relationship:

My wife is unusual in that even if I was upset at her she would still have sex. She tells me she believes that she needs to keep me satisfied to keep me from going out and having extramarital sex. And she's right. She's right. As long as I'm satisfied I won't. I may look. And I tell her that. We had a friend that came over one time. We were talking about going to this male-female strip place and the wife got upset because the man wanted to go . . . he said, "Look, I'm married, not dead!" And that's why I tell my wife, you know, "I'm still gonna look, okay?" I can appreciate someone that I think is beautiful. There's nothing wrong with that.

His wife's distress was important to him because it added to his feelings of rebelliousness and independence. Though she felt "betrayed" by his behavior, Joe felt that he was still being faithful to her because he was not engaging in sexual activity. Although he had visited massage parlors for manual release in his first, "sexless" marriage of seventeen years, for example, he felt that because his new wife was always willing to have sex with him, he could no longer justify such visits.

Psychoanalysis on Passion and Marriage

Despite dreams of lasting romantic love, many people have difficulties sustaining the early passion and excitement of their intimate relationships. Certainly, there are relationships in which both partners experience the wonder and excitement of being with each other, along with sexual passion, for the duration of their marriage, or in which the partners recreate this situation sporadically or ritualistically. On the other hand, there is a great deal of evidence that this feeling is lacking in a substantial number of relationships. Sexual passion is of concern to psychoanalysts who study the psychology of love and intimate relationships, and the question often arises as to "whether sexual passion is a characteristic of romantic falling in love or of the early stages of love relations that is gradually replaced by a less intense, 'affectionate' relationship, or whether it is a basic ingredient of what keeps couples together" (Kernberg 1995: 42).

Some psychoanalysts take the first approach, arguing that passion inevitably fades in dyadic relationships over time. Person, for example, "emphasized that brevity is an essential feature of passionate love. However, the capacity of the two partners for mature object relations helps them to convert the flame of intense emotions into the steady glow of affectionate companionship" (in Akhtar 1996: 158). This more "sober friendship" of a couple is referred to as mature love, and the "cooling" process that occurs in a long-term relationship as an inevitable counterpart to its healthy development. Some psychologists, as well as laypeople, argue that these deep feelings of companionship and intimacy developed over the years are more satisfying than the "adolescent" fires of passion.

The men I have been discussing in this chapter explicitly discussed these changes in their relationship. Yet, although they missed the early passion of the relationship, they did not wish to end their marriage. They also understood their visits to the clubs within this framework. As Jim said of his relationship with his wife, "The funny thing is that when [we] do have sex . . . it's a comforting and joyful sex but it's not erotic and it's not the fantasized sex that you think about when you're in a club. It's not the same. And maybe I don't get that at home and I don't necessarily want that at home . . . It feels to me that one of the reasons that she's upset about me going to the club is that she can't be that for me. And maybe she wants to be that for me." Steven discussed the changes that had occurred in his marriage after fourteen years: "There's more of a bond. More of a sharing. And you get to a point where I believe that you just have to appreciate that honesty and respect and all those old traditional values, I think, grow stronger as the marriage gets older. To the point where the whole physical thing does become less important. You show me someone that's been married fourteen years that says sex is as good as it was when you met. Come on! And if it is, it's unique circumstances . . . what a guy gets in a men's club, he doesn't get at home anymore." In the strip club, he explained, it was important that the final step of actualizing the sexualized relationship was never taken: "That tension, that discovery is still there because the fantasy lives on."

Yet the "boredom" they sometimes felt in their primary relationship was a continuing issue for this set of interviewees. Joe said, "There's variety [in the club] . . . It's not always exactly the same thing. I find that it's a little out of your ordinary from home and I keep telling myself, you know, if my wife would dance like that every once in a while I bet you I wouldn't ever go to those places, okay?" Though Joe made this claim, he also admitted that he became bored with her sexual receptiveness. Similarly, Brian described himself as "satisfied" with his marriage of seventeen years, although he claimed that he wanted far more sex than his wife did. Besides this conflict, he noted that the "number one problem" was a "combination of repetitiveness and boredom":

> If we get into spats about anything, it seems to center around a few things that neither one of us is willing to compromise on . . . the spats become redundant, and the real underlying problem of coming to a compromise never seems to happen. That's where the boredom comes from. I'm tired of arguing over the same thing. We both lead very busy lives, with few commonly shared interests . . . My wife is pretty conservative, not very creative or aggressive sexually. This leads to more redundancy, this time in our lovemaking. It's tough knowing that each time you make love, the outcome will be the same. Same approach, same foreplay, same intercourse, every time. It's become too predictable.

What men hoped for in strip clubs, Steven argued, was to "reignite that spark" that had gone out of their marriage (though without involving their wife in the interactions). The boredom depicted by the interviewees was not simply in regard to the sexual elements of their primary relationship, but with the entire pattern of interaction. Many other men made similar comments, both during the interviews and in the daily interactions I had in the clubs. The idea of variety, significantly, was rarely simply the desire to *view* other naked female bodies. Rather, variety was often meaningful in terms of the interactive nature of the encounters: "building that rapport" and experiencing both oneself and one's partner as "new" and "exciting"

One could conceivably argue that this boredom is evidence of an inability to attain a healthy intimacy with one's partner. Yet, is ideal intimate connection with the other necessarily possible (or even desirable) all of the time? Despite the analytic difficulties in determining what intimacy is or should be, there may be other psychological processes at work that undermine this possibility. Object-relations psychoanalyst Otto Kernberg, for example, argues that it is aggressive forces that eventually undermine intimate relationships, not cultural and social structures (such as an erosion of the sanctity of marriage) or the eventual replacement of passion with friendship in long-term relationships. A mature sexual love relationship, according to Kernberg, will integrate both tenderness and eroticism, but will also involve "all aspects of the ordinary ambivalence of intimate object relations" (1995: 29). This ambivalence stems from the earliest object relation between a baby and its mother. That is, just as "affectionate and generally pleasurable experiences with mother" come to be integrated into libidinal strivings, an aggressive drive is the result of the integration "of a multitude of negative or aversive affective experiences—rage, disgust, and hatred" (21). Aggression against a love object is thus an intrinsic part of erotic desire, and fantasies of penetrating, engulfing, hurting, or destroying the other are always part of intimate relations, and yet can be experienced as pleasurable because they are "contained by a loving relationship" (24). To maintain their erotic bond, a couple must successfully negotiate this ambivalence and develop and maintain a "delicate equilibrium between sadomasochism and love" (82) in their relationship, both sexual and emotional. Although Kernberg's retention of the drive concept is problematic to many modern users of psychoanalytic theory, his idea that aggression is a part of both healthy and pathological object relations is quite important to consider. We do not necessarily need to view aggression as the result of a precultural drive or instinct, but can theorize it as emergent in the context of intimate, dependent relationships.

As emotional intimacy develops between two people, more specific dynamics come into play, specifically, unconscious reenactments of earlier relationships, parental and otherwise.[12] Kernberg writes that the "unconscious wish to repair the dominant pathogenic relationships from the past and the temptation to repeat them in terms of unfulfilled aggressive and revengeful needs result in their reenactment with the loved partner" (1995: 82). Projective identification is the means by which partners induce in each other past impulses and fears. Over time, couples may unconsciously establish an equilibrium in which they "complement each other's dominant pathogenic object relation from the past" (83). The way couples interact in their intimacy can thus be "both frustrating and exciting" and can involve periods of "madness" as well as intensely gratifying experiences for both individuals. Though the outcome of such replays of unconscious scenarios is unpredictable, Kernberg is deeply interested in which couples can continue to grow together at the same time that they maintain their bonds.

To discuss the different ways that couples may maneuver through this complicated terrain, Kernberg elaborates the idea of triangulation. "Direct and reverse triangulations," he writes, "constitute the most frequent and typical unconscious scenarios, which may at worst destroy the couple or at best reinforce their intimacy and stability" (1995: 87). Direct triangulation is "both partners' unconscious fantasy of an excluded third party, an idealized member of the subject's gender—the dreaded rival replicating the oedipal rival." This results in the common conscious or unconscious worry of both genders of being replaced by their sexual partner, leading to emotional insecurity and jealousy. Reverse triangulation, on the other hand, "defines the compensating, revengeful fantasy of involvement with a person other than one's partner, an idealized member of the other gender who stands for the desired oedipal object, thus establishing a triangular relationship in which the subject is courted by two members of the other gender instead of having to compete with the oedipal rival of the same gender for the idealized oedipal object of the other gender" (88). This leads Kernberg to almost humorously conclude that there are "potentially, in fantasy, always six persons in bed together: the couple, their respective unconscious oedipal rivals, and their respective unconscious oedipal ideals" (88). The successful couple, the one that is able to maintain sexual intimacy and exclusiveness, does so "not only by maintaining its obvious conventional boundary but also reasserting, in its struggle against rivals, its unconscious gratification of the fantasy of the excluded third party." Fantasies about "excluded third parties," he writes, "are typical components of normal sexual relations. The counterpart of sexual intimacy that permits the enjoyment of polymorphous perverse sexuality is the enjoyment of secret sexual fantasies that express, in a sublimated fashion, aggression toward the loved object" (88).

Though it may sometimes seem to be so in experience, the couple is never an isolated dyad, even in fantasy. As Kernberg notes: "Mature sexual love—the experiencing and maintaining of an exclusive love relation with another person that integrates tenderness and eroticism, that has depth and shared values—is always in open or secret opposition to the surrounding social group. It is inherently rebellious. It frees the adult couple from participation in the conventionalities of the social group, creates an experience of sexual intimacy that is eminently private and secret, and establishes a setting in which mutual ambivalences will be integrated into the love relation and both enrich and threaten it" (1985: 181). Yet despite its rebelliousness, the couple still needs the group, as "a truly isolated couple is endangered by a serious liberation of aggression that may destroy it." In some instances, "severe psychopathology in one or both participants may bring about the activation of repressed or dissociated, conflictual, internalized object relations," and this may ultimately cause a rupture of the union. In less severe situations, "unconscious efforts by one or both partners to blend or dissolve into the group, particularly by breaching the barrier of sexual exclusiveness, may be a way of preserving the existence of the couple at the risk of invasion and deterioration of its intimacy" (181).

Kernberg thus sees a "built-in, complex, and fateful relationship between the couple and the group" (1995: 182). A couple that becomes isolated from the social group may be torn apart by "the internal effects of mutual aggression": "Marriage may now feel like a prison, and breaking away and joining the group may feel like an escape into freedom." On the other hand, for those individuals who cannot sustain a stable relationship, the group itself may become "a prison" (183). He suggests that whereas short-term triangular relationships (sometimes affairs) may permit "the stabilizing expression of unresolved oedipal conflicts," and thus sustain the marriage, long-term affairs often destroy a couple because the parallel marital and extramarital relationships become similar over time: "They may protect a couple against the direct expression of some types of aggression, but in most cases, the capacity for real depth and intimacy declines" (184).

When a man visits a strip club in anger at his wife, he may in effect be consciously creating a situation of reverse triangulation—displacing aggression and enacting a secret, vengeful fantasy as his wife becomes the excluded third party. In other situations, a man might not be consciously angry at his wife or partner, yet he visits the strip club "on the sneak," expecting and perhaps even hoping to get caught. Regardless of the outcome, his knowledge (or belief) that the visit will cause his wife emotional pain is significant and a reverse triangulation is set up. His interaction with the dancer is not, as Stock writes of commodified sexualized encounters, an example of "the dismembering of sexuality from potentially intimate, mutually vulnerable, human eroticism" (1997: 100). Rather, sexuality remains interpersonal as he brings the dancer, as the other woman, into a preexisting and continuing psychic situation.[13] The potential for an intersubjective encounter in the club means that what happens next is often unknown to the customer. The unknown aspects of the interaction lend excitement to the encounter, at the same time that there is also a comfortable balancing out of the risk; that is, the man knows that sexual activity will almost certainly *not* occur and that he can terminate the interaction at any time.

As mentioned earlier, many cultural representations focus on the excitement and danger of adulterous relationships. Nonmonogamy, argue sociologists Blumstein and Schwartz, "touches the lives of all couples." "Even if they are monogamous," they write, people "wonder about it—what it would be like, and what it would do to their relationship" (1983: 267). Though the men discussed here may not have actually been unfaithful, their behavior was in part motivated simultaneously by wishes to betray and wishes not to betray their wife or partner.

The satisfaction gained for these men from their visits to the clubs was also related to the fact that they held particular cultural beliefs about gender identity, sexuality, and marriage that made such practices meaningful as expressions of freedom and individuality. Thus, though there may be a similar buildup of aggression and a need for deflection in most long-term relationships, not every man becomes a customer of the sex industry, much less strip clubs. The interviewees tended to identify with discourses that associated sexual conquest or sexual desire with masculinity, freedom, and adventure, as discussed in Chapter 3. At the same time, they held particular beliefs about what constituted monogamy for themselves; for example, looking and interacting outside of the marriage was acceptable, whereas sexual release through contact was not. Strip clubs, then, provided a safe space in which to be both married (or committed) and interacting with another woman (often simultaneously or alternatively idealized and degraded), setting up a triangular situation. This in turn was important in the way that it activated particular self-representations that the men identified with and found pleasurable—as a desirable and desiring man, for example.

The difference in class status between the customers and the dancers is also psychologically significant. Strippers are still stigmatized in the contemporary United States, and these particular customers who found the clubs most erotic, exciting, or transgressive (thus becoming regular customers for whom visits were a significant sexual practice) were also those who had married or imagined themselves being married to very "conservative" women. If traditional, middle-class femininity is associated with relative sexual modesty, as it often still is, women who dance nude in front of strangers will have transgressed a significant class boundary regardless of their background and regardless of what kind of club they work in. The men may identify with the dancers and against their wife, again in a rebellious fashion: *We are both morally weaker than she is; we are both more sexually free; we are both more adventurous, independent, and experimental.*

It is important to recognize that whether these visits *actually* caused the wives any emotional pain is to some extent irrelevant in explaining the men's satisfaction. As I did not interview the wives and partners of the male customers, I have no way of knowing whether they felt pain when they found out about the men's visits, how explicit the "don't ask, don't tell" agreements were, or how their protests against the men's practices were actually verbalized and carried out. The significant thing is that these men's *belief* that their partner would feel upset was an intrinsic and important element of their experience, causing them to feel an ambivalent mix of pleasure and guilt, regardless of whether they were *actually* caught or their wife *actually* felt betrayed. In some ways, the experience may be all the more powerful if it remains secretive; after all, not only does socialization require that most sexual activity be hidden, but for some men sexual behavior and sexual excitement have been associated with secrecy (and secret or fantasized identity) in close relationships since they hid their first pornographic magazine under the bed as teenagers.[14] Further, in some situations, the pain or discomfort that the men believed they were causing may even have been more intense in their own fantasies about getting caught than as actually experienced by their wife or partner.

Contextualizing Triangulation

Several questions about culture, power, and history need to be addressed when analyzing such encounters using psychoanalysis. First, strip clubs have not always existed in their current form, and there has been a proliferation of clubs in recent years across the United States. If the motivations of male consumers are somehow psychological, what might account for the changes in the composition of the industry over time, and why might more men be seeking such encounters now in strip clubs? There are a number of social elements that are of course also important to understanding just where these kinds of secret and sexualized relationships take place and among which kinds of participants. A commitment to monogamy in the age of AIDS may certainly be a contributing factor, as may be the growth among men of serial monogamy instead of maintaining one long-term, but not necessarily faithful, marriage. Changing patterns of mobility, and thus commitment, may make relationships and affairs for some men difficult to negotiate and maintain. Strip clubs could be seen to offer a McDonaldized (or "McDisney-ized"),[15] virtual affair, for some customers: predictable (to an extent), efficient (no "games" necessary), calculable (the prices are set up front; sex will not occur), and controlled (there is an easy exit; the effects on the primary relationship are pretty well known). *"Social life? I don't have time for a social life. That's why I come here," Phillip said.* There is also a continuing connection of sexuality and sexual experiences with a kind of last frontier to transcendence and adventure for many Americans. As discussed earlier, strip clubs articulate with certain ideas about masculinity and consumption that appeal to particular men as well, in addition to providing spaces where certain kinds of masculinized leisure can be engaged in without remorse.

Second, without positing some essential difference between men and women in terms of their psychological processes, how can we explain why it is men who visit strip clubs and that similar services do not exist for women on the same scale? Cultural expectations of particular kinds of relationships as well as social inequalities affect people's opportunities, choices, and resulting satisfactions. As mentioned earlier, traditional discourses of masculinity certainly shape the meaning of these men's practices. Also, the historical difference in disposable income between men and women is certainly an issue here, as are the different meanings that individuals place on money (as power, as security, etc.). As more women earn higher salaries, travel alone more frequently on business, and move away from traditional ideologies about passivity in sexual relationships, they may indeed come to desire commodified sexualized services in greater numbers.

Further, women may have developed other ways of fulfilling their needs. For now, the still greater need for many women to become and remain married for financial security, for example, along with cultural ideas about the importance of female virtue may certainly lead to the necessity for women of releasing aggression or creating triangulations in different ways depending on their social position. Sociologist Stacey Oliker found, for example, that married women in traditional relationships developed friendships with other women that fostered both intimacy and a mutual validation of individual activity and inner self—an "ego boost." The women she studied also did marital "emotion work" with their friends; that is, these close friendships allowed the women to express anger and frustration about their relationship and to return to their partner with more peaceable attitudes (1989: 127).

Again, this is not to say that the sexualization of the encounters that the male customers sought in strip clubs was not extremely important. After all, even a man who is interested in conversation is seeking that talk in a setting where women's bodies are being routinely displayed. Though these particular customers were not actively pursuing adulterous sexual affairs, the experiences were sometimes discussed as analogous. At one point during our interview, for example, Jim referred to his experiences in strip clubs as "quickies." Steven used the phrase "falling in love again" to describe such experiences. Thus, these men were often enjoying the *fantasy* of such a transgression and, in effect, creating situations of triangulation. That this would *not* happen with male friends in everyday (nonsexualized) interactions was directly suggested by many of the respondents.

Honesty and Intimacy in Marriage

Whether these encounters are positive or negative for the trajectory of the marriage is inherently difficult to determine; even the men themselves could rarely voice an opinion on this issue. Yet customers who use the sex industry cannot be simply opposed to those who develop some "ideal" monogamous heterosexual relationship. After all, despite the emphasis on communication and honesty in intimate relationships, many people are unable to express particular emotions or desires within the context of their primary relationship. As Blumstein and Schwartz write, "Marriage itself makes couples more deceptive. Couples who marry have traditionally sworn to 'forsake all others,' and it is rare that couples change the agreement, even if they do not always live up to it. Because most non-monogamous husbands and wives have broken their contract rather than revised it, they are forced into dishonesty" (1983: 270). Even when couples have not cheated on each other, they may fantasize about doing so and wish to express those fantasies. As a sex worker I often heard this complaint from men who believed that they could not disclose either the truths of their past or particular desires and fantasies to their wife.

Despite the fact that social changes such as the increasing economic independence of women have raised the possibility of more mutually fulfilling heterosexual relationships, it seems that many individuals still have difficulties negotiating the sexual demands of long-term monogamous relationships. In a recent article British sociologists Duncombe and Marsden draw on Hochschild's concept of emotional labor to discuss the performance of "sex work" by couples. Although I disagree with their decision to use the phrase sex work (seeing many theoretical reasons to distinguish this kind of inner negotiation from actual work in the sex industry), their analysis is useful: "By analogy with emotion work, in doing 'sex work' individuals would 'manage' their emotions according to 'feeling rules' of how sex *ought* to be experienced (Hochschild 1983), to try to attain or simulate (for themselves and / or their partners) a sexual fulfillment they would not feel 'spontaneously': for example, to endure sex, Victorian brides-to-be were exhorted to 'lie back and think of England'; and, more recently, women admit they sometimes fake orgasms, and couples (or women) are advised to 'work' on their fading relationships by restaging romance" (1996: 221). They note a performative aspect to some relationships in which couples admit to "playing the couple game" and "act" happy in the presence of outsiders (221).

Some of the emotion work that takes place in long-term committed relationships covers up a lack of desire. Drawing on a long-term study of heterosexual couples, Duncombe and Marsden argue that there is considerable empirical evidence that individuals are both influenced by ideologies of how sex "ought" to be and also find "they have to 'try' or 'work' or 'force' themselves to have sex." This is not to say that "people live at a constant pitch of sexual disappointment or even desperation," they argue; rather, at some level many long-term couples would recognize these difficulties (1996: 235). Further, they argue that couples are influenced by cultural beliefs about how sex should be: that it should be mutually satisfying, passionate, and so on. Such widespread concern about mutual sexual satisfaction is a recent phenomenon, only really becoming salient since the 1960s, yet it is increasingly influential in how people understand their relationships (DeLamater 1991: 62) and may also be influencing how individuals respond to fading sexual desire for their partner.

Perhaps, then, men who use the sex industry are not necessarily unable to be intimate; rather, many traditional marriages may be successful *because of* an inhibition of certain kinds of intimacy, evidenced by such acknowledged needs for emotion work in long-term relationships. Much popular psychology literature tends toward the idea that if we all just expressed our feelings to each other and did the necessary work, we would suddenly be able to be truly intimate with our partner and be able to maneuver through the vacillations of sexual passion. For some couples this may be true, but it may not be a realistic possibility for every partnership. In some cases an inhibition of intimacy may even be necessary for a particular relationship to continue. Lawrence Blum writes:

> The persistence of human self-interest is of course closely related to intimacy and infidelity. For example, some of the chief matters that spouses tend, by and large out of courtesy, not to discuss with each other are their everyday selfish wishes: not to have to sweep the floor, take care of the kids, or take each other's needs into account; wishes to be taken care of without reciprocation; and certainly their wishes to sample dif-

ferent sexual partners. Does this withholding limit intimacy or permit it? Implicit here also is the matter of aggression. Communication to one's spouse of a fantasy of infidelity is more often an act of hostility than of intimate closeness. In considering instances of infidelity we must, of course, be alert not only to the opportunity of romance with the new partner but also to the anger of the betrayer to the betrayed. (1996: 142)

Some marriages would cease to exist if they were constantly interrogated by the participants. For some people, however, getting a divorce is not an attractive option. For a variety of reasons, then, people find themselves in relationships that don't fulfill all their needs. Should those relationships be abandoned? Or should the participants arrange more creative ways of fulfilling those needs? Even sexual experiences between lovers at an early stage of a relationship can involve different levels of intimacy at different times; there is always the potential for fantasy scenarios, power differentials, and aggression to intrude on the scene.

At times, then, an analysis of such encounters comes down to aesthetics and ideas about authenticity. What is a real relationship? What is real intimacy? Some of these men suggested that appearances (and the real*ness* of those appearances) were more important than the real. Given the importance of being able to "play the couple game" in many social circles, and the willingness of so many couples to cocreate this particular public fantasy, this is not necessarily surprising. Further, some of the men valued lastingness more than absolute honesty. As Charles said: "I love my wife and I value our relationship enormously, therefore I will always avoid doing anything that could jeopardize that. However, sometimes that decision has more to do with the risk of her finding out than following absolute rules . . . The simple fact is that if my wife thought I was anything other than monogamous, there probably wouldn't be a relationship. And I guess the same goes for me. That said, I recognize it's entirely possible she hasn't been monogamous, and I would have no idea. At the end of the day, as long as I never find out, or suspect, and our relationship is the long-term goal, then that's the important thing." Similarly, Steven asked, "What does faithful even mean, Kate? Does it mean I'm faithful in my mind? Does a one-night stand in a hotel room somewhere, years back, mean that I am not faithful to my wife? A year from now? I would say that I am faithful to my wife because I love her and there is no one else I want to be married to and share a life with. I've been married to her for fourteen years and I'll be married to her for fourteen more."

Roger talked at length during our interviews about the importance of marriage, commitment, and the family. When I asked him what he had taught his children about sexuality, a standard question that I posed to interviewees, he said that he hoped to teach them how to "have a stable family relationship." As Roger admitted spending several hundred dollars on his interactions with young dancers in strip clubs each week, lying to his wife about this behavior, and even expressed a (fantasized) interest in having sexual relations with me, his actions did not *seem* to necessarily correspond with his beliefs (or his fantasies, for that matter). Despite his deceitful behavior, however, he *could* be said to have a stable relationship in many ways. He expressed no desire to end the marriage, described his wife and him as happy, and described the marriage as successful. Could his marriage really have been falling apart? Given that this pattern of behavior had been occurring for a long time, I find no reason to doubt his stories or dismiss his claims. For these particular men that I interviewed, intimacy with their wife was something they both desired and felt they had achieved. As mentioned earlier, they did not feel that the encounters they had in strip clubs were more fulfilling and satisfying than their relationship with their wife, and unanimously these men did not want to leave their partner. (Now, whether their partner wanted to leave *them* but could not, or felt herself unsatisfied in the relationship, is a different and important question that requires additional research.)

Certainly, help should be available for men who seek it and who feel that pornography or the sex industry is affecting their ability to have an intimate and loving relationship with their wife. There are men who feel dissatisfied with their relationship and for whom the sex industry is simply a temporary and ineffective panacea. Even given this psychoanalytic perspective on the interviewees' visits to strip clubs, perhaps there are more effective ways for men to discharge the excess aggression in their primary relationship—ways that would cause their partner less pain and would not reinforce the double standard for women, for example. On the other hand, there are indeed individuals who combine a satisfying relationship with commodified sexualized services. I am in no position, and have no desire, to pass judgment on these particular marriages, nor to say whether the sex industry, or strip clubs in particular, are a good thing for relationships. Rather, the answer to this question, in part, depends on how one feels about lastingness, commitment, self-fulfillment, honesty, and authenticity in long-term relationships, and different people prioritize these values in distinct ways.

*

Visits to strip clubs became meaningful for these particular men, in part, as a secret form of sexualized consumption and as a practice that would be considered painful by their wife if exposed. The views the men held about marriage and the ways they practiced marriage made these visits both transgressive and exciting. Here, the men's visits were made meaningful through the relationship these men had with their wife or partner and their (perhaps fantasized) understandings of how she would interpret these visits. This is not just to say that these men have psychically bifurcated women into madonnas and whores, however, though this may indeed contribute to some men's motivations and pleasure. For these particular customers, I have argued, visits to the clubs are related to both a buildup of aggression in isolated, dyadic relationships and to a breakdown in the potential for recognition of Otherness in their partner and themselves. Although these are psychological processes, it is not necessary to assume that either process is natural or inevitable.

Earlier I suggested that the wife's or partner's *actual* pain was irrelevant for my argument about how this particular group of customers made their visits to strip clubs meaningful. Yet her potential pain is not irrelevant in other contexts, and is related to the divisions that have arisen within feminism and within popular discourse on the sex industry. What do these wives feel about their husband's practices? To answer this question needs further research. Certainly, many women married to or partnered with a male customer might be significantly unhappy if they realized the amount of deception that underlies their relationship (and / or the amount of money spent on this kind of entertainment). But, as mentioned earlier, the interviewees suggested that many had already worked out a tacit "don't ask, don't tell" agreement. To see the wives and partners of these male customers as completely ignorant in this situation is to see them as simply passive and to miss the ways they themselves may be duplicitous in the relationships—they may indeed have negotiated arrangements with their husband or partner that feel fair and comfortable to them. On the other hand, to see them as completely and freely consenting to these practices would be ignoring the very real power differentials that still exist in many heterosexual relationships, the force of cultural ideologies about love and marriage, and the different opportunities available in the commercial sex industry for men and women as it now exists.

Though I have focused only on the men's relationships with other women in this chapter, there are other possible psychic scenarios that could play out in such a space. There may certainly be object relations with other men that also influence some men's visits, for example, either in the form of rivalries or desire, and potential direct triangulations between customers and dancers as well. Further, there are undoubtedly complicated psychic scenarios that are being worked out with regard to the customers' children. Numerous customers in these clubs, for example, commented on the proximity of my age to their daughter's, and given the silence surrounding sex in most of their homes, the clubs were perhaps one of the only spaces in which they could work through sexual fantasies regarding these particular forbidden partners. Men also sometimes visited the clubs with their son and father, either for bachelor parties or on more everyday occasions. These visits certainly contain a social element of male bonding; they also involve more complex emotional exchanges.

Just as with any form of consumption, it is too simple to say that visits to strip clubs serve only a compensatory function that inevitably alienates individuals from some true experience of wholeness or from an authentic intimate relationship. Indeed, critiques of the sex industry based on ideologies of intimacy are often coded attempts to legitimize heterosexual monogamy as the standard for all adult relationships. Such claims assume a perfect correspondence between sexuality and emotion that is in fact a product of deeply entrenched cultural ideology. I agree that commodified sexual services and images can at times promote myths and unrealistic ideas about what sex and sexuality *should* be, but this analysis is too simple on its own. Sexuality cannot be so easily removed from vulnerability or from an interpersonal context, and myths and ideologies are not simply absorbed by empty vessels. Rather, psychically and emotionally alive but not wholly reflexive subjects creatively engage with these myths and ideologies in the context of personal histories that are shaped through, but not determined by, cultural forces.

Chapter Eight

Disciplining Erotic Practice

The answer to bad porn isn't no porn. It's better porn.
—Annie Sprinkle, *Herstory of Porn: Reel to Real*

Strip clubs, and strippers, are currently embroiled in legal battles across the nation. Zoning laws instated in New York City in 1995, for example, forced many sexually oriented establishments to either relocate or adapt their operations such that they complied with these kinds of extreme ordinances (Hanna 1998a). Cultural anthropologist Judith Hanna notes that one of the new requirements under these ordinances, that sexual entertainment and materials make up only 40 percent of the business, had rather "humorous consequences" in New York City as adult establishments desperately tried to avoid being regulated out of existence: "G-rated videos on one side of the store, xxx-rated ones on the other; pool tables and dart boards replacing table-dancing tables" (9). One strip club also began to allow minors to enter with parental supervision to avoid the designation of adult entertainment; one can easily imagine the kind of response that received.[1] Yet the regulations that are being imposed across the United States are also a very serious matter, and over the past several years Hanna has testified as an expert witness in defense of strip clubs in fifty court cases in Nevada, Tennessee, Florida, Ohio, Virginia, California, Michigan, Washington, and elsewhere. She writes that she has watched the courts and legislatures "impose restrictions on all aspects of exotic dance, including distance from the audience, degree of nudity, self-touching or touching of a spectator, lighting, types of gesture and movement, whether alcohol may be served, and the proximity of clubs to schools and residences" (8). In and around Laurelton, similar battles are being fought, and as mentioned in Chapter 2, already one of the clubs used in this study has been closed due to zoning ordinances that prohibited it from remaining competitive with the other clubs in the city. Another club I worked in, after being plagued with legal troubles for over two years and facing federal charges that, to me, appeared to be extremely exaggerated, has also been shut down. Studying at home, an anthropologist does not necessarily assume that her field sites will begin disappearing in the space of five years, though this has certainly become my experience.

Anthropologist Gayle Rubin notes several persistent features of thought about sex that are axiomatic in Western culture: sexual essentialism, sex negativity, the fact that sexual acts "are burdened with an excess of significance," the existence of a hierarchical system of sexual value (with married and reproductive heterosexuals at the top), a "domino theory of sexual peril," and the lack of a concept of benign sexual variation (1993: 11).[2] Such axioms affect the way sexual behaviors are understood and policed in medicine and law, as well as the way children are reared (and thus the way adults react to sexual issues). These axioms are thus influential in shaping perceptions of the sex industry—through legal regulations, through moral prohibitions surrounding commodified sexualized services, and through the various personal psychological meanings that such practices have for the participants. Rubin writes that in Western culture, "sex is taken all too seriously." Yet, "If sex is taken too seriously, sexual persecution is not taken seriously enough. There is systematic mistreatment of individuals and communities on the basis of erotic taste or behavior. There are serious penalties for belonging to the various sexual occupation castes. The sexuality of the young is denied, adult sexuality is often treated like a variety of nuclear waste, and the graphic representation of sex takes place in a mire of legal and social circumlocution. Specific populations bear the brunt of the current system of erotic power, but their persecution upholds a system that affects everyone" (35).

Rubin writes that each new "sex scare or morality campaign deposits new regulations as a kind of fossil record of its passage. The legal sediment is thickest—and sex law has its greatest potency—in areas involving obscenity, money, minors, and homosexuality" (1993: 19). Current campaigns against strip clubs (and other adult entertainment establishments and productions) often are based on unsupportable claims that strip clubs increase crime and depreciate property values (i.e., they have adverse secondary effects), are linked to prostitution and the spread of venereal disease, and are harmful to minors and the community (Bukro 1998; Hanna 1998a). Many such campaigns show all the signs of being sex *panics* rather than improvements to the "quality of life" of anyone but a small group of individuals (Barry 1998; Weldon 1998a).

I have argued that strip clubs need to be differentiated from other forms of adult entertainment when discussing customer motivation. At the same time, campaigns *against* strip clubs should be seen as continuous with other attempts to legislate what types of people can engage in which kinds of commercial, sexual, or leisure practices and where they can do so. As writer, activist, and sex worker Jo Weldon writes about the zoning battles in New York City, "the war against strip joints, sex shops, and porn shops in residential districts is really a class war" (1998a). Other writers note that such campaigns are also a war against sexual minorities and sexual practices that are deemed threatening to mainstream morality (Califia 1994; Rubin 1993). Only certain kinds of fetishists (married, reproductive, heterosexual monogamists) have widespread institutional support, and individuals with other desires often find that they must feign accordance with this standard.

Granted, certain kinds of regulations can make strip clubs better workplaces for the employees. Regulations against touching in strip clubs, for example, can protect dancers against unwanted advances from customers and mean that if contact does occur, it is on the dancer's terms.[3] In Laurelton, as in other cities where I worked, such regulations gave the dancers a great deal of control over their transactions. In six years of dancing, I was touched inappropriately *once,* and the customer was promptly removed from the club when I alerted the management. (If only I had been so lucky while waitressing!) Some dancers enjoy lap dancing and other forms of contact; others prefer to maintain a distance between themselves and the customers. In an ideal situation, women could *choose* which kinds of services they offered and to whom and could be assured that they would be supported by the management in their decisions. Unfortunately, few (if any) of the zoning regulations being imposed on clubs around the country are pitched toward improving working conditions for the dancers. Rather, they often are used to harass the employees and are designed to eradicate nude or topless dancing in the communities altogether (Baldas 1998). This can have sometimes devastating consequences for the women (and men) who support themselves and their family by working in the clubs; of course, it may also have the effect of driving up the incomes of the dancers in the remaining clubs or in neighboring communities but not without the costs of continuing stigmatization and ghettoization of certain employees and venues.

Despite any of the problems, strip clubs as they now exist are worth protecting from moralistic and often hypocritical regulations, although discussions about workplace safety and employee benefits and compensation should be welcomed. My support of strip clubs against eradication efforts comes at the same time that I realize there are certain problems with the industry. As they now exist, heterosexual strip clubs are indeed deeply intertwined with existing systems of privilege and power, as I have discussed throughout this text. The takeover of small clubs by large corporations, for example, can eventually lead to less control for dancers and potentially poor working conditions, just as it can in any industry.[4] Also, though women may feel individually empowered by their experiences as dancers, this does not mean that strip clubs do not simultaneously bolster certain kinds of heterosexual male privileges. Interactions in strip clubs often serve to reinforce certain racial, gendered, and classed stereotypes and inequalities, and indeed, the transactions can derive a great deal of erotic power from these relations. The stigmatization that is faced by women working as strippers, or in any other sector of the sex industry, also tends to reproduce existing disadvantages. I have known exotic dancers who have had a difficult time securing loans for housing or transportation or who have been denied custody of their children based on the nature of their employment. Further, many writers have recognized that there are indeed women working in the sex industry not because they enjoy it, but because it is their only option. However, eradicating or more tightly regulating strip clubs to the detriment of the dancers would do nothing to combat these problems, which are related to the organization of labor in late capitalism, to systemic inequalities and prejudices, and to the stigmatization and fear that still surrounds issues of sex and sexuality in the United States.

The sex industry is a potential site for challenging social norms and assumptions about gender, sexuality, desire, and relationships. For many women who have worked as dancers, including myself, strip clubs have led to increased comfort with their own sexuality and with female bodies and to new understandings of female virtue and freedom (Funari 1997; Queen 1997a; Reed 1997; Mattson 1995; Frank 1998, 2002; Johnson 1999). As Margaret Dragu, a former stripper, and A. S. A. Harrison write in *Revelations: Essays on Striptease and Sexuality*, stripping can be "surprisingly conservative," yet "in spite of its conformist ideas about itself and sexuality, it has always been able to make room for visionaries" (1988: 20). Dancing is also a significant form of income for many young women, attracting those wishing to rebel against middle-class norms of femininity, college students and single mothers who want a flexible work schedule and decent pay, drug addicts, writers, artists, and professionals. Because of their marginalized status, strip clubs and other adult entertainment venues attract customers who are sex radicals as well as more conservative men (such as men who typify all women as madonnas or whores, for example). Many women and men, however, still feel a deep and inhibiting shame about their bodies, sexualities, and desires. Some of these individuals have associated the products and services available in the sex industry, including strip clubs, with such feelings; others may feel just as negatively affected by Hollywood films, supermodels, certain religious traditions, or laws against the sexual practices they find enjoyable. As I have mentioned throughout this text, I have come to believe that the problems with strip clubs are not *intrinsic* to the existence of commodified sexualized services, products, or entertainment. It is not the fact that some people choose particular configurations of sex, emotion, work, and money to believe in that should be critiqued, but rather that existing power relations and belief structures may circumscribe some individuals' choices and opportunities more than others'.

Some writers have suggested that changes in sexual mores or in the distribution of economic resources and opportunities might eventually decrease the demand (and supply) for particular kinds of commodified sexualized services. Stacy Reed, for example, argues that more sexual openness in the United States would eventually reduce the demand for topless bars (1997: 184). Likewise, Carol Queen points out that "until the climates in their bedrooms change," sex professionals may be among the only outlets for men with desires that are seen as socially unacceptable by their partner (1997b: 131). On the other hand, more sexual openness could also potentially radically increase the variety of sexual services and products available, as more people begin to feel comfortable with becoming customers or sexual entrepreneurs and as imaginative-ness sparks new marketing ideas. Certainly, the last several decades have seen a growth in products and services aimed at female consumers (heterosexual and otherwise). As Pat Califia writes, though "sweeping social change would probably alter the nature of sex work, the demographics of sex workers, and the wage scale, along with every other kind of human intimacy, I doubt very much that a just society would (or could) eliminate paying for pleasure" (1994: 242). Even in an egalitarian society, she notes, there might still be individuals who are too busy to form long-term intimate relationships, who are uninterested in maintaining one, or who are too unattractive or too stigmatized through age or disability to attract partners. There would probably also still be fetishists who desire specialized services and people who enjoy having the opportunity to pay for, and receive, the exact kinds of interactions they want. Yet such a world might also be one in which sex work is not feared and stigmatized, in which only those individuals who enjoy the work would labor in these venues (as with all other types of work perhaps), and in which misogyny, homophobia, classism, or racism would not *limit* the imaginations and practices of the patrons (male and female, gay and straight) and the opportunities that exist for the providers. Whether one believes that people are actually any better off in such a world ("quality of life"?) would depend, in the end, on how one feels about capitalism and commodification.

Though an egalitarian or sex-positive society would certainly change erotic patterns over time in unforeseeable ways, as erotics are deeply intertwined with material social relations and positionings, it may not be possible, or even desirable, to ever eradicate the play of power in erotic fantasy. As Andrew Ross points out, it is by no means clear "to what extent the conscious, let along the unconscious, register of fantasy is one which is directly affected by, say, progressive changes in the social meaning of the representations or narratives which are the stimulus or source of fantasies" (1989: 200). Even in a perfectly egalitarian world, as I noted earlier, sexual fantasies might still involve eroticized power differentials due to the fact that the very first stirrings of desire are based on the interaction between an infant and its (powerful) adult caretaker. And sexual encounters, whether fantasized or real, involve both the boundaries of the body (inside and outside) and the boundaries of the subject (self and other); as such, ambivalent feelings of danger, defilement, disgust, shame, pleasure, and desire in intimate situations are not likely to be parting ways. Further, as I argued in Chapter 7, intimate attachments of any sort are not based simply on tenderness and passion but also involve moments of hostility and aggression, and this ambivalence will undoubtedly continue to surface in cultural productions and individual practices and fantasies. Theoretically, the answer is thus not a matter of trying to overcome binaries—public and private, body and mind, reality and fantasy, cultural and personal—but of understanding the way each of these oppositions are mutually constitutive, entangled with each other in complicated ways, and, in fact, are created because they are somehow useful to us in making sense of the world. Perhaps what we might work for is a situation where these binaries are not so rigidly fixed and where feelings of shame, disgust, and desire do not congeal into predictable power differentials and hierarchical configurations of sexuality and gender.

In many ways, attempts at eradicating strip clubs rest on their own discourse of "lost authenticity." As with the spread of touristic practices and other forms of modern consumption, we can decry the ways that these commodifications and practices have supposedly changed and eroded earlier, more authentic ways of life or love, or we can explore precisely how these forms of consumption generate pleasure and become meaningful for individual consumers. The political and philosophical crux of the issue of moralistic sex laws and ordinances lies in the idea that there is, or could be, an *authentic* sexuality and that this authentic sexuality can be discerned, legislated, and policed. Throughout this text, in different ways, I have argued for the psychological relativity of the very idea of authenticity and for a view of fantasy as rooted in, yet not necessarily determined by, everyday life.

The Interviewees

Customers

To maintain confidentiality, the men's occupations are listed as executive, professional (requiring higher education; white-collar positions), self-employed professional (consultants, owners of businesses), self-employed, sales, managerial white collar, managerial blue collar, or manual laborer.

Alex: Twenty-eight-year-old white male. Manual laborer. Divorced for one year after a seven-year marriage.

Beck: Fifty-seven-year-old white male. Professional. Married twenty-seven years.

Brett: Forty-one-year-old white male. Self-employed. Single.

Brian: Thirty-eight-year-old white male. Managerial blue collar. Married seventeen years.

Carl: Thirty-seven-year-old white male. Managerial blue collar. First marriage of three years. Currently in second marriage of one year.

Charles: Thirty-three-year-old white male. Executive. Married nine years. British citizen.

Dan: Thirty-one-year-old white male. Self-employed. Engaged.

David: Forty-six-year-old white male. Managerial blue collar. Divorced for three years after an eight-year marriage.

Frank: Forty-five-year-old white male. Executive. First marriage of ten years. Currently in second marriage of five years.

Gary: Forty-four-year-old white male. Sales. Divorced after five-year marriage. Currently in a live-in relationship of ten months.

Glen: Thirty-five-year-old white male. Self-employed. Live-in relationship of three years.

Herb: Thirty-six-year-old African American male. Professional. Married eight years.

Jack: Fifty-year-old white male. Self-employed. Divorced after eleven-year marriage.

Jason: Twenty-nine-year-old white male. Executive. Single.

Jim: Forty-eight-year-old white male. Self-employed professional. Married twenty-three years.

Joe: Forty-one-year-old white male. Managerial blue collar. First marriage of seventeen years. Currently in second marriage of three years.

Kenneth: Forty-six-year-old white male. Professional. Live-in relationship of seventeen years.

Louis: Forty-two-year-old African American male. Self-employed. First marriage of three years. Currently in a live-in relationship of three years.

Matthew: Forty-two-year-old white male. Professional. First marriage of eleven years. Currently in second marriage of one year.

Mick: Thirty-eight-year-old white male. Self-employed professional. First marriage of ten years. Currently in second marriage of four years.

Nick: Fifty-one-year-old white male. Sales. Married thirty years.

Paul: Forty-five-year-old white male. Self-employed. Divorced for one year after a thirteen-year marriage.

Phillip: Thirty-four-year-old white male. Sales. Single.

Roger: Forty-three-year-old white male. Self-employed professional. Married twenty years.

Ross: Forty-year-old white male. Self-employed. Married eight years.

Saul: Thirty-seven-year-old white male. Managerial white collar. Married one year.

Steven: Thirty-eight-year-old white male. Professional. Married fourteen years.

Tim: Fifty-three-year-old white male. Managerial white collar. Married thirty-two years.

William: Thirty-three-year-old white male. Professional. Commuter relationship with a woman for four years.

Zachary: Thirty-year-old white male. Manual laborer. Single.

Employees Only

These men were not counted among the interviewees for statistical purposes. Their interviews were used for background information but not for the analysis of customer motivations.

Eric: Graduate student. Single.

Julius: Thirty-nine-year-old white male. Professional DJ. Single.

Todd: A regular customer of strip clubs that offered lap dancing. This interview is used for comparative purposes but not counted among the thirty primary interviewees.

Notes

Preface: Skin Brings Men

1 This monologue, slightly edited, was taken from an interview with the disc jockey at Tina's Review, during which I asked him to recreate the spiel that he gave me on my first day of work as a dancer at the club.

2 The terms "stripping" and "stripper" are used interchangeably with "dancing" and "dancer" through the text, as this is common practice among individuals involved in the industry. Female employees are also sometimes referred to as "entertainers."

3 Throughout the text, I use the term "American" to refer to citizens of the United States. In *American Culture: Myth and Reality of a Culture of Diversity,* Larry Naylor points out that America and American are well-established and frequently used synonyms for the United States and its citizens. While individuals living in South America, Central America, and the Caribbean Islands may also use the term "American" to identify themselves, Naylor notes that they also frequently identify themselves by virtue of their country of origin—as Canadians, Mexicans, Colombians—and rarely refer to themselves *first* as Americans (1998: viii). As I agree with Naylor that "United Statesians" is not likely to become a popular designation, and as I find "U.S. Americans" to be unwieldy and somewhat redundant given colloquial usage, I choose to refer to U.S. citizens simply as Americans.

4 Statistics for money spent on prostitution are impossible to calculate due to its illegality.

5 Here I do not want to imply that sexual release or even a form of contact always occurs when an individual participates in another realm of the sex industry. In fact, this varies to an extreme extent. However, in theory, each of these different venues is designed to provide for different possibilities. Further, legal regulations often influence (without dictating) how much sexual activity occurs in different contexts and locations and the customers are generally, though not always, aware of this fact.

1. Observing the Observers

1 Sexual release on the premises was prohibited by local and club regulations. Obviously, if a man wished to masturbate in the restroom, this would be difficult to police. Further, there may have been men who used the clubs as a kind of foreplay to later masturbation or sexual activity.

2 The exploratory research for this project was conducted in 1996 at a sixth club in a Midwestern city. At this club I worked as a topless entertainer and conducted interviews with a number of dancers and other sex workers in the city. I also continued to work as an exotic dancer in an upscale club intermittently for several years after my fieldwork was completed. These experiences are the source of some of the insights and examples that inform my work.

3 Auditions vary and a new dancer may be asked to perform on stage during a slow time of the day (especially if she is inexperienced) or simply asked to undress in the dressing room in front of a manager. Some clubs may hire a dancer on the spot without an audition, though this is more likely to happen at a lower-tier club where the management is not as concerned with tattoos, scars, or a standard body type.

   After each shift I recorded my observations of that evening's events, paying particular attention to my interactions with customers, my thoughts and emotions while dancing, and my observations and conversations with other dancers and employees. In addition to the time I spent in the clubs working as an entertainer, I also spent time observing in these clubs and in most of the other existing clubs around the city.

4 Some strip clubs for men have rules prohibiting female customers from entering without a male escort. In many other instances, however, women choose not to visit strip clubs for personal reasons. Few Laurelton women I spoke with during the course of my research who were not involved in sex work had ever entered strip clubs, despite the fact that they were curious about the transactions available to the male customers inside. I expect that the number of female customers will vary by region, type of strip club, age, and so forth.

5 Several other, shorter interviews were conducted with men who claimed that they disliked strip clubs and preferred other forms of adult entertainment, although these are not counted among the thirty primary interviews. Interviews were also conducted with managers, DJs, advertisers, and marketers of the clubs. Informally, my coworkers were also a significant source of information. Quantitative data, in addition to more qualitative research, comparing the male customers of strip clubs to those who preferred other forms of adult entertainment would be extremely useful.

6 Of course, there were times when the club was too busy for conversation, or when my only contact with a given customer was while I was onstage. In

these cases, the customers most likely knew me only as a dancer. During my exploratory research, I was focusing on my coworkers and not yet studying the male customers; thus I could not possibly disclose these details. I gained different kinds of insight from each of these experiences.

7 Despite my caution in this matter, there were still some men who showed up for an interview worried that I might be a prostitute trying to solicit business. Because of this, I dressed very conservatively for the interviews. Although public settings may have influenced personal disclosure somewhat, I found that the men generally talked quite easily and bluntly about private matters even in such public spaces. Interviews usually lasted from two to four hours and two or three follow-up interviews were conducted whenever possible. Some follow-up interviews were conducted over email or by telephone if the respondents were not native to the city. The interviews were structured with open-ended questions and often became conversational as I responded to the men's questions about dancing as well.

8 Offered income levels ranged from a landscaper making $10 an hour to a hospital administrator making $250,000 a year (not counting the additional family income of his wife, who was a doctor). Several authors have noted Americans' tendency to view themselves as middle class regardless of their economic situation or to simply avoid the subject of class altogether (e.g., Mantsios 1995; Ortner 1991). I found it to be a significant indication of this when, after fourteen months of fieldwork and interviewing, I never met anyone who did not *first* describe himself to me as middle class (although afterwards occasionally making further clarifications such as "upper-middle" or "lower-middle" class). Despite this fact, however, many people seemed quite willing and able to draw distinctions between themselves and others and to position other people in categories such as "white trash" or "redneck," especially when asked about individuals who lived or worked in specific locations. The appendix provides more information about the interviewees, including their pseudonyms and occupations.

9 The fact that none of the clubs selected for this study was considered primarily black explains, in part, why only two of the interviewees were African American, despite the fact that the population in Laurelton is around 33 percent African American. The racialized landscape, and its effects on the meanings of visits to strip clubs for the (primarily white) interviewees, is discussed in more depth in Chapter 2.

10 There are several kinds of "regular" customers. First, there are the regulars of particular dancers. These are men who visit the same dancer or dancers repeatedly, developing ongoing relationships with those dancers inside of the clubs. In these cases, if a dancer moves to a different club the man may follow her. I have discussed these relationships in more depth elsewhere (Frank 1998). None of the interviewees saw themselves as this kind of regular at the

time of the interview. On the other hand, most of these interviewees (94 percent) saw themselves as both regular users of strip clubs as a form of entertainment and leisure and as regular visitors to particular *clubs* (rather than dancers). That is, although these men might spend time with their favorite dancers while at the club, they are more loyal to the club than to these relationships (and would probably continue visiting the club even if those dancers moved on). These categories, of course, may overlap and change over time. I refer to the interviewees as regulars in the text for simplicity.

11 Certainly, the fact that I am a woman may have influenced interactions with the male interviewees. This in itself is a source of information, however, rather than a liability. One reader of my early work, for example, suggested that men might speak more forthrightly with a male interviewer; another suggested that the men may have highlighted the more cerebral aspects of their visits because of how they wanted to represent themselves to me. Yet it is important to remember that I was involved in interactions with each of the interviewees before our formal interviews, and often afterwards as well, and that I was perceived as a dancer as well as a researcher. Many of the men made comments such as, "I can tell you this because you're a dancer" and "Excuse my language . . . well, I can say that because you hear it all the time." Perhaps being interviewed by a male would have caused the interviewees to highlight the sexual aspects of their visits even more. Yet there is no reason to think that these interactions would have been any more truthful or authentic, as the interviewees often expressed difficulty in discussing personal issues with other men.

12 Men in groups, for example, were often much more likely to speak in demeaning ways about a dancer's body or to act as if the dancers did not exist as individuals. These same men, however, often would be quite respectful in individual interaction. Further, as many group occasions were bachelor parties, men in groups often spoke detrimentally about marriage and relationships. Singly, however, these same men would profess love for their wife and a great deal of satisfaction with their outside intimate life.

13 Ronai writes: "The roles—dancer, wife, and researcher—often clash with one another. Things become muddled when I try to explain why I am willing to disrobe in front of strange men in the name of research. What is it with me that I am able to do this when others in my culture find the concept untenable? Good wives certainly don't do this to their husbands. Or am I in fact just another dancer with a good line of bullshit, playing the marks?" (1992: 107).

14 In referring to the sex workers' rights movement, I do not wish to imply that there is a homogeneous movement. Rather, there are coalitions of national and local sex workers, activists, academics, customers, and other concerned individuals who work toward the eradication of the stigmatization and criminalization of consensual adult sexualized activity. There are a wide variety of

different perspectives and strategies represented and employed in pursuing this goal, some that I find extremely compelling and others that I find somewhat problematic (though rarely as disturbing as the countermovements to purge communities of sexual expression and services).

15 For MacKinnon, the alienation of female sexuality under male dominance, or patriarchy, could be equated with the alienation of labor under capitalism: "Sexuality is to feminism what work is to Marxism: that which is most one's own, yet most taken away" (1989: 3).

16 Images and performances are not mutually exclusive, of course, and neither are the categories of worker and customer.

17 In feminism and men's studies, Scott MacDonald (1983), John Stoltenberg (1989), David Mura (1987), Harry Brod (1992), and Alan Soble (1992) have theoretically explored men's use of pornography and analyzed it in relation to social configurations of power and gender, each with different conclusions. Few researchers of pornography, however, have conducted the kind of audience-oriented consumption studies that have been undertaken with other forms of consumer culture, such as Radway's (1984) analysis of how women read romance novels. Simon Hardy's *The Reader, the Author, His Woman and Her Lover: Soft Core Pornography and Heterosexual Men* (1998) attempts to rectify this situation by providing the testimony of male consumers of pornography. There is some literature, both popular (Bildstein 1996; Beller 1997; Anderson 1999) and academic (Hanna 1998b; Liepe-Levinson 1998, 2002), that addresses the possible motivations for men's visits to strip clubs, but again, these analyses are provocative but are usually not based on indepth interviews with the customers and do not contextualize the men's consumption patterns in specific clubs or in a broader framework. Katherine Liepe-Levinson's *Strip Show: Performances of Gender and Desire* (2002), for example, draws on a number of ethnographic sources and some interviews with performers and managers to suggest possible customer motivations, but with its impressive range (over seventy different strip clubs and theaters in the United States and Canada for both men and women), it is a very different kind of study. Further, it is beyond the scope of the study, and tangential to her theoretical concerns, to consider the place of such consumption in the consumers' everyday lives and in relation to their outside relationships. See Egan (forthcoming) for an exception.

18 For my purposes here, I will be discussing the male, heterosexual customers of female striptease dancers. There are many different kinds and genders of clients, however, and many different sexualities that are commodified and expressed in the sexual marketplace. Some writers on workplace culture have distinguished between the terms client and customer, pointing out that professions such as medicine and law deal with "patients and clients" and the service industries deal with "customers or passengers." In a book on waitress-

ing, sociologist Greta Paules writes: "This distinction is particularly relevant when addressing issues of power and control, since power relations are generally thought to be reversed between service workers who have clients and those who have customers" (1991: 18). Interestingly, the men who frequent strip clubs were always called customers in my experience, whereas many escorts and prostitutes refer to their patrons as clients. This is indeed partly because of the power differentials involved in these different kinds of labor, as dancers are employees of the club and the customers are choosing within the club confines. Nevertheless, I use the terms client and clienthood when referring to discourses about the commodification of services and their consumers, although I continue to refer to the men as customers as well.

19 Although similar metaphoric comparisons have been made in the past between marriage and prostitution (Engels 1972; MacKinnon 1987), most people would agree that there are significant distinctions that should be made between these institutions, especially in terms of cultural legitimacy. MacKinnon, for example, writes: "feminism stresses the indistinguishability of prostitution, marriage, and sexual harassment" (59). Although this is an interesting rhetorical strategy, it ignores and erases the specificity of each of these practices.

20 Wendy Chapkis began this project of differentiation in *Live Sex Acts* (1997), yet her focus on multiple forms of sex work, across two cultures, is too broad to illuminate the sometimes subtle differences between strip clubs and their social context in the United States (and indeed, this is not her project).

21 I make this distinction because there is a growing sector of the industry that produces pornography for lesbian and bisexual women. Several writers claim that heterosexual women are growing consumers of other sectors of the sex industry as well. Andrew Ross writes: "The male strip join a la Chippendales, the 'Tupperware' parties for buying sex accessories and paraphernalia, the vast readership for romance novels and literary erotica, and the rapidly growing female consumption of visual pornography in magazines, films, and video have all become routine features of popular cultural life for women in the last fifteen years" (1989: 191). There certainly are a growing number of companies that are producing sexual products for female customers such as Candida Royalle's Femme Productions and the woman-oriented Good Vibrations, for example. On the other hand, many of the male strip clubs that exist cater to a gay male clientele and the ones that do not are usually frequented by women in groups, for bachelorette parties or other special occasions, and the services provided are not exactly comparable to those provided to men. There are almost fifty strip clubs in the Laurelton area, yet only three of these feature male dancers and two of these almost exclusively attract male customers. At the clubs that feature female dancers, the number of female customers is small. In the clubs in which I have worked or visited,

I have never seen more than one or two women a night out of the hundreds of male customers, and these women were *generally* escorted by men. Of course, some locations, such as San Francisco, may cater to a larger lesbian crowd than the clubs in the Midwest and the southern states where I worked. Some locations may also attract more heterosexual couples, especially well-known or prestigious clubs. As of yet, however, the kind of spaces and services available for male customers just do not exist for women in any comparable form. The important point here is that there is a difference in the use and availability of commodified sexual services between men and women that may serve to reinforce stereotypes and inequalities in society at large. As the sex industry becomes less stigmatized and the border between female virtue and the expression of female sexual desire less rigidly policed, female customers may come to ask for and receive more high-quality sexual products and services. For an insightful look at how women gain access to the kinds of erotic materials that they desire, see Juffer (1998). For explorations of the spatial and theatrical elements of strip shows for women, see Liepe-Levinson (2002) and Smith (2002).

22 Although intimacy as a concept remains nebulous in the literature, it appears to have several fairly important, interrelated components that are fairly consistently emphasized: emotional (in the sense of positive affect, caring, etc.), spatial (involving bodily interaction and physical proximity, sexual or otherwise), psychological (involving intersubjectivity at some level), and social (involving situated knowledges, verbal sharing, etc.).

23 The tourist gaze is not totalizing, even though it is certainly related to historical configurations of power and privilege. After all, most tourists are also workers in other spheres. All of the men I interviewed worked full time, although they felt differently about their jobs (ranging from being "very satisfied" to "bored and disillusioned").

24 Distinctions can be found between sincerity and authenticity in some of the literature, with authenticity used to imply "natural" feeling and sincerity a deception that can be worked upon oneself (Trilling 1972; Hochschild 1983). The transactions I discuss involve both an interactive element that can be questioned and a psychological element, and I see these as different parts of the same problem rather than seeing the problem of authenticity as replacing the problem of sincerity in modern times, as Trilling does. To mediate between these two terms and two levels, I often use the term realness.

25 The connection of experimental writing with specifically feminist ethnography is one that has been ardently explored by feminists and anthropologists (Stacey 1988; Abu-Lughod 1990; Behar and Gordon 1995). In countering James Clifford's claim that women anthropologists have *not* experimented with unconventional forms of ethnographic writing, Lila Abu-Lughod argues that he ignored "a whole alternative 'women's tradition' within ethnographic

writing," that of the popular ethnographies written by the "untrained wives" of anthropologists (18). In response, Ruth Behar poses the question in *Women Writing Culture:* "What kind of writing is possible for feminist anthropologists now, if to write unconventionally puts a woman in the category of untrained wife, while writing according to the conventions of the academy situates her as a textual conservative?" (Behar and Gordon 1995: 15). It is also certainly debatable that feminist anthropologists may have been conservative textually but politically avant-garde (Abu-Lughod 1990), or that there were indeed marginalized feminist anthropologists writing about culture in experimental ways who have not made the official canon (Behar 1995: 12). Deborah Gordon argues that feminist anthropology itself should be seen as a literary genre, and that this requires and allows us to let go of the reductionist distinction between " 'conventional' realist and 'experimental' ethnography" (1995: 431). Regardless of the line of argument followed, the connections among "feminism, fieldwork, writing, and ethnography" (431) are complex and politically charged.

26 Of course, the practice of writing (and editing and rewriting), whether academic prose or fiction, is itself admittedly untidy and incomplete (Jones 1998); it is not necessarily the same author who sits down in front of his or her computer every day, and these styles are never completely discrete. My argument is not that we should return to a focus on authorial intent, but that we should focus on issues of practice and method in writing as much as we focus on the slipperiness of texts and language.

2. Laurelton and Its Strip Clubs

1 In one locale, a customer might find dancers performing fully nude in a club that serves only soft drinks, but in the next town over find clubs with a liquor license and topless table dancing.

2 Ortner (1991) also discusses the discourse of respectability as a code for social class and as implicated in gender relations.

3 The upscaling of particular cabarets did not mean that stock burlesque or working-class entertainment did not continue to thrive (see Allen 1991).

4 In my own experience, I have found that many of these regulations tend to backfire in terms of preventing physical contact between the patrons and the entertainers. The clubs I have worked in with the minimum of physical contact between the parties have been completely nude clubs that served alcohol and that permitted nude dances from a foot away. With too many restrictions and prohibitions on nudity, a different customer base begins to frequent the clubs, sometimes men who care less about the pleasure of the voyeuristic spectacle and more about purchasing more sexual activities such as lap dances.

5   The names of the city, counties, and clubs have been changed.

6   This combination has recently come under fire in several counties adjacent to the city, however.

7   Dancers were allowed to interact casually with customers when fully clothed (touching hands or arms, giving a kiss on the cheek, etc.) but were not allowed to perform these contacts when nude in any of the clubs in which I worked. They were also prohibited at all times from sitting on a customer's lap. Private nude table dances were allowed as long as the dancers officially maintained at least a foot of distance between themselves and the customer. In Chapter 4, I discuss more of the subtleties of the table dances with regard to contact.

8   I was unable to obtain actual customer and worker demographics for this area, though it is often the case that minority sex workers are more visible to the public. The interviewees were primarily white, however, and this may reflect their fantasies about different locations as much as an actual pattern. The two African American interviewees spoke the most critically about Lawrence Avenue and claimed the most direct experience with the area.

9   In the United States particular historical transformations have given rise to a complex and sometimes contradictory notion of privacy. Further, the gendered ideological split between public and private spheres has a long and significant history (e.g., Coontz 1992; Cancian 1987).

10 Of the other three clubs that I studied, the Panther had changed locations in the city and remodeled several times in recent years and the Pony Lounge had changed management and names several times as well. Although Diamond Dolls and Tina's Revue had also remodeled at particular times, they were also seen as relatively continuous businesses in Laurelton at the time of my fieldwork. The Crystal Palace was an upscale club, though more middle tier than upper tier, but it was located the farthest from downtown and thus did not have the same potential customer base as the others. Although described as a nice, upscale club, the Crystal Palace was never ranked higher than the Panther or Diamond Dolls in my interviews or experiences.

11 As Diamond Dolls considered itself to be in competition with both the Panther Club and the Crystal Palace, management told me that I could not simultaneously dance at either of those other clubs. They did not directly prohibit me from working at smaller clubs, such as Tina's Revue, during that time period.

12 Though these highly public admissions did occur, and seemed to be supportable, none of the customers I formally interviewed, nor any of the hundreds I informally interacted with and discussed the issue, had engaged in such activity. Further, though some dancers had allegedly had sex with athletes, this was not a *service* that was offered inside the club, and many of the stories about sexual activity between athletes and dancers did not involve additional

money exchanging hands and supposedly occurred off-site at parties or in hotel rooms. Indeed, professional athletes generally seem to attract groupies and women quite willing to engage in sexual activity with them for free. Certainly, as part of their business strategy, *some* dancers might also choose to have sex with very famous, wealthy, or generous customers either in the clubs, if possible, or off-site; however, at that point, the entertainment should probably not be considered striptease.

13 In other clubs around the country, different regulations mean that lap dancing or other forms of contact may be allowed, and in this case sexual release may occur in a more public setting. Even so, however, the spatial layout of the room, the lighting, and the behavior of the dancers and customers often means that private spaces for such activity are circumscribed and delineated or even created through customer behavior (not looking at or interacting with other men receiving dances, for example).

14 Literally, the term redneck implies a sunburned neck from working outdoors (something that would be familiar to some of the white working-class locals), though the term is used as well to refer to a particular classed identity and to certain patterns of taste and consumption.

15 Men who were regulars at other clubs, however, also frequently invoked the name Cheers. Beck, for example, said that he stopped going to Diamond Dolls when it was renovated because "it wasn't like Cheers anymore." Instead, he began frequenting the Crystal Palace. Some regulars at the Panther Club said that they had become such good friends with the dancers there that it had "become like Cheers." But whereas some of the regulars termed the more upscale clubs "like Cheers," first-time or occasional visitors almost never did so.

16 This move basically consisted of facing away from the customer and quivering the buttocks quickly, sometimes while slightly bent over.

3. Just Trying to Relax

1 Although two Laurelton clubs provided lap dancing and the possibility of sexual release, and thus did not offer one or the other of nudity or alcohol, these clubs were not nearly as numerous or well-known as the clubs that did not, and neither was selected as a field site.

2 In one of the few studies of prostitutes' clients in the United States, Martin Monto distributed surveys to men who were attending a John's School after being arrested for attempting to hire a prostitute. He found that seeking the services of prostitutes reflected a number of motivations: "an attraction to the illicit nature of the encounter," a desire for kinds of sex that a regular partner would not provide, a tendency to define sex as a commodity, and "a lack of interest in or access to conventional relationships" (2000: 82). Al-

though these spoken motivations differ slightly from those of the men I spoke with who preferred to visit strip clubs, qualitative interviews would probably further elucidate the meanings of these motivations in their social contexts.

3 This is evident in the linguistic changes that have become more prevalent in recent years with industry promoters, especially in regard to upscale clubs— from "sex industry" to "adult entertainment" and from "strippers" to "entertainers." Men who frequented the more upscale clubs were more likely to mention "entertainment" as an important part of their experience. Significantly, upscale clubs are consciously designed to be visually and aurally stimulating, with fast-paced music, multiple stage shows, elaborate lighting and sound systems, and an ingenious use of interior space to maximize voyeuristic possibilities. This particular atmosphere was not necessarily appealing to all customers, as discussed in Chapter 2. The atmosphere itself, however, was indeed a vital aspect of the experience of visiting a strip club no matter what its position on the hierarchy.

4 Urry (1990) has discussed the role of photography in the universalizing of the tourist gaze. The connection of strip clubs to a particular kind of photography—pornography—is unmistakable. Women who do spreads in men's magazines, for example, often get highest billings in the clubs and may become traveling feature dancers who earn significantly more than house dancers. Porn stars also work as traveling features between movies, where they draw male fans to the local strip clubs. Even when interacting with the house dancers or in clubs that do not provide feature entertainment, men often want to see poses that they have often seen before in still pornography or pornographic films and videos.

5 If customers are engaged in touristic practices, dancers are positioned somewhere between "natives" (or part of the site / sight themselves) and service workers / tourist industry employees (helping to create the customers' desired experiences; sometimes also part of the site / sight themselves). Sex work, like tourist employment, has previously been discussed as a form of emotional labor (Ronai 1992; Chapkis 1997; Frank 1998), which means that the work requires an employee to draw on emotional reserves to create a feeling, a mood, or an experience for a customer. Tourist employment, argues sociologist Philip Crang, involves the "co-presence of employees and their customers in the so-called 'service encounters'," and is associated with "moral dilemmas of honesty-dishonesty, trust-distrust, and the seen-unseen." This phenomenon is reflected in dramaturgical or performative metaphors where "workers are said to take on roles, [and] workplaces become stages" (1997: 138).

Drawing on Urry's (1990) distinction between different kinds of tourist gazes, Crang argues that tourism employees both work at producing gazes and become part of them, working at becoming familiar with and to the tourists and also at "providing brief encounters that are memorable enough to be collectable." He writes: "In doing so, tourism workers have to inhabit visual practices that are power-laden, in terms of class relations, histories of ethnic power, and sexuality. But . . . they are not just passive recipients of tourist gazes. They actively respond to them. They may hide from them (finding or constructing places shielded from the gazes); they may masquerade within them (using gazes to facilitate the development of one or more personae); and they may pose through them (using the gaze to send a message)" (1997: 151). The gaze may thus be taken up and used by the tourist employee in creative ways, allowing for diverse experiences of agency, enjoyment, dissatisfaction, self-efficacy, and so on. This certainly corresponds with my own experiences as a dancer and with those narrated by an earlier group of individuals whom I interviewed, all women who worked in various sectors of the sex industry. See Chapkis (1997) for more discussion of the various kinds of sex work as emotional labor.

6 In addition to those discussed in this chapter, there are, of course, other roles that a male customer might consciously play. A man might like to see himself performing as a "big spender," for example, even if that was not necessarily a role that he was able to take on regularly in his everyday life. Some customers also clearly found it enjoyable to take on a protective, almost parental role with some of the dancers, and there are certainly other possibilities as well. In addition, the customers' interactions became meaningful as they drew on self-representations that were simultaneously real and imagined, subjectivities that are both fantasized and experienced as authentic.

7 During my fieldwork I had the opportunity to speak with men who did not enjoy strip clubs and who described the clubs as "boring" and the patrons as "pathetic." Nevertheless, they drew on the same metaphors to explain their experiences in other venues, claiming that actual sexual encounters were more "exciting," that singles bars offered the "real adventure," and so on. Customers at other kinds of adult entertainment venues, of course, will frame their experiences and motivations in ways more specific to those sites as well, and I am not suggesting that all of these customers are seeking the same kinds of experiences or give them the same meanings.

8 By using the term "continuum," I do not want to reify or hierarchically organize sexual practices. In Laurelton (and elsewhere), however, these practices are indeed organized according to their *legality*, with commercialized genital contact (even in the form of a woman "masturbating for hire") being illegal and thus more "risky" in a number of different ways.

9 Indeed, while I was conducting fieldwork I met several men for whom these other venues were the preferred means of spending their money and time. As one man told me, "Why would I spend money to look when I can touch right

across the street? I just don't understand it." Another man, Todd, was used to the lap dancing of the Florida clubs (in which a dancer sits on a man's lap and moves back and forth, sometimes until he has an orgasm). He found the Laurelton clubs "frustrating" because the women "promise sexual satisfaction that is never delivered." Todd usually frequented the lower-tier clubs, where the women were more likely to break the rules against such contact out of financial necessity, or visited the less popular lap dancing clubs that did not serve alcohol. Interestingly, Todd used the same explanation of a respect for monogamy to discuss these activities, and he drew the line at lap dancing: he had been married for fourteen years, did not want to dissolve his marriage, and felt that lap dancing was a way to "have sex without being unfaithful" to his wife.

10 Although I did not have the opportunity to formally interview any handicapped customers, disabled men frequently visit strip clubs. Not only are clubs one of the few legal commodified sexualized outlets, but they also provide human companionship in a society that often stigmatizes the disabled. At every club I worked in, several of the regulars had some form of disability yet were not necessarily treated differently by the dancers. In fact, being regulars, they were often treated with more friendliness and respect than single-visit customers. Similarly, in an article debunking many of the myths about strip clubs, Stacy Reed writes: "Though most gentleman's clubs' clients are strikingly normal, many lonely and awkward men benefit from watching dancers. Sexual voyeurism alleviates some of their suffering. Also, impotent, disabled, and conventionally unattractive men are sexually stigmatized and frequently rejected as partners. One of my old regulars used a wheelchair. Until prejudices subside, he believes such clubs will be his only legal source of sexual interaction" (1997: 185). See also Shuttleworth (2000) for an interesting analysis of disability and the search for sexual intimacy in strip clubs.

11 This technique, of course, had to be abandoned when I began working in Laurelton, as I always wore my wedding ring and was forthcoming about my sexuality and partner when asked.

12 Individuals who identify as part of a community based on nonmonogamous practices.

13 One male reader of this book who worked in the pornography industry mentioned the paradoxical and uncomfortable "side effect" for a man when encountering a woman who was sexually interested and uninhibited in real life: a concomitant worry that he would be unable to please her. The sex industry generally ensures that the woman will at least feign pleasure.

14 In *Femininity and Domination: Studies in the Phenomenology of Oppression,* philosopher Sandra Lee Bartky writes that there is a particular quality to an emotional caregiver's attention that works to raise the recipient's confidence:

"This attention can take the form of speech, of praise, perhaps for the Other's character and accomplishments, or it can manifest itself in the articulation of a variety of verbal signals (sometimes called 'conversational cheerleading') that incite him to continue speaking, hence reassuring him of the importance of what he is saying. Or such attention can be expressed nonverbally, e.g., in the forward tilt of the caregiver's body, the maintaining of eye contact, the cocking of her head to the side, the fixing of a smile upon her face" (1990: 102). This is precisely the kind of attention that dancers give their customers, especially their regulars. These are also traditional examples of deference to someone with greater social power. Many dancers (though certainly not all) are less privileged than their customers. Many times, the customers I interacted with held very conservative views about women's roles in society and had the privilege of being extremely unreflective about those views. In the clubs, though, men are unlikely to be directly challenged about their personal or political beliefs (although the dancers may certainly criticize them later in the dressing room; deference does not automatically imply domination). Further, if a dancer *is* challenging him in some way, a man can simply move on to the next available and attentive woman. Certainly, there is nothing intrinsically wrong with doing such ego-boosting work, or with receiving it. When this kind of emotional support flows in only one direction, however, it may indeed buttress gendered and classed inequalities that already exist at a societal level.

4. The Pursuit of the Fantasy Penis

1 Though the men's encounters are referred to in this chapter as sexual or sexualized, it is important to realize that this is focusing on the customers' perspective. The perspective of a dancer as to the nature of an encounter may or may not match those of her customer at any given moment. There are times when dancing is just a job, when all of her movements and thoughts are focused on the financial transaction (What turns him on? is a question simply asked to figure out how to get him to buy another dance); there are also times when the experience might be mutually erotic, when the dancer might do "deep acting" (Hochschild 1983) to match her customer's emotional state and thus enjoy her job more and / or boost her profits; when a dancer may drift off and be thinking any number of mundane things; or even when a dancer might feel more aroused than the customer for her own reasons. The intersubjective nature of the transactions, and the fact that the men's enjoyment often required that the dancers also express enjoyment, attraction, and arousal, makes the situation quite complicated.

2 Indeed, I have had the opportunity to speak with men who were avid consumers of other types of commodified sexual services and who thought that

the customers of strip clubs were dupes, being "ripped off" by women who were interested only in teasing.

3 John Anderson, personal communication (2001). Similarly, Gary Brooks notes, "There is something relatively moot about the evolutionary biology argument since the entire sociocultural climate has undergone sweeping and radical change in the past one hundred years (a speck of time to evolutionary thinkers)" (1995: 88).

4 See Chapter 6 for an exploration of the way these fantasies play out along the lines of social class.

5 Even though anal sex is obviously just one act in a repertoire of potential sexual activities betweeen same-sex partners, in my experience this was the act most focused on by the customers when they mentioned homosexuality or when they asked for advice about sexual practices.

6 Interestingly, when "bachelors" were divested of their clothing onstage, this usually took place in an atmosphere of homosocial humiliation, as their friends chanted, "Get him!" "Shred him!," and so forth. Bachelor dances and showers, then, because of the exposure involved, required participants to take up vulnerable (and sometimes humiliating) positions and, partly because of this fact, were responded to enthusiastically by some customers and engaged in quite reluctantly by others. Participation rituals of this kind, however, rarely were engaged in by men visiting the Laurelton clubs alone. In other cities and venues, patrons may occasionally be allowed to stage their own exhibition scenes or even masturbate as part of the show (see Liepe-Levinson 2002: 168–169).

7 This is not to say that some men did not want to be *revealed*. If fact, some men did identify with dancers in that they wished themselves to be onstage and the center of attention, the object of desire in a kind of cross-identificatory fantasy. There are other places, however, where men could go if they did want to be recognized for their body and did want to be naked in the presence of a woman.

8 The economic benefits of sex work are often mentioned in treatises on its potentially empowering aspects for the women (Funari 1997; Reed 1997; Morgan 1987; Frank 2002). Sex work, of course, is not *always* experienced as enjoyable or liberating. Many books written by and for sex workers have attempted to acknowledge this complexity (Bell 1994; Pheterson 1989; Delacoste and Alexander 1987; others). In *Reading, Writing, and Rewriting the Prostitute Body*, Shannon Bell examines the discourse of prostitute rights groups to show "two oppositional constructions of the prostitute [sex worker] as a site of politicized resistance and as a site of oppression: empowerment/exploitation." She also examines the work of six North American prostitute performance artists to point out how individuals can "hold both sides of the dichotomy in their own body," thus destabilizing such a binary division of

experience and identity (137). Filmmaker and peep show dancer Vicky Funari writes that "there is no standard sex worker." Each woman has her own reasons for working and responses to the work: "The only safe thing to say is that we're all in it for the money" (28). Certainly there are different social positionings that situate a particular woman such that she chooses to labor in the sex industry and a man such that he has the financial means to procure her services. Regarding the individual transactions, however, many women who work in the sex industry do claim to enjoy the fact that their commodified relationships can be entered into and terminated at will. Money may also be seen as an equalizer: in an article in a New Jersey weekly paper, for example, a dancer is quoted as saying: "Men come here to gain power over women. Meanwhile, we're gaining power over them" (A. Friedman 1998). However, as the meanings of sex work are extremely variable in different places and different times, caution is necessary when generalizing. My own emotional experiences as a dancer were both positive and negative, and I would not be able to categorize sex work as either wholly liberating or wholly exploitative; nor would I want to do so. I have written more about these complexities elsewhere (Frank 2002).

5. "I'm Not Like the Other Guys"

1   Sometimes I use extended quotes from one or two interviewees to illustrate these concerns. For reasons of space, I cannot possibly include every man's comments. Could these concerns about realness have been expressed just because of the particularities of the interview situation? I am highly doubtful of that possibility. After all, I had interacted with all of these men inside the clubs before (and usually after) the interviews and knew the other dancers with whom these customers spent time. Further, I know how other dancers "sold" to different customers in the clubs and worked as a successful dancer for many years; thus, I do not believe that my authenticating strategies were unique. See Chapter 1 for more explanation of my methodological considerations.

2   I purposefully use the masculine pronoun here because the literature nearly always codes the traveler as male and because the interviewees were male. Challenges to this unconscious tendency have been made by Jokinen and Veijola (1997).

3   An example of staged authenticity given by MacCannell is that of a tendency to make the kitchen visible to the patrons of a restaurant, who may be fascinated by being able to watch "cooks at work" (1976: 99).

4   These critiques are wide-ranging. Cohen and Taylor (1976), for example, noted that tourists are capable of "ironically commenting on their disappointment" in not finding authenticity: "they see through the staged authen-

ticity of the tourist setting and laugh about it" (quoted in Rojek 1993: 177). Pearce and Moscardo argue that it is "necessary to distinguish between the authenticity of the setting and the authenticity of the persons gazed upon; and to distinguish between the diverse elements of the tourist experience which are of importance to the tourist in question" (quoted in Urry 1990: 9). Other challenges have been raised regarding the performative aspects of everyday life. Malcolm Crick, for example, has pointed out that all cultures are in some sense "staged"; thus, how is the "apparently inauthentic staging for the tourist" different from this (quoted in Urry 1990: 9)? Others have critiqued the narrative of "lost authenticity." In " 'Getting There': Travel, Time, and Narrative," Barry Curtis and Claire Pajaczkowska argue that "the opposite of tourism is not 'staying at home,' nor travel for self-realization, but the involuntary travel associated with the predicament of the immigrant" (1994: 202). They note that the preoccupation of the literature with authenticity and originality suggests a "nostalgia for earlier times, for times when the relationship of traveler to 'native' was one that produced more cultural difference and certainly more deference" (202). Curtis and Pajaczkowska challenge the very meaning of travel "as a universal symbol of growth, change and dissemination," arguing that historically many people have "been recruited or coerced to travel neither for leisure, not interest nor choice," but rather out of hunger and fear (214). Power relations are thus displaced through a faulty distinction between travel and tourism—both actually very privileged forms of mobility.

5 In *The Managed Heart*, Arlie Hochschild distinguishes between emotion work that we do privately (such as trying to enjoy a party) and that which we do as part of a job (such as summoning up a friendly smile for an irate customer). Jobs that require workers to be in direct contact with the public and to "create and maintain a relationship, a mood, a feeling" in others as part of that job are said to involve emotional labor (Hochschild 1983). People who perform emotional labor must strive to create the feelings in others that their job demands and, at the same time, to manage those feelings in themselves that are not conducive to a successful transaction. When emotional management becomes part of one's job, feelings can "fall under the sway of large organizations, social engineering, and the profit motive" (1983: 19). Emotional labor requires a worker to coordinate mind and feeling, to draw on a deep sense of self to produce a particular state of mind in others, and, like physical labor, can eventually lead to alienation under these circumstances.

6 Quoting Feifer, Urry explains: "The post-tourist knows that he is: 'not a time traveler when he goes somewhere historic; not an instant noble savage when he stays on a tropical beach; not an invisible observer when he visits a native compound.' " The post-tourist "is above all self-conscious, 'cool,' and role-distanced" (1990: 101).

7 As mentioned in Chapter 1, Urry argues that the tourist gaze can take two forms: the romantic and the collective. The romantic form of the tourist gaze has an emphasis on solitude, privacy, and a personal or semispiritual relationship with the object of the gaze (1990: 45). The collective form, on the other hand, relies on the presence of other tourists to create atmosphere and to add excitement and glamour to the experience (46). Lack of authenticity, he writes, tends to be more of a problem under the romantic gaze than for those engaged in the collective gaze, "where congregation is paramount" (34). This distinction becomes quite useful in the discussions raised about authenticity in strip clubs, for, as I have noted throughout, men who visited the clubs in groups often desired quite different kinds of interactions from those who visited singly.

8 In *Ways of Escape,* Chris Rojek also considers the phenomenon of tourism and the problem of authenticity in terms of the desire to escape from the everyday, and like Baudrillard, believes that "escape" has become impossible. He argues that postmodernist thinking about culture as depthless, fragmented, and organized around processes of simulation has several implications for thinking about leisure and tourism, one of which is that authenticity will disappear as a concern. Rojek argues that under modernity, leisure and travel were "seen as spheres of activity in which self-realization could be pursued in a more authentic way than in work and family life" (1993: 6). Yet he also argues that this particular worldview has "decomposed" under postmodernity, bringing with it changes in the organization of touristic practice (208). He writes that tourist forms are now "preoccupied with spectacle and sensation" and that tourist "experience is accompanied with a sense of irony" (134). Although people continue to long for escape because of the anxieties created by the "thorough artificiality of modern life," in postmodern societies leisure "is not the antithesis of daily life but the continuation of it in dramatized or spectacular form" (213). Rojek's tourist, then, still *believes* that he is escaping routine existence, even though this has become impossible.

9 Peggy Phelan (1993) argues that this is the experience for viewers of Cindy Sherman's photographic *Film Stills,* images of women (all herself) in different narrative situations.

10 A customer told me a story about being upset when he saw his first girlfriend nude during high school, as he had seen naked women only in pornographic magazines and strip clubs and "didn't realize that her breasts would fall" when he took off her bra.

11 At other times during the interview Roger categorized me as a dancer instead of an anthropologist. When we were discussing whether dancers might date their customers, for example, he said, "*You* are all stunningly beautiful girls. To even consider that *you* are all running around without male companion-

ship outside the club is ridiculous." This tracking back and forth in terms of how the interviewees perceived me was not uncommon.

12 If there was already a "Kate" on the rotation, I was asked to choose a stage name so that the DJ and managers would not get me confused with another dancer. In these cases, I also provided the customers with my real name.

13 The idea that men who use the sex industry are immature may also influence some of the men's claims to enjoy women's bodies as "works of art." Art is distinguished from pornography, in part, through its association with a refined manner of contemplation: viewers supposedly are not moved to bodily arousal from art. Masturbation, associated with the immature adolescent, is thus a lower form of appreciation.

14 Often, even stage names were self-consciously chosen to be "revealing" of a dancer's fabricated work identity: Kim would be the girl next door; Chloe would be refined and elegant; Gabriella would be exotic. This was not always the case, however, and there was often a difference between types of clubs and types of dancers. At Tina's Revue, a lower-tier club, many of the black dancers chose clearly fanciful names—Peaches, Ecstasy, Tequila, Beauty, and Diamond, for example—and explained that the African American clientele at Tina's liked names that were "exotic." (In fact, one night a customer took me aside and told me that Kate was "no name for a dancer," suggesting that I use the name "Princess" instead.) In the upper-tier clubs, on the other hand, black and white dancers alike usually chose (or were instructed to use) names that were much more "realistic," such as Jessica, Ashley, and Sara.

There are very real reasons why dancers do not like to provide their customers with much information. Many dancers attract stalkers, prank callers, or obsessive individuals, and for this reason they were usually advised by the management not to use their own name and to fabricate a life story. Even in the dressing rooms, real names were often reserved only for dancers who were close friends. The danger of providing customers with too much personal information was openly acknowledged, and in fact provided an alibi when a dancer became caught in a lie. "Well, I had to lie about where I lived when I first met you," I found myself explaining when I accidentally mixed up stories at the first club I worked at, "because I've had men try to follow me home before. But, of course, I know now that you're different." In fact, this type of gradual disclosure itself fostered a kind of intimacy and trust. Over time, a dancer might quite willingly share more and more of her outside life and identity with her regular customers.

15 When working in Laurelton, I was always immediately forthcoming about my name and institutional affiliation (I provided business cards), as well as my marital status (I wore a wedding ring). This was necessary for my research and for my rapport with the men I interviewed; however, for some

customers it clearly disrupted their pleasure in eliciting this information on their own. Other customers doubted the veracity of this actually truthful information.

16 The stigma of a male customer, of course, is quite different from that experienced by a dancer, prostitute, or other sex worker. Because there are a number of socially legitimated occasions in which going to a strip club is acceptable, there are always spaces in which men can talk about their involvement in the industry without fear of disapproval and as a form of masculine display. Further, given the strength of biological and moral notions about male sexuality, going to strip clubs can also be ideologically justified in some cases and to some people as "normal" male behavior. Yet in informal conversations about my project with men I did not meet in the clubs, I found they were usually reluctant to admit to being even infrequent customers until they felt comfortable that I was not going to criticize them. Often, both men and women acted skittish when they heard about my subject, laughing nervously and making jokes before furtively asking me what I *really* thought about men who went to strip clubs. All of the men whose interviews I use in the following analysis, however, are men I met while actually working as a dancer. Because of this, they were already customers when I approached them for an interview. Certainly, they could downplay their involvement, as some men did by telling me that they had "just stopped in on a whim" or by saying that this was "what the business partners wanted to do" and not an activity they would have personally chosen. There was no way for them to completely disavow their customer status when talking to me, however, as they had already slipped money (even if only a dollar or two) into my garter.

17 Again, I am discussing clubs that did not provide for any kind of sexual release on premises. In clubs that allow lap dancing or other forms of dancer-customer contact that might lead to orgasm, the dynamics might be quite different (with an orgasm being authenticating enough).

18 This is not to say that gay men do not ever visit strip clubs featuring female dancers; rather, it is just to point out that they would be approached as straight by the dancers and other members of the audience in such a situation.

19 Here I am using Butler's (1993) reading of realness to discuss performance, and not using these strip club performances to discuss her theory of performativity.

20 There is evidence of concern about the authenticity of emotion in noncommodified intimate relationships as well, and the connection between these two is well worth exploring. In a series of interviews with husbands and wives in the United States, for example, anthropologist Naomi Quinn notes that when individuals narrated their relationship histories they often evidenced a concern as to whether they really loved the person they were

thinking of marrying. She found that they used a "metaphor of love as an *entity* that may or may not be the real thing, so that a person might be fooled into thinking that this love, even their own for someone else, is real when it is actually false" (n.d.: 10). Her interviewees performed mental tests to interrogate their emotions and to decide on the authenticity of their relationships.

21 Here it is important to remember that the customers may be performing desire, arousal, and attachment as well (Frank 1998; Liepe-Levinson 1998, 2002).

22 See Handler and Gable (1997) for a fascinating look at the quest for and commercialization of historical authenticity at Colonial Williamsburg, VA.

6. Hustlers, Pros, and the Girl Next Door

1 Unfortunately, when I contacted *Hustler* to obtain updated statistics on customer demographics, I was unable to find more recent information on education level or occupational status. In 2001, the median age of the readership was 34 and 94 percent male (personal communication with the Sales and Marketing Division of Larry Flynt Productions). The most recent statistics that I received from Playboy Enterprises, Inc. were compiled in the spring of 2001. *Playboy* may have slightly more female readers, as I was given the figure of 17 to 20 percent.

2 When determining class in the interactions that I had in the clubs, I almost always used education and occupation (white collar or blue collar) rather than income, as most conversations that I had with new customers involved the topic of work. Further, as the customers were almost always informed that I was a graduate student, education was a natural topic of conversation as well. This method certainly has its problems, but the situation was such that it was next to impossible for me to get a customer to tell me his income in an exchange in the clubs; it might be inflated, because he was trying to impress me in the club atmosphere, or it might be deflated, as he tried to position himself as a man who "couldn't be hustled." My methodology was such that I could not systematically survey all of the customers who came through the door (nor would this have been acceptable to either the customers or the management). In the interviews, on the other hand, I asked the men to self-designate their class status, along with information about their educational background, occupation, and income. All of the interviewees personally identified themselves as somewhere in the middle class (upper to lower) regardless of income, occupation, or education. One African American man (Louis) said that he had grown up on welfare and one Caucasian man (Ross) said that his parents were "definitely upper class." Both of these men, however, saw themselves as solidly middle class at this time.

3 Interestingly, Gary had developed an ongoing relationship with a dancer

named Angie several years earlier, and helped finance her breast implants. He justified this by saying, "Now Angie, for instance, had to get a boob job because she had two kids at a young age and her boobs just stretched out, like, you know, they really were very unattractive. So I think she did it for a warranted reason."

4 In some ways this is again illustrative of Urry's (1990) distinction between the romantic and the collective gazes in terms of motivation, pleasure, and desire.

5 This need for distance from "outside" women, for some customers, was expressed in other ways as well. I danced for one day under the name Cathy, for example, and after three men told me that this was their wife's name and they felt strange about interacting with me because of it, I selected the name Ryan instead. On the other hand, some customers desired women who *were* similar to the outside women in their lives in appearance or behavior (the girl next door who could be your neighbor or the cashier in the local ice cream shop).

6 The men did not always simply distinguish between upper- and lower-tier clubs. Jason, a regular at the upper-tier Diamond Dolls, critiqued the Panther for being too "business-oriented," for example, saying it was not a place where one could really become "friends" with the dancers.

7 Again, because my own access to the spaces was limited by race, I did not have much opportunity to speak with customers who preferred the black clubs in Laurelton. I hope to do so in future work.

8 The customers, as noted earlier, fantasized that the dancers led wild sexual lives, were victims of abuse, and possessed particular dark knowledges about the world. I use the word fantasized here to highlight the fact that these beliefs were often held despite the men's lack of proof. Obviously, some dancers do indeed lead wild sexual lives and are victims of varied kinds of abuse; this is also true of some secretaries, professors, and housewives! Yet these beliefs were motivating for the male customers in particular ways and colored exchanges both inside and outside the clubs. People who do not know me well have difficulty believing that I was a nude dancer, given the signs of middle-class acceptability with which I often move around the world (an advanced degree, business clothes, etc.), and the confusion that ensues as they try to make sense of a married sex worker academic points to the kinds of preconceived binaries at work (and play) in commodified sexualized exchanges.

9 In *Imperial Leather* Anne McClintock argues that psychoanalysis "needs to take another, long look at the body of the working-class woman" (1995: 82). She argues that the splitting of women into madonnas and whores has its origins in the class structure of the Victorian household, not in a universal

archetype (87). Some critics, she writes, "see the doubled image of women as arising out of an archetypal doubling in consciousness that can be transcended by a defiant act of aesthetic will. Can we not, however, more properly see this doubled image of women that haunts the glossy surfaces of male Victorian texts as arising less from any archetypal doubling in the male unconscious than from the contradictory (and no less patriarchal) doubling of class that was a daily reality in the households and infancies of these upper-middle-class men?" (95). McClintock's argument is provocative and implies that this splitting is not inevitable, universal, or simply pathological; rather, it is an erasure of the role of the working-class woman in the everyday lives of upper-middle-class individuals. To discuss the material underpinnings of Freud's supposedly universal psychoanalysis is not to disavow that there are unconscious processes at work; rather, it can provide us with a richer psychoanalysis.

10 This term is used here in the psychoanalytic sense.

11 Even in a category such as pornography, of course, there are boundaries that are drawn and redrawn. As Laura Kipnis argues, the humor found in *Hustler* "seems animated by the desire to violate what Douglas describes as 'pollution' taboos and rituals . . . a society's set of beliefs, rituals, and practices having to do with dirt, order, and hygiene (and by extension, the pornographic)" (1996: 143). The social transgressions of *Hustler* are thus quite different from those of *Playboy*. There is a recent series of hardcore pornographic films from Extreme Associates that exploits the allure of this phenomenon. The films, entitled "Cocktails," were directed by a woman and feature female performers drinking various mixtures of bodily fluids—saliva, semen, enema fluids, urine, and so on.

7. The Crowded Bedroom

1 The term monogamy in this chapter is used in its colloquial sense to mean sexual exclusivity within a dyadic partnership.

2 This comparison can also be seen in the work of Friedrich Engels and his followers, work that has often informed feminist arguments but that did not present itself explicitly as such originally. For Engels, bourgeois marriage was an inauthentic relation because of its connection to the holding of private property. Whereas in the working classes, partnerships could be formed through sentimental bonds, in the middle classes marriage was always one of "convenience," often turning into "the crassest prostitution" (1972: 102).

3 The married men discussed in this chapter are Roger (married 20 years); Nick (married 30 years); Beck (married 27 years); Mick (first marriage 10 years; second marriage 4 years); Herb (married 8 years); Tim (married 32 years);

Saul (married 1 year); Brian (married 17 years); Jim (married 23 years); Charles (married 9 years); Steven (married 14 years); and Joe (first marriage 17 years; second marriage 3 years). Kenneth was in a long-term, live-in relationship with a woman (17 years). Three recently divorced men also fit this pattern when they were married: David, Alex, and Paul. Further, three of the younger, unmarried men in my sample—William, Jason, and Zachary—anticipated a traditional marriage to a conservative woman and talked at length about the importance of this fantasized relationship. Two other married men, Ross and Louis, saw their encounters in strip clubs as important because they were secret and sexualized, and also noted that their wife would be very upset if (and when) she found out. These men are not included in this particular group, however, as they claimed that they were staying in their relationship only because of their children. Gary fit this pattern while in his relationship with his first wife; however, in his current relationship he said that he was staying with her only for financial reasons, and thus I do not count him in this pattern either.

4 Some of these men admitted to having had extramarital affairs in the past, yet still considered themselves faithful to their wife. Most, however, expressed little interest in the active pursuit of sexual contact and release (commodified or not) outside of their primary relationship. In Laurelton there is a wide range of sexual activity that can be purchased and all of these men admitted that they knew how to do so if they desired.

5 Whereas there may be a tendency for individuals to represent their marriage in particularly positive ways to outsiders, these men's patterns of behavior were fairly consistent (based on their self-reports, my observations, and the observations of other dancers) and their marriages were almost all long term. Longevity, of course, is not the only test of a marriage—and indeed may be meaningless for some individuals who place value on other aspects of a partnership such as honesty or mutual self-fulfillment. It is, however, quite important for a large number of individuals.

6 Some men volunteered stories about "experimenting" with prostitution, massage parlors, or lingerie shops. When they did so, they more than simply stated this fact; rather, they often told lengthy stories about these experiences and why they did not "work" for them. They also spent a significant amount of money in strip clubs, enough that it is fairly safe to say that they received a different kind of service in this environment that they specifically enjoyed.

7 Many men used this exact phrase. My fieldwork and interviewing was done during the Clinton administration and this was a reference to President Clinton's policy on homosexuality in the military.

8 Elsewhere I have problematized the idea of "true" intimacy in relationships (Frank 1998). There are many difficulties in defining a term like intimacy, which is used both academically and colloquially in a wide variety of ways.

Throughout this book, I use the term as I interpret the authors that I focus on do: as involving more than just bodily contact and including conscious commitments as well as emotional, spatial, psychological, and social components.

9 Only two of the interviewees had a wife who openly approved of their being regular customers. Both of these couples considered themselves swingers and had negotiated a marriage that was nonmonogamous but that seemed to involve a high level of honesty. I spoke with one of the wives on the phone on several occasions and set up an interview with the other (which was subsequently cancelled when her husband was abruptly transferred out of the city). This was a rare experience, however. Of course, some men visited strip clubs during bachelor parties or for special occasions with their wife's knowledge and consent. Yet it seemed as if these more "legitimate" visits also only sustained the men's excitement if they were in some sense prohibited, and I often heard guests at bachelor parties say that they were "just there for the guys" or that they were bored or uninterested in the proceedings, albeit for different reasons. Not every man fit the pattern I am discussing here, then, but secrecy about visiting the clubs alone was often important to other men as well. Many of the customers with whom I interacted in the clubs on a daily basis laughingly (and sometimes guiltily) admitted that their wife did not know where they were and would not be told.

10 Interestingly, he tried to keep his visits to the Crystal Palace secret from the dancers at the Panther, and vice versa. As I was the only dancer who worked in both places simultaneously, he believed that I was privy to information that he was uncomfortable having shared, and he asked me not to speak about his visits to the other dancers. Several other dancers, however, knew about his behavior but pretended not to when in his company.

11 Jim, for example, made a comment during our first interview about my skirt being short (knee length!) and said: "Maybe part of the reason for me having this interview with you is that I would love to have sex with you. And I don't know what that makes you think, but it's probably true." At the same time, however, Jim stressed that he was a faithful husband and did not make any other overt propositions during our encounters.

12 Though Kernberg (1995) relies heavily on a traditional oedipal story of development, we do not need to accept this as a universalized process to appreciate the process of projective identification. Further, despite the assumption of heterosexuality implied by such a story, there is no necessary reason to believe that the processes he discusses would not be significant in other kinds of relationships as well, sexual or not.

13 A possible objection might be raised here that such a statement relies on a coherent, "true" self that supposedly resides within each individual. Yet, as Jessica Benjamin notes, we should not "confuse the category of the epistemological, thinking subject with that of the self as a locus of subjective experi-

ence, unconscious as well as conscious." She writes: "The term *subject* as it is used in psychoanalysis refers to such a locus of experience, one that need not be centrally organized, coherent, or unified. Yet it can still allow continuity and awareness of different states of mind, can still feel more or less real or alive, can be more or less capable of recognizing or feeling the impact of the other" (1995: 13).

14 Indeed, sex was not something that was openly talked about in these men's current family contexts. In every interview I asked the men what they had taught their children about sex (if they had children; if not, what they planned to teach them). Of all the men who had children and fit this pattern, only one had spoken with them about sex (and this was Mick, talking to his twenty-something stepson about married life!). Most of those with younger children were not even sure if their wife had done so.

15 Sociologist George Ritzer (1993) has discussed the process of McDonaldization in the contemporary United States as an extension of Weber's principles of rationality to ever more aspects of social and consumer life.

8. Disciplining Erotic Practice

1 See Liepe-Levinson 2002 for a more detailed discussion of this campaign in New York City.

2 According to Rubin, sexual essentialism is "the idea that sex is a natural force that exists prior to social life and shapes institutions," that sex is "eternally unchanging, asocial, and transhistorical" (1993: 9). Sex negativity is the idea that sex is a "dangerous, destructive, negative force," sinful unless used for reproductive purposes (11). The domino theory of sexual peril refers to the need to maintain an imaginary line between which human sexual behaviors are "safe, healthy, mature, legal, or politically correct" and those that are "the work of the devil, dangerous, psychopathological, infantile, or politically reprehensible" (14).

3 As many of my interviewees noted, certain regulations about touching were also desirable to many of the customers.

4 Dancers are certainly not passive in dealing with the clubs. In 1998, a group of five hundred exotic dancers won a class action suit against the Mitchell Brothers O'Farrell Theatre in San Francisco for back wages and benefits. Dancers at the Lusty Lady Theater in San Francisco successfully organized and are now represented by the Service Employees International Union. In Anchorage, Alaska, dancers have also organized to receive union representation (Steinberg 1998). Unfortunately, these movements have been slow and beset with many difficulties and much opposition from both club owners and the unions. Julia Query's film, *Live Nude Girls Unite* (2000), chronicles the struggle to form a union at the Lusty Lady.

Bibliography

Abrahams, Roger D. 1986. "Ordinary and Extraordinary Experience." In *The Anthropology of Experience*, ed. Victor Turner and Edward Bruner. Urbana: University of Illinois Press.

Abu-Lughod, Lila. 1990. "Can There Be a Feminist Ethnography?" *Women and Performance* 9:1–24.

Akhtar, Salman. 1996. "Love and Its Discontents: A Concluding Overview." In *Intimacy and Infidelity: Separation-Individuation Perspectives*, ed. Salman Akhtar and Selma Kramer, 145–78. Northvale, NJ: Jason Aronson.

Akhtar, Salman, and Selma Kramer, eds. 1996. *Intimacy and Infidelity: Separation-Individuation Perspectives*. Northvale, NJ: Jason Aronson.

Alexander, Priscilla. 1987. "Prostitution: A Difficult Issue for Feminists." In *Sex Work: Writings by Women in the Sex Industry*, ed. Frederique Delacoste and Priscilla Alexander, 184–214. Pittsburgh: Cleis Press.

Allen, Robert C. 1991. *Horrible Prettiness: Burlesque and American Culture*. Chapel Hill: University of North Carolina Press.

Allison, Anne. 1993. "Dominating Men: Male Dominance on Company Expense in a Japanese Hostess Club." *Genders* 16: 1–16.

———. 1994. *Nightwork: Sexuality, Pleasure, and Corporate Masculinity in a Tokyo Hostess Club*. Chicago: University of Chicago Press.

———. 1996. *Permitted and Prohibited Desires: Mothers, Comics, and Censorship in Japan*. Boulder, CO: Westview Press.

Ample, Annie. 1988. *The Bare Facts: My Life as a Stripper*. Toronto: Key Porter Books.

Anderson, Brett. 1999. "Film Strip." *Washington City Paper*, January 15, 22–31.

Baldas, Tresa. 1998. "Prostitution Convictions Fought, Motion Claims 1st Amendment Protects Sex Talk." *Chicago Tribune*, July 24.

Barry, Dan. 1998. "Topless Bars Threatened by 'Quality of Life' Drive." *New York Times*, April 29.

Barthes, Roland. 1972. *Mythologies*. New York: Hill and Wang.

Bartky, Sandra Lee. 1990. *Femininity and Domination: Studies in the Phenomenology of Oppression*. New York: Routledge.

Baudrillard, Jean. 1981. *Simulacra and Simulation*. Ann Arbor: University of Michigan Press.

Bederman, Gail. 1995. *Manliness and Civilization: A Cultural History of Gender and Race in the United States, 1880–1917*. Women in Culture and Society, ed. Catharine R. Stimpson. Chicago: University of Chicago Press.

Behar, Ruth, and Deborah Gordon, eds. 1995. *Women Writing Culture*. Berkeley: University of California Press.

Bell, Laurie, ed. 1987. *Good Girls / Bad Girls: Feminists and Sex Trade Workers Face to Face*. Toronto: Seal Press.

Bell, Shannon. 1994. *Reading, Writing, and Rewriting the Prostitute Body*. Bloomington: Indiana University Press.

——. 1995. *Whore Carnival*. New York: Autonomedia.

Beller, Thomas. 1997. "In the Company of Men." *Elle* 13, no. 3: 146.

Bendix, Regina. 1997. *In Search of Authenticity: The Formation of Folklore Studies*. Madison: University of Wisconsin Press.

Benjamin, Jessica. 1986. "A Desire of One's Own: Psychoanalytic Feminism and Intersubjective Space." In *Feminist Studies / Critical Studies*. Bloomington: Indiana University Press.

——. 1995. *Like Subjects, Love Objects: Essays on Recognition and Sexual Difference*. New Haven: Yale University Press.

Berger, John. 1972. *Ways of Seeing*. London: Penguin.

Berger, Maurice, Brian Wallis, and Simon Watson, eds. 1995. *Constructing Masculinity*. New York: Routledge.

Berk, Richard, Paul R. Abramson, and Paul Okami. 1995. "Sexual Activities as Told in Surveys." In *Sexual Nature, Sexual Culture*, ed. Paul R. Abramson and Steven D. Pinkerton, 371–86. Chicago: University of Chicago Press.

Bildstein, Jay. 1996. *The King of Clubs*. New York: Barricade Books.

Bishop, Ryan, and Lillian Robinson. 1998. *Night Market: Sexual Cultures and the Thai Economic Miracle*. New York: Routledge.

Blum, Lawrence D. 1996. "Egocentricity and Infidelity: Discussion of Ross's Chapter 'Male Infidelity in Long Marriages: Second Adolescences and Fourth Individuations.'" In *Intimacy and Infidelity: Separation-Individuation Perspectives*, ed. Salman Akhtar and Selma Kramer, 131–44. Northvale, NJ: Jason Aronson.

Blumstein, Phillip, and Pepper Schwartz. 1983. *American Couples: Money, Work, Sex*. New York: Morrow.

Bocock, Robert. 1993. *Consumption*. New York: Routledge.

Bordo, Susan. 1993. *Unbearable Weight: Feminism, Western Culture, and the Body*. Berkeley: University of California Press.

———. 1999. *The Male Body: A New Look at Men in Public and in Private.* New York: Farrar, Straus and Giroux.

Bourdieu, Pierre. 1984. *Distinction: A Social Critique of the Judgement of Taste.* Cambridge, MA: Harvard University Press.

Bright, Susie. 1997. *Susie Bright's Sexual State of the Union.* New York: Simon and Schuster.

Bringle, Robert G., and Bram P. Buunk. 1991. "Extradyadic Relationships and Sexual Jealousy." In *Sexuality in Close Relationships,* ed. Kathleen McKinney and Susan Sprecher, 135–53. Hillsdale, NJ: Lawrence Erlbaum.

Brod, Harry. 1992. "Pornography and the Alienation of Male Sexuality." In *Rethinking Masculinity: Philosophical Explorations in Light of Feminism,* ed. Larry May and Robert A. Strikwerda, 149–65. Lanham, MD: Rowman and Littlefield.

Brooks, Gary R. 1995. *The Centerfold Syndrome: How Men Can Overcome Objectification and Achieve Intimacy with Women.* San Francisco: Jossey-Bass.

———. 1997. "The Centerfold Syndrome." In *Men and Sex: New Psychological Perspectives,* ed. Ronald F. Levant and Gary R. Brooks, 28–60. New York: Wiley.

Brooks, Siobhan. 1997. "Dancing toward Freedom." In *Whores and Other Feminists,* ed. Jill Nagel, 252–55. New York: Routledge.

Brown, Karen M. 1991. *Mama Lola: A Vodou Priestess in Brooklyn.* Berkeley: University of California Press.

Bukro, Casey. 1998. "Adult Entertainment May Face Tough Rules." *Chicago Tribune,* February 3.

Burana, Lily. 2001. *Strip City.* New York: Talk Miramax.

Butler, Judith. 1993. *Bodies That Matter: On the Discursive Limits of Sex.* New York: Routledge.

Califia, Pat. 1994. *Public Sex: The Culture of Radical Sex.* Pittsburgh: Cleis Press.

Campbell, Colin. 1987. *The Romantic Ethic and the Spirit of Modern Consumerism.* Oxford: Basil Blackwell.

———. 1995. "The Sociology of Consumption." In *Acknowledging Consumption,* ed. Daniel Miller, 96–126. London: Routledge.

Cancian, Francesca M. 1987. *Love in America: Gender and Self-Development.* New York: Cambridge University Press.

Cash, W. J. 1941. *The Mind of the South.* New York: Vintage.

Chancer, Lynn Sharon. 1993. "Prostitution, Feminist Theory, and Ambivalence: Notes from the Sociological Underground." *Social Text* (winter): 143–72.

———. 1998. *Reconcilable Differences: Confronting Beauty, Pornography, and the Future of Feminism.* Berkeley: University of California Press.

Chapkis, Wendy. 1997. *Live Sex Acts: Women Performing Erotic Labour.* London: Cassell.

Chodorow, Nancy J. 1995. "Gender as a Personal and Cultural Construction." *Signs: Journal of Women in Culture and Society* 20: 516–44.

———. 1999. *The Power of Feelings: Personal Meaning in Psychoanalysis, Gender, and Culture.* New Haven: Yale University Press.

Clifford, James. 1986. "Introduction: Partial Truths." In *Writing Culture: The Poetics and Politics of Ethnography,* ed. James Clifford and George E. Marcus. Berkeley: University of California Press.

Cohen, S., and Taylor, L. 1976. *Escape Attempts: The Theory and Practice of Resistance in Everyday Life.* Harmondsworth: Penguin.

Connell, R. W. 1995. *Masculinities.* Berkeley: University of California Press.

———. 2000. *The Men and the Boys.* Berkeley: University of California Press.

Coontz, Stephanie. 1992. *The Way We Never Were: American Families and the Nostalgia Trap.* New York: Basic Books.

Cornwall, Andrea, and Nancy Lindisfarne. 1994. *Dislocating Masculinity: Comparative Ethnographies.* London: Routledge.

Cowie, Elizabeth. 1992. "Pornography and Fantasy: Psychoanalytic Perspectives." In *Sex Exposed: Sexuality and the Pornography Debate,* ed. Lynne Segal and Mary McIntosh, 132–52. New Brunswick, NJ: Rutgers University Press.

Crang, Phillip. 1997. "Performing the Tourist Product." In *Touring Cultures: Transformations of Travel and Theory,* ed. Chris Rojek and John Urry, 137–54. London: Routledge.

Cressey, Paul G. 1932. *The Taxi-Dance Hall: A Sociological Study in Commercialized Recreation and City Life.* Chicago: University of Chicago Press.

Curtis, Barry, and Claire Pajaczkowska. 1994. "'Getting There': Travel, Time, and Narrative." In *Traveller's Tales: Narratives of Home and Displacement,* ed. George Robertson, Melinda Mash, Lisa Tickner, Jon Bird, Barry Curtis, and Tim Putnam, 199–215. London: Routledge.

Davis, Laurel R. 1997. *The Swimsuit Issue and Sport: Hegemonic Masculinity in Sports Illustrated.* Albany: State University of New York Press.

Delacoste, Frederique, and Priscilla Alexander. 1987. *Sex Work: Writings by Women in the Sex Industry.* San Francisco: Cleis Press.

DeLamater, John. 1991. "Emotions and Sexuality." In *Sexuality in Close Relationships,* ed. Kathleen McKinney and Susan Sprecher, 49–70. Hillsdale, NJ: Lawrence Erlbaum.

D'Emilio, John, and Estelle B. Freedman. 1988. *Intimate Matters: A History of Sexuality in America.* New York: Harper and Row.

Devereux, George. 1967. *From Anxiety to Method in the Behavioral Sciences.* Paris: Mouton.

di Mauro, Diane. 1995. *Sexuality Research in the United States.* New York: Social Science Research Council.

Dines, Gail, Robert Jensen, and Ann Russo, eds. 1998. *Pornography: The Production and Consumption of Inequality.* New York: Routledge.

Douglas, Mary. 1966. *Purity and Danger: An Analysis of Concepts of Pollution and Taboo.* New York: Praeger.

Dragu, Margaret, and A. S. A. Harrison. 1988. *Revelations: Essays on Striptease and Sexuality.* London, Ontario: Nightwood Editions.

Dudash, Tawnya Renee. 1993. "Emerging Feminist Discourses among Dancers at a San Francisco Peepshow." Master's thesis, San Francisco State University.

Duncombe, Jean, and Dennis Marsden. 1996. "Whose Orgasm Is This Anyway? 'Sex Work' in Long-term Heterosexual Couple Relationships." In *Sexual Cultures: Communities, Values, and Intimacy,* ed. Jeffrey Weeks and Janet Holland, 220–38. London: Macmillan.

Dworkin, Andrea. 1981. *Pornography: Men Possessing Women.* London: Women's Press.

———. 1997. *Life and Death: Unapologetic Writings on the Continuing War Against Women.* New York: Free Press.

Eco, Umberto. 1986. *Faith in Fakes: Essays.* 1967. London: Secker and Warburg.

Edwards, Susan S. M. 1993. "Selling the Body, Keeping the Soul: Sexuality, Power, the Theories and Realities of Prostitution." In *Body Matters: Essays on the Sociology of the Body,* ed. Sue Scott and David Morgan, 89–104. Washington, DC: Falmer Press.

Egan, R. D. Forthcoming. "Eyeing the Scene: The Uses and (Re)Uses of Surveillance Cameras in an Exotic Club." *Journal of Critical Sociology.*

Ellis, Carolyn, and Michael G. Flaherty, eds. 1992. *Investigating Subjectivity: Research on Lived Experience.* Newbury Park: Sage.

Engels, Friedrich. 1972. *The Origin of the Family, Private Property, and the State.* New York: Penguin.

Erenberg, Lewis A. 1984. *Steppin' Out: New York Nightlife and the Transformation of American Culture.* Westport, CT: Greenwood Press.

Farley, M., and V. Kelly. 2000. "Prostitution: A Critical Review of the Medical and Social Sciences Literature." *Women & Criminal Justice* 11, no. 4: 29–64.

Feifer, N. 1986. *Tourism in History.* New York: Stein and Day.

Foucault, Michel. 1975. *Discipline and Punish: The Birth of the Prison.* Trans. Alan Sheridan. New York: Vintage.

———. 1978. *The History of Sexuality, Volume I: An Introduction.* New York: Vintage.

Frank, Katherine. 1998. "The Production of Identity and the Negotiation of Intimacy in a 'Gentleman's Club.'" *Sexualities* 1, no. 2: 175–202.

———. 2000. "The Management of Hunger: Using Fiction in Writing Anthropology." *Qualitative Inquiry* 6, no. 4 (December): 474–88.

———. 2002. "Stripping, Starving, and Other Ambiguous Pleasures." In *Jane Sexes It Up: True Confessions of Feminist Desire,* ed. Lisa Johnson. New York: Four Walls, Eight Windows.

Frankenberg, Ruth. 1993. *White Women, Race Matters: The Social Construction of Whiteness.* Minneapolis: University of Minnesota Press.

French, Dolores, with Linda Lee. 1988. *Working: My Life as a Prostitute.* New York: Dutton.

Freud, Sigmund. 1950. "Contributions to the Psychology of Love: The Most Prevalent Form of Degradation in Erotic Life." In *Collected Papers,* ed. Joan Riviere, 4: 203–16. 1912. London: Hogarth Press.

Friedman, Andrea. 1996. "'The Habitats of Sex-Crazed Perverts': Campaigns against Burlesque in Depression-Era New York City." *Journal of the History of Sexuality* 7, no. 2: 203–38.

Friedman, Andrew. 1998. "Student Bodies: Why Smart Girls Strip." *Long Island Voice,* 15–21.

Funari, Vicky. 1997. "Naked, Naughty, Nasty: Peep Show Reflections." In *Whores and Other Feminists,* ed. Jill Nagel, 19–35. New York: Routledge.

Gamman, Lorraine, and Merja Makinen. 1994. *Female Fetishism.* New York: New York University Press.

Gilbert, Jeremy, and Ewan Pearson. 1999. *Discographies: Dance Music, Culture, and the Politics of Sound.* London: Routledge.

Gilfoyle, Timothy J. 1992. *City of Eros: New York City, Prostitution, and the Commercialization of Sex, 1790–1920.* New York: Norton.

Ginsburg, Faye, and Anna Lowenhaupt Tsing, eds. 1990. *Uncertain Terms: Negotiating Gender in American Culture.* Boston: Beacon Press.

Gonos, George. 1976. "Go-go Dancing: A Comparative Frame Analysis." *Urban Life* 5: 189–220.

Good, Glenn E., and Nancy B. Sherrod. 1997. "Men's Resolution of Nonrelational Sex across the Lifespan." In *Men and Sex: New Psychological Perspectives,* ed. Ronald F. Levant and Gary R. Brooks, 181–204. New York: Wiley.

Gordon, Deborah A. 1995. "Conclusion: Culture Writing Women: Inscribing Feminist Anthropology." In *Women Writing Culture,* ed. Ruth Behar and Deborah Gordon, 457. Berkeley: University of California Press.

Greenwald, Harold. 1958. *The Elegant Prostitute: A Social and Psychoanalytic Study.* New York: Walker and Company.

Gutmann, M. 1996. *The Meanings of Macho: Being a Man in Mexico City.* Berkeley: University of California Press.

Haden-Guest, Anthony. 1997. *The Last Party: Studio 54, Disco, and the Culture of the Night.* New York: Morrow.

Halberstam, Judith. 1998. *Female Masculinity.* Durham, NC: Duke University Press.

Handler, Richard, and Eric Gable. 1997. *The New History in an Old Museum: Creating the Past at Colonial Williamsburg.* Durham, NC: Duke University Press.

Hanna, Judith Lynne. 1998a. "Analysis: The First Amendment and Exotic Dance." *National Campaign for Freedom of Expression Quarterly* (autumn): 8–9.

——. 1998b. "Undressing the First Amendment and Corsetting the Striptease Dancer." *Drama Review* 42: 38–69.

——. 1999. "Toying with the Striptease Dancer and the First Amendment." In *Play and Culture Studies, Vol. 2,* ed. Stuart Reifel. Greenwich, CT: Ablex.

Haraway, Donna J. 1991. *Simians, Cyborgs, and Women: The Reinvention of Nature.* New York: Routledge.

Hardy, Simon. 1998. *The Reader, the Author, His Woman and Her Lover: Soft-Core Pornography and Heterosexual Men.* London: Cassell.

Hart, Angie. 1994. "Missing Masculinity? Prostitutes' Clients in Alicante, Spain." In *Dislocating Masculinity: Comparative Ethnographies,* ed. Andrea Cornwall and Nancy Lindisfarne, 48–65. London: Routledge.

———. 1998. *Buying and Selling Power: Anthropological Reflections on Prostitution in Spain.* Boulder, CO: Westview Press.

Harvey, David. 1990. *The Condition of Postmodernity.* Cambridge, England: Blackwell.

Herdt, Gil, and Robert Stoller. 1990. *Intimate Communications: Erotics and the Study of Culture.* New York: Columbia University Press.

Hochschild, Arlie Russell. 1983. *The Managed Heart: Commercialization of Human Feeling.* Berkeley: University of California Press.

Illouz, Eva. 1997. *Consuming the Romantic Utopia: Love and the Contradictions of Capitalism.* Berkeley: University of California Press.

Jackson, Peter. 1993. "Towards a Cultural Politics of Consumption." In *Mapping the Futures: Local Cultures, Global Change,* ed. Jon Bird, Barry Curtis, Tim Putnam, George Robertson, and Lisa Tickner, 207–28. New York: Routledge.

Jackson, Peter, and Nigel Thrift. 1995. "Geographies of Consumption." In *Acknowledging Consumption: A Review of New Studies,* ed. Daniel Miller, 204–37. London: Routledge.

Jarrett, Lucinda. 1997. *Stripping in Time: A History of Erotic Dancing.* London: Pandora.

Jensen, Robert. 1998. "Using Pornography." In *Pornography: The Production and Consumption of Inequality,* ed. Gail Dines, Robert Jensen, and Ann Russo, 101–46. New York: Routledge.

Johnson, Merri Lisa. 1999. "Pole Work: Autoethnography of a Strip Club." In *Sex Work and Sex Workers: Sexuality and Culture, Volume 2,* ed. B. Dank and R. Refinetti, 149–57. New Brunswick, NJ: Transaction Publishers.

Jokinen, Eeva, and Soile Veijola. 1997. "The Disoriented Tourist: The Figuration of the Tourist in Contemporary Cultural Critique." In *Touring Cultures: Transformations of Travel and Theory,* ed. Chris Rojek and John Urry, 23–51. London: Routledge.

Jones, Stacey Holman. 1998. "Turning the Kaleidoscope: Revisioning an Ethnography." *Qualitative Inquiry* 4, no. 3: 421–41.

Jones, Vanessa E. 2001. "Baremarket: Stripper Chic Flavors R & B, Hip-hop Videos." *Boston Globe,* April 22.

Juffer, Jane. 1998. *At Home with Pornography: Women, Sex, and Everyday Life.* New York: New York University Press.

Kappeler, Susanne. 1986. *The Pornography of Representation.* Minneapolis: University of Minnesota Press.

Kapsalis, Terri. 1997. *Public Privates: Performing Gynecology from Both Ends of the Speculum.* Durham, NC: Duke University Press.

Keichline, S. 2001. "Stripped of Athletic Status." *Daily Titan,* California State University, Fullerton, March 16, 2001.

Kempadoo, Kamala, and Jo Doezema, eds. 1998. *Global Sex Workers: Rights, Resistance, and Redefinition.* New York: Routledge.

Kennedy, Duncan. 1993. *Sexy Dressing, Etc.* Cambridge, MA: Harvard University Press.

Kernberg, Otto F. 1995. *Love Relations: Normality and Pathology.* New Haven: Yale University Press.

Kimmel, Michael. 1996. *Manhood in America: A Cultural History.* New York: Free Press.

——. 1997. "Masculinity as Homophobia: Fear, Shame and Silence in the Construction of Gender Identity." In *Toward a New Psychology of Gender,* ed. Mary Gergen and Sara Davis. New York: Routledge.

Kipnis, Laura. 1996. *Bound and Gagged: Pornography and the Politics of Fantasy in America.* New York: Grove Press.

Kristeva, Julia. 1982. *Powers of Horror: An Essay on Abjection.* New York: Columbia University Press.

Lasch, Christopher. 1977. *Haven in a Heartless World: The Family Beseiged.* New York: Basic Books.

Lemoncheck, Linda. 1985. *Dehumanizing Women: Treating Persons as Sex Objects.* New Jersey: Rowman and Allenheld.

Lerum, Keri A. 1993. "Is It Exploitative If I Like It? Commercial Sex Workers Compare Notes with Feminists and the Social Problems Industry." Master's thesis, University of Washington.

Levant, Ronald F., and Gary R. Brooks, eds. 1997. *Men and Sex: New Psychological Perspectives.* New York: Wiley.

Liepe-Levinson, Katherine. 1998. "Striptease: Desire, Mimetic Jeopardy, and Performing Spectators." *Drama Review* 42: 9–37.

——. 2002. *Strip Show: Performances of Gender and Desire.* New York: Routledge.

MacCannell, Dean. 1976. *The Tourist: A New Theory of the Leisure Class.* New York: Schocken Books.

MacDonald, Scott. 1983. "Confessions of a Feminist Porn Watcher." *Film Quarterly* 36: 10–16.

MacKinnon, Catharine A. 1987. *Feminism Unmodified: Discourses on Life and Law.* Cambridge, MA: Harvard University Press.

——. 1989. "Sexuality, Pornography, and Method: Pleasure under Patriarchy." *Ethics* 99 (January): 314–46.

——. 1993. *Only Words.* Cambridge, MA: Harvard University Press.

Manderson, Lenore. 1995. "The Pursuit of Pleasure and the Sale of Sex." In *Sexual Nature, Sexual Culture,* ed. Paul R. Abramson and Steven D. Pinkerton, 305–29. Chicago: University of Chicago Press.

Manderson, Lenore, and Margaret Jolly, eds. 1997. *Sites of Desire / Economies of Pleasure: Sexualities in Asia and the Pacific.* Chicago: University of Chicago Press.

Mantsios, Gregory. 1995. "Media Magic: Making Class Invisible." In *Race, Class, and Gender in the United States: An Integrated Study,* ed. Paula S. Rothenberg, 409–17. New York: St. Martin's Press.

Marcus, George E., and Michael M. Fischer. 1986. *Anthropology as Cultural Critique: An Experimental Moment in the Human Sciences.* Chicago: University of Chicago Press.

Marx, Karl. 1978. "Economic and Philosophic Manuscripts of 1884." In *The Marx-Engels Reader,* 2d ed., ed. Robert Tucker, 66–125. New York: Norton.

Massey, Doreen. 1993. "Power-Geometry and a Progressive Sense of Place." In *Mapping the Futures: Local Cultures, Global Change,* ed. Jon Bird, Barry Curtis, Tim Putnam, George Robertson, and Lisa Tickner, 59–69. New York: Routledge.

Mattson, Heidi. 1995. *Ivy League Stripper.* New York: Arcade.

McCaghy, Charles H., and James K. Skipper. 1969. "Lesbian Behavior as an Adaptation to the Occupation of Stripping." *Social Problems* 17: 262–70.

McClintock, Anne. 1995. *Imperial Leather: Race, Gender, and Sexuality in the Colonial Contest.* New York: Routledge.

McElroy, Wendy. 1995. *XXX: A Woman's Right to Pornography.* New York: St. Martin's Press.

McKean, Philip Frick. 1989. "Towards a Theoretical Analysis of Tourism: Economic and Cultural Involution in Bali." In *Hosts and Guests: The Anthropology of Tourism,* ed. Valene Smith, 199–38. Philadelphia: University of Pennsylvania Press.

Meridian, Reese. 1997. "Special Report: It's a Black Thing . . . Or Is It?" *Exotic Dancer Bulletin* (fall): 52–54.

Michael, Robert T., John H. Gagnon, Edward O. Laumann, and Gina Kolata. 1994. *Sex in America: A Definitive Survey.* Boston: Little, Brown.

Miller, Gale. 1978. *Odd Jobs: The World of Deviant Work.* Englewood Cliffs, NJ: Prentice-Hall.

Miller, Richard K., Terri C. Walker, and Christen E. Pursell. 1998. *The 1998 Entertainment and Leisure Market Research Handbook.* Norcross, GA: Richard K. Miller and Associates.

Miller, William Ian. 1997. *The Anatomy of Disgust.* Cambridge, MA: Harvard University Press.

Misty. 1973. *Strip.* Toronto: New Press.

Mizejewski, Linda. 1999. *Ziegfeld Girl: Image and Icon in Culture and Cinema*. Durham, NC: Duke University Press.

Moffat, Michael. 1989. *Coming of Age in New Jersey: College and American Culture*. New Brunswick, NJ: Rutgers University Press.

Morgan, Peggy. 1987. "Living on the Edge." In *Sex Work: Writings by Women in the Sex Industry*, ed. Frederique Delacoste and Priscilla Alexander, 21–28. San Francisco: Cleis Press.

Monto, M. A. 2000. "Why Men Seek Out Prostitutes." In *Sex for Sale: Prostitution, Pornography, and the Sex Industry*, ed. R. Weitzer, 67–84. New York: Routledge.

Mulvey, Laura. 1975. "Visual Pleasure and Narrative Cinema." In *The Sexual Subject: A Screen Reader in Sexuality*, ed. John Caughie and Annette Kuhn, 22–34. London: Routledge.

Mumford, Kevin J. 1997. *Interzones: Black / White Sex Districts in Chicago and New York in the Early Twentieth Century*. New York: Columbia University Press.

Mura, David. 1987. *A Male Grief: Notes on Pornography and Addiction*. Minneapolis: Milkweed Editions.

Myerhoff, Barbara. 1978. *Number Our Days*. New York: Simon and Schuster.

Nagel, Jill, ed. 1997. *Whores and Other Feminists*. New York: Routledge.

Naylor, Larry L. 1998. *American Culture: Myth and Reality of a Culture of Diversity*. Westport, CT: Bergin and Garvey.

Nead, Lynda. 1992. *The Female Nude: Art, Obscenity, and Sexuality*. London: Routledge.

Oliker, S. J. 1989. *Best Friends and Marriage: Exchange among Women*. Berkeley: University of California Press.

Orbuch, Terri L., and John H. Harvey. 1991. "Methodological and Conceptual Issues in the Study of Sexuality in Close Relationships." In *Sexuality in Close Relationships*, ed. Kathleen McKinney and Susan Sprecher, 9–24. Hillsdale, NJ: Lawrence Erlbaum.

Ortner, Sherry B. 1991 "Reading America: Preliminary Notes on Class and Culture." In *Recapturing Anthropology: Working in the Present*, ed. Richard G. Fox, 163–90. Santa Fe, NM: School of American Research Press.

Paglia, Camille. 1992. *Sex, Art, and American Culture*. New York: Vintage Books.

Pateman, Carole. 1988. *The Sexual Contract*. Stanford: Stanford University Press.

Paules, Greta Foff. 1991. *Dishing It Out: Power and Resistance among Waitresses in a New Jersey Restaurant*. Philadelphia: Temple University Press.

Pearce, Philip L. 1982. *The Social Psychology of Tourist Behavior*. Oxford: Pergamon Press.

Pearce, Philip L., and Gianna M. Moscardo. 1986. "The Concept of Authenticity in Tourist Experiences." *Australian and New Zealand Journal of Sociology* 22: 121–32.

Peiss, Kathy. 1983. " 'Charity Girls' and City Pleasures: Historical Notes on Working-Class Sexuality, 1880–1920." In *Powers of Desire: The Politics of Sexual-*

ity, ed. Ann Snitow, Christine Stansell, and Sharon Thompson, 74–87. New York: Monthly Review Press.

Penley, Constance. 1997. "Crackers and Whackers: The White Trashing of Porn." In *White Trash: Race and Class in America,* ed. Matt Wray and Annalee Newitz, 89–112. New York: Routledge.

Perlman, Daniel, and Beverly Fehr. 1987. "The Development of Intimate Relationships." In *Intimate Relationships: Development, Dynamics, and Deterioration,* ed. Daniel Perlman and Steve Duck, 320. Newbury Park, CA: Sage.

Phelan, Peggy. 1993. *Unmarked: The Politics of Performance.* New York: Routledge.

Pheterson, Gail. 1989. *A Vindication of the Rights of Whores.* Seattle: Seal Press.

Powdermaker, Hortense. 1950. *Hollywood: The Dream Factory: An Anthropologist Looks at the Movie Makers.* Boston: Little, Brown.

Prewitt, Terry J. 1988. "The Exposed Exotic Dancer: A Semiotic of Deception in Porno-active Ritual." In *Semiotics 1988,* ed. Terry Prewitt, John Deely, and Karen Haworth, 241–47. New York: University Press of America.

——. 1989. "Like a Virgin: The Semiotics of Illusion in Erotic Performance." *American Journal of Semiotics* 6, no. 4: 137–52.

Prus, Robert. 1996. *Symbolic Interaction and Ethnographic Research: Intersubjectivity and the Study of Human Lived Experience.* New York: State University of New York Press.

Queen, Carol. 1997a. *Real Live Nude Girl.* Pittsburgh: Cleis Press.

——. 1997b. "Sex Radical Politics, Sex-Positive Feminist Thought, and Whore Stigma." In *Whores and Other Feminists,* ed. Jill Nagel, 125–35. New York: Routledge.

Quinn, Naomi. 1997. "Research on the Psychodynamics of Shared Understandings." In *A Cognitive Theory of Cultural Meaning,* ed. Claudia Strauss and Naomi Quinn, 189–209. New York: Cambridge University Press.

——. N.d. "Love and the Experiential Basis of American Marriage." Unpublished manuscript.

Radway, Janice A. 1984. *Reading the Romance: Women, Patriarchy, and Popular Literature.* Chapel Hill: University of North Carolina Press.

Reed, Stacy. 1997. "All Stripped Off." In *Whores and Other Feminists,* ed. Jill Nagel, 179–88. New York: Routledge.

Reisman, Judith. 1991. *"Soft Porn" Plays Hardball: Its Tragic Effects on Women, Children, and the Family.* Lafayette, LA: Huntington House Publishers.

Richardson, Laurel. 1989. "Secrecy and Status: The Social Construction of Forbidden Relationships." In *Gender in Intimate Relationships: A Microstructural Approach,* ed. Barbara J. Risman and Pepper Schwartz, 108–19. Belmont, CA: Wadsworth.

Ritzer, George. 1993. *The McDonaldization of Society: An Investigation into the Changing Character of Contemporary Social Life.* Thousand Oaks, CA: Pine Forge Press.

Ritzer, George, and Allan Liska. 1997. "McDisneyization and Post-Tourism." In *Touring Cultures: Transformations of Travel and Theory,* ed. Chris Rojek and John Urry, 96–109. London: Routledge.

Rojek, Chris. 1993. *Ways of Escape: Modern Transformations in Leisure and Travel.* Lanham, MD: Rowman and Littlefield.

Rojek, Chris, and John Urry, eds. 1997. *Touring Cultures: Transformations of Travel and Theory.* London: Routledge.

Ronai, Carol Rambo. 1992. "The Reflexive Self through Narrative: A Night in the Life of an Erotic Dancer / Researcher." In *Investigating Subjectivity: Research on Lived Experience,* ed. Carolyn Ellis and Michael G. Flaherty, 102–24. Newbury Park, CA: Sage.

Ronai, Carol Rambo, and Carolyn Ellis. 1989. "Turn-ons for Money: Interactional Strategies of the Table Dancer." *Journal of Contemporary Ethnography* 18: 271–98.

Ross, Andrew. 1989. *No Respect: Intellectuals and Popular Culture.* New York: Routledge.

Ross, John M. 1996. "Male Infidelity in Long Marriages: Second Adolescences and Fourth Individuations." In *Intimacy and Infidelity: Separation-Individuation Perspectives,* ed. Salman Akhtar and Selma Kramer, 107–30. Northvale, NJ: Jason Aronson.

Rotundo, E. Anthony. 1993. *American Manhood: Transformations in Masculinity from the Revolution to the Modern Era.* New York: Basic Books.

Rubin, Gayle S. 1993. "Thinking Sex: Notes for a Radical Theory of the Politics of Sexuality." In *The Lesbian and Gay Studies Reader,* ed. Henry Abelove, Michele Aina Barale, David M. Halperin, 3–44. New York: Routledge.

Russo, Ann. 1998. "Feminists Confront Pornography's Subordinating Practices." In *Pornography: The Production and Consumption of Inequality,* ed. Gail Dines, Robert Jensen, and Ann Russo, 9–36. New York: Routledge.

Salutin, Marilyn. 1971. "Stripper Morality." *Transaction* 8, no. 3 / 4: 12–22.

Sanday, Peggy R. 1990. *Fraternity Gang Rape: Sex, Brotherhood, and Privilege on Campus.* New York: New York University Press.

Schaefer, Eric. 1999. *Bold! Daring! Shocking! True! A History of Exploitation Films, 1919–1959.* Durham, NC: Duke University Press.

Scheper-Hughes, Nancy. 1992. *Death without Weeping: The Violence of Everyday Life in Brazil.* Berkeley: University of California Press.

Schlosser, Eric. 1997. "The Business of Pornography." *U.S. News & World Report* (February 10): 42–50.

Schmidt, Gunter. 1998. "Sexuality and Late Modernity." *Annual Review of Sex Research* 9: 224–41.

Schur, Edwin M. 1988. *The Americanization of Sex.* Philadelphia: Temple University Press.

Sedgwick, Eve Kosofsky. 1988. *Between Men: English Literature and Male Homosocial Desire.* New York: Columbia University Press.

Segal, Lynne. 1990. *Slow Motion: Changing Masculinities, Changing Men.* New Brunswick, NJ: Rutgers University Press.

———. 1994. *Straight Sex: Rethinking the Politics of Pleasure.* Berkeley: University of California Press.

Segal, Lynne, and Mary McIntosh, eds. 1992. *Sex Exposed: Sexuality and the Pornography Debate.* New Brunswick, NJ: Rutgers University Press.

Shaviro, Steven. 1993. *The Cinematic Body.* Minneapolis: University of Minnesota Press.

Shuttleworth, Russell P. 2000. "The Pursuit of Sexual Intimacy for Men with Cerebral Palsy." Ph.D. diss. University of California, Berkeley.

Simmel, Georg. 1978. *The Philosophy of Money.* 1907. Trans. Tom Bottomore and David Frisby. London: Routledge.

Singer, Linda. 1993. *Erotic Welfare.* New York: Routledge.

Skeen, Dick. 1991. *Different Sexual Worlds: Contemporary Case Studies of Sexuality.* Lexington, MA: Lexington Books.

Skeggs, Beverley. 1997. *Formations of Class and Gender: Becoming Respectable.* London: Sage.

Smith, Clarissa. 2002. "Shiny Chests and Heaving G-Strings: A Night Out with the Chippendales." *Sexualities* 5, no. 1: 67–89.

Soble, Alan. 1992. "Why Do Men Enjoy Pornography?" In *Rethinking Masculinity: Philosophical Explorations in Light of Feminism,* ed. Larry May and Robert A. Strikwerda, 135–47. Lanham, MD: Rowman and Littlefield.

Stacey, Judith. 1988. "Can There Be a Feminist Ethnography?" *Women's Studies International Forum* 11: 21–27.

Steinberg, David. 1998. "Some Room of Their Own: Dancers Win Claim against Mitchell Brothers, Organize in Anchorage." *Comes Naturally* 73.

Stock, Wendy. 1997. "Sex as Commodity: Men and the Sex Industry." In *Men and Sex: New Psychological Perspectives,* ed. Ronald F. Levant and Gary R. Brooks, 100–132. New York: Wiley.

Stoltenberg, John. 1989. *Refusing to Be a Man: Essays on Sex and Justice.* New York: Meridian.

Strauss, Claudia. 1990. "Who Gets Ahead? Cognitive Responses to Heteroglossia in American Political Culture." *American Ethnologist* 17: 312–28.

Strauss, Claudia, and Naomi Quinn. 1997. *A Cognitive Theory of Cultural Meaning.* Cambridge, England: Cambridge University Press.

Symons, Donald. 1995. "Beauty Is in the Adaptations of the Beholder: The Evolutionary Psychology of Human Female Sexual Attractiveness." In *Sexual Nature, Sexual Culture,* ed. Paul R. Abramson and Steven D. Pinkerton, 80–118. Chicago: University of Chicago Press.

Thompson, William E., and Jackie L. Harred. 1992. "Topless Dancers: Managing Stigma in a Deviant Occupation." *Deviant Behavior: An Interdisciplinary Journal* 13: 291–311.

Tiefer, Leonore. 1995. *Sex Is Not a Natural Act and Other Essays.* Boulder, CO: Westview Press.

Tierney, John. 1998. "The Big City: Monkeys, Strippers, and the Dow." *New York Times,* November 9.

Tocqueville, Alexis de. 1956. *Democracy in America.* New York: Penguin.

Tolich, Martin B. 1993. "Alienating and Liberating Emotions at Work: Supermarket Clerks' Performance of Customer Service." *Journal of Contemporary Ethnography* 22: 361–81.

Travers, Andrew. 1993. "An Essay on Self and Camp." *Theory, Culture and Society* 10: 127–43.

Trilling, Lionel. 1972. *Sincerity and Authenticity.* Cambridge, MA: Harvard University Press.

Tucker, Hazel. 1997. "The Ideal Village: Interactions through Tourism in Central Anatolia." In *Tourists and Tourism: Identifying with People and Places,* ed. Simone Abram, Jacqueline Waldren, and Donald V. L. Macleod. Oxford, UK: Berg.

Turner, Victor, and Edward Bruner. 1987. *The Anthropology of Experience.* Urbana: University of Illinois Press.

Tuzin, Donald. 1995. "Discourse, Intercourse, and the Excluded Middle: Anthropology and the Problem of Sexual Experience." In *Sexual Nature, Sexual Culture,* ed. Paul R. Abramson and Steven D. Pinkerton, 257–75. Chicago: University of Chicago Press.

Tyler, Stephen A. 1986. "Post-Modern Ethnography: From Document of the Occult to Occult Document." In *Writing Culture: The Poetics and Politics of Ethnography,* ed. James Clifford and George E. Marcus. Berkeley: University of California Press.

Urry, John. 1990. *The Tourist Gaze: Leisure and Travel in Contemporary Societies.* London: Sage.

Vance, Carole S. 1984. "Pleasure and Danger: Toward a Politics of Sexuality." In *Pleasure and Danger: Exploring Female Sexuality,* ed. Carole S. Vance, 1–27. Boston: Routledge and Kegan Paul.

Vogler, Candace. 1998. "Sex and Talk." *Critical Inquiry* 24: 328–65.

Watney, Simon. 1987. *Policing Desire: Pornography, AIDS, and the Media.* Minneapolis: University of Minnesota Press.

Weitzer, Ronald. 2000. *Sex for Sale: Prostitution, Pornography, and the Sex Industry.* New York: Routledge.

Weldon, Jo. 1998a. "Baring My Teeth (and Whatever Else I Like)." *Vixen* 1, no. 1: np.

———. 1998b. "Pornography: The Production and Consumption of Inequality. Book Review." *Vixen* 1, no. 5: 9–11.

Wharton, Amy S. 1993. "The Affective Consequences of Service Work: Managing Emotions on the Job." *Work and Occupations* 20: 205–32.

Williams, Linda. 1989. *Hard Core: Power, Pleasure, and the Frenzy of the Visible.* Berkeley: University of California Press.

———. 1992. "Pornographies On / Scene, or Diff'rent Strokes for Diff'rent Folks." In *Sex Exposed: Sexuality and the Pornography Debate,* ed. Lynne Segal and Mary McIntosh, 233–65. New Brunswick, NJ: Rutgers University Press.

Williams, Raymond. 1976. *Keywords: A Vocabulary of Culture and Society.* New York: Oxford University Press.

Williamson, Judith. 1980. *Consuming Passions: The Dynamics of Popular Culture.* London: Marion Boyars.

Wolf, Margery. 1992. *A Thrice-Told Tale: Feminism, Postmodernism, and Ethnographic Responsibility.* Stanford: Stanford University Press.

Žižek, Slavoj. 1989. *The Sublime Object of Ideology.* London: Verso.

Films Cited

Query, Julia. *Live Nude Girls Unite.*

Sprinkle, Annie. *Herstory of Porn: Reel to Real.*

Adult entertainment. *See* Sex industry

Adventure, 99–108. *See also* Fantasy

Affairs, 110; fantasies of, 92, 249–252, 262–263, 265–266

Aggression. *See* Male sexuality; Marriage

AIDS, 129; customers' fear of, 108

Allen, Robert, 42, 48

Allison, Anne, 16, 23, 144, 196, 247

Amateurs, 188, 210, 214

Antipornography feminism, 15, 48–49. *See also* Feminism

Authenticity, 33–35, 38, 49, 153–154, 201, 291 n.24; and commodification, 117, 189–197, 278; customer claims to, 180–189; customer cynicism about, 182–184, 198–201; customer perceptions of, 205–220; and identity, 195–197; and postmodernity, 35; in relationships, 269–271, 304 n.20; and tourism, 34–35, 175–179, 201, 302 n.8; as value or taste, 194–196, 211

Barthes, Roland, 209–210

Bartky, Sandra, 297 n.14

Baudrillard, Jean, 177–179

Beauty, 111, 123, 149–150, 215–217

Bederman, Gail, 98

Bell, Shannon, 15

Bendix, Regina, 34

Benjamin, Jessica, 24, 309 n.13

Bildstein, Jay, 85, 88, 99

Blum, Lawrence, 268

Blumstein, Philip, 263, 267

Boorstin, Daniel, 175

Bordo, Susan, 20, 111, 126

Breast implants, 179, 205–206

Brooks, Gary, 125, 143

Brown, Karen M., 37

Burlesque, 26, 39, 42–44, 48; Minsky brothers and, 48

Butler, Judith, 142, 197

Cabarets, 44

Califia, Pat, 15, 242, 278

Campbell, Colin, 177

Chancer, Lynn, 16

Cheers, 70, 180

Chodorow, Nancy, 21–22

Class. *See* Social class

Commodification, 117–118, 133, 153–154, 186–189, 193–194, 278; of intimacy, 27, 190–191

Comstock, Anthony, 43

Connell, R. W., 19

Consumption, 40, 137–138; as distinction, 43–45, 63–68; in late capitalism, 25, 94, 201. *See also* Masculinity

Cooch dance, 42

Crang, Phillip, 176, 199, 295 n.5

Cressey, Paul, 47

Customers: desire for safety, 99–108, 110, 247–248; focus on, 1–4, 16–19; as performers, 138–139, 151–153; types of, 28, 287 n.10

Dancer-customer relationships: authenticity in, 189–201, 303 n.14; intimacy in, 27–28; power in, 153–154

Desire, 23; to be looked at, 115; in marriage, 267–268; performances of, 141, 151–153, 199–201. *See also* Sexuality

de Tocqueville, Alexis, 53

Devereux, George, 8, 13

Dines, Gail, 204

Dragu, Margaret, 277

Duncombe, Jean, 267, 268

Dworkin, Andrea, 15, 17

Eco, Umberto, 200

Edwards, Susan, 18, 115

Emotional labor, 119, 176, 189, 267, 297 n.14, 301 n.5. *See also* Labor

Erenberg, Lewis, 43, 46

Escape. *See* Leisure

Ethnography: critique of, 35–38; feminist, 291 n.25; power dynamics in, 3

Fantasy, 21–24, 30, 35, 98, 150, 174, 225–228, 260–263, 272, 278–279; as commodity, 45, 138; of danger and transgression, 72–75, 101–103, 136, 250

Farley, Melissa, 154

Feminism, 14–19, 36, 242; backlash, 96; and male gaze theory, 29–31; "sex wars" in, 14–16

First Amendment, 51–52

Flaneur, 34–35, 101, 221

Foucault, Michel, 20

Foxworthy, Jeff, 69

Frankenburg, Ruth, 55, 57

Freud, Sigmund, 223–224

Friedman, Andrea, 48

Funari, Vicky, 197

Gender: ambiguity, 140; and consumption, 24, 265–266; performances of, 139–141; as simulacra, 179; and visibility, 29–30, 59, 221. *See also* Masculinity

Gender identity. *See* Masculinity

Gender relations: as economic, 185–186; in everyday life, 96–98; in workplace, 95–96, 109

Good, Glenn, 147

Hanna, Judith L., 51, 273

Harrison, A. S. A., 277

Hart, Angie, 16

Harvey, David, 25, 40, 58, 178

Hefner, Hugh, 50, 130

Heterosexuality, 140–143, 188. *See also* Sexuality

Hochschild, Arlie, 27, 176, 189, 267, 301 n.5

Homosexuality, 128–129, 142

Hustler magazine, 188, 203

Intersubjectivity, 24, 138

Interviewees, 7–8. *See also* Customers

Intimacy, 27–28, 213, 242–243, 245–246, 260–263, 267–271, 308 n.8; commodification of, 27, 190–191; intimacy scripts, 47

Jackson, Peter, 59

Jarrett, Lucinda, 43, 49

Jokinen, Eeva, 101

Kennedy, Duncan, 115
Kernberg, Otto, 260–262
Kimmel, Michael, 21
Kipnis, Laura, 203

Labor: of customers, 31; of dancers, 31, 153–154, 199–200, 209–210, 275, 295 n.5, 298 n.1. *See also* Emotional labor
Lee, Gypsy Rose, 48
Leisure, 24–32, 35, 88, 93, 199; public voyeurism as, 41–52. *See also* Touristic practices
Lesbianism, 45
Liepe-Levinson, Katherine, 30, 138, 141, 152, 289 n.17
Liska, Allan, 177–178

MacCannell, Dean, 175, 211
MacKinnon, Catharine, 15
Male gaze, 29–31
Male sexuality: aggressiveness, 48–49, 127–129, 154–155; customer beliefs about, 127–134. *See also* Sexuality
Marriage, 106–107, 241, 267–271; aggression in, 260–263; boredom in, 259–260; sex in, 148–151; and sex industry, 242–246; and visits to strip clubs, 241–246, 258–265; women and, 266
Masculinity, 19–23, 91, 97–98, 100–101, 111–120, 133–134, 140–141, 143–144, 194; and development of sexualized entertainment, 41–52; and hegemonic masculinity, 19, 98
Masculinizing practices, 19–20, 28, 134, 154–156
Massey, Doreen, 59
Masturbation, 54, 108
McClintock, Anne, 221, 306 n.9
Men: competition between, 63–65, 111–112, 143; in friendships, 109–110. *See also* Masculinity
Methodology, 1–14, 286–287 nn.2–7
Meridian, Reese, 219–220
Miller, William, 224
Mizejewski, Linda, 44
Model artist shows, 41
Money, 59, 75, 117, 191, 194, 266
Monogamy, 106, 124, 241–242, 244, 253–257, 264–267
Morality, 53–54, 223–224, 244, 264
Mulvey, Laura, 29
Mumford, Kevin, 43, 46

Naylor, Larry, 285 n.3
Nudity, 135–138, 216; customer fantasies of, 104, 136

Objectification, 36. *See also* Male gaze
Oliker, Stacey, 110, 266
Otherness, 32, 34, 42, 47, 74–75, 259–260

Participant observation, 5–7
Penley, Constance, 114
Phelan, Peggy, 196
Playboy, 50, 67, 105, 123, 130, 204
Playboy clubs, 50
Pornography, 22, 14–18, 23, 29, 30, 111, 203–204; customer use of, 105, 187, 244
Positionality, 1–4, 9–14, 36, 288 n.11
Postmodern culture, 29, 35, 61
Post-tourists, 177; customers as, 182–184
Power, 20, 31–32, 115–120, 266; in customer-dancer interactions, 153–154; in sex industry, 14–19, 23, 276–279
Professionalism, 209–214
Propriety. *See* Respectability

Prostitution, 41, 43; customers' fantasies about, 64–66, 73, 222–223; customers' use of, 105, 186–187, 294 n.2

Psychoanalysis, 22–24, 196–197; feminist, 21–23; Lacanian, 23–24; and marriage, 257–263; object relations, 24

Queen, Carol, 15, 277
Quinn, Naomi, 304 n.20

Race, 5, 42–43, 46, 57–58, 68–69, 71–72, 217–220; whiteness, 45
Realness, 34, 193, 195, 201
Reed, Stacy, 277
Regulars. See Customers
Regulations, 40, 48–51, 53–55, 100, 135, 273–276; about touching, 134–135; customer desire for, 107–108, 244; and social class, 48, 51
Reisman, Judith, 242
Religion, 53–54, 107
Respectability, 43–45, 207, 214–227
Ritzer, George, 177–178
Rojek, Chris, 35, 101, 201, 221, 302 n.8
Ronai, Carol, 11
Ross, Andrew, 98, 121, 278
Rubin, Gayle, 274

Salutin, Marilyn, 26
Schmidt, Gunter, 138
Scores, 99
Secrecy, 92; of sexual fantasies, 113; of visits to strip clubs, 244–252, 264–265
Sedgwick, Eve, 142
Sex, 86–87, 137–138, 148–151, 274; meaning freedom or escape, 32, 129, 133
Sex hormones, 125
Sex industry, 2, 23–25, 33, 137–138, 154–155; in Laurelton, 52–58

Sex tourism, 32
Sexual desire / performance, 141–151
Sexuality, 21–23, 104–105, 122, 243, 263, 274; in anthropology, 22; and masculinity, 110–117; and respectability, 44–45. See also Male sexuality; Sociobiology
Sex work. See Sex industry
Sex workers: agency of, 14–16, 42, 120
Sherrod, Nancy, 147
Sincerity. See Authenticity
Skeggs, Beverly, 207
Slumming, 46–47, 50, 101–103
Social class: and attraction, 208–209, 224–228; and the body, 66–68, 206–207, 211–212, 216–217, 228; of customers, 69–71, 75–76, 204, 287 n.8, 305 n.2; and taste, 207–208, 211
Sociobiology, 122–126
Spatial practices, 40–41, 58–75
Sprinkle, Annie, 15, 39
Staged authenticity, 176
Stigma, 18, 149, 304 n.16; around nudity, 131; of customers, 116–117; of dancers, 13, 113–114, 225, 276
Stock, Wendy, 137, 243, 263
Strip clubs: as different from work and home, 90–99; differentiation from other forms of adult entertainment, 17, 24–27; distinctions between, 25, 55–58, 204, 210–220; as entertainment, 87–88; as part of sex industry, 51–52, 275; as place to experience sexual desire without expectations, 144–150; as providing acceptance, 108–115; services offered in, 26, 57; as sites of adolescent fantasy, 146–148; as sites of triangulation, 265–266, 272
Stripping: as deviance, 49; as work, 4, 120. See also Labor
Subjectivity, 36, 19–24, 194–197

Surveillance. *See* Visibility

Symons, Donald, 123–124

Table dances, 27, 134–135

Taste. *See* Authenticity

Taxi dance halls, 47

Tiefer, Leonore, 146

Tourism, 36. *See also* Authenticity; Touristic practices

Tourist gaze, 29; romantic and collective, 29, 302 n.7

Touristic practices, 28–33, 90, 93, 119, 215. *See also* Tourist gaze

Travers, Andrew, 200

Triangulation, 261–266

Urry, John, 28–29, 90, 101, 177, 208, 221, 295 n.4

Veijola, Soile, 101

VIP rooms, 62–66, 68. *See also* Spatial practices

Visibility: of customers, 62–64, 72–74, 138–139, 144; pleasure in looking, 29, 89–90; and power, 30–31, 59; in social science, 36. *See also* Slumming

Voyeurism, 47, 95; academic, 103; as leisure practice, 41–43

Watney, Simon, 128

Weldon, Jo, 275

Women: class distinctions between, 203, 207, 221–226, 264; as consumers in the sex industry, 18, 52, 286 n.4, 290 n.21; reactions to partners' visits to strip clubs, 245, 253–255, 264, 271–272; as symbols of respectability, 43–45, 216

Youthfulness, 146–150, 214

Ziegfeld Follies, 44–46

Katherine Frank is Assistant Professor of Cultural
Anthropology at College of the Atlantic.

Library of Congress Cataloging-in-Publication Data
Frank, Katherine.
G-strings and sympathy : strip club regulars and
male desire / by Katherine Frank.
p.   cm.
ISBN 0-8223-2981-6 (cloth : alk. paper)
ISBN 0-8223-2972-7 (pbk. : alk. paper)
1. Striptease. 2. Striptease—Social aspects.
3. Men—Sexual behavior. I. Title.
PN1949.S7 F73 20002
792.7—dc21   2002005516